THE
BURNING GIRL

Also by
MARK BILLINGHAM

Sleepyhead

Scaredy Cat

Lazybones

Mark Billingham

THE
BURNING GIRL

wm

WILLIAM MORROW
An Imprint of HarperCollins*Publishers*

This book is a work of fiction. The characters, incidents, and dialogue are drawn from the author's imagination and are not to be construed as real. Any resemblance to actual events or persons, living or dead, is entirely coincidental.

Lyrics from 'Bigmouth Strikes Again' reproduced by kind permission of Morrissey and Sanctuary Records.

This book was originally published in Great Britain in 2004 by Little, Brown, an imprint of Time Warner Book Group UK.

FIRST U.S. EDITION

Printed on acid-free paper

Library of Congress Cataloging-in-Publication Data

Billingham, Mark.
    The burning girl / Mark Billingham.—1st ed.
        p. cm.
    ISBN 0-06-074526-6
    1. Police—England—London—Fiction. 2. London (England)—Fiction. 3. Organized crime—Fiction. 4. Murder for hire—Fiction. 5. Gangsters—Fiction. I. Title.

    PR6102.I44B87 2005
    823'.92—dc22

                                                            2004065479

05 06 07 08 09 ❖/RRD 10 9 8 7 6 5 4 3 2 1

For
Hilary Hale

'And now I know how Joan of Arc felt,
Now I know how Joan of Arc felt,
As the flames rose to her Roman nose,
And her Walkman started to melt . . .'

'Bigmouth Strikes Again' – The Smiths

PROLOGUE

NEARLY HALF OF ALL NEW BUSINESSES FAIL WITHIN THE FIRST THREE YEARS!

'DON'T BE ONE OF THE UNLUCKY ONES!'

Dear Local Businessman

As businessmen ourselves, we know only too well the risks involved in getting a new venture off the ground. We know too that as your business has already begun to establish itself, you must certainly be determined to succeed. We can make sure that happens.

We are a company specialising in protecting the small business-man. We can take care of everything, so that you need never worry about anything again. We can offer **guaranteed** peace of mind for a reasonable monthly premium.

Our rates begin at £400 per month, but if you should find your-self in short-term difficulty for any reason, payments may be offset at a cost to be negotiated. Compare our terms with any you might find elsewhere, but make sure that you **talk to some of our other clients first**. We're sure you will decide that ours is a service you cannot afford to be without.

Our reputation ensures that from the moment you go into busi-ness with us, you will be free to run your shop, restaurant or company, secure in the knowledge that we are there to handle any problem that may arise.

We can be contacted **24 HOURS A DAY** on the mobile phone number you will be given today by our representative.

Call us right now and buy yourself some peace of mind!

FEBRUARY

THE PRICE OF
BEING HUMAN

Later, Carol Chamberlain would convince herself that she had actually been dreaming about Jessica Clarke when she got the first call. That the noise of the phone ringing had dragged her awake; away from the sound and the smell of it. The fuzzy picture of a girl running, the colours climbing up her back, exploding and flying at her neck like scarves of gold and crimson.

Whether the dream was imagined or not, she'd begun to see it all again the moment she'd put down the phone. Sitting on the edge of the bed, shivering; Jack, who had stirred only momentarily, dead to the world behind her.

She saw it all.

The colours were as bright, and the sound as clear and crisp as it had been that morning twenty years before. She was certain of it. Though Carol had not been there, had not seen any of it with her own eyes, she had spoken to everyone, *everyone* who had. Now she believed that when she ran over it in her mind, when she imagined it, she was seeing it all exactly as it had happened . . .

The sound – of the man's feet on the grass as he climbed the slope, of his tuneless humming – was drowned out by the noise from the playground. Beneath the high-pitched peaks of shouts and screams was a low throb of chatter and gossip, a wave of conversation that rolled across the playground and away down the hillside, towards the main road.

The man listened to it as he got nearer, unable to make out anything clearly. It would almost certainly be talk about boys and music. Who was in and who was out. He could hear another sound, too: the buzz of a lawn-mower from the far side of the school where a team of gardeners was working. They wore green boiler-suits, and so did he. His was only missing the embroidered council logo.

Hands in his pockets, cap pulled down low on his head, he walked around the perimeter of the playground to where the girl and a bunch of her friends were gathered. A few of them were leaning back on the metal, cross-hatched fence, bouncing gently against it, relaxed.

The man removed the secateurs from his belt and squatted, inches away from the girls on the other side of the fence. With one hand, he began snipping at the weeds that sprouted around the base of a concrete fence post. With the other, he reached into his pocket for the can of lighter fluid.

It had always been the smell, more than anything, that had worried him. He'd made sure the can was full and there was not the faintest hiss or gurgle as he squeezed, as the jet of fluid shot from the plastic nozzle through the gap in the fence. His concern was that some hint of it, a whiff as it soaked into the material of the blue, knee-length skirt, might drift up on the breeze and alert the girl or one of her friends.

He needn't have worried. By the time he'd laid the can down on the grass and reached for the lighter, he'd used half the fuel at least, and the girls had been too busy chattering to notice anything. It surprised him that for fifteen seconds or more the girl's skirt smouldered quietly before finally catching. He was also surprised by the fact that she wasn't the one who screamed first . . .

Jessica had only one ear on Ali's story about the party she'd been to and Manda's tale of the latest tiff with her boyfriend. She was still thinking about the stupid row with her mum that had gone on the whole weekend, and the talking-to she'd been given by her father before he'd left for work that morning. When Ali pulled a face and the others laughed, Jessica joined in without really appreciating the joke.

It felt like a small tug at first, and then a tickle, and she leaned forward to smooth down the back of her skirt. She saw Manda's face change then, watched her mouth widen, but she never heard the sound that came out of it. Jessica was already feeling the agony lick at the tops of her legs as she lurched away from the fence and started to run . . .

Long distant from it now, Carol Chamberlain imagined the panic and the pain – as shocked as she always was at the unbearable events unfolding in her mind's eye.

Horribly quickly. Dreadfully slowly . . .

An hour before dawn, it was dark inside the bedroom, but the searing light of something unnatural blazed behind her eyes. With hindsight, with *knowledge,* she was everywhere, able to see and hear it all.

She saw girls' mouths gape like those of old women, their eyes big and glassy as their feet carried them away from the flames. Away from their friend.

She saw Jessica carve a ragged path across the playground, her arms flailing. She heard the screams, the thump of shoes against asphalt, the sizzle as the hair caught. She watched what she knew to be a child move like a thrown firework, skittering across a pavement. Slowing down, fizzing . . .

And she saw the face of a man, of *Rooker,* as he turned and jogged away down the slope. His legs moving faster and faster. Almost, but not quite, falling as he careered down the hill towards his car.

Carol Chamberlain turned and stared at the phone. She thought about the anonymous call she had received twenty minutes earlier. The simple message from a man who could not possibly have been Gordon Rooker.

'I burned her . . .'

ONE

The train was stationary, somewhere between Golders Green and Hampstead, when the woman stepped into the carriage.

Just gone seven on a Monday night. The passengers a pretty fair cross-section of Londoners heading home late, or into the West End to make a night of it. Suits and *Evening Standard*s. The office two-piece and a dog-eared thriller. All human life, in replica football kits and Oxfam chic and Ciro Citterio casuals. Heads bouncing against windows and lolling in sleep, or nodding in time to Coldplay or Craig David or DJ Shadow.

For no good reason other than it was on the Northern Line, the train lurched forward suddenly, then stopped again a few seconds later. People looked at the feet of those opposite, or read the adverts above their heads. The silence, save for the tinny basslines bleeding from headphones, exaggerated the lack of connection.

At one end of the carriage, two black boys sat together. One looked fifteen or sixteen but was probably younger. He wore a red bandanna, an oversized American football jersey and baggy jeans. He was laden with rings and necklaces. Next to him was a much smaller boy, his younger brother perhaps, dressed almost identically.

To the man sitting opposite them, the clothes, the jewellery, the *attitude* seemed ridiculous on a child whose expensive trainers didn't even reach the floor. The man was stocky, in his early forties, and wore a battered brown leather jacket. He looked away when the bigger boy caught him staring, and ran a hand through hair that was greyer on one side than the other. It looked, to Tom Thorne, as if the two boys had blown their pocket money in a shop called 'Mr Tiny Gangsta'.

Within a second or two of the woman coming through the door, the atmosphere in the carriage had changed. From buttoned-up to fully locked-down. English, *in extremis* . . .

Thorne looked at her just long enough to take in the headscarf and the thick, dark eyebrows and the baby cradled beneath one arm. Then he looked away. He didn't quite duck behind a newspaper, like many of those around him, but he was ashamed to admit to himself that this was only because he didn't have one.

Thorne stared at his shoes, but was aware of the hand that was thrust out as the woman stood over him. He could see the polystyrene cup, the top of it picked at, or perhaps chewed away. He could hear the woman speak softly in a language he didn't understand and didn't need to.

She shook the cup in front of his face and Thorne heard nothing rattle.

Then it became a routine: the cup held out, the question asked, the plea ignored and on to the next. Thorne looked up as she moved away down the carriage, feeling an ache building in his gut as he stared at the curve of her back beneath a dark cardigan, the stillness of the arm that supported her baby. He turned away as the ache sharpened into a stab of sorrow for her, and for himself.

He turned in time to watch the older boy lean across to his brother. Sucking his teeth before he spoke. A hiss, like cats in a bag.

'I really hate them people . . .'

Thorne was still depressed twenty minutes later when he walked out of the tube station on to Kentish Town Road. He wasn't feeling much better by the time he kicked the door of his flat shut behind him. But his mood would not stay black for long.

From the living room, a voice was suddenly raised, sullen and wounded, above the noise of the television: 'What bloody time d'you call this?'

Thorne dropped his bag, took four steps down the hall and turned to see Phil Hendricks stretched out on the sofa. The pathologist was taller, skinnier and, at thirty-three, ten years younger than Thorne. He was wearing black, as always – jeans and a V-neck sweater – with the usual assortment of rings, spikes and studs through most of the available space on and around his face. There were other piercings elsewhere, but Thorne wanted to know as little about those as possible.

Hendricks pointed the remote and flicked off the television. 'Dinner will be utterly ruined.' He was normally about as camp as an armoured car, so the joky attempt at being queeny in his flat Mancunian accent made Thorne smile all the more.

'Right,' Thorne said. 'Like you can even boil an egg.'

'Well, it *would* have been ruined.'

'What are we having, anyway?'

Hendricks swung his feet down to the floor and rubbed a hand back and forth across his closely shaved skull. 'Menu's next to the phone.' He waved a hand towards the small table in the corner. 'I'm having the usual, plus an extra mushroom bhaji.'

Thorne shrugged off his jacket and carried it back out into the hall. He came back in, bent to turn down the radiator, carried a dirty mug through to the kitchen. He picked up Hendricks' biker boots from in front of the sofa and carried *them* out into the hall.

Then he picked up the phone and called the Bengal Lancer . . .

Hendricks had been sleeping on Thorne's sofa-bed since just after Christmas, when the collection of mushrooms growing in his own

13

place had reached monstrous proportions. The builders and damp-proofers were supposed to be there for less than a week, but as with all such estimates the reality hadn't quite matched up. Thorne was still unsure why Hendricks hadn't just moved in with his current boyfriend, Brendan – he still spent a couple of nights a week there as it was. Thorne's best guess was that, with a relationship as on and off as theirs, even a temporary move would have been somewhat risky.

He and Hendricks were a little cramped in Thorne's small flat, but Thorne had to admit that he enjoyed the company. They discussed, fully and frankly, the relative merits of Spurs and Arsenal. They argued about Thorne's consuming love of country music. They bickered about Thorne's sudden and uncharacteristic passion for tidiness.

While they were waiting for the curry to arrive, Thorne put on a Lucinda Williams album. He and Hendricks argued about it for a while, and then they began to talk about other things . . .

'Mickey Clayton died as a result of gunshot wounds to the head,' Hendricks said.

Thorne peered across at him over the top of his beer can. 'I'm guessing that wasn't one of your trickier ones. What with most of his head plastered all over the walls when we found him.'

Hendricks pulled a face. 'The full report should be on your desk tomorrow afternoon.'

'Thanks, Phil.' He enjoyed taking the piss, but, aside from being just about his closest friend, Hendricks was the best pathologist Thorne had ever worked with. Contrary to appearances, and despite the sarcasm and the off-colour jokes, there was no one better at understanding the dead. Hendricks listened as they whispered their secrets, translating them from the mysterious language of the slab.

'Did you get the bullet?' Thorne asked. The killer had used a nine-millimetre weapon; what was left of the bullets had been found near the previous victims, or still inside what was left of their skulls . . .

'You won't need a match to tell you it's the same killer.'

'The X?' It had been obvious when the body had been discovered the previous morning. The nylon shirt hoiked up to the back of the neck, the blood-trails running from two deep, diagonal cuts – left shoulder to right hip and vice versa.

'Still not sure about the blade, though. I thought it might be a Stanley knife, but I reckon it could be a machete, something like that.'

Thorne nodded. A machete was the weapon of choice with a number of gangland enforcers. 'Yardies or Yakuza, maybe . . .'

'Well, whoever's paying him, he's enjoying the work. He shoots them pretty quickly afterwards, so I can't be a hundred per cent sure, but I think he does his bit of creative carving while they're still alive.'

The man responsible for the death of Mickey Clayton, and three men before him in the previous six weeks, was like no contract killer Thorne had ever come across or heard about. To these shadowy figures – men who were willing to kill for anything upwards of a few thousand pounds – anonymity was everything. This one was different. He liked to leave his mark. 'X marks the spot,' Thorne said.

'Or X as in "crossed out".' Hendricks drained his can. 'So, what about you? Good day at the office, dear?'

Thorne grunted as he stood up. He took Hendricks' empty can and went through to the kitchen to get them both fresh ones. Staring aimlessly into the fridge, Thorne tried in vain to remember his last good day at the office . . .

His team – of which Hendricks was the civilian member – at the Serious Crime Group (West) had been seconded to help out the Projects Team at SO7 – the Serious and Organised Crime Unit. It had quickly become apparent that *organised* was one thing this particular operation was not. The resources of SO7 were stretched paper thin – or at least that was their story. There *was* a major turf war between two old family firms south of the river, and an escalation in a series of ongoing disputes among Triad gangs that had seen three shootings in one week and a pitched battle on Gerrard Street. All the same, Thorne suspected that he and his team were basically there to cover other people's arses.

There was nothing in it for him. If arrests were ever made, the credit would go elsewhere, and anyway, there was precious little satisfaction in chasing down those responsible for getting rid of pondlife like Mickey Clayton.

The series of fatal 'X' shootings – of which Clayton's was the fourth – was a major assault on the operations of one of north London's biggest gangland families, but the simple fact was that the Projects Team hadn't the first idea who was doing the assaulting. All the obvious rivals had been approached and discounted. All the usual underground sources had been paid and pumped for information, none of which had proved useful. It became clear that a major new operation had established itself and was keen to make a splash. Thorne and his team were on board to find out who they were. Who was paying a contract killer, quickly dubbed the X-Man, to hurt the Ryan family?

'He's making life hard for himself, though, isn't he?' Thorne started talking from the kitchen and continued as he brought the beers into the living room. 'This X thing, this signature or whatever it is, it limits what he can do, where he can do it. He can't just ride up on a motor-bike or wait for them outside a pub. He needs a bit of time and space.'

Hendricks took a can. 'He obviously puts a lot of effort into his work. Plans it. I bet he's bloody expensive.'

Thorne thought Hendricks was probably right. 'It's still cheap though, isn't it? When you think about it. To kill someone, I mean. Twenty, twenty-five grand's about top whack. That's a damn sight less than the people putting out the contracts pay for their Jeeps and top-of-the-range Mercs.'

'What d'you reckon I can get for a couple of hundred quid?' Hendricks asked. 'There's this mortuary assistant at Westminster who's getting on my tits.'

Thorne thought about it for a second. 'Chinese burn?'

The laugh was the first decent one that Thorne could remember sharing with anyone for a few days . . .

'How can it be the Yardies?' Hendricks said when he'd stopped giggling. 'Or Yakuza? We know our hitman's not black or Japanese . . .'

A witness claimed to have seen the killer leaving the scene of the third murder and had given a vague description of a white male in his thirties. The witness, Marcus Moloney, was an 'associate' of the Ryan family, and not what you'd call an upright citizen, but he seemed pretty sure about what he'd seen.

'It's not that simple,' Thorne said. 'It might have been, ten years ago, when people stuck to their own, but now they don't care so much and the freelancers just go where the work is. The Triads use Yardies. Yardies work with the Russians. They nicked a gang of Yakuza last year for recruiting outside schools. They were as good as giving out application forms; signing up Greek lads, Asians, Turks, whoever.'

Hendricks smiled. 'It's nice to see that they're all equal-opportunities employers . . .'

Thorne grunted, and the two of them settled back into saying nothing for a few minutes. Thorne closed his eyes and picked at the goatee he'd grown towards the end of the previous year. The beard created the illusion of a jawline and covered up the scar from a knife wound.

The puckered line that ran diagonally across Thorne's chin was the only visible reminder of a night six months before when he'd both begged for his life and prayed for death to come quickly. There were other scars, easier to disguise, but far more troublesome. Thorne would reach into his gut in the darkness and finger them until they reopened into wounds. He could imagine the scab forming then, blood black across the tender flesh. The crust that would itch and crumble beneath his fingernails, exquisite and agonising, for him to poke and pick at . . .

Lucinda Williams sang softly about an all-consuming lust, her voice sweet and saw-toothed at the same time, rising like smoke above a single acoustic guitar.

Thorne and Hendricks both started slightly when the phone rang.

'Tom?' A woman's voice.

Thorne sank back into his armchair with the phone. He shouted across to Hendricks deliberately loud enough for the caller to hear, 'Oh Christ, it's that mad old woman who keeps phoning me up . . .'

Hendricks grinned and shouted back, 'Tell her I can smell the cat food from here!'

'Come on then, Carol,' Thorne said. 'Tell me what's been happening in glamorous Worthing. Any "cat stuck up tree" incidents or Zimmer-frame pile-ups I should know about?'

The woman on the other end of the line was in no mood for the usual banter. 'I need to talk to you, Tom. I need you to listen . . .'

So, Thorne listened. The curry arrived and went cold, but he didn't even think about it. He could tell as soon as she started to talk that something was seriously wrong.

In all the time he'd known Carol Chamberlain, Thorne had never heard her cry before.

TWO

'I presume you tried 1471 . . .?'

She raised her eyebrows. Asked if he thought she was a complete idiot.

Thorne shrugged an apology.

When he had first met Carol Chamberlain the previous year, he had taken her for a frumpy, middle-aged woman with too much time on her hands; a frumpy, middle-aged woman he had mistakenly assumed to be the mother of one of his constables.

She still claimed not to have forgiven him.

Ex-DCI Carol Chamberlain had arrived in Thorne's office on a humid July morning seven months earlier, and turned the hunt for a sadistic rapist and killer on its head. She was a member of what had become known as the Crinkly Squad – a unit made up of former officers brought out of retirement to work on cold cases. Chamberlain hadn't needed a great deal of persuading to come back. Having done her thirty years, she'd been forced out of the Met – to her way of thinking at least – prematurely, and felt, at fifty-five, that she still had a good deal to offer. The first case she'd worked on had thrown up information that had changed the course of Thorne's investigation, and it would turn out later, his life. The cold case – now anything *but* cold – had quickly been taken away from her, but Thorne had kept in touch and he and Chamberlain had quickly grown close.

Thorne wasn't sure precisely *what* Carol Chamberlain got from her relationship with him, but he was happy to give whatever it was in exchange for her directness, her sound advice and a bullshit detector that seemed to get sharper with age.

Looking at her now across the table, remembering that first impression of her, Thorne wondered how he could have made so gross a misjudgement . . .

Chamberlain held up the dirty cream envelope for Thorne to see, and then tipped it, emptying the ashes on to the table. 'These arrived yesterday morning.'

Thorne picked up a fork and nudged the tines through the blackened scraps of material. He was careful not to touch any of it with his bare hands, but he didn't know why he was bothering. He wasn't sure yet if he was going to do anything about this. The pieces crumbled even as the fork touched them, but he could see that one or two fragments still retained their original blue colour.

'I'll hang on to these.' He picked up a menu and used the edge of it to scrape the ashes back into their envelope.

Chamberlain nodded. 'It's serge, I think. Or heavy cotton. Same material that Jessica Clarke's skirt was made out of . . .'

Thorne thought about what she was saying, what she'd begun to tell him the previous night on the phone. He remembered a little of the case, remembered the outrage, but most of the details were new to him. He asked himself if he'd ever heard such a horrific story.

If he had, he couldn't remember when.

'What sort of sick sod does that to a kid?' Thorne said. He glanced around, anxious not to alarm those at the nearby tables.

Chamberlain waited until he turned back, looked him in the eye. 'One who's getting paid for it.'

'*What?*'

'We thought it was some sort of headcase; everybody did. Us and the schools and the papers, all getting jittery, waiting for him to do it again. Then we found out that Jessica Clarke was the wrong girl . . .'

'How d'you mean, "wrong"?'

'The girl standing next to her in the playground that day was called Alison Kelly. She was one of Jessica's best friends. Same height, same colour hair. She was also the youngest daughter of Kevin Kelly.' She looked at Thorne as though expecting a reaction. She didn't get one.

Thorne shook his head. 'Should I . . .?'

'Let me run you quickly through how it was in 1984. You'd have been about what . . .?'

Thorne did the mental calculation. 'I'd've been about to come out of uniform,' he said. 'About to get married. Sowing the last of my wild oats, probably. Going to clubs, going to gigs . . .'

'You lived in north London, right?'

Thorne nodded.

'Well, chances are that any club you went to was owned by one of the big firms, and the Kellys were the biggest. There were others taking control of the south-east, and there were a few independents knocking about, but the Kellys had a stake in most things north of the river . . .'

As Thorne listened, it struck him that her normal, measured tone had become hesitant; the neutral accent had slipped, allowing her native Yorkshire to emerge. He'd heard it before, when she was angry or excited. When she was fired up about something. If he hadn't already known, he'd have guessed that something had shaken her badly.

'The Kellys were based in and around Camden Town. There were other firms, other families in Shepherd's Bush and Hackney, and they sorted things out between them most of the time. There was the occasional bit of silliness – a couple of shootings a year – but it was no worse than it had ever been. Then, in 1983, someone took a pop at Kevin Kelly . . .'

'Put out a contract?'

'Right, but for one reason or another they didn't get him. Whatever message they were trying to send wasn't understood. So, they went after his daughter.'

'And didn't get her either. Jesus . . .'

'Kelly got the message this time though. A dozen people died in the three weeks after the Jessica Clarke incident. Three brothers from one family were shot in the same pub one night. Kevin Kelly more or less wiped the opposition out.'

Thorne picked up his cup. The coffee was stone cold. 'Leaving Mr Kelly and his friends with most of north London to themselves . . .'

'His friends, yes, but not Kelly. It was like the attempt on his daughter knocked the guts out of him. Once the competition was out of the way, he retired. Upped sticks, just like that. He took his wife, his daughter and a couple of million, and walked away from it.'

'Sounds like a good move . . .'

Chamberlain shrugged. 'He dropped dead five years later. Just gone fifty.'

'So, who ran things once Kelly joined the pipe-and-slippers brigade?'

'Well, it was really just a family in name only. Kelly had no brothers or sons. He handed his entire operation over to one of those friends we were talking about: a particularly nasty piece of work called William Ryan. He was Kelly's number two, and . . .' Chamberlain saw the look on Thorne's face and stopped. 'What?'

'When you've finished the history lesson, I'll bring you up to date.'

'Fair enough.' Chamberlain put down the teaspoon she'd been fiddling with for the past ten minutes.

Thorne pushed back his chair. 'I'm going to get another cup of coffee. Do you want anything?'

They'd met in a small, Greek café near Victoria Station. Chamberlain had caught the train from Worthing first thing that morning, and was planning to get back as quickly as she could.

Standing at the counter, waiting to order, Thorne glanced over at her. He thought that she'd lost a little weight. Ordinarily, he knew that she'd have been delighted, but things seemed far from ordinary. The lines across her face were undisguised. They showed when she looked up and smiled across at him. An old woman suddenly . . . and frightened.

Thorne carried a tray back to the table: two coffees, and a baklava for them to share. He got stuck in straight away and, between mouthfuls, told Chamberlain about the SO7 operation. About the present-day organised-crime set-up in north London. About the as-yet-unidentified challenge to a powerful gangland boss named Billy Ryan . . .

'It's lovely to hear that Billy's done so well for himself,' Chamberlain said.

Thorne was delighted at the sarcasm and the smile. That was more like the Carol Chamberlain he knew. 'Oh, he's done *very* well. And Ryan's certainly *is* a family firm: brothers and cousins all over the shop, plus a son and heir, Stephen.'

'Stephen. I remember him. He'd have been five or six when all this happened . . .'

'Well he's a big boy now. A winning individual by all accounts.'

Chamberlain had picked up the spoon again. She tapped it against her palm. 'Billy married Alison Kelly later on.'

'Kevin Kelly's daughter? The one who . . .?'

She nodded. 'The one who Gordon Rooker *meant* to set fire to. The one he mistook Jessica Clarke for. Her and Billy Ryan got married just before Kelly died, if I remember rightly. It made the old man happy, but it was never going to last. She was a lot younger than he was. Just turned eighteen, I think. He'd have been mid-thirties, with a kid already . . .'

'Not exactly made in heaven then.'

'I think it lasted a year or two. Once everything went pear-shaped, Billy got back together with whichever tart he'd had Stephen with. Married her as soon as the divorce from Alison came through.'

23

Thorne pointed his spoon towards the last piece of baklava. 'I'm eating all of this. Don't you . . .?' She shook her head and he helped himself. 'Tell me about Rooker,' he said.

'There's not a huge amount to tell. He confessed.'

'That always helps.'

By now, the smile was long gone. 'Seriously, Tom, it was about as simple a case as I ever worked on. I was the DI. I took his first statement.'

'And what did you think?'

'It seemed to fit. Rooker wasn't unknown. What he did at that school, to that girl, was well out of the ordinary, admittedly, but he was someone who'd do pretty much anything, or any*body*, if the price was right.'

Thorne had come across far too many people like that. He was coming across more of them all the time. 'Did he say who was paying it?'

'He never went as far as to name anyone, but he didn't have to. We knew that he'd worked for a few of the smaller firms before. He may even have been involved in the failed contract on Kevin Kelly. Also, we knew that Rooker *liked* to burn people. It hadn't been proved, but he was in the frame for a contract job in 1982. Someone, probably Gordon Rooker, tied the boss of a security firm to a chair and emptied a can of lighter fluid into his hair . . .'

'What a charmer.'

'Actually, he was. Or *thought* he was. Bastard was flirting with me in that interview room.' She stopped, swallowed, as if trying to take away a sour taste. 'Like I said, it was simple. Rooker pleaded guilty. He got life. And, as of yesterday, when I called to check, he was still in Park Royal Prison.'

Thorne stretched out a hand and placed it over hers for a few seconds. 'He was still there about three hours ago. When *I* called.'

The smile returned for a moment, but it looked a little forced. 'Thanks, Tom.'

'What about Jessica?'

Chamberlain's eyes flicked away from Thorne's face and she stared past him, out of the café's front window. 'The burns were major. It was a year before she could go back to school.'

'What about now? What does she . . .?'

She shook her head, her voice barely above a whisper. 'You didn't really expect a happy ending, did you, Tom?'

'One would be nice,' Thorne said after a few moments. 'Just occasionally . . .'

She turned back to him and her face softened, as if he were a child asking for something that she couldn't possibly afford.

'She threw herself off a multi-storey car park on her sixteenth birthday . . .'

Muslum Izzigil had been swearing pretty solidly for ten minutes when the two boys walked into his shop.

He was working his way through an enormous pile of tapes, all returned the night before and each one needing to be rewound. People returning videos without bothering to rewind them were the bane of his life. He took a tape out of the machine, slammed it into a box, reached for another. 'Lazy bastards . . .'

He glanced across at the two boys who were flicking through the boxes in the 'used/for sale' bins near the door. He held up one of the tapes and pulled a face. 'How hard is it to rewind? Huh?' One boy looked blankly back at Izzigil, while his friend whispered something and began to laugh. Izzigil hit the rewind button for the umpteenth time and leaned back against the counter. He looked up at the screen, watched a minute or two of an Austin Powers movie, then turned his attention back to the boys.

'New releases over this side,' he said, pointing. 'We haven't got it, film is free next time. Same as Blockbuster.'

The two boys were pulling display boxes from racks in the adult section, leering at the pictures on the back. One boy rubbed a box against his crotch, stuck out his tongue and licked his lips.

'Hey . . .' Izzigil began to gesture. 'Don't mess.'

The boys quickly pulled a couple more boxes from the rack, carried an armful across to the counter and dropped them down. One was almost a foot taller than his mate, but they were both stocky. They wore baseball caps and puffa jackets, the same as Izzigil saw the black kids wearing, hanging around Shopping City on a Saturday afternoon . . .

'Got anything with Turkish birds in?' the taller boy asked.

The other boy leaned on the counter. 'He likes women who are really hairy . . .'

Izzigil felt himself redden. He said nothing, began to gather up the display boxes that the two boys had dropped and piled them up.

'Whatever you've got, I hope it's a damn sight better than this.' The shorter boy reached into his jacket, produced a plain black video box, and slammed it down hard on the counter. 'I rented this from you the other day.'

Izzigil looked at the box, then shook his head. 'Not from here. My boxes are different, look . . .'

'You trying to stitch me up?' the boy said.

'We want our fucking money back, mate . . .'

The smell reached Izzigil then. He almost retched, and let his hand drop below the level of the counter. 'You should go before I call the police . . .'

The taller boy picked up the box, opened it and shook the turd out on to the counter.

Izzigil stepped back. '*Christ!*'

The taller boy began to laugh. His friend pulled a mock-serious face. 'That film's shit, mate . . .'

'Get the fuck out of my shop!' Izzigil reached beneath the counter, but before he could lay his hand on the pool cue the shorter boy had leaned across and a knife was suddenly inches from the shopkeeper's face.

'You were given a letter . . .'

'What letter? I don't know about a letter.'

'Some friends of ours gave you a fucking letter. You were offered the chance to behave like a businessman and you didn't take it. So, now we won't be wasting any more money on fucking notepaper. Clear enough for you?'

Izzigil nodded.

'Now we stop messing about. Next time we might stop by when you're upstairs giving your hairy old lady one, and your son's down here, minding the shop . . .'

Izzigil nodded again, watched over the boy's shoulder as his friend moved slowly around the shop, tipping display cases on to the floor, casually pulling over bins. He saw a customer put one hand on the door, then freeze and move quickly away when he glimpsed what was happening inside.

The boy with the knife took a slow step backwards. He cocked his head and slipped the knife into the back pocket of his jeans. 'Someone will pop round in the next week or two to go over things,' he said.

Izzigil's hand tightened around the pool cue then. He knew it was much too late to be of any use, but he squeezed it as he watched the two boys leave.

On the screen above him, Austin Powers was dancing to a Madonna song as Izzigil came slowly around the counter and walked towards the front of the shop. He pressed himself against the window and looked both ways along the street.

'Muslum . . .?'

Izzigil turned at his wife's voice and took a step back into the shop. He saw her eyes suddenly widen and her mouth drop open, and he turned back just as the black shape rushed towards the window. Just as the world seemed to explode with noise and pain and a terrible waterfall of glass.

They walked slowly back along Buckingham Palace Road, towards the station. It was the middle of the lunch hour, and people were queuing out of the doors of delis and coffee-shops. February was starting to bite and Thorne's jacket was zipped up to the top, his hands thrust right down into the pockets.

'How's Jack doing?'

Chamberlain stopped for a second to let a girl dart across the pavement in front of her. 'He's the same.' They moved off again. 'He tries to be supportive, but he didn't really want me to go back to it. I know he worries that I'm taking on too much, but I was going mental stuck in the house.' She looked at herself in a shop window, ran fingers through her hair. 'I couldn't give a shit about gardening . . .'

'I meant about these phone calls. That letter.'

'He doesn't know about the letter and he slept through all but one of the calls. I told him it was a wrong number.' She pulled the scarf she was wearing tighter around her throat. 'Now I'm more or less hovering over the bloody phone all night long. It's almost worse on the nights when he *doesn't* ring.'

'You're not sleeping at all? It's been going on for a bloody fortnight, Carol . . .'

'I catch up in the day. I never slept much in the first place.'

'What's he sound like?' Thorne asked.

She answered quickly and simply. Thorne guessed that she'd known the questions he would ask, because they were the ones *she* would have asked.

'He's very calm. Like he's telling me things that are obvious. Like he's reminding me of things I've forgotten . . .'

'Accent?'

She shook her head.

'Any thoughts as to his age?'

She carried on shaking it.

'Look, I know this is going to sound strange, but I'm not sure why you didn't just call the police.'

She started to speak, but Thorne stopped her.

'I mean the local lads. This is just some nutter, Carol. It's a kid pissing you about. It's someone who's read some poxy true-crime book and hasn't got anything better to do.'

'He knows things, Tom. Things that never came out. He knows about the lighter that was dropped at the scene, which brand of fuel was used . . .'

'It's someone Rooker spent time with inside, then. Rooker's told him to wind you up when he's got out.'

She shook her head. 'There's no reason for Rooker to send anyone after me. He confessed, remember. Anyway, Rooker bloody well *liked* me.'

'He had a relationship with you. You were the one who interviewed him. Which is why *you're* the one being targeted now, and not whoever the SIO was.'

'I think it's just because I'm next in line. The DCI on the case left the force well before I did. He emigrated to New Zealand ten years ago. He'd be a damn sight harder to track down than I was.'

It made sense, but Thorne had one other suggestion. 'Or maybe, whoever it is knows that you were . . . *affected* by what happened to Jessica.'

She looked up at him, concerned. 'How would anyone know that? How do *you* know . . .?'

They walked on in silence for fifty yards or so before Thorne spoke again. 'Are you worried that you put the wrong man away, Carol? Is that what this is about?'

'No, it isn't. Gordon Rooker burned Jessica Clarke. I know he did.'

They didn't speak again until they reached the station.

Halfway across the concourse she stopped and turned to him. 'There's no need to bother waiting. I've got quarter of an hour until the next train back.'

'It's fine. I don't mind.'

'Get back to work. I like to potter about a bit anyway. I'll buy a magazine, get myself sorted. I'm a fussy old bat like that.'

'You're not fussy.'

She leaned forward to kiss him on the cheek. 'Cheeky sod.'

Thorne sighed and broke their embrace. 'I don't quite know what you expect me to do about this, Carol. There's nothing *I* can do officially that anybody else couldn't.'

'I don't want you to do *anything* officially.'

He saw then, despite the light-hearted tone and the banter of a few moments before, just how rattled she really was. The very last thing she wanted was to let the powers-that-be see it, too. He couldn't believe that they'd take her off the Cold Case Unit, but there were plenty who thought the Met should not be using people who'd be better off queuing up in the post office.

'Right,' Thorne said eventually. 'But it's OK for me to waste *my* time.'

Chamberlain pulled a large handbag on to her small shoulder and turned on her heels. 'Something like that . . .'

Thorne watched her disappear inside WH Smith.

Walking back towards the underground, he thought about scars that you hid, and those that you showed off. Scars bad enough to make you jump off a car-park.

THREE

These rooms always had one thing in common. The size might vary, the style was usually governed by age, and the decor was dependent on the whim of budgets or the inclination of the top brass. But they invariably had the same smell. Chrome and tinted glass or flaking orange plasterboard. Freezing or overheated. Intimate or anything but. Whatever the place was like, that smell would tell you where you were with a sack over your head. Thorne could sniff it up and name its constituent parts like a connoisseur: stale cigarette smoke, sweat and desperation.

He looked around. This one had a bit of everything – a fresh coat of magnolia, the fumes charged up by the heat coming off radiators a foot thick. There was a snazzy new system of coloured chairs. Blue for visitors, red for inmates . . .

Most chairs were occupied, but a few red ones remained vacant. A black woman in the next row but one glanced across at him. The seat opposite her was empty. She smiled nervously, her eyes crinkling behind thick glasses, and then looked away before Thorne had a chance to smile back. He watched the woman beam as a young man –

her son, Thorne guessed – swaggered towards her. The man grinned, then checked himself slightly, looked around to see if anyone had noticed him drop his guard.

Thorne checked his watch: just before ten. He needed to get this over with as quickly as possible and get back to the office. He'd called DC Dave Holland earlier, on his way west across London, towards HMP Park Royal . . . 'I need you to cover for me,' he'd said. 'Tell Tughan I'm off seeing a snout, or that I'm following up a hunch, or whatever. You know, some "copper" bollocks . . .'

'Do I get to know what you're really doing?'

'I'm doing someone a favour. I should be back by lunchtime if the traffic's all right, so . . .'

'Are you *driving*? When did you get the car back?'

Thorne knew what was coming. He was stupid to have let it slip. 'I got it back late yesterday,' he'd said.

The car in question, a pulsar-yellow BMW, was thirty years old, and Thorne had parted with a good deal of money for it the year before. Thorne thought it was a classic. Others preferred the term 'antique'. Holland, in particular, never missed an opportunity to take the piss, having maintained from the moment he'd seen it that the car was a big mistake. He'd gone to town when it had spectacularly failed its MOT and disappeared into the garage a fortnight earlier.

'How much?' Holland had asked, gleeful.

Thorne had cursed as he'd caught a red light. He'd yanked up the handbrake. 'It's an old car, all right? The parts are expensive.' Not only were they expensive, but there seemed to be a great many of them. Thorne couldn't remember them all, but he could recall the growing feeling of despair as they were cheerfully reeled off to him. For all Thorne knew about what was going on under the bonnet, the mechanic might just as well have been speaking Serbo–Croat.

'Five hundred?' Holland had said. 'More?'

'Listen, she's old, but she's still gorgeous. Like one of those actresses that's knocking on, but still tasty, you know?' As the car was a BMW,

Thorne had tried to come up with a German actress who would fit the bill. He had failed. Felicity Kendal, he'd said as he pulled away from the lights. Yeah, that'll do.

'She?' Holland had sounded hugely amused.

'*She's* like Felicity Kendal.'

'People who call their car "she" are one step away from a pair of string-back driving gloves and a pipe . . .'

At the noise of the chair opposite him being scraped backwards, Thorne looked up and saw Gordon Rooker dropping on to the red seat. Thorne had never seen a picture, or been given a description, but there was no mistaking him.

'Anyone sitting here?' asked Rooker, a gold tooth evident as he smiled.

He was sixty, give or take a year or two, and tall. His face was thin and freshly shaved. The skin hung, leathery and loose, from his neck, and a full head of white hair had yellowed above the forehead with a lifetime's fags.

Thorne nodded towards the green bib that Rooker wore, that *all* the prisoners wore on top of the regulation blue sweatshirts. 'Very fetching,' he said.

'We've all got to wear these now,' Rooker said. 'A few places have had them for ages, but a lot of governors, including the one here, thought they were demeaning to the prisoners, which is all very splendid and progressive of them. Then a lifer in Gartree swaps places with his twin brother when nobody's looking and walks out through the front door. So, now it has to be obvious who's the prisoner and who isn't, and we all have to dress like prize prats when we have visitors. You think I'm making this up, don't you?'

The voice was expressive and lively. The voice of a pub philosopher or comedian, nicely weathered by decades on forty roll-ups a day. While Rooker was speaking, Thorne had taken out his warrant card. He slid it across the table. Rooker didn't bother to look at it.

'What do you want, Mr Thorne?' He held up a hand. 'No, don't bother, let's just have a natter. I'm sure you'll get round to it eventually.'

'I'm a friend of Carol Chamberlain.'

Rooker narrowed his eyes.

'She'd've been Carol Manley when you knew her . . .'

The gold tooth came slowly into view again. 'Did that woman ever make commissioner? I always reckoned she had it in her.'

Thorne shook his head. 'She was a DCI when she retired. That was seven or eight years ago.'

'She was a decent sort, you know?' Rooker looked away, remembering something. His eyes slid back to Thorne. 'I'm not surprised she got married; she was a good-looking woman. Still fit, is she? Is she a game old bird?' He leaned across the table. 'Do you like 'em a bit older?'

Whether the suggestive comments were an attempt to unsettle or to bond, Thorne ignored them. 'She's being *bothered*. Some lunatic is sending letters and making calls . . .'

'I'm sorry to hear that.'

'Whoever he is, he claims to be the person responsible for the attempted murder of Jessica Clarke.' Thorne looked hard at Rooker, studied his face for a reaction. 'He reckons he was the one who burned her, Gordon.'

There was a reaction, no question, but Thorne had no idea what Rooker was so amused about.

'Funny?' Thorne asked.

'Pretty funny, yeah. Like I said, I'm sorry about Miss Manley, or whatever she's called now, being bothered, but it's a laugh when you get your own personal nutter, isn't it? It's taken him long enough, mind you, whoever he is . . .'

'You're telling me you don't know who this person is?'

Rooker turned up his palms, tucked them behind his bib. 'Not a fucking clue.'

If he'd been asked at that instant to put money on whether Rooker was telling the truth, Thorne would happily have stumped up a few quid.

'I've had plenty of letters over the years,' Rooker continued, grinning. 'You know, the ones in green ink where they've pressed so hard that the pen's gone through the paper. People who want me to tell them stuff, so they can have a wank over it or whatever. I've had a few mad women and what have you, writing steamy letters, saying they want to marry me . . .'

A case the year before – when Thorne had first encountered Carol Chamberlain – had begun with just that sort of letter. It had not been genuine, but plenty were, and Thorne never ceased to be amazed, and sickened, by them. 'Well, Gordon, you're obviously quite a catch.'

'But this is different, right? This is sort of like a stalker in reverse. He can't stalk *me*, so he's stalking somebody else, somebody who was involved in it all, and he's *pretending* to be me. Pretending he did what I did . . .'

Thorne decided it was time to stop pissing about. 'So he *is* pretending then, is he? Because that's basically why I'm here. To make sure.'

The cockiness, the *ease*, melted slowly back into the lines of Rooker's face. The shoulders drooped forward. The voice was low and level. *Matter of fact . . .*

'You can be sure. I set fire to that girl. That's basically why *I'm* here.'

For half a minute, Thorne watched Rooker stare down at the table-top. His scalp was visible, pink and flaking beneath the white hair. 'Like you said, though. He's waited a long time, this nutter. Why *have* you been here so long, Gordon?'

The animation returned. 'Ask the fucking judge. Miserable arse-hole's dead by now, if there's any justice.' He laughed, humourlessly, at his own joke. 'Like he'd know justice if it bit him in the bollocks.'

'It was a high-profile case,' Thorne said. 'You were always going to get sent down for a long one.'

'Listen, I wasn't expecting a slap on the wrists, all right? Look at what some of these bastards get away with now, though. Blokes who've carved up their wives are getting out after ten years. Less sometimes . . .'

Without an ounce of sympathy, knowing that he deserved every second he spent banged up, Thorne could nevertheless understand the point that Rooker was making. The twenty-year tariff – or 'relevant part of the sentence' – he'd been handed was more than twice many so-called 'life sentences' Thorne had seen doled out.

'There's no fairness to it,' Rooker said. 'Twenty years. Twenty years on fucking VP wings . . .'

Thorne tried not to smirk: Vulnerable Prisoners. 'Are you still *vulnerable* then, Gordon?'

Rooker blinked, said nothing.

'Still dangerous, though, apparently. Twenty years and still a Cat. B? You can't have been a very good boy.'

'There have been a few incidents . . .'

'Never mind, eh? Almost done, aren't you?'

'Three months left until the twenty's up . . .'

Thorne leaned back, glanced to his right. The black woman caught his eye as she fished a crumpled tissue out of her handbag. He turned back to Rooker. 'It's a coincidence, don't you reckon? This bloke turning up now, claiming responsibility.'

Rooker shook his head. 'I doubt it. This is the best possible time to get the attention, isn't it? When I'm coming up for release. For *possible* release. Mind you, if he thinks they're going to let me out, he's dafter than I thought.'

'What is it, a DLP?'

Rooker nodded. Once the tariff was completed, the Discretionary Lifer Panel of the Parole Board could recommend release to the Home Secretary. The panel comprised a judge, a psychiatrist and one other professional connected to the case, a criminologist or a probation officer. The review, unlike normal parole procedure, involved an oral hearing, and the prisoner could bring along a lawyer, or a friend, to represent him.

'I've got no sodding chance,' Rooker said. 'I've already had a couple of knockbacks in as many years.' He looked at Thorne, as if expecting some sort of explanation or reassurance. He received neither. 'What have I got to do? I've been to counselling, I've gone on Christ knows how many courses . . .'

'Remorse is important, Gordon.' The word seemed almost to knock Rooker back in his seat. Thorne leaned forward. 'These people are big on that, for some mysterious reason. They like to see some victim empathy, you know? Some shred of understanding about what it is that you actually *did* to your victim, to her family. Maybe they don't think you're sorry enough, Gordon. What do you reckon? Maybe that's the question they want answering. Where's the remorse?'

'I held up my hand to it, didn't I? I confessed.'

'It's not the same thing.'

The scrape of Rooker's chair as he pushed himself back from the table was enough to make Thorne wince. 'Are we done?' Rooker asked.

Thorne eased his own chair back and looked again to his right, where the black woman was now sobbing, the tissue pressed against her mouth. He caught the eye of the man sitting opposite her.

The man looked back at Thorne like he wanted to rip his head off.

As promised, Tom Thorne had rung as soon as he'd left the prison. He'd told her briefly about his meeting with Rooker. She'd heard everything she'd hoped to hear, and yet the relief which Carol Chamberlain had expected was slow in coming.

She sat at her desk, in the makeshift office she and Jack had rigged up in the spare room the year before. It was less cluttered than it had been then, a lot of junk transferred to the top of the wardrobe and stuffed beneath the spare bed, box-files piled on top of what used to be a dressing-table. It was now used as a bedroom only once or twice a year when Jack's daughter from his first marriage made the effort to visit.

Jack shouted up to her from downstairs. 'I'm making some tea, love. D'you want some?'

'Please.'

Chamberlain could never understand those colleagues – *ex*-colleagues – who insisted that they couldn't remember certain cases. She was bemused by those who struggled to recall the names and faces of certain rapists and murderers; or their victims. Yes, you forgot a file number, or the colour of a particular vehicle, of course you did, but the *people* stayed with you. They stayed with *her* at any rate.

And she knew that they stayed with Tom Thorne, too. She recalled him telling her once that the faces he could *never* forget were those he'd never seen. The ones belonging to the killers he had never caught. The smug faces he imagined on those that had got away with it.

Perhaps those who claimed *not* to remember had developed some technique for forgetting; some trick of the trade. If so, she wished that she'd been a bit closer to some of them, spent a few more nights in curry houses or out on the piss. If she had, they might have passed the secret on to her.

For reasons she wasn't ready to admit to herself, she hadn't wanted to pull the Jessica Clarke files officially, to draw any attention to herself or to the case. Instead, she'd called in a favour, gone down to the General Registry in Victoria, and taken a quick look while an old friend's back was turned. Within a few seconds of opening the first battered brown folder, she could see that she'd remembered Gordon Rooker perfectly. The face in the faded black-and-white ID photo was exactly as she'd been picturing it since the night when she'd received that first phone call . . .

'*I burned her . . .*'

It was *still* the face she pictured now, despite the two decades that had passed. She'd tried, since speaking to Thorne, to age the image mentally, to give it the white hair and lines that Thorne had described, but without any success.

She guessed this was the way memory worked . . .

A colleague on the Cold Case Unit, now a man in his early sixties, had worked on the Moors Murders case. He told her that when he thought about Hindley and Brady, he still saw those infamous pictures of them, smug and sunken-eyed. He could never imagine the raddled old man and the smiling, mumsy brunette.

Bizarrely, Carol Chamberlain *needed* to remember Rooker's face. She equated this total recall of him with the confidence she had in his guilt. It was an illogical, ridiculous collision of ideas, and yet, to her, it made perfect sense. His face, the one she knew every inch of, was the face of the man she saw kneeling by the fence. His face, the one she remembered smiling across an interview room, was the face of the man she saw running away, exhilarated, down the hill, away from the school.

She clung to that memory now, her grip stronger since the call from Thorne. Of course, there had been doubt, and she knew, from his question about Rooker at the station, that Thorne had sensed it. It had sprouted in the dark and pushed as she'd sat shivering. It had grown like a weed, forcing its way up through the cracks in a slab as she'd lain awake.

'*I burned her . . .*'

Now, thankfully, that doubt was dying. It had begun to shrivel from the moment she'd picked up the phone and made that call to Thorne. Now Thorne had been to see Rooker and heard him confirm it. Heard him *confess* it, *again* . . .

There was relief, but it could never be complete, for while the remembrance of Rooker's face was oddly comforting, there was also the face of Jessica Clarke to consider.

Chamberlain had seen photos; snaps of a smiling teenager, pale skin and dark hair down past her shoulders. She could still see the hands of the parents trembling as they lifted wooden picture frames from a sideboard, but the girl's face – the smooth, *perfect* face she'd had before – had been all too easy to forget.

She could hear Jack coming upstairs with the tea. She tried to blink the image away.

She always remembered Gordon Rooker exactly as he had been the first time she'd laid eyes on him. She was cursed to remember Jessica Clarke the same way.

At the end of the day, Thorne climbed into the BMW with a damn sight more enthusiasm than he'd had when getting into it eleven hours before. He pulled out of the car park of the Peel Centre, and for the next few minutes drove on autopilot. Most of his attention was focused on the far more important task of choosing the right music. The car had a six-disc CD multichanger mounted in the boot, and Thorne relished the time he spent once a week rotating the discs, making sure his selections gave him a good choice, but also a decent balance. There'd generally be something from the early years of country music and something more contemporary – Hank Williams and Lyle Lovett were the bookends at the moment. Sandwiched between them would be a couple of compilations, sometimes a soundtrack, and usually an alt country outfit he was getting into – Lambchop maybe, or Calexico. And there was *always* a Cash album.

He scanned through the choices available. It was important that he make the right one, to carry him through the thirty-minute drive and deliver him home in a different mood. He needed to drift a little, to lose himself in the music and let at least some of the tension bleed away.

The problem was Tughan . . .

Half a mile shy of Hendon, Thorne had settled for *Unchained*. By the time Cash's vocal came in on 'Sea of Heartbreak' and he was smacking his palms against the steering wheel, Thorne was starting to feel much better. As well as it was possible to feel, given the current procedural set-up. The current personnel . . .

He drove east for a while, then cut south, crossing the North Circular and heading towards Golders Green.

Thorne had clashed with Nick Tughan on a case four years previously, and he'd thanked all the deities he didn't believe in when their paths had finally separated. While Thorne had been part of the new team established at the Serious Crime Group, Tughan had found other tits to get on at SO7. Now he was back as part of the investigation into the Ryan killings, the investigation with which Thorne and his team were supposed to cooperate. He was back giving Thorne grief. Worst of all, the slimy fucker was back as a DCI.

Though they hadn't set eyes on each other for four years, their relationship had picked up exactly where it had left off. It had been neatly encapsulated in their first, terse exchange in the Major Incident Room at Becke House:

'Thorne . . .'

'Tughan . . .'

'I'll settle for "Sir" or "Guv" . . .'

'What about "twat"?'

If an officer were to get physical, to throw a punch, for example, at another officer of equal or subordinate rank, things could get a tad sticky. If he were to throw that punch – and break a nose, or maybe a cheekbone – even if he just handed out a good, hard slap, to a *superior* officer – a DCI, say – he would be in a world of very deep shit. Thorne was thinking about just how unfair this was when his mobile began to ring.

He took a deep breath when he saw the name on the caller ID.

'Tom . . .?' Auntie Eileen, his father's younger sister. 'Listen, there's no need to panic . . .'

Thorne listened, glancing in the rear-view mirror, swerving across the road and pulling up in a bus lane. He listened as buses and cabs drove around him, deaf to the swearing of the irate drivers, to the bark and bleat of their horns. He listened, feeling sick, then scared, and finally fucked off beyond belief.

He ended the call, dragged the car through a U-turn, and accelerated north, back the way he'd come.

The scorch mark rose up the wall behind the cooker and licked a foot or so across the ceiling. The patterned wallpaper had bubbled, then blistered, where the grease that had accumulated over the years had begun to cook the dried paste and plaster beneath. The windows in the kitchen were open, had been for several hours, but still the stench was disgusting.

'No more fucking chip pans,' Thorne said. 'We get rid of *all* the pans, *all* the oil in the place.'

Eileen looked rather shocked. Thorne thought it was his language but then realised when she spoke that it was more than that.

'We should disconnect the *cooker*,' she said. 'Better still, we should get someone to come and take the bloody thing away . . .'

'I'll get it organised,' Thorne said.

'Why don't you let me?'

'I'll sort it.'

Eileen shrugged and sighed. 'He *knows* he's not supposed to come in here.'

'Maybe we should put a lock on the door in the meantime.' Thorne began walking around the room, opening cupboards. 'He was probably hungry . . .'

She nodded. 'He might well have missed his lunch. I think he's been swearing at the Meals on Wheels woman.'

'They don't call it Meals on Wheels any more, Eileen.'

'He called her a "fucking cow". Told her to "stick her hot-pot up her fat arse".' She was trying not to laugh, but once she saw Thorne giving in to it, she stopped bothering to try.

With the tension relieved, they both leaned back against worktops. Eileen folded her arms tight across her chest.

'Who called the fire brigade?' Thorne asked.

'*He* did, eventually. Once he worked out that it was the smoke alarm going off, he hit the panic button. For a while, I don't think he could remember what the noise was.'

Thorne let his head drop back, looked up at the ceiling. There was a spider's web of smoke-stained cracks around the light fitting. He knew very well that, some mornings, his father had trouble remembering what his shoes were for.

'We really need to think about doing something. Tom?'

Thorne looked across at her. For years, Eileen and his father had not been close, but since the Alzheimer's diagnosis two years earlier, she had been a tower of strength. She'd organised virtually everything, and though she lived in Brighton, she still managed to get up to his father's place in St Albans more often than Thorne did from north London.

Thorne felt tired and a little light-headed, exhausted as always by the combination punches of gratitude and guilt.

'How come they called *you*?' he asked.

'Your father gave one of the firemen my number, I think . . .'

Thorne raised his arms and his voice in mock-bewilderment. 'My number's on all the contact sheets.' He started looking in cupboards again. 'Home *and* mobile.'

'He can always remember my number, for some reason. It must be quite an easy one . . .'

'And why did it take *you* so long to ring? I could have got here well before you.'

Eileen walked across to him, let a hand drop on to his forearm. 'He didn't want to worry you.'

'He knew I'd be bloody furious with him, you mean.'

'He didn't want to worry you, and then *I* didn't want to worry you. The fire was already out by the time they called, anyway. I just thought I'd better get here first, tidy up a bit.'

Thorne tried to shut the cupboard door, but it was wonky and refused to close properly, however hard he slammed it.

'Thanks for doing that,' he said, finally.

'We should at least *talk* about it,' she said. 'We could consider the options.' She pointed towards the cooker. 'We've been lucky, but maybe now's the time to think about your dad going somewhere. We could get this place valued, at the very least . . .'

'No.'

'I'm worried he might start going off; you know, getting lost. There was a thing on the radio about tagging. We could get one of those tags put on him and then at least if he *did* forget where he was . . .'

'That's what they do to juvenile offenders, Eileen. It's what they put on bloody muggers.' He moved past her and into the narrow hall. He glared at himself briefly in the hall mirror, then leaned on the door to the living room and stepped inside.

Jim Thorne sat forward on a brown and battered armchair. He was hunched over a low coffee-table, strewn with the pieces of various radios he'd taken apart and was failing to put together again. He spoke without looking up.

'I fancied chips,' he said. He had more of an accent than Thorne. The voice was higher, and prone to a rattle.

'There's a perfectly good chippy at the end of the road, for Christ's sake . . .'

'It's not the same.'

'You *love* the chips from that chippy.'

'I wanted to *cook* 'em.' He raised his head, gestured angrily with a thick piece of plastic. 'I wanted to make my own fucking chips, all right?'

Thorne bit his tongue. He walked slowly across to the armchair next to the fire and dropped into it.

He wondered whether this was the point at which the disease moved officially from 'mid' to 'late' stage. Maybe it wasn't defined by anything clinical at all. Maybe it was just the first time that the person with the disease almost killed themselves . . .

'Bollocks,' his father said to nobody in particular.

It had been a struggle up to now, no question, but they'd been managing. The practical difficulties with keys and with mail and with money; the disorientation over time and place; the obsession with trivia; the complete lack of judgement about what to wear, and when to wear it; the drugs for depression, for mood swings, for the verbally

44

abusive behaviour. Still, his father hadn't wandered away and fallen into a ditch yet. He hadn't started knocking back bleach like it was lemonade. He hadn't *endangered* himself. Until now . . .

'You know you're supposed to stay out of the kitchen,' Thorne said.

Then came the two words the old man seemed to say most often these days. His 'catchphrase' he called it, in his better moods. Two words spat out or dribbled, sobbed or screamed, but mostly mumbled, through teeth grinding together in frustration: 'I forgot.'

'I know, and you forgot to turn the cooker off. The rules are there for a good reason, you know? What happens if you forget that knives are sharp? Or that toasters and water aren't meant to go together . . .?'

His father looked up suddenly, excitement spreading across his face as he latched on to a thought. 'More people die in their own homes than anywhere else,' he said. 'Nearly five thousand people a year die because of accidents in the home and garden. I read it. More in the living room than in the kitchen, as a matter of fact, which I thought was surprising.'

'Dad . . .' Thorne watched as concentration etched itself into his father's features and he began to count off on his fingers and thumbs.

'Falls are top of the list, if I remember rightly. "Impact accidents", they're called. Electrocution's another good one. Fire, obviously. Choking, suffocation, DIY incidents . . .'

'Why didn't you give them my number to call?'

His father continued to count off, but began mouthing the words silently. After half a minute or so he stopped, and went back to poking about among the coils and circuits scattered across the table.

Thorne watched him for a while. 'I'll stay the night,' he said.

The old man grinned and got to his feet. He reached into his pocket and produced a crumpled five-pound note. He held it out, waved it at Thorne. 'Here you go. Here's some . . . bugger . . .' He closed his eyes, struggling to find the word. 'A piece of the stuff people buy things with . . .'

'What do I want money for?'

'*Money!*'

'What do I want it for?'

'To nip down the road and get us some chips. I still haven't had my fucking dinner yet . . .'

He lay awake in the dark, thinking about the burning girl.

He'd never really *stopped* thinking about her, for one reason or another, not for any significant length of time, but lately, for obvious reasons, she'd been on his mind a great deal. The colours and the smells, which had understandably faded over the years, were suddenly more vivid, more pungent than they had been at any time since it had all happened. Not that he'd had much more than a second or two back then to take it all in. Once the flames had taken hold, he'd had to be away sharpish, down that hill towards the spot where he'd parked the car. He'd moved almost as quickly as the girl herself.

The rest of it – the girl's face and what have you – had been filled in afterwards. He'd seen it, swathed in bandages, splashed across every front page and every television screen. Later, he'd seen what she looked like with the bandages off; it was impossible to tell how her face had been before.

It was funny, he thought. *Ironic.* If he *had* seen her face that day at the playground, he would have realised she wasn't the one. Afterwards, of course, nobody would mistake her for anyone else ever again.

He drifted, eventually, towards sleep. Thoughts giving way to fuzzy pictures and feelings . . .

He remembered her arms flailing in the instant before she began to run, as though it were nothing more serious than a wasp. He remembered the sound of her shoes on the playground as he turned away. He remembered feeling like such a fucking idiot when he realised she was entirely the wrong girl.

Thorne spent most of the night writhing across nylon sheets, sinking into the ludicrously soft mattress in his father's spare room and drag-ging back the duvet which had slid away from him down the natural slope of the bed. He felt like he'd only just got off to sleep when his phone rang. He checked his watch and saw that it was already gone nine-thirty. At the same instant that he began to panic, he remembered that he'd called Brigstocke the night before to tell him what was going on. They wouldn't be expecting him at the office.

He reached down towards where the phone lay chirping on top of his clothes. His neck ached and his arms were freezing.

It was Holland. 'I'm in a video shop in Wood Green,' he said. 'We've got two bodies, still warm. And that's not the title of one of the videos . . .'

FOUR

The uniformed constable who'd been first on the scene was sitting at a small table in a back room, next to a teenage boy whom Thorne guessed was Muslum Izzigil's son. Thorne stared across at them from the doorway. He couldn't decide which of the two looked the younger, or the most upset.

Holland stood at Thorne's shoulder. 'The boy ran out into the street when he found them. Constable Terry was having breakfast in the caff opposite. He heard the boy screaming.'

Thorne nodded and closed the door quietly. He turned and moved back into the shop, where screens had been hastily erected around the bodies. The scene of crime team moved with a practised efficiency, but it seemed to Thorne that the usual banter – the dark humour, the *craic* – was a little muted. Thorne had hunted serial killers; he had known the atmosphere at crime scenes to be charged with respect, even fear, at the presentation, the *offering up*, of the latest victim. This was not what they were looking at now. This was almost certainly a contract killing. Still, there was an odd feeling in the room. Perhaps it was the fact that there were two bodies. That they had been husband and wife.

'Where was the boy when it happened?'

'Upstairs,' Holland said. 'Getting ready for school. He didn't hear anything.'

Thorne nodded. The killer had used a silencer. 'This one's a little less showy than the X-Man,' he said.

Muslum Izzigil was sitting against the wall between a display of children's videos and a life-sized cardboard cut-out of Lara Croft. His head was cocked to one side, his eyes half-open and popping. A thin line of blood ran from the back of his head, along freshly shaved jowls, soaking pink into the collar of a white nylon shirt. The body of his wife lay, face downwards, across his legs. There was very little blood, and only the small, blackened hole behind her ear told the story of what had happened. Or at least, some of it . . .

Which one had he killed first? Did he make the husband watch while his wife was executed? Did the wife die only because she had tried to save her husband?

Thorne looked up from the bodies. He noticed the small camera in the corner of the shop. 'Too much to hope for, I suppose?'

'*Far* too much,' Holland said. 'The recorder's not exactly hard to find. It's over there underneath the counter. The shooter took the tape with him.'

'One to show the grandchildren . . .'

Holland knelt and pointed with a biro to the back of the dead woman's neck. 'Twenty-two, d'you reckon?'

Thorne could see where the blood was gathering then. It encircled her neck like a delicate necklace, but it was pooling, sticky between her chin and the industrial grey carpet. 'Looks like it,' he said. He was already moving across the shop towards the back room. Towards what was going to be a difficult conversation . . .

Constable Terry got to his feet when Thorne came through the door. Thorne waved him back on to his chair. 'What's the boy's name?'

The boy answered the question himself: 'Yusuf Izzigil.'

Thorne put him at about seventeen. Probably taking A levels. He'd gelled his short, black hair into spikes and was making a decent enough job of growing a moustache. The hysteria which Holland had mentioned, which had first alerted the police, had given way to a stillness. He was quiet now, and seemingly composed, but the tears were still coming just as quickly, each one pushed firmly away with the heel of a hand the instant it brimmed and began to fall.

He started to speak again, without being asked. 'I was getting ready upstairs. My father always came down just after eight o'clock, to deal with the tapes that had been returned in the overnight box. My mother came down to help him get things set up once she'd put the breakfast things away.' He spoke well, and slowly, with no trace of an accent. Thorne realised suddenly that the maroon sweater and grey trousers were a uniform, and guessed that the boy went to a private school.

'So you heard nothing?' Thorne asked. 'No raised voices?'

The boy shook his head. 'I heard the bell go on the door when someone opened it, but that isn't unusual.'

'It was a bit early, though, wasn't it?'

'We often have customers who come in on their way to work, to pick up a film that's been returned the night before.'

'Anything else . . .?'

'I was in the bathroom after that. There was water running. If not, I might have heard something.' His hand went to his face, pressed and wiped. 'They had silencers on their guns, didn't they?'

It was an odd thing to say. Thorne wondered if perhaps the boy knew more than he was telling, but decided it was probably down to seeing far too many of the shitty British gangster movies his father kept on the shelves.

'What makes you think there was more than one of them, Yusuf?'

'A week ago two boys came in. About the same age as me, my father said. They tried to scare him.'

'What did they do?'

'Pathetic stuff, threats. Dog mess in a video case. Throwing a litter

50

bin through the window.' He pointed towards the shopfront, where a thick black curtain now ran across the plate-glass window and front door, rigged up to hide the activity within from the eyes of passers-by. 'There was a letter first. My father ignored it.'

'Did he keep the letter?'

'My mother will have filed it somewhere. She never throws anything away.'

The boy realised what he'd said, and blinked slowly. The hand that went to his face stayed there a little longer this time. Thorne remembered the sign he'd seen stuck to the front of the till: *You are being recorded.* 'Did your father get it on tape? The incident with the two boys?'

'I should think so. He recorded everything, but it won't be there any more.'

Thorne asked the question with a look.

'Because he used the same few tapes over and over again,' Yusuf said. 'Changed them half a dozen times every day, and recorded over them. He was always trying to save money, but this business with the videotapes was really stupid, considering that we *sold* the bloody things. Always trying to save money . . .'

The boy's head dropped. The tears that came were left to run their course, the hands that had been wiping them away now clutching the countertop.

'You're not a child, Yusuf,' Thorne said. 'You're far too clever to buy any of my bullshit, so I won't give you any, all right?' He glanced back towards the screens, towards what lay behind them. 'This is not about an argument, or an affair, or an unpaid bill. I'm not going to tell you that I can catch whoever did this, because I don't know if I can. I *do* know I'm going to have a bloody good try, though.'

Thorne waited, but the boy did not look up. He gave a small nod to Terry, who stood and put an arm on Yusuf's shoulder. The constable said something, a few murmured words of comfort, as Thorne closed the door behind him.

51

He arrived back in the shop in time to see the black curtain swept aside and DCI Nick Tughan stepping through it like a bad actor.

'Right. What have we got?' Tughan was a stick-thin Irishman with less than generous lips. His short, sandy hair was always clean, and the collars crisp beneath a variety of expensive suits. 'Who's filling me in . . .?'

Thorne smiled and shrugged: Me, given half a chance, you tosser. He was happy to see Holland walking across to do the honours, clearly not relishing the task, but knowing that he'd earn himself a drink later. A pint sounded like a good idea, even at eleven o'clock in the morning. Including the Izzigils, there were a dozen people inside the small shop, which, combined with the heat coming off the SOC lights, had turned the place into a sauna very quickly. Keen to get some air, Thorne stepped towards the front door, just as another person pushed through the curtain. This one was dressed from head to foot in black himself.

'What happened to you last night?' Hendricks asked.

Thorne sighed. He'd completely forgotten to call and tell Hendricks he'd be stopping over at his old man's. 'I'll tell you later . . .'

'Is everything all right?'

'Yeah, fine . . . just my dad.'

'Is he OK?'

'He's a pain in the arse . . .'

'I stayed up. You should have called.'

'Oh, that's sweet.' It was Tughan's voice. The DCI was standing over the bodies of Muslum and Hanya Izzigil, a mock-sweet smile on his face. 'No, really, it's very touching that he's worried about you . . .'

Thorne was still spitting blood ten minutes later when Holland joined him on the pavement outside the shop.

'If ever there was an incentive to solve a case . . .'

'Right,' Thorne said. 'Get shot of the slippery bugger.'

'Mind you, he had a point. It *was* touching . . .'

Thorne turned, ready to let off some steam, but the broad grin on

Holland's face softened the scowl on his own. He let out a long, slow breath and leaned back against the shop window. 'You look rough, Dave . . .'

Thorne had seen DC Dave Holland do a lot of growing up in recent years, no more so than since his daughter had been born. The floppy blond hair had been cut shorter recently, which put a couple of years on him, and the lines around his eyes had added a few more. Thorne knew that very few coppers stayed fresh-faced for long. Those that did were lucky or lazy, and Holland was neither of those things. He'd saved Thorne's life the year before, and the circumstances – the dark, depraved intimacies which the pair of them had witnessed and experienced – had rarely been talked about since the resulting court case.

'I'm utterly knackered,' Holland said.

Thorne looked at the gingerish stubble dotted across the pale and slightly sunken cheeks. Maybe the change in him was due to responsibility as much as experience. A few years ago, and particularly during his girlfriend's pregnancy, Holland hadn't shown a great deal of either.

'Is it the baby?'

'Actually, it's Sophie,' Holland said. 'It's probably hormones or something, but she's at me three or four times a night demanding sex.'

'*What?*'

'Of *course* it's the baby! Have you had a sense-of-humour bypass?'

'I didn't get a lot of sleep myself. I was staying at my dad's place.'

'Sorry, I forgot. How's he doing?'

'I reckon he'll be the death of me before he manages to kill himself.'

On the other side of the road, a small crowd had gathered to stare at the comings and goings at Izzigil's video shop. The café from which Constable Terry had run to see what all the screaming was about had now become a convenient vantage-point. The owner was cheerfully scurrying around, serving coffee and pastries to those who wanted to sit outside and gawp.

Holland took out a packet of ten Silk Cut. He scrounged a light from a woman walking past with a pushchair.

'How long's that been going on?' Thorne asked, nodding towards the cigarette. He hadn't smoked in a long time, but would still happily have killed for one.

'Since the baby, I suppose. It was fags or heroin.'

'Well, you're in the right place for that . . .'

North of Finsbury Park, Green Lanes straightened into a strut of what had become known as the Harringay Ladder. Looking at the bustle around its shops and businesses at that moment, it was easy to see the area for what it was: one of the busiest and certainly one of the most racially diverse areas of the city. Of course, that did not explain the presence of armed police on its streets. A fierce gun-battle in those same streets six months earlier had left three men dead, and shown the other side of the area only too clearly. Harringay was home to a number of gangs operating within the Turkish community. According to figures from the National Criminal Intelligence Service, they were in control of over three-quarters of the seventy tonnes of heroin that passed through London every year. They protected their investments fiercely.

'Does Tughan think it's about smack?'

Holland wasn't listening. 'Sorry . . .?'

Thorne pointed back to the shop. 'The Izzigils. Does our gangland expert in there think this is a turf war?'

'Actually, he thinks it's the Ryans.'

'Eh?'

'He seems to think that this is a message from Billy Ryan to who-ever's been knocking his boys off. A "declaration", he reckons.'

'That's a bit of a leap, isn't it?' Thorne said. 'What's he base that on?'

'No idea. He seems pretty convinced, though.'

Thorne closed his eyes as smoke from Holland's cigarette drifted across his face. 'It makes sense on one level, I suppose.'

'What?'

'The Ryans were always going to work out who was after them long before we did.'

Thorne watched as two officers carrying body-bags moved towards the front door. Hendricks had obviously finished his preliminary examination. Thorne moved to follow the officers back inside, murmuring to Holland as he passed: 'Listen, the fact that Hendricks is staying at my place . . . Are people making cracks about it?'

Holland was enjoying a long drag. He laughed so much that he began to choke.

Thorne had spent the last three years based at the Peel Centre in Hendon, and his familiarity with it, with Becke House in particular, had bred a good deal of contempt. The building – a dun-coloured, three-storey blot on an already drab landscape – had once housed dormitories for recruits. The beds had given way to open-plan incident rooms and suites of poky offices, but there were still plenty of fresh faces to be spotted around the place, with the Metropolitan Police cadets now housed in another building within the same compound.

It always struck Thorne as strange that the Serious Crime Group should be based where it was, hand in glove with a cadet-training centre. He remembered arriving back late one afternoon, a year or so earlier, and bumping into a uniformed cadet as he turned from locking his car. He'd spent the previous few hours trying to explain to an old woman why her son-in-law had taken an axe to her daughter and grandchildren. The look on Thorne's face that day had stopped the cadet dead in his tracks, hacking off his cheery greeting mid-sentence and sending the blood rushing from his smooth cheeks . . .

The meeting was taking place in the office that Russell Brigstocke was reluctantly sharing with Nick Tughan. The SO7 Projects Team was based in a collection of Portakabins at Barkingside, where Tughan and his team still spent a fair amount of time, but since the joint operation had begun, there'd been something of a shake-up on the third floor of Becke House. Holland and DC Andrew Stone now shared *their* office part time with two DCs from Serious and Organised Crime, leaving the third office to Thorne and DI Yvonne Kitson. The latter spent most of her time in the Incident Room, collating information alongside office manager DS Samir Karim and their opposite numbers from SO7. So, more often than not, Thorne had his office, such as it was, to himself.

'Right,' said Tughan. 'Game on. I think we've got ourselves a war . . .'

Tughan's Irish accent could switch between syrupy and strident. Today, it went right through Thorne. He remembered the scrape of Gordon Rooker's chair across the floor of the visiting room at the Royal.

Tughan leaned against the desk in a vain effort to make his superiority appear casual. He held up a piece of paper inside a transparent plastic jacket. 'This was found among the dead man's paperwork. There are photocopies for each of you.'

Brigstocke and Kitson already had their copies. Holland, Stone and Thorne moved forward and took theirs from the desk.

'This letter isn't dated,' continued Tughan, 'but, according to the son, it was delivered by hand five or six weeks ago.'

'Late Christmas present . . .' Stone said, looking for the laugh, a little too full of himself, as usual.

Tughan ignored him, pressed on. 'It's nothing we haven't seen before. Subtler than some I've come across – lots of stuff about the dangers facing new businesses. But basically it's a simple protection scheme. Only problem is they were moving in on someone who was already protected.'

'"They"', Thorne said, 'being Billy Ryan.'

'To the best of my knowledge, yes.'

'The "best of your knowledge"?'

Tughan smiled thinly and turned away from Thorne. 'We're moving forward on the basis that this letter originated from the Ryan family, or from criminals closely associated with them.'

Thorne let it go, but it still bothered him. It wasn't like threatening letters were sent out on headed notepaper. How could Tughan be so sure that this one came from the Ryan family?

Thorne caught Brigstocke's eye, but the DCI did not allow him to hold it for very long. Brigstocke's attitude to the entire SO7 operation basically involved keeping his head down until they disappeared. Thorne had a lot of time for the man – he was hard and principled, caught far too often between those above and below him – but he still had an irritating predilection for hedging his bets. At the same time, of course, Thorne was well aware that his own refusal to do the same thing had often landed him in plenty of trouble . . .

Yvonne Kitson was less afraid than some to speak her mind. 'It doesn't make a lot of sense,' she said. 'They send a threatening letter. They send the bully boys round to chuck a bin through the window. Then they have the owners *killed*?'

Holland looked up from the letter. 'Right, that's quite an escalation, sir.'

'It's not complicated,' Tughan said. His smile took him way over the line that separated informative from patronising. 'This was a straightforward campaign of intimidation. It might well have got nasty eventually, but it wouldn't have gone as far as killing. Then the Ryans discovered that the video shop was protected by the same people responsible for the murder of Mickey Clayton and the others. The same people that are paying the X-Man.'

'A bit coincidental, isn't it?' Holland asked.

Tughan had been waiting for this. 'I don't think so . . .'

'It was the letter,' Thorne said. 'That's what started everything.'

'It was *probably* the letter.' Tughan couldn't keep the irritation off his face at having his thunder stolen. 'It doesn't really matter now how it started . . .'

Thorne took Tughan's expression as his cue to get stuck in. 'Whoever was protecting Izzigil's business took major offence at the Ryans trying to move in.'

'Major offence?' Holland said. 'That's putting it bloody mildly. They've had four of Billy Ryan's top men killed.'

Brigstocke agreed: 'Whatever happened to breaking somebody's legs?'

'It's about a lot more than territory now,' Thorne said. 'It probably always was. We're presuming they're Turks, right? Whoever's been hitting the Ryans . . .'

'We can't presume anything,' Tughan said. 'The fact that the video business was Turkish needn't be significant.'

'It *needn't* be, no. But I still think it is.'

'We've heard nothing from the NCIS . . .'

'They're not infallible. We're probably talking about somebody relatively new here. Maybe an offshoot of an existing gang.'

'Granted, it's a Turkish area, but other groups might still try their luck.'

'They'd be idiots if they did . . .'

'The Ryans did.'

'Right,' Thorne said. 'And look what they got for their trouble.'

Tughan seemed to decide suddenly that a physical barrier between himself and Thorne might be a good idea. He moved behind the desk and slid into the chair. He looked at his computer, affecting an air of thoughtfulness, but, to Thorne, it seemed more like regrouping.

'We're assuming that on one side we've got the Ryans, right?' Thorne continued quickly before Tughan had a chance to pull him up: 'If we assume that on the other side we've got an as yet unknown Turkish operation, it all starts to add up. If you're a newish gang, looking to establish yourself, you don't go up against the big Turkish gangs that have already got the area sewn up. Not if you want to be around in six months' time. You so much as start sniffing around one of those big heroin operations and they'll wipe you out, right?'

If anybody disagreed, they were keeping quiet about it.

'What makes more sense, if you're looking to make a splash, is to go up against somebody else completely. Somebody unconnected with local business or local territory. When that letter dropped on to the doormat in that video shop, somebody saw an opportunity to expand in a different direction altogether; to send out a message to the gangs around them without getting anybody's back up. This lot, whoever the hell they are, probably see the Ryans as a soft target.'

Tughan had been typing something. He raised his eyes from his computer screen and smiled. 'Somebody should tell Billy Ryan that.'

There wasn't a trace of a smile from Yvonne Kitson. 'And the Izzigils . . .'

'So who are they?' Stone asked. 'If we want to stop a war, we'll need to know who's up against who.'

Tughan stabbed at a key, leaned back in his chair. 'I think DI Thorne might well be right when he suggests that we're dealing with a Turkish – or possibly Kurdish – group here. I'm liaising with the NCIS, specifically the Heroin Intelligence Unit . . .'

Thorne shook his head. 'I told you, I can't see that this is about heroin. This is about not shitting on your own doorstep.'

'Is that a technical term?' Brigstocke asked. 'I must have missed that seminar.'

Thorne smiled. 'I've seen a couple of Guy Ritchie films.'

Tughan raised his voice a little, bridling slightly, as always, at any exchange that rose above the funereal. 'I'm confident that we will establish the identity of this gang quickly. We will find something connecting them to the video rental business, or we might get a lead from Turkish community leaders in the area . . .'

'Only the ones with a death wish,' Brigstocke said.

'One way or another, things are much clearer now than they were.' Tughan brandished the letter whose implied threats had probably been the catalyst for at least six deaths. 'We've made a real breakthrough today.'

Thorne's mood blackened in an instant. He remembered the film of tears across a pair of dark eyes, red around the rims.

A real breakthrough . . .

He doubted that Yusuf Izzigil would see things in quite the same way.

They drove back from the restaurant in virtual silence.

As always, Jack stayed well within the speed limit as he steered the Volvo through streets that were still slick after an early evening downpour. The short journey was one that they tried to make at least once a month – sometimes more if there was a birthday or anniversary to be celebrated. Jack always drove, always stuck to half a bitter while they waited for the table, and a glass of wine with the meal.

'Are you cross with me?' Carol said, eventually.

'Don't be silly. I was just worried.'

'It's like I spoiled your evening.'

'You couldn't help it. What happened, I mean. You didn't spoil my evening.'

Carol turned away from him and stared out of the window. She could still taste the vomit at the back of her throat. Instinctively, she looked again to make sure there was none on her blouse.

'You must be coming down with something,' Jack said. 'I'll call the quack first thing.'

Carol nodded without shifting her gaze from a scratch on the car window, from the darkness moving past it.

It had come over her from nowhere as she was digging into her spaghetti – a heat that had prickled and spread quickly – until she'd had to throw down her fork and rush to the toilet. She'd emerged ten minutes later, pale and with a weak smile that had fooled nobody: not the manager, who offered to call a doctor and assured her that the meal was on the house, and least of all her husband. Jack had shrugged at the waiters and smiled. He'd taken her arm: 'Come on, love. You're white as a sheet. We'd best make a move . . .'

60

Carol knew full well what the trouble was. This was the first physical symptom of a virus that had been lurking inside her, waiting for the chance to blossom since the day she'd handed over her warrant card. She'd tried to ignore it on other occasions, when an unfamiliar reaction to something had forced her to ask the question.

Have I stopped being a copper *inside*?

She knew what the answer was. The cold-case stuff was Mickey Mouse; it was just playing at what she used to do for real. Now, she could feel doubt, worry, pain, anger. And fear. She felt them all in a way she never had for those thirty years she'd spent watching other people feel the same things. She felt like a *civilian*. And she hated it.

She knew that this was all about Gordon Rooker. The reassurance that had come from Thorne's visit to the Royal had lasted no more than a couple of hours. God, it was all so bloody stupid. After all, the facts were pretty obvious: Rooker was locked up; Rooker was guilty; whoever had been phoning her and sending the letters was some nutcase who, by the look of it, had probably stopped now anyway.

It hadn't been facts, though, that had made her throw up. She needed to deal with the feelings. She needed to deal with the *panic*.

She needed to start behaving like a real copper again.

'It's definitely not the food,' Jack said as he slowed to turn into their quiet crescent. 'How many times have we eaten in that place over the years . . .?'

Hendricks was already asleep by the time Thorne got in, just after eleven. As Thorne crept past the sofa-bed towards the kitchen, Elvis, his psychotic cat, jumped down from where she'd been curled up on Hendricks' feet and followed him. While he waited for the kettle to boil, Thorne poured some cat munchies into a grubby plastic bowl and told Elvis one or two things about his day. He'd rather have talked to his friend, who was a marginally better conversationalist, but the snoring from the next room made it clear just how well away Hendricks was. Thorne didn't want to wake him. He knew that Hendricks had probably had a fairly tough day himself.

Up to his elbows in the cadavers of Muslum and Hanya Izzigil.

Drinking his tea at the kitchen table, Thorne thought about those who would spend the coming night sleepless. Those with money worries or difficulties at work, or relationship problems. It was odd what could keep some people awake, while a man who dealt in death – usually one that had been anything but peaceful – could sleep like a baby. He thought about Dave Holland, bleary-eyed at 4 a.m., who would tell him just how ludicrous *that* expression was.

Of course, he didn't know what went on in Phil Hendricks' *dreams* . . .

Thorne hadn't slept brilliantly himself since the night he'd come so close to death the year before. There had been nightmares, of course, but now it was just as if his body had adapted and required less sleep. Most nights he'd get by on four or five hours and then collapse into something approaching a coma when he took a day off.

Having removed his shoes, Thorne carried them, and what was left of his tea, towards the bedroom. On the way through the darkened living room he picked up his CD Walkman and a George Jones album. He held the bedroom door open for Elvis, and watched as she hopped back up on to Phil Hendricks' legs.

'Sod you, then,' Thorne said.

He padded into his bedroom with his tea, his shoes and his music, and closed the door behind him.

It was a sudden change in the light, no more than that.

Carol Chamberlain saw it reflected in the dressing-table mirror as she sat taking her make-up off. She'd washed most of it off earlier, rubbing cold water into her face in the toilets at the Italian restaurant. Trying to stop the dizziness and to bring back a little colour to her cheeks.

Jack was moving around downstairs. Locking up, pulling out plugs. Keeping them safe . . .

She sat in her night-dress and stared hard at herself. It was time to sort her hair out, and maybe shift a few pounds though, at fifty-six, that was a damn sight harder than it used to be. She could try to get back to how she was when they'd taken the job away from her: her 'fighting weight', Jack called it.

Leaning closer towards the mirror, cream smeared across her fingers, she saw the light change. A glow – pink at first, then orange – that crept through a gap in the curtains and lit up the room behind her. She opened her mouth to call out Jack's name, then closed it and pushed back her chair. As she walked towards the window, she saw the glow reaching up and illuminating the bare branches of the copper beech at the end of the drive. She knew more or less what she was going to see when she reached the far side of the room and looked out. She wondered if he'd be there. She hoped that he would be . . .

He was already looking up when she pulled back the curtains, standing motionless next to the car, the can of lighter fluid white against his gloved hand.

Waiting for her.

For a few long, still seconds they stared at each other. The flames were not spectacular, and the light danced only across the dark material of the man's anorak. The blaze never threatened to break up the shadow, blue-black beneath the hood that was pulled tight around his head.

The fire was already beginning to spread across the Volvo's bonnet. It drifted down around its edges, into its mouldings, where the lighter fluid had run and dripped. Still, the words, sprayed in fuel and spelled out now in flame, were clear enough.

I burned her.

Carol heard locks being thrown back downstairs, and saw the man's head turn suddenly towards the front door. He took a step away from the car, then looked up at Carol for another moment or two before he turned and ran. She had seen nothing, *could* see nothing of his face, but she knew very well that he had been smiling at her.

A few seconds later, Jack burst out of the front door in his vest. He ran, arms raised and mouth gaping, on to the front lawn. Carol half-saw him turn to look up, at the same moment she moved away from the window and back into the heart of the room.

FIVE

Thorne had never conducted an interview alongside Carol Chamberlain before and, although this was in no sense official, he still felt slightly odd, sitting there next to her, waiting for Rooker to be brought in. He looked around the small, square room and imagined himself, for no good reason he could think of, as a father, sitting with his wife. He remembered the sobbing black woman he'd seen on his last visit. He pictured himself and Chamberlain as anxious parents waiting for their son to be marched in.

The door opened and an officer led Rooker into the room. He looked angry about something until he saw Chamberlain; then, a broad smile appeared.

'Hello, sexpot,' he said.

Thorne opened his mouth to speak, but Chamberlain beat him to it. There was an edge to her voice that Thorne could not recall hearing before.

'One more out-of-order remark and I'll come round this table and tear off what little you've got left between your legs that hasn't already withered away. Fair enough, Gordon?'

Rooker's smile wobbled a little, but it was back in place as he pulled back his chair and plonked himself down at the table. The officer moved towards the door. 'Give us a shout when you've finished,' he said.

'Thanks,' Thorne said, looking up. 'I thought you'd retired, Bill.'

The officer opened the door, turned back to Thorne. 'Got a year or two left yet.' He nodded towards Rooker. 'Feels like I've been in here as long as this cunt.' He quickly looked across to Chamberlain, reddening slightly. 'Sorry, I didn't . . .'

Chamberlain held up a hand. 'Don't apologise. That sounds about right to me . . .'

Rooker cackled. The officer stepped out of the room, letting the door swing shut, hard, behind him.

'This is getting to be a habit,' Rooker said. He produced a tobacco tin from behind the green bib and removed the lid. 'Twice in a week, Mr Thorne. I don't have family who come as often as that.' He teased out the strands of tobacco, laid them carefully into a Rizla and rolled it pin-thin. 'Nothing *like* as often as that . . .'

In fact, it had been just over a week since Thorne had first encountered Gordon Rooker. And seven days since Carol Chamberlain had stared down from her bedroom window at the man who was claiming Gordon Rooker's crime as his own.

Rooker lit his roll-up. He picked a piece of tobacco from his tongue and looked across at Chamberlain. 'I thought *you'd* retired,' he said.

'That's right.'

'Living out in the sticks with a houseful of cats, listening to *The Archers* . . .'

'What do you know about where I live?'

Rooker turned to Thorne. 'If she's not on the job any more, what are we doing here?'

By 'here', Rooker meant the Legal Visits Room. It was normally reserved for confidential interviews, for meetings with police officers or solicitors, for official business. Thorne was content to keep things *unofficial* . . . for now. He had seen no real reason to go to Brigstocke and certainly not to Tughan. The connection between Rooker and Billy Ryan was twenty years old and tenuous at best to the SO7 inquiry, *and* he'd promised Carol Chamberlain that he'd try to sort things out on his own time. He'd discreetly pulled a few strings and called in a favour or two to ensure that he, Chamberlain and Gordon Rooker could discuss one or two things in private.

'What we talked about a week ago,' Thorne said, 'it's escalated.'

Rooker looked, or *tried* to look, serious. 'That's a shame.'

'Yes, it is.'

'I told you last time . . .'

'I'll forget the rubbish you told me last time and pretend we're starting from scratch, OK? This has to be down to some fuckwit you've done time with, or somebody who's written to you. You told me all about some of the letters you get, right?'

'Right.'

'So, any bright ideas, Gordon?'

Rooker took three quick drags. He held the smoke in and let it out very slowly on a sigh. 'I've got to have some sort of protection,' he said.

Thorne laughed. '*What?*'

'Word got around after you were here last time . . .'

Thorne shrugged. He'd obviously opted for privacy a little too late. 'You've not exactly been popular for quite a while now, Gordon. Talking to a copper isn't going to make much difference.'

'You'd be surprised . . .'

Chamberlain's voice was quieter than when she'd spoken before, but the edge had sharpened. 'If you've got something to say, Rooker, you'd best say it.'

Another drag. 'I want this parole. I really need it to go my way this time.'

'And?' Thorne stared blankly across the table at Rooker. 'Not a lot we can do about *that*.'

'Bollocks. It's down to the Home Office. You can get it done if you want to.'

'Why would we want to?'

'I need a guarantee that I'm getting out . . .'

'Don't want much, do you?'

'It'll be worth it.'

'Unless you're telling us who Jack the Ripper was and where Lord Lucan and Shergar are holed up, I doubt we'd be interested.'

Rooker didn't seem to find that funny.

'What about these letters?' asked Chamberlain. 'The phone calls. That's what we're here to talk about.'

Rooker stared down at the ashtray.

'Whoever's doing this has been to my *house* . . .'

'I want protection.' Rooker looked up at Thorne. 'After I'm out.'

'Protection from who?' Chamberlain said.

'New identity, national insurance number, the lot . . .'

'Billy Ryan,' Thorne said.

'Maybe . . .'

'Is Billy Ryan going to come after you?'

'Not for the reason you think.'

'So why should we give a toss?'

'I can give him to you.'

Thorne blinked. This was interesting. This was far from tenuous. He avoided eye contact with Chamberlain, refused to show Rooker anything, kept his voice casual. 'You're going to grass up Billy Ryan?'

Rooker nodded.

'Grass up the Ryans,' Chamberlain said, 'and you really *will* be a target.'

'That's why I want protection.'

It was a straightforward piece of gangland logic, and Thorne could see the sense of it. 'Get Ryan before he gets you. That it?'

'Don't make out like you wouldn't like to put him away. He's a piece of shit and you know it.'

'And you're a fucking saint, are you, Gordon?'

'It's him or me, isn't it? What would you do?'

'After what you did at that school, what you did to that girl . . . I'm inclined to let Billy Ryan have you.'

Rooker's head dropped and stayed down as he stubbed out what was left of his cigarette. He ground the butt into the ashtray until there appeared to be nothing left of it at all. For a moment, Thorne wondered if he'd palmed it, like a magician. When Rooker finally looked up, the cockiness had gone. The lines in his face had deepened. He seemed suddenly tense. He looked like a frightened old man.

'I didn't burn the girl,' he said. 'It wasn't me.'

Thorne saw Chamberlain's hands clench into fists on the table, white across her knuckles as she spoke. 'Don't piss me about. Don't you bloody dare piss me about . . .'

Rooker licked his lips and repeated himself.

And Thorne believed him. It really was that simple. All that struck him as odd was that Rooker seemed so reluctant, so hesitant about his denial. Surely things were arse about face. Thorne remembered how, a week before, the man sitting opposite him had admitted to setting a fourteen-year-old girl on fire as easily as he might own up to nicking lead off a roof. Now, he was taking it back, denying he'd had anything to do with it, and it was as if it were the hardest thing in the world.

It was like he was confessing his innocence.

Dave Holland and Andy Stone got along, but no more than that. A year or so ago, when they'd first begun working together, Holland had resented Stone's easy charm, and bridled at his place as the young pretender – pretender to *what* he was never sure – feeling threatened. They'd kicked along well enough since then, though there were still times when the ease with which his fellow DC told a joke or wore a suit made him want to spit.

'I feel like shit warmed up,' Stone said.

Holland looked up from the computer screen and smiled. 'Caning it again last night, were you?'

'Still sweating Carlsberg and Sea Breezes.'

Holland raised an eyebrow. 'Cocktails?'

'I was with a very classy lady, mate . . .'

Holland was at least self-aware enough to admit that now, with a baby to think about, his resentment had distilled into plain, old-fashioned jealousy.

'I bet I still had more sleep than you, though,' Stone said.

'Right . . .'

Holland had more or less grown used to the physical fatigue. He could happily nod off at pretty much any time, and was not beyond catnapping in the Gents' after a really bad night. It was mentally that he was still finding things tough. There was a fuzziness about his thinking these days, a reluctance to go in any direction other than the path of least resistance. There was a time, back before the baby and the rough patch they went through even before that, when Sophie would badger him about being the kind of straightforward, head-down, career copper that his old man had been. She didn't have to bother these days, and she knew it. Holland didn't have the mental energy to do a great deal else.

And there was the way the baby made him feel: the sheer, fucking size of the love and the terror. Looking down at her sometimes, he could feel his heart swell and his sphincter tighten at the same time.

Holland closed his eyes for a few seconds. He could remember so vividly the first time he'd walked into a CID suite. He could recall virtually every moment of that first case he'd worked on with Tom Thorne. He saw in perfect detail the clothes he'd been wearing on a particular occasion in Thorne's car, or in the office when they got a break in the case. It was only the excitement of it, which he knew had been intense, that seemed suddenly distant and hard to imagine . . .

'Where's that plum from SO7, anyway?' asked Stone. 'He's never here when he's needed, is he?'

They were going through the paperwork and computer data relating to what had quickly emerged as the less than legitimate business activities of Muslum Izzigil's video shop. When one or two members of Brigstocke's team had expressed surprise that video piracy was still big business, they had been subjected to Tughan at his most patronising: 'Five thousand copies from one stolen master tape, knocked out at a couple of quid a pop. You might be looking at half a million per year per film. It's not quite up there with heroin, but there's a damn sight less risk and you don't tend to get put away for so long.'

Some, notably Thorne, had remained sceptical. Then again, Thorne was sceptical about *everything* that came out of Tughan's mouth, and there was certainly evidence that pointed towards a sophisticated smuggling operation. There was no such evidence leading them to whoever was running it; whoever Muslum Izzigil – among many others in all likelihood – had been fronting for; whoever had reacted so aggressively when Billy Ryan had tried to muscle in on their territory.

Whoever was paying the X-Man . . .

There was a DC from SO7 who, theoretically at least, was supposed to be working with Holland and Stone, but whenever there were paper-trails to slog through, urgent meetings would materialise back at Barkingside, or mysterious sources would suddenly need chasing up on the other side of London.

'They're taking the piss, aren't they?'

Holland found it hard to disagree with Stone's assessment. He was about to chip in with a comment of his own when something on the screen caught his eye. He stared at it for a few seconds, scrolled back to check something else, then held up a hand, beckoning Stone from the other side of the room. 'Come and look at this, Andy.'

'What?'

'A name.' He highlighted two words on the screen for Stone to look at, moved to a different page and highlighted the same words again.

Stone stared down at the screen from behind his shoulder. 'Just a name,' Holland said. 'Nothing to tie it to anything dodgy, as yet.'

'There wouldn't be. These fuckers are too clever for that.'

'Maybe . . .'

'Definitely. We won't catch 'em with Windows 2000, I can tell you that.'

Holland grunted. 'Well, whoever they are, their name just keeps cropping up . . .'

'I was a dead man,' Rooker said.

Chamberlain leaned back in her chair, waiting. Thorne moved in the opposite direction. 'Don't get existential on us, Gordon. Keep it simple and keep it honest. All right?'

'I was fucked, all right? That simple enough? Whoever did the girl made it look like me. I was known for stuff like that, wasn't I? For using lighter fuel . . .'

'"Whoever did the girl". I take it you can't tell us who that was?'

'I can tell you who paid for it. I can tell you whose idea it was to kill a kid.'

'We knew that. We knew it was one of the other firms who . . .'

'You knew fuck all.'

Next to him, Chamberlain sat stock still, but Thorne could feel the tension radiating off her. He asked the question slowly: 'So, who was it then?'

This was Rooker's big moment. 'It was Billy Ryan. That's why I can give him to you. Billy Ryan put the contract out on Kevin Kelly's little girl.'

A pause, but nothing too dramatic before Thorne asked the obvious question: 'Why?'

'It wasn't complicated. He was ambitious. He wanted to take on the smaller firms, but Kelly wouldn't have it. He thought things were fine as they were. Billy reckoned Kevin was losing his edge.'

'So he tried to take over?'

'Billy wanted what Kevin had. *More* than Kevin had. He'd tried to get him out of the way earlier but fucked it up.'

Thorne remembered Chamberlain's gangland history lesson: the failed attempt on Kevin Kelly's life a few months before the incident at the school. 'Were you anything to do with that, Gordon?'

'I'm not getting into anything else. Point is, the Kelly family *thought* I was.'

'So, Billy targets his boss's daughter, but whoever he's paying tries to kill the wrong girl.'

'Yeah, that got fucked up as well, but it still worked. Kevin Kelly goes mental, wipes out anybody who's so much as looked at him funny, then hands the whole fucking business over to Billy Ryan and walks away. It couldn't have gone better.'

Thorne saw Rooker flinch slightly when Chamberlain spoke. 'I'm not sure Jessica Clarke or her family would have seen things in quite the same way.'

'How come you know any of this?' Thorne asked.

'Because Billy Ryan asked me to do it, didn't he? I was the perfect person to ask. I'd done a bit of freelance stuff for one or two people, a few frighteners and what have you . . .'

'You're telling us that Ryan offered you money to kill Kevin Kelly's daughter.'

'*A lot* of money . . .'

'And you turned the job down.'

'Fuck, yes. I don't hurt kids.'

Chamberlain groaned. 'Jesus, this stuff makes me sick. It always comes down to this "noble gangster" bollocks. "We only hurt our own", and "it was only business", and "anybody who touches kids should be strung up". He'll be telling us how much he loves his mum in a minute . . .'

Rooker laughed, winked at her.

The room wasn't warm, and up to this point Thorne had kept his leather jacket on. Now he stood and dropped it across the back of his chair. Chamberlain stayed where she was. Thorne guessed that her smart, grey business suit was new. He thought she might have had her hair done as well, cut a little shorter and highlighted, but he'd said nothing.

'I hope this isn't an obvious question,' Thorne said. 'But why did you confess?'

'Billy Ryan made sure that every face in London thought I'd done it. I was well stitched up. That lighter they found by the fence was left there deliberately.' He looked at Chamberlain. 'You saw what Kevin Kelly did to the people he *guessed* were responsible. Imagine what he'd have done to me. I had Kelly after me for what he thought I'd tried to do to his Alison, *and* Billy after my blood because I was the only person who knew who'd really set it all up.' He turned back to Thorne. ' I was a marked man.'

'So, prison was a preferable option, was it?'

Rooker took the lid off his tobacco tin. He put the cigarette together without looking down, and spoke as if he were trying to explain the mysteries of calculus. 'I thought about running, pissing off to Spain or further, but the idea of spending years looking over my shoulder, shitting myself every time the doorbell went . . .'

Chamberlain shook her head. She glanced at Thorne and then looked back to Rooker. 'I'm not buying this. You'd be just as much of a marked man in prison.'

Rooker put down his half-finished roll-up. 'Do you think I didn't know that?' He reached down and gathered up the bottom of the bib and the sweatshirt underneath, then hoisted them up above sagging, hairy nipples to reveal a jagged scar running across his ribs. 'See? I was a marked man from the moment I walked into Gartree, and Belmarsh, and this place . . .'

'So why not just take your chances outside?'

'It's on my terms in here. I'm not scared of it.' He pulled down the sweatshirt, smoothed the bib across his belly. 'On the outside it could be anyone who's on a big pay-day to take you out. It's the bloke who wants to know the time. The bloke taking a piss next to you, asking you for a light, whatever. In here, I know who it's going to be. I can see it coming and I can protect myself. I've had a couple of scrapes, but I'm still breathing. That's how I know I did the right thing.'

Thorne watched Rooker's yellow tongue snake out and moisten the edge of the Rizla. He rolled the cigarette, slid it between his lips and lit up. 'You did the right thing by Billy Ryan as well. You never grassed him up.'

'I wasn't a *complete* fucking idiot.'

Chamberlain drummed her fingers on the table. 'That "honour among thieves" shite again.'

'So why now?' Thorne asked.

'Listen, it was you who came to see me, remember. Started me thinking about this. Started people round here whispering.'

'*Why now, Rooker?*'

Rooker removed the cigarette from his mouth, held it between a nicotine-stained finger and thumb. 'I've had enough. I'm breathing, but the air tastes of stale sweat and other men's shit. I'm arguing with rapists and perverts about whose turn it is to change channel or play fucking pool next. I've got a grandson who's signing forms with West Ham in a few weeks. I'd like to see him play.' He blinked slowly, took a drag, flicked away the ash. 'It's time.'

Chamberlain stood up and moved towards the door. 'That's all very moving, and I'm sure it's just the kind of stuff the parole board loves to hear.'

Rooker stretched. 'Not so far, it isn't. That's why I need a bit of help . . .'

'I still don't see why you confessed to the attempted murder of Jessica Clarke. You could have got yourself safely banged up by putting yourself in the frame for any number of things. That security manager you tied to a chair and set light to, for instance. Why claim that you tried to kill a fourteen-year-old girl?'

Thorne had the answer. 'Because you're less of a marked man on a VP wing. Right, Gordon? You're harder to get at.'

Rooker stared, and smoked.

There was a knock, and the prison officer put his head round the door, offered tea. Thorne accepted gracefully and Chamberlain declined. The officer bristled a little at Rooker's request for a cup but disappeared quietly enough at the nod from Thorne.

'So, who was it?' Chamberlain said.

Thorne knew that she was thinking about the letters, about the calls, about the man she'd thought was smiling up at her from her front garden.

'If it wasn't you who took Billy Ryan's money, you must have some idea who did.'

Rooker shook his head. 'Look, I haven't got a clue who this nutter is who's been pestering you . . .'

'Who burned Jessica Clarke?' Chamberlain asked.

'I haven't got the faintest, and that's the truth. I don't know anyone who *would* have done it. Who *could* have. Over the years, I've started to wonder if maybe it was Billy himself . . .'

They sat in the car for a minute, saying nothing. When Thorne leaned forward to turn the key, Chamberlain suddenly spoke.

'What did you make of all that?'

Thorne glanced at her, exhaled loudly. 'Where do you want to start?'

'How about with Rooker getting himself put away for something he didn't do?'

'I've heard similar stories once or twice,' Thorne said. 'I suppose if you've got a headcase like Billy Ryan on your back . . .'

'Twenty years, though?'

'Yeah, well, he didn't bank on that, did he?'

Chamberlain turned her head, stared out across the car park.

'You not convinced?' Thorne asked.

She spoke quietly, without looking at him. 'I haven't got the foggiest bloody idea. I'm not far away from a free bus pass, and, to be honest, I'm no better at working out what goes on in the heads of people like Gordon Rooker than I was when I first pulled on a uniform.'

Thorne started the car. As he pulled out of the car park his mind drifted back to how their interview with Rooker had ended. Thorne had almost gasped when he'd suddenly remembered something else from Chamberlain's history lesson. 'Hang on, didn't Ryan *marry* Alison Kelly a few years after all this happened?' Chamberlain had nodded. 'He tries to kill her, pays someone to set fire to her, maybe even does it himself . . . and then marches her down the aisle as soon as she's old enough?'

'That was the perfect fucking touch,' Rooker had said. 'That was good business, wasn't it? The heir marrying the daughter, like he was cementing alliances.' He had chuckled at the sight of Thorne shaking his head in disbelief, then nodded towards Carol Chamberlain. 'She'll tell you about Billy Ryan. She knows him. She knows what he's like.'

Chamberlain had remained silent.

Rooker stared at Thorne through a sheet of blue smoke. 'Billy Ryan's *cold* . . .'

SIX

On Monday morning, just after ten-thirty, Tughan stuck his head round the door, scanned the bodies in the Major Incident Room, and backed out again, his face like a smacked arse.

Holland checked his watch.

Samir Karim shuffled his sizeable backside along the edge of a desk and leaned in close to him. 'Someone's in trouble,' he said.

Holland nodded. He knew who Karim was talking about. Behind an adjacent desk, DI Yvonne Kitson had her head buried in a thick, bound manuscript. 'What you reading, Guv?' he asked.

Kitson looked over the top of a page and held up the latest edition of the *Murder Investigation Manual*. A weighty set of strategies, models and protocols produced by the National Crime Faculty. It was, in theory at least, required reading for all senior investigative officers, and covered everything from crime-scene assessment and media management to offender profiling and family liaison.

If there was a 'book' by which homicide detectives were supposed to do things, this was it.

'Having trouble sleeping?' Holland asked.

Kitson smiled. 'It's not exactly holiday reading, but it doesn't hurt to keep up with the latest guidelines, Dave.'

'Trouble with guidelines for solving murders is that they're only really any use if the murderers are following some of their own.'

'You know who you sound like, don't you?' Kitson said.

Holland knew very well, and thought that maybe there was still hope for him, after all. It struck him as odd that people had taken to talking about Tom Thorne without using his name . . .

As if on cue, the man himself walked through the door looking almost as angry as Tughan had been a few moments before . . . and still was, judging by his expression as he loomed at Thorne's shoulder.

'You've kept a lot of people waiting, DI Thorne.'

Thorne spoke to the room, without so much as a glance towards Nick Tughan. 'I'm sorry. The car wouldn't start . . .' He caught the beginnings of a smirk on the most likely face. 'And neither should you, Holland. I'm not in the mood.'

'OK, we've wasted enough time,' Tughan said. 'Core-team briefing in my office. Five minutes . . .'

While Tughan spoke, Thorne let his mind drift. He was taking it all in, but he was thinking about other things . . .

Thinking about Yvonne Kitson for one. He'd seen the copy of the *Murder Manual* that she was cradling as he'd walked into the Incident Room. It was like her to stay on top of things; she was someone who Thorne had always admired for her ability to juggle her responsibilities at work and at home. Those responsibilities had shifted somewhat since the previous summer, when her husband had found out about the affair she'd been having with a senior officer and walked out with the three kids. She had the kids back at home now, but she was a changed person. Before, she'd been moving effortlessly upwards. Now, she was clinging on. Thorne could see the difference in her face. She seemed to be hanging on every one of Tughan's words, but Thorne was pretty sure he wasn't the only one thinking about other things . . .

His mind drifted on to his father. He needed to talk to him, to see how everything was going. Perhaps it would be easier if he just called Eileen.

Then, he started thinking about why, nearly three days after he and Chamberlain had been to Park Royal prison, he still hadn't told Tughan what Gordon Rooker had told them.

All over the weekend Hendricks had kept bringing it up, looking at him as if he were an idiot, nagging him about it while they slobbed out in front of *The Premiership* . . .

'You want to get Billy Ryan yourself, don't you?' Hendricks had said. 'You want to catch whoever set fire to that girl. Whoever as good as killed her . . .'

'Heskey is such a bloody donkey. Look at that . . .'

'You're an idiot, Tom.'

'I do *not* want to get him myself.'

'So why haven't you told anybody about Rooker?'

Thorne knew no more than that it was because of his relationship with Chamberlain, and, OK, to a degree because of the one he had with Tughan. He had also virtually convinced himself that Rooker's information, his *offer*, related to a case that was twenty years old. It was not *strictly* relevant to the investigation into the killings of Mickey Clayton, the Izzigils and the others. He would, of course, have fucking *loved* to nail Billy Ryan on his own, but he didn't have the first idea how . . .

Tughan was talking about Dave Holland and Andy Stone. He commended them on the work that had thrown up the all-important name. Thorne focused on what Tughan was saying, but noticed how pissed off Holland looked at having to share any credit with Andy Stone.

'The NCIS have been working on this for us over the last forty-eight hours,' Tughan said, 'and we now have a decent bit of background on the Zarif family.'

Tughan was leaning against the front of the desk. Brigstocke stood to the left of it, arms folded. There were maybe a dozen people facing them, crammed into the small office: the senior officers from Team 3 at the Serious Crime Group (West), together with their opposite numbers from SO7.

'The Zarif family would appear to be model citizens,' Tughan said. 'Each property they own or have a stake in, every business interest we've been able to establish – minicabs, a chain of video outlets, haulage, van hire – are all completely legal. Not even a parking ticket.'

'Par for the course, right?' Brigstocke said.

Tughan nodded towards one of his DCs, a squat, bearded Welshman named Richards. Thorne's heart sank as Richards started to address them. He'd been stuck in the corner of a pub with him a day or two into things and been less than riveted.

'Think of it as three concentric circles,' Richards said.

Not caring if it was spotted or not, Thorne closed his eyes. The tedious little tit had given him the 'concentric circles' speech in the pub. Cornering him next to the fruit machine, he'd explained – in ten minutes when it could easily have been covered in two – the basic way a gangland firm, or family, operated. There were the street gangs: the robbers and the car-jackers and those who'd shove a handgun in a child's face for the latest mobile phone or an MP3 player. Then came the institutionalised villains: those controlling loan-sharking operations, illegal gambling, arms-smuggling, credit-card fraud. Finally, there were the tycoons: the seemingly legitimate businessmen who ran huge drug-trafficking empires and money-laundering networks, and who behaved as if they were respectable captains of industry.

'Think of three concentric circles,' Richards had said, an untouched half of lager-top in his fist. 'They all touch and bleed into one another, but the points where they actually meet are always shifting, impossible to pin down.' He'd smiled and leaned in close. 'I like to think of them as concentric circles on a target . . .'

Thorne had nodded, like he thought that was a great idea. He preferred to visualise the circles as ripples moving out across dirty water. Like when a turd hits the bottom of a sewer-pipe.

He was jolted back from dull remembrance to even duller reality by Richards talking about 'footsoldiers'. Thorne rubbed his eyes, let his hand fall over his mouth to cover the aside to Sam Karim: 'Jesus, he thinks he's in an episode of *The Sopranos* . . .'

'The Izzigil video shop is a good example of how it works,' Richards said. 'The name Zarif appears on the deeds of the property, and on the paperwork at Companies House; and the vehicles that theoretically distribute the perfectly legal videotapes are leased from their company. But there's nothing tying them to anything illegal going on in those premises and they can't be held responsible for what the people who hire their vans and lorries get up to.'

Tughan cleared his throat, took over: 'There are three brothers. We'll distribute photos as soon as we have them.' He glanced down at his notes. 'Also a sister, and probably plenty of cousins and what have you knocking about. At this stage, even the NCIS don't know a great deal about them. They're Turkish Kurds, been here a couple of years, kept their heads down.' He looked up from his clipboard. 'Getting their feet under the table. Main business premises and homes in the area you'd expect, between Manor House and Turnpike Lane.'

A voice from the back of the room: 'Little fucking Istanbul . . .'

Tughan smiled for about half a second. 'Now they've got themselves established, it seems like they're looking to expand. And poor old Billy Ryan's on the receiving end.'

'Let's bring a bit of pressure to bear,' Brigstocke said. 'See just how well established they are.'

Tughan pushed himself upright, tugged at the sharp creases in the trousers of his suit, dropped his clipboard down on to the desktop. 'Right, DS Karim, DC Richards, let's get some Actions organised and allocated . . .'

As the briefing broke up, Thorne was amazed when Tughan stepped over and spoke almost as if the two of them didn't hate the sight of each other.

'Fancy coming to see Billy Ryan?' Tughan asked.

'What about the Zarifs?'

'We'll give that a day or two. Get ourselves a bit of ammunition first.'

'Right.'

'At the moment, the Ryans are four–two down. Let's go and see how they're coping with getting spanked, shall we?'

Thorne nodded, thinking that the surprises were coming thick and fast. *Four–two down.* It was tasteless, but still, *any* joke from Nick Tughan was firmly in *X-Files* territory . . .

They said virtually nothing as they sat in Tughan's Rover, heading towards Camden Town, the music from the stereo conveniently too loud to allow casual conversation. They took what was more or less Thorne's usual route home, south through Hampstead and Belsize Park, through one of the most expensive areas of the city towards what was arguably still the trendiest, though the combat-wearing media brigade in Hoxton or Shoreditch might have welcomed the argument. They drove past the development on the site of Jack Straw's Castle, the coaching inn on Hampstead Heath named after one of the leaders of the Peasants' Revolt and once a favourite haunt of Dickens and Thackeray. Now, on certain nights of the week, gay men who liked their sex casual, and perhaps even dangerous, would gather there in darkened corners before disappearing on to the Heath with strangers.

'Dick-ins of a completely different sort,' Phil Hendricks had said.

They parked in front of a snooker hall behind Camden Road Station, a few streets away from Billy Ryan's office. Thorne was hugely relieved to escape from Tughan's car, deciding that, although his own taste in music had irritated a few people in its time, he wouldn't wish Phil Collins on his worst enemy. The man was perhaps second only to Sting in terms of smugness and his capacity to make you pray for hearing loss. As they walked towards Ryan's place, Thorne couldn't help wondering if gangland enforcers ever considered using a Phil Collins album as an alternative to pulling people's teeth out and drilling through their kneecaps . . .

Getting in to see the managing director of Ryan Properties was much like getting in to see any other successful businessman, save for the fact that the receptionist had tattoos on his neck.

'Wait there,' he said. Then, 'Not yet.' And finally, 'Go in.'

Thorne wondered whether he spoke only in two-word phrases. When he and Tughan eventually strolled into Billy Ryan's office, Thorne gave the receptionist a pithy, two-word phrase of his own. He watched as Billy Ryan stood and greeted Tughan like a respected business rival. Tughan shook Ryan's hand, which Thorne thought was distinctly fucking unnecessary, and when he himself was introduced he did no such thing, which Ryan seemed to find amusing.

Thorne recognised the two other men present from photos. Marcus Moloney had risen quickly through the ranks and was known to be one of Ryan's most trusted associates. The younger man was Ryan's son Stephen.

'Shall we crack on, then?' Ryan said.

As the five men sat – Tughan and Thorne on a small sofa and the others on armchairs – and while drinks were offered and refused, Thorne took the place and the people in. They were in one of the two rooms above an office furniture showroom from which Ryan ran his multi-million-pound empire. It was spacious enough, but the decor and furnishings were shabby – ironic, considering what they knocked out from the premises downstairs, which, of course, Ryan also owned. Thorne wondered whether the man was just tight or genuinely didn't care about high-quality leather and chrome.

In his twenty-five years on the job, and never living more than a mile or two away from where he now sat, Thorne had come across the name William John Ryan with depressing frequency. But, up to this point, he had miraculously avoided any direct dealings with him. Staring at him in the flesh for the first time, across a low table strewn with a variety of newspapers and magazines – the *Daily Star, House & Garden*, the *Racing Post, World of Interiors* – Thorne was grudgingly impressed by the way the man presented himself.

Ryan's complexion was ruddy, but the mouth was small and sensitive. When he spoke, his teeth remained hidden. The red cheeks were closely shaved and looked as if they might have been freshly boiled. The scent of expensive aftershave hung around him, and something else – hairspray, maybe, judging by the way the sandy hair, turning to white in places, curled across the collar of his blazer. Thorne thought he looked a little like a well-preserved Van Morrison.

'I presume you've made no progress in catching this maniac,' Ryan said.

Ryan's Dublin accent had faded a little over the years but was still strong enough. Tughan turned his own up a notch or two in response. Thorne couldn't tell if it was deliberate or not.

'We're following up a number of promising leads,' Tughan said.

'I hope so. There needs to be a result on this, you know.'

'There will be . . .'

'This man has butchered friends of mine. I have to assume that, until he's caught, members of my own family might well be at risk.'

'That's probably a fair assumption.'

Moloney spoke for the first time. 'So do something about it.' His voice was low and reasonable, the face blank and puffy below thinning, dirty-blond hair. 'It's fucking outrageous that you aren't offering Mr Ryan's family any protection.'

Ryan spotted the look on Thorne's face. 'Something funny?' he asked.

Thorne shrugged. 'Not laugh-out-loud funny.' He looked at Moloney. 'More ironic, seeing as it's Mr Ryan's family that's normally *offering* the protection. Then again, "offering" isn't really the right word . . .'

Now it was Stephen Ryan's turn to chip in: 'Cheeky cunt!' The son was thought by many to have become the muscle of the Ryan operation. Though he had his old man's features, as yet unsoftened, the voice was very different, and not just in tone. Thorne knew very well that Stephen had been sent to an exclusive private school. His accent was pure Mockney.

Thorne smiled at Stephen's father. 'Nice to see that the expensive education was well worth it.'

Ryan returned what in some lights could be mistaken for a smile. He looked at Tughan, nodded at Thorne: 'Where did you find this one?'

Tughan glanced at Thorne as if he were wondering the same thing himself. 'We'll make this quick, Mr Ryan,' he said. 'We just wanted to check that nothing else has cropped up at your end since we last spoke.'

'Cropped up?'

'Any other thoughts, you know? Theories about who might be . . . attacking your business.'

'I told you last time, and every time before that . . .'

'You might have thought of something since then. Heard something on the grapevine, maybe.'

Ryan leaned back in his chair, spread his arms wide across the back of it. Thorne could see that his shoulders were powerful beneath the cashmere blazer, but, looking down, he was amazed at the daintiness of the feet. Ryan was supposed to have been a fair amateur boxer in his younger days but also, bizarrely, had something of a reputation as a ballroom dancer. Thorne stared at the small, highly polished loafers, at the oddly girlish, silk socks . . .

'I don't know who's doing this. I wish I did . . .'

Thorne had to admit that Ryan lied quite brilliantly. He even managed to plaster a sheen of emotion – something like sadness – on to his face, masking what was clearly nothing more noble than anger, and a desire for brutal vengeance. Thorne glanced at Moloney and Stephen Ryan. Both had their heads down.

'I have no bloody idea who it is,' Ryan repeated. 'That's what you're supposed to be finding out.'

Tughan tugged at the material of his trousers, crossed one leg over the other. 'Has anybody else remembered anything? An employee, maybe . . .?'

It was 'employee' that made Thorne smile this time. If Ryan spotted it, he didn't react. He shook his head, and for fifteen seconds they sat in silence.

'What about these leads you mentioned?' Stephen Ryan looked at Thorne like he was a shit-stain trodden into a white shagpile.

'Thank you,' Thorne said. 'We'd almost forgotten. Does the name Izzigil mean anything at all?'

Shaking heads and upturned palms. Stephen Ryan ran a hand across his closely cropped black hair.

'Are you sure?'

'Is this now a formal interview?' Moloney asked. 'We should get the brief in here, Mr Ryan.'

Ryan raised a hand. 'You did say this was just a chat, Mr Tughan.'

'Nothing sinister,' Tughan said.

Thorne nodded, paused. 'So, that's a definite "no" on Izzigil, then?' He nodded to Tughan, who reached into his briefcase and took out a couple of ten-by-eights.

'What about these?' Tughan asked.

Thorne pushed aside the papers and magazines, took the pictures from Tughan and dropped them on to the table. 'Does anybody recognise these two?'

Sighs from Stephen Ryan and Marcus Moloney as they leaned forward. Billy Ryan picked up one of the pictures, a still from CCTV footage on Green Lanes, taken nearly three weeks earlier: a fuzzy shot of two boys running; two boys they presumed to have been running away from Muslum Izzigil's video shop, having just hurled a four-foot metal bin through the window.

'Look like any pair of herberts up to no good,' Ryan said. 'Ten a fucking penny. Marcus?'

Moloney shook his head.

Stephen Ryan looked over at Thorne, eyes wide. 'Is it Ant and

Dec?' He cackled at his joke, turning to share it with Moloney.

Tughan gathered up the pictures and pushed himself up from the sofa. 'We'll get out of your way, then . . .'

Moloney and Stephen Ryan stayed where they were as Billy Ryan showed Tughan and Thorne out. The receptionist gave Thorne a hard look as he passed. Thorne winked at him.

Ryan stopped at the door. 'What this arsehole's doing, the cutting, you know? It's not on. I've been in business a long time, I've seen some shocking stuff.'

'I bet you have,' Thorne said.

Ryan didn't hear the dig, or chose to ignore it. He shook his head, looking thoroughly disgusted. 'Fucking "X-Man" . . .'

It didn't surprise Thorne that Ryan knew exactly what it was that the killer did to his victims. Three of them had been found by Ryan's own men, after all. The nickname, though, was something else – something that, as far as Thorne was aware, had been confined to Becke House. Obviously, Ryan was a man with plenty of contacts, and Thorne was not naïve enough to believe that they wouldn't include a few who were eager to top up a Metropolitan Police salary.

Thorne asked the question as if it were an afterthought. 'What does the name Gordon Rooker mean to you, Mr Ryan?'

There was a reaction, no question. Fleeting and impossible to define. Anger, fear, shock, amazement? It could have been any one of them.

'Another arsehole,' Ryan said, eventually. 'And one who I haven't had to think about for a very long time.'

The three of them stood, saying nothing, the smell of aftershave overpowering close-up, until Ryan turned and walked quickly back towards his office.

The light had been dimming when they'd arrived. Now it had gone altogether. Turning the corner into the unlit side-street, Thorne was disappointed to see that the Rover didn't at least have a window broken.

'Who's Gordon Rooker?' Tughan asked.

'Just a name that came up. I was barking up the wrong tree . . .'

Tughan gave him a long look. He pressed a button on his keyring to unlock the car, walked round to open the driver's door. 'Listen, it's almost five and I signed us both out for the rest of the day anyway. I'll drop you at home.'

Thorne glanced through the window and saw the empty cassette box between the seats. The idea of a balding millionaire bleating about the homeless for another second was simply unbearable.

'I'll walk,' he said.

SEVEN

Thorne cut up Royal College Street, where a faded plaque on a flaking patch of brickwork identified a house where Verlaine and Rimbaud had once lived. By the time he came out on to Kentish Town Road it had begun to drizzle, but he was still glad he'd refused Tughan's offer of a lift.

As Thorne walked past some of the tattier businesses that fringed the main road, his thoughts returned to Billy Ryan. He wondered how many of the people who ran these pubs, saunas and internet cafés were connected to Ryan in some way or another. Most probably wouldn't even recognise the name, but the working lives of many, honest or not, would certainly be touched by Ryan at some stage.

He thought of those who looked up to Ryan. Those in the outer circles who would be looking to move towards the centre. Did those likely lads, keen to trade in their Timberland and Tommy Hilfiger for Armani, have a clue what they might be expected to do in return? Could they begin to guess at what the softly spoken ballroom dancer had once been – might still be – capable of?

'I've seen some shocking things . . .'

Just before the turning into Prince of Wales Road, Thorne nipped into a small supermarket. He needed milk and wine, and wanted a paper to see what the Monday night match was on Sky Sports. Queuing at the till, he became aware of raised voices near the entrance and walked over. A uniformed security guard was guiding a woman of forty or so towards the doors, trying to move her out of the shop. He was not taking any nonsense, but there was still some warmth in his voice: 'How often do we have to do this, love?'

'I'm sorry, I can't help it,' the woman said.

The security guard saw Thorne coming over and his eyes widened. We've got a right one here . . .

'Do you want a hand?' Even as Thorne said it, he hadn't quite decided who he was offering the help to.

Though the woman had three or four fat, plastic bags swinging from each hand, she was well dressed. 'It's something I feel compelled to do,' she said, revealing herself to be equally well spoken.

'What?' Thorne asked.

The security guard still had a hand squarely in the middle of the woman's back and was moving her ever closer to the door. 'She pesters the other customers,' he said.

'I tell them about Jesus.' The woman beamed at Thorne. 'They really don't seem to mind. Nobody gets annoyed.'

Thorne slowly followed the two of them, watching as they drifted towards the pavement.

'People just want to do their shopping,' the security guard said. 'You're holding them up.'

'I have to tell them about Him. It's my job.'

'And this is mine.'

'I know. It's fine, really. I'm so sorry to have caused any trouble.'

'Don't come back for a while this time, OK?'

With a shrug and a smile, the woman hoisted up her bags and turned towards the street. Thorne moved to the exit and watched her walking away.

The security guard caught his eye. 'I suppose there are worse crimes . . .'

Thorne said nothing.

He'd arrived home to a note from Hendricks saying that he was spending the night at Brendan's. Thorne had put the frozen pizza he'd picked up from the supermarket in the oven. He flicked through the *Standard*, watched *Channel Four News* while it was cooking . . .

Now, five minutes into the second half, Newcastle United and Southampton appeared to have settled for a draw. It was chucking it down on Tyneside and the St James' Park pitch was slippery, so there were at least the odd hideously mistimed tackle and some handbags at ten paces, but that was as exciting as it got.

Thorne snatched up the phone gratefully when it rang.

'Tom . . .?'

'You not watching the football, Dad?' Time was, the TV coverage of a match would be swiftly followed by ten minutes of amateur punditry over the phone with the two of them arguing about every dodgy decision, every key move. That all seemed a lifetime ago.

'Too busy,' his dad said. 'Different game I'm concerned about, anyway. You got your thinking cap on?'

'Not at this very moment, no . . .'

'All the ways you can be dismissed at cricket, if you please. I've made a list. There's ten of them, so come on.'

Thorne picked up the remote, knocked the volume on the TV down a little. 'Can't you just read them out to me?'

'Don't be such a cock, you big fucker.' He said it like it was a term of endearment.

'Dad . . .'

'Stumped and hit wicket, I'll give you them to start . . .'

Thorne sighed, began to list them: 'Bowled, LBW, caught, run out. What d'you call it . . . hitting the ball twice? Touching the ball . . .?'

'No. *Handling* the ball.'

'Right. Handling the ball. Listen, I can't remember the other two . . .'

His father laughed. Thorne could hear his chest rattling. 'Timed out and obstructing the field. They're the two that people can never remember. Same as Horst Bucholz and Brad Dexter.'

'*What?*'

'They're the two in *The Magnificent Seven* that nobody can ever remember. So, come on then. Yul Brynner, I'll give you him to start . . .'

Southampton scrambled a late winner five minutes from the final whistle, just about the time when Thorne's dad began to run out of steam. Not long after, he put down the handset, needing to fetch a book, to check a crucial fact. A minute or two into the silence that followed, Thorne realised that his father had forgotten all about the call and wasn't coming back. He'd maybe even gone upstairs to bed.

Thorne thought about shouting down the phone, but decided to hang up instead.

EIGHT

An attractive young woman placed menus on the table in front of them.

'Just two coffees, please,' Thorne said.

Holland looked a little disappointed, as if he'd been hoping to put a spot of breakfast on expenses. After the waitress had gone, Holland scanned the menu: 'Some of this stuff sounds nice. You know, the Turkish stuff.'

Thorne glanced around, caught the eye of a dour, dark-eyed individual sitting at a table near the door. 'I can't see us eating here too regularly, can you?'

When the coffees arrived, Thorne asked, 'Is the owner around?' The waitress looked confused. 'Is Mr Zarif available?'

'Which?'

'The boss. We'd like to speak to him . . .'

She picked up the menus and turned away without a word. Thorne watched her drop them on to the counter and stamp away down the stairs at the back of the room.

'She can say goodbye to her tip,' Holland said.

The café was at the Manor House end of Green Lanes, opposite Finsbury Park, and not a million miles away from where Thorne had once been beaten up by a pair of Arsenal fans. It was small – maybe six tables and a couple of booths – and the blinds on the front door and windows made it a little gloomier than it might have been. The ceiling was the only well-lit part of the room, the varnished pine coloured gold by the glow from dozens of ornate lanterns – glass, bronze and ceramic – dangling from the wooden slats and swinging slightly every time the front door opened or closed.

Holland took a sip of coffee. 'Maybe he's got a thing about lamps.'

Thorne noticed the slightly incongruous choice of background music and nodded towards the stereo on a shelf behind the counter. 'And Madonna,' he said.

They both looked up at the sound of heavy footsteps on the stairs. The man who emerged around the corner and walked towards their booth was big – bulky as much as fat – and round-shouldered. A blue-and-white-striped apron was stretched across his belly, and his hands were tangled in a grubby-looking tea-towel as he struggled to dry them.

'Can I help you?'

Thorne took out his warrant card and made the introductions. 'We'd like to have a word with the owner.'

The man edged behind the table, squeezed himself in next to Holland and sat down. 'I am Arkan Zarif.'

Thorne was happy for Holland to kick off and listened as he told Zarif that they were investigating a number of murders, including that of Muslum Izzigil, and that they needed to ask him some questions regarding his various business interests. Zarif listened intently, nodding almost constantly. When Holland had finished, Zarif thought for a few seconds before suddenly breaking into a smile and holding out his hands: 'You need proper coffee. *Turkish* coffee.'

Holland raised a hand to refuse, but Zarif was already shouting across to the waitress in Turkish.

'Mr Izzigil was murdered just up the road from here,' Holland said. Zarif shook his head. 'Terrible. Many murders here. Lots of guns.'

He had a strong Mediterranean accent, his face folding into concentration as he spoke. Though olive-skinned, Thorne could see that the rest of his colouring was unusual. His eyes were a light green beneath his heavy brows. His hair was dark with oil, and the stubble across his jowls was white, but Thorne could see from the thick moustache, and the wisps around his ears, that his natural colour was a light, almost orangey brown.

'You have to speak with my son,' he said.

'About Mr Izzigil's murder?'

'These business interests. My sons are the businessmen. They are *great* businessmen. Just two years after we come here and they buy this place for me. How's that?' He held out his arms, his smile almost as wide as they were.

'So who is the owner of this place?' Holland asked. 'Of all the other businesses?'

Zarif leaned forward. 'OK, here it is. See, I have three sons.' He held up his fingers, as if Thorne and Holland would find it as hard to understand some of the words as he did to find them. 'Memet is the eldest. Then Hassan and Tan.' He nodded towards the waitress who was watching from behind the counter, smoking. 'Also my daughter, Sema.'

Thorne caught movement near the door and turned to see the man who had clocked him earlier rising to leave. It didn't look like he'd settled his bill. Zarif gave him a wave as he went.

'Memet runs things here,' Zarif said. 'Deliveries and everything else.'

Holland scribbled in his notebook. He'd never quite lost the habit. 'But it's in your name?'

'The café was a present from my sons.' He leaned back against the red plastic of the booth as his daughter put three small cups of steaming coffee on the table. She said something to Zarif in Turkish and he nodded. 'I love to cook, so I spend my time in the kitchen. My wife helps, and Sema. Chopping and peeling. *I* do all the cooking, though.' He poked himself in the chest. '*I* pick out the meat . . .'

'Is Memet here?' Thorne asked.

Zarif shook his head. 'Gone out for the day.' He picked up his coffee cup, pointed with it towards the street. 'Next door is Hassan's minicab office, if you want. My other two sons are usually in there. I'm certain they just play cards all day.' He took a slurp of the coffee and with a grin gestured for Thorne and Holland to do the same. 'Good?'

'Strong,' Thorne said. 'Zarif Brothers owns a number of video shops, is that right?'

Another proud smile. 'Six or seven, I think. More, maybe. They get me all the latest films, the new James Bond . . .'

'Muslum Izzigil was the manager of one of those shops a quarter of a mile up the road. He and his wife were shot in the head.'

Zarif's eyes widened as he swallowed his coffee.

'Did your sons not mention that to you, Mr Zarif?'

The daughter began talking loudly to him in Turkish from behind the counter. Zarif held up his hands, spoke sharply to her, then turned at the noise of the door opening. The irritation instantly left his face: 'Hassan . . .'

The door closed. Several of the lanterns clinked against one another. Thorne turned to see two young men moving purposefully across the room. He was in little doubt they'd been summoned from next door by the customer who'd just left. One of the men stopped at the counter and began talking in a low voice to Sema. The other marched across to the end of the booth.

'My old man's English isn't so good,' he said.

Thorne looked at him. 'It's fine.'

Another stream of Turkish, this time from the son to the father.

Thorne held up a hand, put the other on Arkan Zarif's beefy forearm. 'What's he saying?'

Zarif rolled his eyes and began to slide out of the booth. 'I'm being sent back to the kitchen,' he said.

Holland caught Thorne's eye, disturbed at losing control of the interview. 'Hang on . . .'

Zarif turned back to the table. 'You want more coffee?'

'It's fine,' Thorne said, answering Zarif and Holland at the same time.

As Arkan disappeared down the stairs, Hassan slid into his place. With a wave, he beckoned to his sister for his own cup of coffee. He leaned back and stuck out his chin.

Rooker lay on his bunk, glued to the TV that was bolted to the wall in the corner, swearing at *Trisha*. Mid-morning was virtually written in stone. If the subject was a very good one, he *might* defect to *Kilroy*, but it was always a lot more polite and BBC. The people on *Trisha* were usually not too bright and a damn sight more likely to swear and row.

This morning's was especially good: 'Problems with Intimacy' . . .

There was some poof banging on about how he'd never been able to tell his kids that he loved them and a woman who couldn't bear her husband putting his arm around her in the street. Rooker decided that they ought to try crapping next to a child molester or showering with rapists.

He'd spent well over a third of his life in prison but had never got used to the proximity of some of those he'd been locked up with. He remembered reading about how all animals needed a certain amount of territory – even rats or rabbits or whatever – a bit of space that was all theirs, or they'd start to go mad, attacking each other. Fucking rabbits going mental! Plenty of people inside *did* lose it, of course, plenty of them *big time*, but he was surprised it didn't happen more often. He was amazed that a lot more prison officers didn't die every year.

Thinking about it – and he'd had plenty of time to think about it – he'd been wary of getting close to others at school. Changing rooms made him uncomfortable. He'd go home dirty after games rather than jump in the showers with the rest of them. He often wondered if this distance he felt from other kids was why he had ended up in his particular line of work . . .

On the show, Trisha asked the woman if she loved her husband, even though she hated him touching her in public. 'Yeah, I love him sometimes,' she said. 'Other times, I could kill him.'

Rooker laughed along with the studio audience. He knew that the difference between him and most people who said things like 'I could kill him' was that he really could do it. He could remember what it was like to put a gun to someone's head, to pull a knife across a throat, to pour lighter fuel into some poor bastard's hair . . .

The programme finished and he stepped out on to the landing. He could smell lunch coming as he walked down to the floor. You could always smell the food going in one direction or the other.

'DLP going for it this time, d'you reckon? Rooker?' Alun Fisher had served three years of a five-year tariff for causing death by dangerous driving. He had a history of drug abuse and mental illness. His refusal to eat properly meant that he spent as much time on the prison's healthcare wing as he did in the VP Unit. 'Bound to approve you, this time. You'll be counting the days, yeah?'

Rooker grunted, stared across at the card school in the corner. He *was* feeling confident this time. They were bound to go for the deal, considering what he was offering. He could probably afford to pick up one of the pool cues and bash Fisher's head in and they'd *still* send a police limo to pick him up.

'You're going to have it sweet on the outside,' Fisher said. 'That's what everybody reckons. You'll be looked after 'cos you never grassed.'

Rooker stared at him.

Fisher nodded and grinned, the teeth blackened and rotten from years of drug use. 'Never fucking grassed . . .'

'The business was Mr Izzigil's. Our company owns the building which is looked after by a letting agency. I didn't actually know him.' Hassan

Zarif had the same accent as his father, but the grammar and vocabulary were virtually faultless. Two years here and already their native language had become their second. It was clear that, in all sorts of ways, the Zarif boys were quick learners. 'My brother popped in occasionally, I think, and perhaps Izzigil would give him a film or two as gifts. Disney films for his children . . .'

'Right,' Thorne said.

'Zarif Brothers owns the property, but the video business was Mr Izzigil's.'

Holland failed to keep the sarcasm from his voice. 'You said that.'

Zarif cocked his head, put a finger into the empty metal ashtray, and slowly began to spin it on the tabletop. He was in his early twenties – tall, with a mop of thick, black hair which sat high on his head. A pronounced chin marred the brooding looks and was emphasised by the polo neck he wore under a heavy, brown leather jacket with a fur collar. He sighed slightly at having to state the obvious again. 'He rented out movies.'

'That's not what paid for his son's school,' Thorne said. 'Or the nice new Audi in his garage.'

Zarif shook his head, spun the ashtray.

'He had over thirty thousand pounds in a building society "wealth management" service,' Holland said.

'Some people have no vices . . .'

Thorne leaned across, gently nudged the ashtray to one side. 'So, you've no idea at all why anybody would want to put a bullet in his head? And put one in his wife's head for good measure.'

Zarif clicked his tongue against the roof of his mouth, as if he were trying to decide exactly how to answer.

Thorne knew that this meeting was as important for the young man sitting opposite him as it was for them. Hassan Zarif knew he was safe, at least for the time being. This was about making impressions. He wouldn't want to appear obstructive, but he had a natural cockiness, and a place in the world he thought he'd earned the hard way. It was a tricky balance to strike, but while he played the part of concerned local businessman, he also had a message to send. He wanted to let them know, nicely, of course, that neither he nor the rest of them were to be pissed around.

'Maybe he fucked the wrong man's girlfriend,' Zarif said.

From behind the counter, Zarif's sister began to laugh. Thorne glared at her, none too keen on the joke, but saw that she was actually laughing at something Zarif's friend was saying to her. He turned back to Zarif. 'As we told your father, we're investigating a number of recent murders.'

'It's a dangerous city.'

'Only for some people,' Thorne said.

Zarif smiled, held up his hands. 'Listen, I've got stuff to do, so . . .'

Thorne asked his questions, played the game. He had his own message to send and wasn't overly concerned with subtlety.

'Do you have any information that might assist us in investigating the death of Mickey Clayton?'

Zarif shook his head.

'Or Sean Anderson?'

'No.'

The X-Man's victims. 'Anthony Wright? John Gildea?'

'No and no.'

Thorne reached into his jacket, pulled out some change. He dropped a couple of pound coins on to the table. 'That's for the coffee.'

Outside, it was raining. They walked quickly back towards Thorne's BMW.

'Seems to me,' Holland said, 'that we spend a lot of time going to see these fuckers, asking them questions, listening to them tell us they don't know anything, and then leaving again.'

Thorne looked into the park as they walked alongside it. The trees were shiny and skeletal. 'Same as it ever was . . .'

'He was so full of shit,' Holland said. '"Disney films for the kids?"

They'd have been involved somewhere in supply, delivery, all of it. They'd have taken a massive cut of Izzigil's earnings, *on top* of what they got out of the piracy, out of the smuggling operation . . .'

Finsbury Park wasn't Thorne's favourite green space. He'd been to a few gigs there over the years, though – the Fleadh to see Emmylou Harris, Madstock once with a WPC he fancied. When the Sex Pistols reformed and played there, back when he was still living with his wife, he'd been able to hear every word from their back garden in Highbury, which was over a mile away . . .

Holland was grimacing. 'That coffee was shit as well,' he said. 'It tasted like something you'd find in a Gro-Bag.'

Thorne laughed. 'It's an acquired taste.'

'Listen, d'you fancy having a pint later? The Oak, if you like, or we could go into town . . .'

'Sophie letting you out for the night, is she?'

'Happy to see the back of me, mate. I'm getting on her nerves a bit, I think. Fuck it, I'm getting on my *own* nerves . . .'

They'd reached the car. Thorne unlocked it and climbed in before leaning across to unlock Holland's door. 'Can we do it another night? I'm busy later.'

Holland dropped into the passenger seat. The rain had left dark streaks across the shoulders of his grey jacket and at the tops of his trousers. The suit was starting to look a little tired, and Thorne knew that Holland would go into M&S at some point soon to buy another one that was exactly the same.

'Hot date?' Holland asked.

Thorne smiled when the engine turned over first time. 'Not remotely . . .'

NINE

Leicester Square after dark was right up there with the M25 at rush hour or the Millwall ground, in terms of places that Thorne thought were best avoided.

The buskers and the occasional B-list film premiere made little difference. For every few smiling tourists, there was someone lounging against the wall outside one of the cinemas, or hanging around in the corner of the green, with a far darker reason for being there. For every American family or pair of Scandinavian backpackers there was a mugger, or a pickpocket, or just a pissed-up idiot looking for trouble, and the crappy funfair only seemed to bring out the vultures in greater numbers.

'I pity the uniformed lads working round here tonight,' Chamberlain said.

There were plenty of places in the city that were alive with the promise of something. Here, there was only a threat. If it wasn't for the stench of piss and cheap burgers, you'd probably be able to *smell* it.

'The only good thing about this place,' Thorne said, 'is the rent you can get for it on a sodding Monopoly board . . .'

A quarter to seven on a Tuesday night, and the place was heaving. Aside from those milling around, taking pictures or taking cameras, there were those moving through the square on their way to somewhere more pleasant. West towards Piccadilly and Regent Street beyond. South towards the theatres on the Strand. East towards Covent Garden, where the street entertainment was a little artier, and the average burger was anything but cheap.

Thorne and Chamberlain moved through the square on their way to a brightly lit and busy games arcade, slap-bang between Chinatown and Soho. They passed partially steamed-up windows displaying racks of Day-Glo, honey-glazed chickens and leathery squid which drooped from metal hooks like innards.

'How sure are you that he's going to be there?' Chamberlain asked.

Thorne ushered her to the left, avoiding the queue outside the Capital Club. 'Billy was under investigation well before things turned nasty. We know near enough everything he gets up to. We know all his routines.'

Chamberlain quickened her pace just a little to keep up. 'If Ryan's half the character I think he is, I wouldn't be surprised if he knows quite a lot about you, too.'

Thorne shivered ever so slightly, but gave her a grin. 'I'm so glad you came along to cheer me up . . .'

They cut off the square and walked to a Starbucks on the other side of the street from the arcade. They didn't have to wait long before Ryan appeared. Halfway through their coffees, they watched as one of the heavy glass doors was opened for him, and Ryan moved slowly down the short flight of steps towards the street. Marcus Moloney was at his shoulder. A few paces behind were a pair of Central Casting thugs who looked as though they might enjoy shiny objects and the sound of small bones breaking.

As Thorne approached from across the street – heavyset and with his hands thrust into the pockets of his leather jacket – Ryan took half a step back and reached out an arm towards one of the gorillas behind him. He recovered himself when he recognised Thorne: 'What do you want?'

Thorne nodded past Ryan towards the arcade. It was packed with teenagers, queuing to ram their pound coins into the machines. 'I was just a bit bored, and I'm a big fan of the shoot-'em-ups. This one of your places, is it?'

Moloney looked up and down the street. 'Looking for a discount, Thorne?'

'Is that how you try to get coppers on the payroll these days? A few free games of Streetfighter?'

Ryan had recognised Thorne, but had failed to recognise the woman with him. 'Grab-a-Granny night, is it?' He looked Chamberlain up and down. 'Don't tell me she's on the job. I thought coppers were supposed to look *younger* these days . . .'

'You're a cheeky fucker, Ryan,' Chamberlain said.

Then Ryan *did* recognise her. Thorne watched him grit his teeth as he remembered exactly what had been happening the last time their paths had crossed.

'You looked a bit jumpy a minute ago,' Thorne said. He nodded towards the two bodyguards. 'These two look a touch nervous as well. Worried that whoever did Mickey Clayton and the others might come after you, are you, Mr Ryan?'

Ryan said nothing.

A group of young lads burst out through the arcade doors, the noise from inside spilling momentarily on to the street with them: the spatter and squeal of guns and lasers, the rumble of engines, the beat of hypnotic techno . . .

Moloney answered Thorne's question: 'They can fucking well *try* . . .'

'I wonder what I might find,' Thorne said, 'if I were to put you up against that wall over there and pat you down.'

Moloney looked unconcerned. 'Nothing worth the trouble.'

'Trouble?'

Moloney sighed heavily and stepped past him. Thorne watched him walk a few yards up the street. He took out a mobile phone and began to stab angrily at the keypad. Thorne turned back to see the pair of heavies stepping up close to their employer, who was looking into the distance. Ryan was trying hard *not* to look at Carol Chamberlain.

'You remember Carol?' Thorne said. 'DI Manley, as she'd have been when you last saw her.'

'It took you a moment, though, didn't it?' Chamberlain took a step to her left, placed herself in Ryan's line of vision.

'That would have been the Jessica Clarke case, wouldn't it, Mr Ryan?'

'I don't think it's quite come back to him,' Chamberlain said. 'The girl who was set on fire? These things can slip your mind, I understand that.'

'It was Gordon Rooker who got sent down for that, wasn't it? I think we were talking about him a few days ago, weren't we, Mr Ryan?'

The wind was rushing up the narrow street. It lifted the hair from the collar of Ryan's overcoat as he spun around. 'I'll say the same thing I said then, in case *your* memory's playing up. I haven't had the displeasure of thinking about that piece of shite for a long time.'

'That's funny,' Thorne said. 'Because he's been thinking about you. He specifically asked me to say "hello" . . .'

Ryan's mouth tightened and his eyes narrowed. Thorne reckoned it was more than just the wind that was slapping him around the face.

'So . . . hello,' Thorne said.

Thorne saw the relief flood suddenly into Ryan's face. He watched him step quickly past him the instant he heard the noise of the engine. Thorne turned to see a black people-carrier roar up to the kerb and screech to a halt. The door was already open and Stephen Ryan jumped out.

Thorne gave Ryan's son a wave and received a cold stare in return.

Stephen shrugged as his father barged past him. 'Sorry . . .'

'Where the *fuck* have you been?'

Billy Ryan climbed into the car without looking back. He was quickly followed by his son and the two heavies, who pushed past Thorne and Chamberlain without any delicacy. As Moloney marched up, the driver's window slid down. Thorne recognised the receptionist he'd exchanged pleasantries with at Ryan's office.

'Sorry, Marcus. Traffic's fucked all over the West End.'

Moloney ignored him and moved to the rear door. With one foot already inside the car, he looked at Thorne. 'Careful you don't get shot . . .'

Thorne opened his mouth, took a step towards the car.

Moloney pointed over Thorne's shoulder towards the arcade: 'The shoot-'em-ups . . .' He pulled the door shut and the car moved quickly away from the kerb.

'What was all that "hello" business?' Chamberlain asked.

Thorne watched Ryan's car turn the corner and disappear. 'Politeness costs nothing. What time's your train?'

'Last one's just before eleven.'

'Let's get some food . . .'

Marcus Moloney downed almost half his Guinness in one go. He set the glass down on the bar and leaned back in his chair.

'Tough day, mate?' said the man next to him.

Moloney grunted, picked up the glass again. It wasn't so much the day as the last few hours. First the business outside the arcade, and then the fallout: all the way back to Ryan's place in Finchley, Moloney had been given an earful. Whatever it was that Thorne and the woman had been going on about, it had got his boss very wound up. As if things weren't tense enough already, with everything that was going on. Still, Ryan was safe at home now, taking it all out on his wife. She'd be doing what had to be done. She'd be making all the right noises, massaging his ego and anything else he fancied, and thanking Christ that he still hadn't found out about the landscape gardener who was giving her one three times a week.

Moloney downed some more of the Guinness. His pager was on, as always, but his time was his own for a few precious hours and he was keen to unwind a little.

He had known plenty of coppers like Thorne before . . . With the bent ones, it was easy. You knew what made them tick, what got them off. Not that Thorne was necessarily incorruptible; everybody had their price. Moloney saw it offered and accepted every day. Problem was, Thorne was the sort who would take the dirty money, do what was asked of him for a while and then blow up in everyone's face. Do something stupid because he hated himself. It didn't matter if he was bent or not – and it was easy enough to find out. Thorne had to be watched. He was definitely going to cause them trouble.

Moloney drained his glass, waved it to get the barman's attention, and nodded for another. The man on the chair next to him got up and asked where he could find the Gents'. Moloney pointed the way and asked if the man wanted a drink. The offer was graciously accepted. While he waited for the beers, Moloney looked around the crowded bar: plenty of faces. He drank in here pretty often, and one or two of the regulars who knew him had already said hello, or offered to buy him a drink, or held up a glass and waved from the other side of the room.

A lot of people wanted to know him.

The fact that none of them did, that so few people *really* knew him, was becoming harder to deal with lately. He was definitely drinking more, flying off the handle at the slightest thing, on the job and at home. It was all down to this war. Things had ratcheted up once the murders had started. What the Zarifs were doing, what Ryan was going to do in return, was the real test . . .

The man came back from the Gents' and took his seat at the bar. Moloney handed him his pint of lager. When his Guinness had settled and been topped up, he raised the glass.

'Good health,' Moloney said.

★

Thorne and Chamberlain had shared a bottle and a half of red wine with their dinner, and the thickening head may have had something to do with his reaction, his *over*-reaction, when he'd walked into the living room. The smell had hit him the second he'd opened the outer door.

'Fucking hell, Phil. Not in my flat . . .'

'It's only a bit of weed. I'm not shooting up. Jesus . . .'

'Do it round at Brendan's.'

Hendricks had needed to make a real effort not to laugh, and not just because he was stoned. 'Take a day off, why don't you?'

Thorne stalked off towards the kitchen. 'I fucking wish . . .'

Waiting for the kettle to boil, Thorne had calmed down and tried to decide whether to apologise or just pretend the argument had never happened. He'd recently discovered that, within the City of London, a pregnant woman in need of the toilet was still legally allowed to piss in a policeman's helmet. That dope should still be against the law was, he knew, only marginally sillier.

'Make us a piece of toast while you're in there,' Hendricks had shouted.

'*What!?*'

'I'm kidding.' Then, Hendricks hadn't been able to stop himself laughing any more.

If he was honest, it was the associations that went with dope-smoking that riled Thorne. He'd tried it a couple of times at school and, even then, passing an increasingly soggy joint around and talking about how great the shit was and how they all had the munchies seemed ridiculous to him. The drugs being taken in the corners of playgrounds these days were more dangerous, but there was none of that palaver. The kids just dropped a pill and got on with it.

There was also the fact that his ex-wife had liked the occasional joint, provided, so it turned out, by the creative-writing lecturer she'd later left him for. Thorne had smelled it on him, the day he'd walked up his own stairs and dragged the skinny sod out of his own bed. Why he hadn't punched him or put in an anonymous call to the Drugs

Squad was still something Thorne occasionally woke up wondering about.

Thorne had mumbled something approaching an apology as he'd carried his tea into the living room. Hendricks had smiled and shaken his head.

They sat listening to the first Gram Parsons album. Thorne was wide awake and watched as Hendricks grew drowsier, then perked up, then began to wilt again . . .

'The shit we have to deal with is the price we pay for being human,' Hendricks announced, out of the blue.

Thorne slurped his tea. 'Right . . .'

'The difference between us and dogs or dolphins or whatever.' Hendricks took a drag of his joint. He was starting to sound a little like someone stoned on a sketch-show. 'We're the only animal that has an imagination . . .'

'As far as we know . . .' Thorne said.

'As far as we know, yeah. And all the dark, dark shit that gets done to people, the killing and the torture, started off as pictures in some weirdo's head. It all has to be *imagined*.'

Thorne thought about what Hendricks was saying. It made sense, though how some of the horrors they'd both encountered over the years had ever been imagined by *anybody* was beyond him. 'So?'

'So . . . that's the flipside of all the beautiful stuff. We get people who imagine great works of art and books and gardens and music, but the same imagination that creates *that* can also imagine the Holocaust, or setting fire to kids, or whatever.'

'All right, Phil . . .'

'You want one, you have to live with the other.'

They sat in silence for a while.

Finally, Hendricks leaned forward to stub out what was left of the joint, and to sum up: 'Basically . . . you want Shakespeare, you also get Shipman.'

Dark as the conversation had become, Thorne suddenly found the

110

concept strangely funny. 'Right.' He nodded towards the stereo. 'Serial killers are the price we pay for country music.'

A massive grin spread slowly across Hendricks' face. 'I think . . . *that* . . . is a very tough choice . . .'

Moloney had decided to make a night of it. He strutted out into the freezing car park at closing time, full of Guinness and full of himself. 'Don't worry, I know a few places where we can still get a drink.' Moloney chuckled and threw an arm around the shoulder of his new best friend. 'Actually,' he said, 'I know *plenty* of fucking places.'

His drinking partner expressed surprise that Moloney was planning to drive. He asked him if he was worried about being pulled over.

Moloney unlocked the Jag. 'I've been stopped a few times.' He winked. 'It's not normally a problem . . .'

'After you've been drinking?'

'They tend to look the other way . . .'

'Nice to have a bit of influence,' said his friend.

'Better than nice. Get in . . .'

They drove south through Islington, crossing the Essex Road and heading towards the City. The traffic was light and Moloney put his foot down at every opportunity. 'This place I'm taking us, behind the Barbican, there's usually a bit of spare knocking about as well. We lay out a few quid, they'll give us a good night. Up for that?'

It was as the Jag was moving far too fast towards the roundabout at Old Street that the man in the passenger seat placed the muzzle of the Glock against Moloney's waist.

'Go left and head for Bethnal Green . . .'

'What? Fuck . . .'

The gun was rammed into Moloney hard enough to crack a rib, to push him against the driver's side door. He cried out and struggled to keep his feet on the pedals.

Moloney drove, following the instructions he was given, body seizing up and mind racing. He knew that there was no way he could reach his own gun. He knew that nobody had a clue where he was. He knew, now, that he was not a brave man. Every breath was an effort. Any attempt to speak resulted in another jolt of agony as the gun was jammed hard against the broken rib.

The traffic and the lights melted away behind them as Moloney steered the Jag off a quiet road and on to a narrow, rutted path. They crossed slowly over a stretch of black water, still, like motor oil, on either side of a graffiti-covered bridge.

'Pull up over there.'

As soon as the car was stationary, the man raised the gun and pressed it against Moloney's ear. He leaned across to the dashboard and turned off the headlights.

Moloney closed his eyes. 'Please . . .'

He felt the man's hand reach inside his jacket, move slowly around until it had located, and removed, the gun. He opened his eyes when he heard the door open, craned his head round to watch as the man moved behind the car.

The gunman tapped on the driver's side window with the gun. He took a step away from the car as Moloney opened the door. 'Move over to the other side,' he said.

Moloney did as he was told, gasping in pain as he lifted himself up and over the gearstick. 'Why?'

The man slid into the driver's seat. He closed the car door behind him. 'Because I'm right-handed,' he said.

Then Moloney felt his guts go, and everything began to happen very quickly.

The gun was in his ear again, and a hand was twisting him over on to his front, pushing his head across the back of the seat. The hand was reaching down, scrabbling for something, and the seat suddenly dropped back until it was almost flat. The hand began gathering up Moloney's jacket and the shirt beneath and pushing it up his back.

'You're making such a fucking mistake . . .' Moloney said.

Then, in a rush, the breath was sucked up into him, as the man with the gun began to cut.

Thorne woke with a start, disorientated. He could hear music, and Hendricks was looming above the bed in his boxer shorts, holding something out to him and mouthing angrily.

As he tried to sit up, Thorne realised that he'd fallen asleep with his headphones on. He turned off his Walkman, blinked slowly and moaned: 'What time is it?'

'Just gone three. It's Holland, for you . . .'

Thorne reached out for his mobile, the ringing of which he'd been unable to hear, but which had clearly woken Hendricks up.

'Thanks,' Thorne said.

Hendricks grunted and sloped out of the bedroom.

'Dave?'

Holland began to speak, but Thorne knew without being told that there was another body. Holland just needed to tell him which side it belonged to.

Thorne had no way of knowing it, but as he steered the BMW through the deserted streets towards the murder scene, he was following almost exactly the same route as the dead man had done a few hours earlier. Down to King's Cross and then east. Along the City Road and further, through Shoreditch and into what, forty years before, had been Kray territory. The streets of east London were much safer then, if some people were to be believed.

Marcus Moloney might well have agreed with them.

The car was parked on an area of waste ground, no more than a hundred yards from the Roman Road. Here, the Grand Union Canal ran alongside a rundown piece of parkland called Meath Gardens and the railway line divided Globe Town from Mile End.

A man, asleep on a narrowboat moored further up the canal, had heard the gunshots. He'd come along five minutes later with his dog to investigate.

Thorne parked the car, walked across to do some investigating of his own.

The silver Jag was brightly lit by a pair of powerful arc-lights that had been set up on either side of it. Its doors were open. Thorne didn't know whether that's the way they had been found.

'Sir . . .'

Thorne nodded as he passed a DC from SO7 walking quickly in the opposite direction. As he got nearer to the car, he could make out the shape of the body, folded across the front seat, like a suit carrier. Every few seconds, the white hood of a SOCO bobbed into vision through the rear windscreen. Stepping to the side, Thorne could see Holland and Stone huddled near the front wing. Holland glanced up, threw him a look he couldn't read, but which definitely didn't bode well. There were more SOCOs working in the footwells and on the back seats. There were stills and video cameramen. There were three or four other officers with their backs to him, talking on the edge of the canal bank.

The lights showed up every scratch, every mark on the car windows, every speck and gobbet of brain matter glued to the glass with blood.

Thorne grabbed a bodysuit from a uniform who was handing them out like free gifts. 'Dave . . .'

Holland made to come over, then stopped and nodded towards the group of officers who were now walking back in the direction of the car. There were three men in suits of varying quality: Brigstocke, Tughan and a senior press officer called Munteen. It was the man in uniform who Thorne was most surprised, and horrified, to see there. He couldn't recall the last time he'd encountered Detective Chief Superintendent Trevor Jesmond at a crime scene.

Jesmond pulled his blue overcoat tighter around him. 'Tom.'

'Sir.'

Thorne broke the short but awkward silence that followed. He nodded towards the car. 'The Zarifs have really upped the stakes now. Marcus Moloney's in a different league from Mickey Clayton and the others. It's going to get a bit tasty from here . . .'

He looked at Russell Brigstocke, and received the same look he'd got from Holland.

'The stakes have certainly been upped,' Jesmond said, 'but not for the reasons you're assuming . . .'

'Oh?' Thorne glanced at Tughan, who was studying the gravel.

Jesmond looked as drawn, as defeated, as Thorne had ever seen him. 'Marcus Moloney was an undercover police officer,' he said.

TEN

Thorne left the Moloney murder scene as the sun was coming up and drove through streets that were showing the first faltering signs of life. He spent a couple of hours at home – showered, changed and had some breakfast – but he was still getting through on what little sleep he'd managed before being woken by Hendricks with the phone call.

Driving towards Hendon, he couldn't decide whether the *heaviness* he felt was due to the lack of sleep, the wine from the night before or the memory of the atmosphere on that canal bank. The change in those who hadn't known the truth about Moloney was clear to see as soon as word had got around. The volume had fallen; the movements in and around the Jag had become a fraction more delicate. Bodies were always accorded a measure of respect, but that measure tended to vary. Dead or not, a gangland villain was treated by the police a little bit differently to a fellow officer.

Thorne hated that 'one of our own' nonsense, but he understood it. The life of a police officer was clearly worth no more or less than that of a doctor or a teacher or a shop assistant. But it wasn't doctors, teachers and shop assistants who had to pick up the bodies, inform the next of kin and try to catch those responsible. Yes, sometimes the self-righteous anger when a policeman died could make his skin crawl, and the speeches made by senior officers could sound horribly false, but Thorne told himself he could see it all for what it really was. There was nothing false about the relief and the fear, nor about anger at feeling both of those things.

Nothing false about 'there but for the grace of God' . . .

It was early, but Thorne knew Carol Chamberlain would be up and about. She needed to know that *everything* had changed. He called her as he hit the North Circular and told her about Marcus Moloney.

'Well, he certainly had me fooled,' she said.

'Me too,' Thorne admitted. And neither of them was stupid.

Moloney was clearly a committed and brilliant undercover officer, but still, it bothered Thorne that he hadn't sensed something. *Anything*. There was a lot of crap talked about 'instinct', but if there was one thing Thorne was certain of, it was that instinct was unreliable. He certainly possessed it himself, but it came and went, failing him at all the wrong moments, as inexplicable as a striker's goal drought or a writer's block. And it had landed him in the shit plenty of times over the years . . .

Occasionally, Thorne felt like he could look into a killer's eyes and see exactly what was on his mind. See all those dark imaginings that Hendricks had been talking about the night before. Sometimes, Thorne thought he could spot a villain by the way he smoked a cigarette. Other times, he wouldn't know the enemy if he was wearing a ski-mask and carrying a sawn-off shotgun.

'How come you *didn't* know?' Chamberlain asked. 'About Moloney?'

Thorne didn't have an answer, and by the time he hung up on Chamberlain and pulled into the compound at Becke House, he was extremely pissed off about it. Why *hadn't* Tughan told him? It was a fucking good question.

★

The answer wasn't particularly satisfactory: 'It wasn't deemed necessary, or prudent . . .'

'Talk English,' Thorne said. He turned to Brigstocke. He and Tughan had both stood up when Thorne had come marching into the office without knocking. 'Russell, did you know?'

Brigstocke nodded. 'It wasn't to go below DCI level,' he said. 'That was the decision.'

Tughan sat back down again. Thorne could see a copy of the *Murder Investigation Manual* on the desk in front of him. 'Moloney's role as an undercover officer was strictly on a "need to know" basis,' he said, as if he'd just read the phrase in the book.

Thorne sighed, leaned back against the door. 'Did he have a wife? Kids?'

Brigstocke nodded again, just once.

'Have they been told he was carved up and shot in the head? Or is that on a "need to know" basis, too?'

'Close the door on the way out,' Tughan said, looking away.

'A few things suddenly make a lot more sense, though,' Thorne said. 'I wondered how you could be so certain that the Izzigil murders were down to Ryan. How you knew where that threatening letter had come from. Obviously you had a hotline . . .'

Tughan slammed a piece of paper on to the desktop. 'Why the hell is everything always about you, Thorne? An officer has been killed. You just said it: "*carved up and shot in the head*". The fact that you hadn't been told that he was a police officer is pretty fucking unimportant, wouldn't you say?'

Brigstocke was no great admirer of Tughan himself, but his expression told Thorne that he thought the DCI had a point . . .

And as Thorne calmed down, he could see Tughan's point too. He felt a little ashamed of the outburst, of the sarcasm. He walked across the office, dragged a spare chair over to the desk and dropped into it. He was relieved to see that Tughan didn't object.

'How long had Moloney been in there?'

'Two years, more or less,' Tughan said.

Thorne was amazed it had been so short a time. 'He got where he was in the organisation pretty bloody quickly.'

Tughan nodded. 'He was bright, and Billy Ryan liked him. Stephen Ryan treated him like an older brother . . .'

'He was doing a pretty good job,' Brigstocke said.

Tughan corrected him: 'He was doing a *very* good job and, with him dead, it's all been worse than useless.'

'Hang on,' Thorne said. 'In two years he must have put together a fair bit of evidence against Ryan.'

'More than a "fair bit", but Moloney was the key witness. He would have been the one standing up in court. All the evidence was based on conversations *he'd* had, things *he'd* seen, or been told. We've got sod all that'll stand up without him.'

'What about the Izzigil killings? He knew about that, right? There must be something . . .'

Tughan picked at something on his chin. He was freshly shaved, rash-red from the razor, but Thorne could see a small patch of sandy stubble that he'd missed to the left of his Adam's apple. 'He knew about it *afterwards*. He knew something was being planned a few days before it happened but couldn't find out who was being hit or who'd been given the contract.'

'It was true Ryan liked to have Moloney around,' Brigstocke said. 'But there were others he trusted to get the really dirty work done.'

'Stephen?' Thorne suggested.

'Yeah, Stephen,' Tughan said, 'and others.'

Thorne thought about how hard it must have been for DC Marcus Moloney. Once the killings had started, he'd been caught in an impossible position. He'd have wanted to dig around, to try to find out the names of the people Ryan was planning to have killed so that he could tell his colleagues at SO7. He'd also have known full well that if he *did* go sniffing around after information he wasn't meant to have, he ran the risk of exposing himself and ruining everything.

And later – after Muslum and Hanya Izzigil had been killed – had he felt somehow responsible?

'We can still get Ryan,' Thorne said.

The other two men in the room looked at him with renewed interest. This was what Thorne had been putting off, but now was the perfect moment. He'd told Chamberlain on the way in that he was going to have to come clean about what they'd been up to. He hadn't realised it was going to be quite this important.

'How?' Tughan asked.

'I've got a witness.'

Tughan smiled. It was the perfect moment for him, too. 'Is this where you tell me about Gordon Rooker?'

Thorne just about stopped his jaw dropping. '*What?*'

'You must think I'm fucking stupid, Thorne. All that crap when we saw Billy Ryan about "barking up the wrong tree". *You* have been, but only by treating me like a mug.'

'Hang on . . .'

'I did some homework, none of it particularly taxing. I know all about your trips to Park Royal, both alone and with ex-DCI Chamberlain.'

Thorne glanced at Brigstocke, got a look back that said he'd known about *this* as well.

'It had nothing to do with this case,' Thorne said. 'There was no connection.'

'There is now, though, right?'

'That's what I'm trying to tell you . . .'

'Which is why you were hassling Billy Ryan outside one of his arcades last night?' Tughan seemed to enjoy watching the puzzlement that Thorne knew was spreading across his face. 'I knew about it while it was happening.'

Thorne cast his mind back to the previous evening. He remembered Moloney walking away from them, talking angrily on his mobile. Thorne had thought he'd been calling for the car . . .

'Right, let's hear it . . .'

So Thorne told them the whole story, ancient and modern. He told them about the calls to Carol Chamberlain and about his visits to Gordon Rooker. He told them about Jessica Clarke and about Rooker's revelation regarding her attacker. He told them about Rooker's offer . . .

'Why's he waited twenty years?' Brigstocke asked.

It was the first of many questions – all of the obvious ones which Thorne had asked himself, and Gordon Rooker. He gave the answers he'd been given: tried to explain why Rooker had confessed to such a heinous crime; why a man like him was able to survive better inside than on the street; why he had decided that he had to make sure Billy Ryan would not be waiting for him on the outside.

'So, we get him out, offer him witness protection, and he will testify against Billy Ryan for the attempted murder of Jessica Clarke?'

'Rooker knows all sorts of stuff,' Thorne said. 'He'll tell us everything, and he'll tell the court everything.'

Rain was starting to come down outside. The drops were heavy but not yet concentrated. For a few moments the noise of their sporadic tapping against the window was the only sound in the room.

'Who's making these calls to ex-DCI Chamberlain and getting creative with lighter fuel in her front garden?' Tughan sounded sceptical. 'We're presuming he's the man who really set fire to the girl, are we?'

'I don't know,' Thorne admitted.

'It's a bit bloody coincidental, don't you think?'

'Rooker denies all knowledge of it.'

'There's a shock.' Tughan looked to Brigstocke. 'Russell?'

'Some crony of Rooker's? An ex-con, maybe? Someone he's been in contact with . . .?'

Thorne tried not to sound impatient. 'We've got time to check all of this,' he said. 'Look, Billy Ryan as good as killed that girl, and we've got a chance to nail him for it. Christ knows, he's done plenty of other things, but we can *get him* for this. It's got to be worth considering.'

Thorne stopped himself adding: *We should do it for Marcus Moloney.* But only just . . .

The rain was falling harder now, beating out a tattoo against the glass.

'Obviously, people a damn sight higher than me are going to be doing the considering,' Tughan said. 'A damn sight higher than Jesmond even . . .' He took a breath and reached for the phone.

As he and Brigstocke got up and headed towards the door, Thorne thought about what Brigstocke had known and had chosen not to pass on. He wondered if he should have a chat with him about whose side they were supposed to be on. He decided it was probably not the right time.

By lunchtime in the Royal Oak, the mood of the team had lightened a little, though it might just have been the power of beer.

The Oak was the team's regular, but for no other reason than proximity. No one could remember a time when it hadn't been full of coppers, so no one could swear that they were the reason for the atmosphere, or the lack of it. It wasn't that Trevor, the cadaverous landlord, hadn't made an effort. He'd decorated the front of the lacquered-pine bar with Polaroids of various female regulars, all hoisting up their T-shirts to reveal bras or bare breasts. Elsewhere, he'd gone for a Spanish theme, with a good deal of fake wrought iron, a couple of sombreros gathering dust on a shelf above the bar, and two days a week when he cut up pork pies and Scotch eggs into small pieces and called it a tapas menu.

There was no Tughan, Kitson or Brigstocke in the pub, but most of the others were there. They raised a glass to Marcus Moloney. His death had eased a little of the tension between the Serious Crime Group mob and their counterparts from SO7. They were understandably united in their resolve to bring to justice those responsible for his death. For *all* the recent deaths.

Thorne applauded the sentiment, even if that's all it was. He hoped

122

that the cracks wouldn't begin to show again too soon. He pushed away a half-eaten plate of chicken and chips as Holland slid in next to him with a tray of drinks. By now, everyone had moved on to Coke, mineral water or orange juice. Thorne, feeling himself starting to wilt a little, poured out his can of Red Bull. He glanced up at Holland and remembered the invitation he'd turned down. 'Did you go for that beer last night? Sounded like you were set on a major session?'

'Just had a couple in here with Andy.' He nodded towards the other side of the bar where Andy Stone, Sam Karim and a female DC from SO7 were deep in conversation. 'Good job I didn't, really. Bearing in mind what time we were called out.'

'I wasn't exactly stone-cold sober myself at four o'clock this morning,' Thorne said. 'Given what was down by that canal, it was probably a good thing . . .'

'Found out something brilliant in here last night, though.' Holland grinned and inched his chair a little closer to Thorne's. 'You know Andy Stone reckons he has quite a bit of success with the women . . .?'

Thorne followed Holland's gaze: Stone and the female DC seemed to be getting on extremely well. '*Yes* . . .?' Thorne stretched the word out.

'He told me one of his tricks. He'd had a bit more to drink than me . . .'

'I'm listening,' Thorne said.

'He keeps a book on philosophy in his car.' Holland laughed as Thorne's eyes widened. 'Seriously. On the passenger seat, or down by the tapes, or wherever. Girl gets in . . . "*Oh what's this?*" . . . Picks it up, has a look, she's convinced Stone's a deep thinker.' There was a pause, then Thorne almost snorted Red Bull down his nose. 'This is the worst bit,' Holland said, 'it fucking works.'

Thorne laughed even harder, wiped the drink from his jacket. He looked up when he heard a familiar Mancunian accent.

Hendricks was pointing at the can of Red Bull. 'That stuff won't wake you up if you apply it externally,' he said.

'What are you doing up here? I thought you had Moloney's PM to do.'

Hendricks glanced at his watch. 'Starting in a couple of hours. There's a queue of corpses out the bloody doors down at Westminster Morgue.'

Holland got up to make room for Hendricks and headed for the Gents'.

'Tughan wanted to see me over the road.' Hendricks dropped into the chair Holland had vacated. 'He wanted a preliminary report.'

'Well? Do I get to hear it?'

Hendricks looked confused. 'What d'you think I came here for?'

'Go on, then . . .'

'Moloney died from gunshot wounds to the head. Almost certainly a nine mil. No bullets found in the car, so I'll have to dig them out to be certain.'

'Same pattern of knife wounds?'

'Yeah . . .'

Thorne had heard Hendricks sound *more* certain. 'Not sure?'

'I'm still not convinced I know what sort of blade he's using. It could be a filleting knife. Also, the cuts weren't quite as neat as they were on Clayton and the others.'

'Perhaps he had less time.'

'Right. And maybe Moloney struggled a bit more than some of the other victims.'

'This is the first time he's done it in a car, remember. He had less room to manoeuvre than he did with the others . . .'

Hendricks nodded. It all made perfectly good sense.

'You'd say it *was* the same killer, though,' Thorne said. 'The X-Man.'

It was a few seconds before Hendricks gave a nod that said '*probably*'. Enough time for Thorne to find himself wondering if they hadn't got things arse about face. They were assuming that the Zarifs had targeted the Ryans again and killed Marcus Moloney, unaware that he was a police officer. But there was an equally plausible possibility . . .

'What if the killer knew *exactly* what Moloney was?'

'Sir?' It was Holland, back from the Gents'.

The more Thorne articulated it, the more convinced he became. He thought back to the previous night, in the street outside the games arcade: Moloney on the phone, not to Billy Ryan's driver, as Thorne had thought, but to Nick Tughan. Making the last call he was ever going to make. Unaware that his cover had been blown . . .

'I think they found out he was a copper,' Thorne said. 'With what was going on, with what had happened to the others, they had a perfect way to get rid of him, didn't they? I think Billy Ryan killed Moloney.'

Thorne reached for his mobile to make the call to Tughan. Before he could start dialling, it began to ring.

It was Russell Brigstocke.

'Tom? We've just had a call from the Central Middlesex Hospital . . .'

Thorne didn't quite take it all in. He just heard the key word and immediately thought: Dad.

'Up by Park Royal.'

The initial relief quickly gave way to mild panic. 'What's happened?' Thorne guessed what the answer would be before Brigstocke gave it.

'Somebody tried to kill Gordon Rooker.'

ELEVEN

Thorne could think of better places to be on a sunny morning. He hated hospitals for all the obvious reasons, as well as for a few others unique to the job he did – to some of the cases he'd worked . . .

He shuffled his chair a little closer to the bed. Holland was sitting next to him. On the other side of the bed, a prison officer relaxed in a tatty brown armchair.

'You're a lucky bastard, Gordon,' Thorne said.

Rooker had been attacked two days earlier, an hour or so after Thorne and Chamberlain had confronted Ryan in the street, and four hours before Marcus Moloney had been murdered. Thorne had presumed it had been the confrontation with Ryan which had prompted him to do something about Rooker, but now he realised that it could not have been organised in the time. It had to have been Thorne's earlier meeting with Ryan in his office, when he'd first mentioned Rooker's name, that had sparked things off.

He'd certainly touched a raw nerve . . .

Thorne tried to picture Ryan as he'd stood in the street outside his arcade, the wind whipping across his face. Ryan had stood there and smiled when Thorne had offered the greeting from Rooker, safe in the knowledge that a special greeting of his own had already been arranged. Rooker in the evening; Moloney later that night. Two problems solved within hours of each other.

What was it Rooker had said? *Billy Ryan's cold . . .*

Rooker tried to lift himself up the bed a little. He grimaced in pain. 'Define lucky,' he said.

The improvised shiv – actually a sharpened paintbrush – which Alun Fisher had stuck into his belly during an art class had somehow missed every vital organ in Rooker's body. He'd lost a lot of blood, but the surgery had been about patching him up rather than saving his life.

Rooker settled back. 'Lucky that I'm alive, but it's hardly fortunate that certain parties have got wind of things, is it?'

Thorne decided that it wouldn't do Rooker any good to know who was responsible for mentioning his name to Billy Ryan.

'Told you I'd be marked, though, didn't I?' Rooker said. 'Now I've got even more reason to make sure the fucker gets put away.'

Rooker's hair was lank and his skin was the colour of a week-old bruise. The gold tooth still glinted in his mouth, but half of the top set was missing, the bridge sitting in a glass on the bedside cabinet. A drip ran into his left arm and an oxymeter peg was attached to the index finger. His right wrist was connected, rather less delicately, to a prison officer, one of two on a rotating bedwatch. The officer, skull and chin neatly shaved, sat with his head in a paperback.

Rooker raised the handcuffs, lifting his and the officer's arm. 'Fucking ridiculous, isn't it?' The prison officer didn't even look up. 'Like I'm going to do a runner. Like somebody's going to spring me. Like who?'

Holland smiled. 'Got no friends, Gordon?'

'See any flowers?'

'Friends, acquaintances . . . we'll have to check all of that,' Thorne said. 'One or two people are still bothered by this bloke turning up out

127

of the blue and claiming responsibility for what happened to Jessica Clarke.'

'Check what you like,' Rooker said. 'I can't help you. I tell you what, though: if it *is* the bloke who did it, who *really* did it, we both know who can give you his name.'

The small room was strangely half lit. The curtains had been drawn against the dazzling sunshine, filtering it through thin, brown and orange nylon. A dirty amber light moved across the pale walls, softening the metallic gleam of the dressing-trolley and the drip-stand.

'Tell me about Alun Fisher,' Thorne said.

With what few teeth were left in his upper jaw, Rooker bit down hard on his bottom lip. 'He's nothing. A fucking little tosspot . . .'

Thorne heard the prison officer chuckle quietly and glanced across. It wasn't clear whether it was Rooker or his book that he was finding so funny.

'A little tosspot with a smack habit . . .'

Thorne could see where it was going. 'And a drug debt, right?'

'A fucking big one. Three guesses who he owes the money to . . .'

'So Fisher just walks up to you in the middle of a class?' Holland said. 'Stabs you, just like that, while you're doing your Rolf Harris bit?'

'I thought you could see it coming,' Thorne said. 'That's what you told me last time. If someone was going to have a pop at you, you'd know about it . . .'

Rooker sniffed, cast his eyes to the right. 'Well, *somebody* looked the other fucking way, didn't they? Took their eye off the ball. These teachers in the Education Department don't get paid much, do they? Or maybe a screw fancied a new car, a holiday for the wife and kids . . .'

If the prison officer was upset, he wasn't showing it. Park Royal was already carrying out an inquiry into exactly what had gone wrong, while Alun Fisher sat in a segregation cell waiting to see what they were going to do with him. Having fucked up and left Gordon Rooker breathing, he was probably more worried about what Billy Ryan was going to do. He might suddenly find that his debt had increased in all sorts of ways.

'So are you going to press charges?' Holland asked.

'Not much point, is there? They'll move Fisher to another prison. Might as well try to get through the rest of the time without any hassle.'

'Up to you,' Thorne said.

Rooker moved his hand and began scratching the top of his leg. The prison officer raised his head, waited a few seconds, then yanked the hand back down to the mattress.

'What you were saying about checking my friends,' Rooker said. 'How long is all this going to take? The sooner they get everything sorted out, you know, and arranged, the quicker we can start talking. Right? This has been going on too long already . . .'

Thorne knew what Rooker meant, realised that he was reluctant to talk specifically about protection, and evidence, and *Ryan*, with the prison officer in the room.

'It won't be a quick decision,' Thorne said. 'They've only been considering the position seriously for the last couple of days.'

Rooker shook his head. 'Right. That's typical. Maybe, if they'd considered it a bit earlier, I might not have had a fucking paintbrush jammed in my guts . . .'

Thorne knew that was probably his fault. He looked at the indignant expression plastered across Rooker's yellowish chops. He could remember feeling guiltier. From the corner of his eye, he saw the prison officer look up when Holland's mobile rang. The DC checked the caller ID, stood up and took the phone out of earshot to answer it.

'You're supposed to turn those off in here,' Rooker said. 'They can interfere with medical equipment, you know. Fuck up the machines . . .'

The prison officer spoke for the first time: 'Shame you're not wired up to a couple then. Might have done us all a favour.'

Thorne couldn't help smiling. 'How long's he going to be here for?'

'We'll get him shifted back to the healthcare wing tomorrow, with a bit of luck,' the officer said. 'It's a level-three unit. They've got all the facilities, all the medication for any infection or what have you . . .'

Rooker looked less than delighted, but it made sense. The prison would want him back as soon as possible. The officers would be wanted back where they could be of more use, and the hospital would be glad to get shot of any patient who needed guards.

Thorne heard the single, short tone as Holland ended the call and turned to ask him. 'What?'

'That was DCI Tughan. He wants me to give you a message. You're not going to like it . . .'

'Fuck . . .'

Thorne could guess what the message would be. They must have turned down Rooker's offer. There hadn't been enough time for it to get up as high as it needed to go. It must have been blocked at a lower level. It would be interesting to find out exactly *where* . . .

Thorne stood and pulled on his jacket. 'It's not looking too promising, Gordon.'

He saw the prison officer smirk, and return to his book.

Thorne managed to make it through to the end of the day without having it out with Nick Tughan. He lost himself in a pile of unread memos, Police Federation junk mail and case updates from investigations he'd been working on before this one.

He then spent an evening in front of the TV without calling Tughan at home.

By lunchtime on Friday, just when he thought he'd given up on the idea, he found himself cornering Tughan in the Incident Room, spoiling for a fight. Sam Karim, who had been talking to Tughan when Thorne had marched over, made himself scarce pretty bloody quickly. Tughan leaned across a desk, flicking through the *Murder Investigation Manual* that seemed to have become his Bible.

'Answer in there, is it?' Thorne asked.

Tughan glanced up. 'What do you want, Tom?'

Thorne wasn't 100 per cent sure. 'Why didn't they go for it?'

'All the obvious reasons.'

'Such as?'

'Oh, come on. Russell and I raised a number of concerns when you first brought it to our attention. When you *eventually* brought it to our attention . . .'

It was clear to Thorne that Tughan was as riled up as ever. 'This was a genuine chance to get Ryan for something and make it stick.'

'Right. On the word of a man who confessed to it twenty years ago, and who suddenly decides to change his story . . .'

'Ryan is panicking. He's seriously fucking rattled. Why else would he try to get Gordon Rooker out of the way after all this time?'

Tughan went back to the manual. He licked a finger and began to flick through the pages. He was trying to slow things down, to put a foot on the ball. 'Securing the release of a potentially dangerous prisoner is not something to be undertaken if there is any room for doubt.'

'He'd be released into our custody, for fuck's sake.'

'The last thing we need is a compensation case for wrongful imprisonment.'

'How could Rooker claim compensation for that? He *confessed*.'

Tughan looked at him as if he were an idiot. 'If a decent lawyer gets a sniff of what's going on, that confession might suddenly turn out to have been all but beaten out of him . . .'

'These are just excuses.'

Tughan turned over another page.

'You're just pissed off because *I* came up with a way to nail Billy Ryan.'

'I think you should get back to work . . .'

'Same thing with the idea that it was Ryan who killed Moloney. Is anybody actually *pursuing* that line of inquiry?'

The colour began to rise above Tughan's button-down collar. 'What's that supposed to mean?'

'Ryan had the perfect cover. He knew exactly what the X-Man did to his other victims. His men found two of the bodies, for fuck's sake.'

'I know all this . . .'

'All he had to do was make sure that whoever killed Moloney used the same type of gun and carved the X. It was a piece of piss . . .'

'We're looking into it.'

Thorne snorted. 'Right, but not too hard. Because it came from me.'

Tughan slammed the manual shut. It sounded as though he was trying hard to keep his voice down. '*Me* again. There's over fifty officers working on this case . . .'

'Don't give me that fucking "team player" speech.' Thorne leaned forward, gripped the edge of the desk. 'It's all well and good as long as *you're* the captain of the team. That's the truth.'

'I'm not going to stand here and listen to this.' Tughan picked up the manual and waved it angrily at Thorne. 'Who do you think you're talking to?'

Thorne stepped back from the desk, laughing in spite of his anger. 'What? Are you going to throw the book at me?'

For a few seconds, Tughan glared. Then, he dropped his eyes, gave a smile some room on his face. He opened the manual again and leafed through it until he found the page he was looking for. 'Maybe just a bit of it,' he said. Tughan snatched up a pen, dragged it hard across the page, and tore it out. He hesitated for just a second before stepping forward and pressing it hard against Thorne's chest. 'Something to think about.'

Thorne grabbed at the torn-out sheet while Tughan stamped out of the room. Tughan had underscored one section hard enough to go through the paper . . .

'The modern-day approach to murder recognises the fact that there is no longer the place for the "lone entrepreneur" investigating officer.'

Hendricks was working late. For the second night in a row, Thorne sat alone in front of the TV, trying to regain some equilibrium. It rankled that Tughan was choosing to ignore perfectly sound ideas, but, more than anything, Thorne couldn't cope with the idea that Ryan was going to get away with it. Yes, Tughan might nail him one day for drugs offences, or fraud, or bloody tax evasion. Who knew, perhaps even the Zarifs would get him?

But he wouldn't have paid for Jessica Clarke . . .

Thorne brooded for most of the evening, then shouted at a TV chef for a while until the sourness began to dissipate and he started to feel better. Fuck it, February was almost over and spring was around the corner. He was thinking about maybe picking up his dad, driving down to Eileen's place in Brighton for the weekend, when the phone rang.

'Are you watching ITV?' Chamberlain asked.

'I was going to call you. The Rooker thing's a non-starter . . .'

'Put it on,' she demanded.

Thorne reached for the remote, changed the channel and turned up the volume.

A female reporter was talking straight to camera. Thorne watched, not clear what he was supposed to be seeing, until the camera cut away from the reporter and the story was told in a series of related shots . . .

An empty playground. A group of schoolgirls gathered at a bus stop. A can of lighter fluid.

Thorne felt his guts jump.

'He tried to do it again,' Carol Chamberlain said. 'He tried to burn another girl.'

MARCH

THE WEIGHT OF
THE SOUL

TWELVE

Thorne pulled up outside the house and sat for five minutes. It felt like the longest pause for breath he'd taken in a while. The time had passed in a flurry of activity, mindless and otherwise: seven days between the attempt to kill one young girl, and this, a visit to the father of another who had died almost twenty years earlier.

Seven days during which the powers-that-be had quickly changed their minds about Gordon Rooker's offer . . .

Thorne waited until the engine had ticked down to silence and it had begun to get cold in the car before he got out and walked towards the house. It was in the centre of a simple Victorian terrace on the south side of Wandsworth Common, not far from the prison. Thorne rang the bell and took a couple of steps back down the path. There were lights on in most of the houses: people settling down to eat, or getting ready for a Friday night out. The place would probably fetch around half a million. It was certainly worth much more now than it had been fifteen years ago, when the Clarkes had moved back here from Amersham. Back from where Jessica had gone to school.

The man who answered the door nodded knowingly while Thorne

was still reaching into a pocket for his warrant card. 'Don't bother,' he said, stepping away from the door. His voice was thin, and a little nasal. 'What else would you be?'

Ian Clarke had been on the phone within an hour of that first news report. He'd sounded angry and confused. He'd insisted on being told the details, had demanded to know exactly what was being done. Thorne sensed that he'd calmed down a little during the week that had followed.

'Thanks for coming. There might be some tea on the way, with a bit of luck . . .'

'That'd be great . . .'

'We've got some Earl Grey, I think . . .'

'Monkey tea's fine.'

The tea delivered, Mrs Clarke announced that she had work to do. She smiled nervously as she stepped out of the room. She was wearing what, to Thorne, seemed like the look people gave to seriously ill patients before closing doors behind them in hospitals.

'Emma runs her own catering business,' Clarke said. He pointed towards the ceiling. 'She's got a small office at the top of the house.'

'Right. What about your daughter?'

There was the shortest of awkward pauses before Clarke responded. 'Isobel?'

Thorne nodded. The *second* daughter.

'Oh, she's around somewhere.'

Clarke had split from his first wife in 1989, three years after Jessica's death and almost immediately after they'd moved back to London from Buckinghamshire.

Thorne had seen it plenty of times with bereaved parents. It was often impossible to deal with the guilt and the anger and the blame. Impossible to look into the eyes of a husband or wife and not see the face of a lost child.

'No more news, then?' Clarke asked. He ran a hand across his skull. He'd lost a fair amount of hair and cut the remaining grey brutally short. It emphasised the chiselled features and lively, blue eyes that belied his age. Thorne knew that he had to be in his early fifties at least, but he looked maybe ten years younger.

Thorne shook his head. 'Only the same stuff rehashed to sell a few more papers. None of it's coming from us, I'm afraid.'

'Witnesses? Descriptions? It was a busy street, for God's sake.'

'Nothing's changed since I last spoke to you on the phone. I'm sorry.'

'I know I don't really have a right to be told anything at all. I'm grateful . . .'

Thorne waved away the thanks and the implicit apology. For a few seconds they drank their tea and stared into the flame-effect gas fire. On the mantelpiece, Thorne could see postcards, cigarettes, a party invitation in a child's handwriting. The large wooden mirror above reflected a watercolour on the wall behind him.

Clarke caught Thorne studying it. 'That was Jessica's mother's,' he said. 'One of the few things I got to keep.'

Clarke was sitting on a lived-in leather armchair. Thorne was adjacent, on the matching sofa. They were both leaning forwards, mugs of tea on their knees.

'It's like the old joke, then?' Clarke said, suddenly changing tack. 'About the police having their toilets stolen.'

Thorne smiled. 'Right . . .'

Though Thorne obviously understood, Clarke trotted out the tawdry punchline anyway: 'You've got nothing to go on.'

'We need a bit of luck,' Thorne said. 'We *always* need a bit of luck.'

Clarke put down his mug and stood up. 'And if he tries to do it to another girl, would that count as a bit of luck?' He smiled and walked past Thorne to draw the curtains.

Thorne was struck again by how good Clarke looked for his age, though the fleecy blue tracksuit top may have been helping to create the illusion. He was grateful for finding something with which to break the slightly awkward silence. 'You look pretty fit,' he said. He patted his belly. 'I could do with shifting this.'

Clarke walked round the sofa, dropped back into his armchair. 'I manage a leisure centre,' he explained.

Thorne nodded, thinking that actually, it explained nothing. Most hairdressers had terrible hair, and he'd known plenty of dishonest coppers. 'Listen, we're making an assumption,' he said. 'We're assuming that this recent incident is connected, in some way, to the attack on your daughter.'

Clarke pulled at his lip with a finger and thumb. 'Obviously. It's the same . . . *kind* of attack. Whoever this lunatic is, he must be aware of what happened to Jess. He must have read about it . . . yes?'

'Yes. Or there could be other connections.'

'Could there?'

'I said we're making an assumption.'

'Other connections, right.' Quickly: 'Such as?'

Clarke had been correct when he'd said that he had no right to be told anything, but Thorne knew bloody well that there was no other reason for him to be sitting in the man's living room. He'd *come* to tell him.

'It's possible that the man found guilty of attempting to murder your daughter in 1984 was not in fact the man responsible.'

Clarke gave a short bark of a laugh. '*What?* Because some psycho's gone out and bought himself a can of lighter fluid?'

'No . . .'

'That's bloody ridiculous.'

'Hang on, Mr Clarke.'

'So, if a prostitute gets cut up in Leeds tomorrow night that means Peter Sutcliffe's innocent, does it?'

'We had good reason to believe that Gordon Rooker was innocent *before* the attack last week.'

The skin tightened across Clarke's jaw at the mention of Rooker's name. 'I presume that "good reason" is some bloody police euphemism, yes? Like when doctors say "as well as can be expected" when somebody's on their deathbed. Yes? Am I right? Because, don't forget, we're talking about the man who confessed to setting my daughter on fire.'

'Yes, I know.'

'The man who *confessed*.'

'He's withdrawn that confession.'

'Well, he's a bit *fucking* late . . .' Clarke slapped both palms hard against his legs, and grinned as if he'd been half joking, but there'd been no mistaking the venom in his voice. He reached behind the armchair. 'Hang on,' he said. He found a switch, and flicked on an uplighter. 'Best to lift the gloom a bit.'

Thorne looked up at the soft circle of light on the ceiling. 'You're right. Of course you are. It's *very* fucking late . . .'

'So, you think the man who attacked the girl last week is the man who really attacked Jess?'

'We've got to consider the possibility.'

'Where's he been for the last twenty years, then?'

It was, of course, the obvious question and Thorne had only obvious answers. 'Living abroad, maybe. In prison for something else . . .'

'And he's doing this now, because . . .?'

'Because he's worried that Rooker's about to come out. He's trying to make us look stupid, tell us we got it wrong. Or he's trying to claim credit that should rightfully be his. I don't honestly know, Mr Clarke.'

'The toilet joke again . . .'

'Pretty much, yeah.'

For want of anything else to do, Thorne brought the mug to his lips and tipped it back, though he knew full well that the tea was finished. 'Listen, we don't know who this man is, or if he *is* the man who attempted to murder your daughter, and neither, so he says, does Gordon Rooker.'

'So, you don't believe *everything* he says?'

'What he *does* say is that he knows who is responsible for what happened to Jessica. He knows who paid the money, and he's going to tell us.'

'It was some gangster.' Clarke said it as if it were in inverted commas. 'I was told, unofficially, that no one could be one hundred per cent sure which one, but that he was probably killed shortly after what he did to Jess. Right?'

Thorne saw Clarke's expression start to darken when he didn't answer him instantly. He knew that the water was suddenly getting deep and that he shouldn't wade in any further. 'I'm sorry, but I can't really go into . . .'

Clarke held up his hands. He understood.

'I just wanted you to be clear about something,' Thorne continued. 'If Rooker comes out of prison, it's only so that the man who was behind what happened to your daughter can go *in*.'

Clarke pondered this for a minute. He turned his chair towards the fire, held his hands towards it. Thorne thought that it had suddenly become a lot colder. He also thought: How can he stand to look into a fire? What does he see when he stares into the flames?

'You should have a picture of Jess,' Clarke said, suddenly.

The smallest of shivers crept across the nape of Thorne's neck. He felt as if the man opposite him had somehow known what he was thinking. He watched as Clarke got up and walked across to a pine chest in the corner of the room. Photos in assorted metal frames were scattered across the top.

'Right . . .'

'A reminder.'

Clarke picked up a small frame, began removing the clips that held the picture in place. 'This is a good one.' He removed the glass and took out the photograph. He waved it at him.

Thorne stood and moved across the room to take the picture from Clarke's outstretched hand. Clarke handed it over and stepped towards the door. 'That's the "before". You need the "after" as well. I don't keep any out down here because they upset Isobel. That's the *only* reason.'

He left the room. Thorne heard him running up the stairs, heard a door open and close.

You should have a picture of Jess . . .

Thorne thought about how Clarke had said it. As though it were a simple piece of good advice that would aid his well-being. *You should check your cholesterol. You should keep up your pension payments. You should have a photo of my dead daughter.*

Thorne knew that Clarke was well aware that this visit was not procedural. This was not part of any inquiry, and nor was the offer of the photograph. This was something Ian Clarke wanted *Thorne* to have. Thought he *should* have . . .

When he heard a door close upstairs, Thorne stepped out into the hallway and waited near the front door. Now seemed as good a time as any to be making a move.

Clarke jogged quickly down the stairs and pressed a small black book into Thorne's hands. 'I thought you might want to look at her diary. It doesn't matter if you don't. Let me have it back either way when you've finished with it.'

'Right, of course . . .'

Clarke handed over the photo with a small nod. Thorne took it with barely a glance, afraid of staring. Of being *seen* to stare. When he looked back at Clarke, it was clear from the man's expression that this was a reaction he'd seen a hundred times before.

'There were gangsters at her funeral,' he said. 'Murderers and drug barons and men who get paid to hurt people. They came to show their respects after she'd killed herself.' He spoke calmly, though the anger was clear enough, like something moving behind a muslin curtain. 'It was a gorgeous day when we buried her, a really stunning day. We all said how that was Jess's doing, because she loved the good weather so much, and then that lot turned up in dark suits and sunglasses like something out of *Reservoir Dogs* and ruined everything. Kevin Kelly and his tarty wife, and that other one who'd taken over . . . Ryan. A bunch of them. All standing there, sweating, with huge wreaths. One of them spelled out her name, for pity's sake. Hovering with tasteless fucking wreaths for my little girl, who'd died because her friend happened to be a gangster's daughter . . .'

Thorne was finding it hard to look at him. Rubbing his thumbs across the shiny surface of the photo in his hands. Nodding when it felt as though he should.

'We worked our arses off to send Jess to that school, to raise the money for the fees. What did Kelly have to do? How many people did he have to kill or rob to send that little . . . to send his little girl to that school?'

Thorne saw a figure appear on the landing at the top of the stairs: a teenage girl with long, ash-blond hair.

Clarke turned when he saw Thorne raise his eyes. 'Isobel . . .'

Thorne was unsure whether Clarke was talking to the girl or introducing her. He couldn't help but wonder how much she looked like her half-sister. He wanted to look at the photo to check, but the picture on top was of Jessica after her attack, and Thorne felt unable to move it, to slide the photo of her *unscarred* to the front . . .

'Hello,' he said.

The girl tugged at a corner of her sweater, muttered a sullen greeting in return. Clarke gave Thorne a weary, parental shrug. 'She's thirteen,' he said by way of explanation. Then his face changed. 'She'll be fourteen in a couple of weeks . . .' He reached past Thorne to open the front door.

Thorne toyed with some cod response about kids growing up too fast, but before he had a chance to make it, Clarke stepped in close and lowered his voice. 'This man, whoever he is, attempted to murder Jess. You said that. You said it a couple of times, actually.'

'Sorry, I don't . . .'

'He didn't *attempt* to murder her, Mr Thorne. He murdered her.' Clarke looked Thorne in the eyes as he spoke.

Thorne instinctively looked away, but then, ashamed, forced himself to meet Clarke's eyes again.

'It took a couple of years for her to die, but he murdered her.'

There was little to say except 'goodbye', so they both said it, and let the front door close between them.

Thorne glanced back. Through the frosted squares of red, blue and green glass in the front door, he could make out the shape of Ian Clarke climbing slowly up the stairs towards his daughter.

The crowd at the bus stop is just that at first: a crowd; massed, indistinguishable, and not just because of the quality of the film. A tight knot of people bunched on the pavement, bundled up against the cold weather or, in the case of the girls, huddled into a gang, a million things to talk about while they wait for the bus.

There is no sound, but it isn't hard to imagine the screams, the shouts of anger and incomprehension.

The knot unravels in a moment, people wheeling or jumping away, revealing the man for the first time. An old woman points at him, pulls at the sleeve of the woman with the pushchair standing next to her. Girls cling to one another, to blazers and bags, as the man, his face hidden inside the hood of a dark anorak, turns and jogs casually away up the street . . .

Hendricks appeared from the kitchen. 'The food'll be ready in a couple of minutes,' he said.

Thorne got off the sofa and ejected the tape from the VCR. While he was up, he grabbed the bottle of wine from the mantelpiece and refilled Carol Chamberlain's glass.

'Nothing from any other angles?' she said.

Thorne shook his head as he swallowed from his own glass. 'These are the best pictures we could get.' CCTV footage seemed to play an increasingly large part in most investigations these days. Often, the cameras were no more than a deterrent, and a pretty unsuccessful one at that. The crack dealers on Coldharbour Lane and the heroin mules around Manor House knew exactly where they were and treated them with the same disdain they might accord a traffic warden. Most of the time, they would happily go about their business in full view of the camera, knowing just when to turn a head or angle a shoulder to avoid the incriminating shot, then wink at the lens when the deal was done. Once in a while, though, Thorne would find himself staring at more significant footage: grainy, black-and-white pictures of armed robbers, of killers, or, more disturbingly, of those about to become their victims.

In this case, a potential victim who got lucky.

'It doesn't make sense,' Chamberlain said. 'How did he ever think he'd get away with it? If, God forbid, he hadn't been rumbled. If that girl hadn't seen what he was doing with the lighter fluid and he'd managed to set her alight . . .'

'Even if he had, he might still have got away,' Thorne said. 'People would have been far more concerned with helping the girl. You know as well as I do that by and large people are afraid to do anything. They don't want to be the have-a-go hero who gets shot, or gets a knife stuck in him.'

Chamberlain stared into her glass. 'Why a bus stop, though? Why the different MO?'

'There's a lot more security around schools now,' Hendricks said. 'He'd've been lucky to find a school like Jessica Clarke's, where he could just march up to the playground.'

She shook her head. 'The middle of Swiss Cottage at four o'clock in the afternoon? It's stupid. The place was heaving.'

Hendricks leaned his head back into the kitchen to check on something for a second. 'He obviously wanted to make a splash.'

'Do you think it's the same bloke?' Thorne stared hard at Chamberlain.

'Yes, I'm fairly certain. It looked like the same anorak . . .'

Thorne shook his head. 'No, I don't mean that. Do you think it's the same man who set fire to Jessica Clarke twenty years ago?'

There was no quick answer. 'He didn't look . . . old,' she said. 'I know you couldn't see his face. It was more the way he held himself, I suppose.'

'You're thinking about Rooker, about somebody like he is,' Thorne said.

'I know . . .'

'Suppose this man was in his early twenties back then. He'd only be in his early forties now.'

'It was seeing him run away. It seemed wrong, somehow, for the man I was imagining.'

'He *jogged* away,' Thorne said. 'Even if he was in his fifties, or sixties even, that's not out of the question, is it?'

Hendricks carried his glass across the room and topped it up. 'Just jogging away, casually, like he did, makes a lot of sense. It's the right thing to do if you don't want to draw attention to yourself, if you don't want to look like you're legging it away from something . . .'

From the kitchen, the timer on Thorne's cooker suddenly buzzed. Hendricks put down his wineglass and went to do whatever was necessary.

'If it *is* him,' Chamberlain said, 'is Billy Ryan behind what he's doing now?'

'God knows, but, if he is, I haven't got the first idea why.'

Hendricks swore loudly. Either dinner was ruined or he'd burned himself.

'You all right in there, Delia?' Thorne shouted.

There was another bout of slightly more subdued swearing.

Chamberlain laughed. 'It smells good, whatever it is.' She drained her glass, glancing at her watch in the process.

'Listen, why don't you stay the night?' Thorne asked. 'We can sort out a bed . . .'

'No, I'm going to get the last train. If you can give me a taxi number . . .'

'It's no trouble, really. I'm sure Jack can make his own breakfast.'

She shook her head and took a step towards the kitchen.

Thorne put a hand on her shoulder. 'When we get Ryan, he's going to tell us who took his money twenty years ago and burned Jessica. He's going to give me a name.' He pointed towards the VCR. 'If it was this bloke, I'll get him. If it wasn't this bloke, and whoever it was is still alive, I'll get *him*. Then, I'll get this bloke as well. That's a promise, Carol . . .'

When Chamberlain looked at him, her expression a mixture of gratitude and amusement, Thorne realised that his hand had moved from her shoulder. In his effort to reassure her, he'd been gently rubbing her back in small circles. She raised her eyebrows comically. 'So, this offer to stay the night,' she said. 'What exactly did you have in mind?'

Ian Clarke sat on the sofa, his arm around his wife. He stared across the room in the direction of the television.

He cried once a year on his first daughter's birthday. The day that was also the anniversary of her death. For the rest of the time, everything was kept inside, squashed and pressed inside, his ribs, like the bars of a cage, holding in the thoughts and feelings and dark desires.

He sat still, going over the details of Thorne's visit, the things that were said, feeling as if his ribs might crack and splinter at any moment.

His wife laughed softly at something on the television and nestled her head into his chest. His hand moved automatically to her hair. He stared at a small square of white wall a foot or so above the screen. From time to time, he could hear a gentle thud on the ceiling as his second daughter moved around upstairs.

Thorne lay awake in bed, wondering if it was simply indigestion he was suffering from, or something a little harder to get rid of.

Enjoyable as the evening had been, he'd been happy to see Carol call for a cab. And he'd been relieved when, later, Hendricks had decided to leave the clearing up until the morning and get an early night.

The uncertainty that surrounded every aspect of the Billy Ryan/Jessica Clarke case had squatted next to him all evening, like an unwanted dinner guest. Now he felt it pressing him down into the mattress as he stared up at the Ikea light fitting he hated so much.

Not knowing was the worst thing of all.

In the course of some of the cases he'd investigated over the years,

Thorne had learned things, seen things, understood things that, given the choice, he'd have preferred to avoid. Still, in spite of all the horrible truths he'd been forced to confront, he preferred knowledge to ignorance, though the dreadful weight of each was very different.

Beneath the duvet, his hand drifted down to his groin. He fiddled around half-heartedly for a few minutes, then gave up, unable to concentrate.

He began to think about the photos of Jessica Clarke, out in the hallway inside his leather jacket. He pictured the image of her blasted and puckered face pressing against the silk lining of the pocket. He thought about the diary in his bag, waiting for him.

It was reading he'd postpone until another night . . .

Reaching across for his Walkman, he pulled on the headphones and pressed play: *The Mountain*, Steve Earle's 1999 collaboration with the Del McCoury Band. He rubbed at the tightness in his chest, deciding that it almost certainly *was* indigestion.

It was impossible to stay down for too long, listening to bluegrass.

THIRTEEN

'You're looking a bit better, Gordon,' Holland said.

Rooker grunted. 'It's all relative, isn't it?'

'OK then,' Stone said. 'You look better than a bag of shit, but not quite as good as Tom Cruise. How's that?'

The prison officer who had been standing behind them took a step forward, leaned down. 'Can we hurry this up?'

They were gathered around a table in the small office-cum-cubicle in a corner of the visits area. A TV and VCR had been set up. Holland was stabbing at a button, trying to cue up the tape.

Without looking at him, Stone waved a piece of paper towards the prison officer. 'Don't worry, it's not a long list.' The paper was waved in Rooker's direction. 'He isn't exactly your most popular guest, is he?'

This was part of the checking-up that Thorne had spoken about to Tughan when the doubts about Rooker were first raised. While Stone and Holland had headed into HMP Park Royal, others on the team were looking at those who had recently moved in the opposite direction; those who might have associated closely enough with Gordon Rooker to do him a favour on the outside . . .

The list Stone was brandishing contained the names of all those who had been to the prison to see Rooker in the last six months. If the man who had made the calls to Carol Chamberlain, and perhaps been responsible for the attack in Swiss Cottage, had cooked up something with Rooker, chances were the plans would have been hatched in the visiting area. Something *could* have been organised via the telephone, but it was highly unlikely. As a Category B prisoner, any calls made by Gordon Rooker would, at the very least, be randomly monitored. If Rooker had an accomplice, Thorne felt sure that his name would be on the visitors list.

'It's easy to check names and addresses,' Thorne had told Holland, 'but I want you to go through them with Rooker in person, get any extra information you can from him. See how he reacts when you show him the pictures. Let's make absolutely sure we're not being pissed about . . .'

Copies of the visiting area's security tapes had been requested from the prison, sifted through and edited until the team was left with a sequence no more than a few minutes long. This was the tape which Holland, Stone and Rooker were about to watch . . .

'Here we go,' Holland said, leaning back from the video recorder.

Stone patted Rooker on the shoulder. 'This is very much a high-lights package, Gordon. And we want you to provide the commentary, all right?'

Rooker picked up a pair of glasses from the table and inched his chair a little closer to the screen.

Out of the screen-snow came a series of clumsily cut-together shots, the images jumping disconcertingly from one to the next: half a dozen individuals walking into the visiting area, depositing bags and coats on or beneath chairs and sitting down. Each a different size in frame, slid-ing or slumping behind the narrow tables – not a single one of them looking particularly pleased to be there . . .

'Cath, my eldest daughter.' Rooker pointed and spoke while Holland scribbled. On the screen, a dark-haired woman in her late thirties sat down. She wore jeans and a sweatshirt. If she'd been wearing a bib, she might have been a prisoner. 'Her son's being taken on by West Ham . . .'

A jump-cut replaced the woman on the screen with another. In her early seventies, probably. A buttoned-up green overcoat. Handbag clutched in front of her on the table. 'My mother's youngest sister, Iris. Pops by every now and again to tell me who's died . . .'

A man, around the same age as Rooker. Arms moving animatedly as he spoke. Dirty grey suit and hair the same colour. 'Tony Sollinger, an old drinking mate. He got in touch with Lizzie out of the blue, told her he wanted to come in. Insisted on telling me he had cancer, for some fucking reason . . .'

A woman, anywhere between fifty and seventy. Hair hidden beneath a patterned headscarf. Saying little. 'Speak of the devil. The wife . . . the *ex*-wife, as near as dammit, on her annual visit . . .'

From somewhere on the wing behind them came a sudden howl of what might have been rage, or pain, or neither. Holland and Stone both turned. The prison officer didn't so much as raise his head.

'You can see why people aren't queuing up to visit, though,' Stone said. 'It's hardly fucking Alton Towers.'

The prison officer looked like he was laughing, but he did it without making any noise.

'Wayne Brookhouse,' Rooker continued. 'He used to go out with my youngest.' A man in his early twenties. Dark, curly hair and glasses. Lighting a cigarette from the nub-end of another. 'My daughter never bothers, so he comes in, tells me what she's been up to. Supposed to be a mechanic, probably just a cut-and-shut merchant. Ducks and dives, but he's a decent lad . . .'

A black man, fortyish. Very tall and smartly dressed. A short-sleeved white shirt and dark tie. 'Simons, or Simmonds, or something. Fucking prison visitor. I reckon deep down they're all after some sort of thrill, but he's harmless enough. It's better than talking to some of the beasts in here . . .'

152

And finally, the most recent visitor. A broad-shouldered man, a little shorter than average. Hair greying at the sides. Sitting very still and staring at the top of Gordon Rooker's bowed head.

Stone laughed, turned from the image of Tom Thorne and looked at Holland. 'Christ, this one really looks like a nasty piece of work.'

Then white noise, until the tape ended and began to rewind.

Holland put away his notebook. Stone leaned back in his chair and turned to Rooker. 'Five real visitors in six months. Looks to me like you've been all but forgotten, mate.'

Rooker stood up. 'That's what I'm hoping . . .'

He turned and walked out of the door. The prison officer calmly stood and followed, picking the dirt from beneath his fingernails with the edge of a laminated ID badge.

'It's gone very quiet around here,' Kitson said.

Thorne had to agree. He knew that she wasn't just talking about the fact that many of the team had taken lunch early and gone over to the Oak. 'I think, as far as the Swiss Cottage thing goes, it's going to get a lot bloody quieter,' he said. 'Things *might* pick up, if somebody makes a decision about Billy Ryan . . .'

Since they'd changed their minds about Gordon Rooker, the joint operation had divided itself, somewhat less than perfectly, into two distinct strands. There was, understandably, a major emphasis being placed on catching the man who'd tried to set light to the girl in Swiss Cottage, but that investigation hadn't turned up anything within the all-important first twenty-four hours. In spite of the time and location of the attack, there wasn't a single useful description. The man's face had been hidden beneath the hood of his anorak, while witness accounts of height and build had varied as much as might be expected, bearing in mind the thick, cold-weather clothing and hunched posture of the attacker.

The girl herself was already back at school, while her mother was cashing in, discussing her daughter's lucky escape and the shocking ineptitude of the police on any TV or radio show that would have her. Her daughter had been selected, as far as anyone could ascertain, completely at random. Another brick wall. It wasn't that the leads weren't going anywhere. There simply weren't any in the first place.

Meanwhile, whether he was connected to what had happened in Swiss Cottage or not, there was still Billy Ryan. While a case against him was being built behind prison walls, there was uncertainty about how those on the ground should proceed.

Nick Tughan was all for the softly-softly approach. There was still the dispute with the Zarif brothers to be dealt with, and Tughan didn't think there was anything to be gained by confronting Ryan directly about Rooker, or about Jessica Clarke. For once, Thorne had been largely a spectator when things had come to a head in the middle of the previous week.

'We're working with Rooker,' Tughan had said. 'We're putting the evidence against Ryan together, but while that's happening there's still the minor matter of a gang war going on. My first responsibility is to make sure there's no more killing.'

Brigstocke had gone in studs-up. 'Come on, Nick. This is hardly about saving innocent lives, is it?'

Tughan reacted angrily. 'Tell me Hanya Izzigil wasn't innocent. Tell me Marcus Moloney wasn't.'

Brigstocke had looked at his feet, then sidelong at Thorne. He hadn't got off to a very good start . . .

'We don't know what Ryan's going to do next.' Tughan had wandered to the window then and looked out across the North Circular. 'He tried to sort Rooker out and he screwed it up. He's going to have to respond to Moloney's murder sooner or later. It's been nearly a fortnight . . .' He turned and held up a hand before Thorne could say anything. 'Even if it *was* him who had Moloney killed, it's going to look bloody funny if he doesn't retaliate, isn't it?'

'Why don't we press him on Moloney, then?' Brigstocke had asked. 'Why don't we press the fucker on a lot of things?'

'This isn't just about Ryan, by the way. Whatever happens, I want the Zarifs as well.'

'Obviously, but we're talking about Billy Ryan, and right now there's a lot of sitting about on our arses. We should be trying to disrupt his operations.'

The commanding view of cars and concrete was obviously too much for Tughan to resist. After a few moments' thinking, or pretending to think, he turned back to the window. 'Let's just wait . . .'

Brigstocke had let out a weary sigh. 'Rooker might not be enough, Nick. I think we should get everything we can.'

There was only ever going to be one side Thorne was on, and he couldn't resist chipping in for very long. 'You were the one who said Rooker was unreliable.' He had taken a step to his left so that he could at least see the side of Tughan's face. 'Don't you think a jury might agree with you? However good the evidence is, Rooker just might not be a credible witness. Ryan's legal team are going to be doing their best to make him look anything *but* credible. It can't hurt to go after something else to back him up, can it?'

Brigstocke had held up his hands. 'I don't see how it can.'

'Let's just remind Ryan that we haven't forgotten him,' Thorne had suggested. 'Stir things up a bit . . .'

Now, days later, sitting in his office with Yvonne Kitson, Thorne was still smiling about what Tughan had said next: 'That's what you're good at, isn't it, Tom? Stirring things up. You're a spoon on legs.'

Kitson spun her chair around to face him. 'Is Brigstocke winning the argument, d'you reckon?'

'Russell gives as good as he gets,' Thorne said, 'but he needs a prod every now and again. I reminded him that *he* was a DCI as well, and he got a bit shirty.' Kitson laughed. 'I think he might just go over Tughan's head . . .'

Thorne looked across at Kitson and suddenly remembered a moment sitting in the same office with her the year before. He'd been watching her eat her lunch, staring as she took her sandwiches from the Tupperware container and unwrapped the foil. He'd thought she had everything under control . . .

Thorne's stomach growled. Karim was bringing him back a cheese roll from the pub. Surely even the Oak's culinary wizard couldn't fuck *that* up.

'What are you doing for lunch, Yvonne . . .?'

Before she could answer, there was a knock, and Holland put his head round the door. He came in, followed by Andy Stone, and together they gave Thorne a rundown on the morning's session at Park Royal.

Thorne looked at the pictures – stills from the tape they'd shown Rooker – laid out on his desk in front of him. 'Well, I think we can safely discount the wife, the daughter and the auntie,' he said.

Holland pulled a face. 'I'm not being funny, but couldn't any one of them have been passing messages between Rooker and somebody else?'

Thorne was not known as the belt-and-braces type. In this case, though, it was better to play it safe. 'Right, sod it,' he said. 'With the exception of the old lady, have a word with all of them.'

As he and Holland were leaving, Stone turned back with a grin. 'Are you sure you don't want us to check the old woman out? She looks pretty dodgy to me.'

Thorne nodded. 'Right. The gap between perception and reality.' He looked innocently at Stone. 'I'm sure some of the great philosophers have got plenty to say on the subject, Andy.'

Holland fought back a laugh as he quickly stepped out of the room. Stone looked blank as he turned and followed him, leaving Thorne unsure as to whether or not he'd cottoned on.

'What was all that about?' Kitson asked.

Thorne was still grinning, highly pleased with himself. 'Just something Holland told me about Andy Stone and his winning ways with the opposite sex.'

'Right. He's a bit of a shagger, isn't he?'

'Apparently. I never seem to meet any, but if some people are to be believed, women are falling over themselves to jump into bed with coppers all of a sudden . . .'

It took Thorne a second to realise what he'd said, and who he'd said it to. When he looked across at Kitson, the colour had already reached her face.

'Sorry, Yvonne . . .'

'Don't be stupid.'

He nodded. Stupid was exactly how he felt. 'How is everything?'

'Oh, you know. Shitty . . .' She smiled and spun her chair towards her desk.

'How're the kids doing?'

The chair came slowly back around again. She obviously wanted to talk. 'The eldest's been playing up a bit at school. It's hard to know whether it's anything to do with what's been happening, but I still manage to convince myself that it is. I try and tell myself not to be so bloody stupid and guilty *all* the time. Then one of them bangs their head, or twists an ankle playing football, and it feels like it's my fault . . .'

The phone on Thorne's desk rang, and Kitson stopped talking.

It was the security officer at the gatehouse. He told Thorne that somebody had driven up to the barrier and was asking to see him.

In point of fact, the woman – so the duty officer had explained – had not come to see him specifically. He just happened to be the highest-ranking member of Team 3 in the building at the time. It was a piece of luck, both good and bad, that Thorne would reflect on for a long time afterwards.

The woman stood as he came down the stairs into the small reception area. Thorne nodded to the officer on the desk and walked across to her. She was in her mid-thirties, he guessed, and tallish, certainly as tall as he was. Her hair was the colour of the cork pin-board on the wall behind his desk, her complexion as pale as the wall itself. She wore smart grey trousers with a matching jacket, and, for no good reason, Thorne wondered if she might be a tax inspector.

'Did you find a parking space?' he asked. On second thoughts, he never imagined civil servants to be quite so attractive . . .

She nodded and held out a hand, which Thorne took. 'I'm Alison Kelly,' she said.

Perhaps the stunned expression on Thorne's face looked a lot like ignorance. She repeated her name, then explained exactly who she was. 'Jessica Clarke was my best friend. I was the one she got mistaken for.'

Thorne released her hand, slightly embarrassed at having held on to it for so long. She didn't seem overly bothered. 'Sorry, I know who you are. I just wasn't expecting you to walk in, or to . . . I just wasn't expecting you.'

'I probably should have called.'

They looked at each other for a second or two. Thorne could feel the eyes of the duty officer on them.

'Right, then.' *What do you want?* This would perhaps have been a little brusque, but it was all Thorne was thinking. Rather than ask the question, though, he looked around, as if searching for a place where they could talk in private. 'I'm sure I can find us somewhere where we can chat, or whatever.' He pointed to the exit. 'Unless you'd rather go for a walk or something . . .?'

She shook her head. 'It's bloody freezing out there.'

'Spring's not far away . . .'

'Thank God.'

Becke House was an operational HQ, as opposed to a fully functioning station, and, as such, it had no permanent interview suite. There was a small room to the right of the reception desk that was occasionally used in emergencies, or to store booze whenever a party was thrown. A table and chairs, a couple of rickety cupboards. Thorne opened the door, checked that the room was unoccupied and beckoned Alison Kelly inside.

'I'll see if I can organise some tea,' he said.

She moved past him and sat down, then began speaking before he'd closed the door. 'Here's what I know,' she said. Her voice was deep and unaccented. Just the right side of posh. 'You're not getting anywhere trying to find the man who squirted lighter fluid all over that girl in Swiss Cottage ten days ago.' She paused.

Thorne walked across to the table and sat down. 'I'm not quite sure what you're expecting me to say to that . . .'

'Three days before *that* happened, somebody tried to kill the man who's in prison for burning Jess, by stabbing him in the gut with a sharpened paintbrush. It's pretty obvious that there's a connection. Something's going on.'

'Do you mind me asking how you know all these things?'

She gave a small shake of her head. More as if she couldn't be bothered to answer than as if she was actually refusing. Then she continued to demonstrate just how much she *did* know. 'Even if you weren't aware that the man who did the stabbing owed Billy Ryan a load of money, you'd have to be an idiot not to work out who was behind it.' She tucked a few loose strands of hair behind her ear. 'Ryan was *clearly* responsible.'

'Clearly,' echoed Thorne.

'He wanted Rooker killed for the obvious reasons.'

The obvious reasons. Thorne was relieved to discover that she didn't know *absolutely* everything . . .

'Though why he should choose now to get revenge for what Rooker did twenty years ago is anybody's guess.'

Thorne was disturbed and excited by the bizarre and abrupt conversation. He felt oddly afraid of this woman. Her attitude fascinated him, and pissed him off.

'You said, "the man who's in prison for burning Jess". That's a bit odd, don't you think? You didn't say, "the man who burned Jess". It just seems a strange way of putting it.'

She looked blankly at him.

159

'Have you got any reason to think that Gordon Rooker *isn't* the man responsible?' Thorne asked.

She couldn't conceal the half smile. 'There *is* something going on, isn't there?'

Thorne felt pretty sure he'd just walked into an elaborate verbal trap. There was clearly even more going on behind Alison Kelly's green eyes than he'd begun to suspect.

Now she wasn't even trying to hide the smile. 'That's the other thing I know,' she said. 'That you're not going to tell me anything.'

The time for politeness had long since passed. 'What is it you want, Miss Kelly?' Thorne immediately saw the front for what it was, but only because he noticed it crack and slip a little: there was a softening around the jaw, and in the set of her shoulders.

'You aren't the only one who wasn't expecting me to walk in here,' she said. 'I needed a bloody big glass of wine before I drove up. I've been sitting in the pub opposite, surrounded by coppers, getting some Dutch courage.' The smile suddenly seemed nervous. The voice had lost any pretence at confidence or authority.

'I want to know what that girl did,' she said. 'What her *friends* did at that bus stop that saved her. I want to know what it was that alerted them. What it was that *we* didn't see, that we didn't do.'

'I really don't think there's much point . . .'

'The first thing I knew was when Jess ran at me, and I stepped out of the way. Do you understand that? All I could do was watch it, then.' Her voice was barely above a murmur, but it seemed to echo off the shiny white walls. 'I heard the crackle when it reached her hair. Then I smelled it. Have you ever smelled it? I mean, have you ever smelled anything *like* that?

'I wasn't actually sick. I felt like I was going to, like I was going to heave, but I didn't. Not then. Now, just the thought of it . . . just the smell of a match being struck . . .'

She looked, and sounded, disorientated. She was an adult in a playground. A child in a police station.

'That could have been my hair. *Should* have been my hair . . .'

Thorne opened his mouth, but nothing came quickly enough.

'I want to know why Jess wasn't all right, like that other girl was. Why wasn't she? I want you to tell me what we could have done to save her.'

Thorne turned *Eastenders* up just enough to drown out the noise of Hendricks singing in the bathroom. He pulled Elvis on to his lap, flicked through the sports pages of the *Standard* folded across the arm of the sofa. He couldn't stop thinking about what Alison Kelly had said. He wasn't the only one who couldn't cope with ignorance . . .

Alison Kelly's need for certainty sprang from something a little deeper seated than his own, though. There'd been plenty of things he would have done differently, given half a chance, but not too many bad things for which he felt *responsible*. She'd had twenty years of blame and guilt. Each had fed off – yet perversely fattened – the other, until they'd become the twin parasites that defined her.

Thorne asked himself how much better off Alison Kelly really was, than the girl who'd been mistaken for her.

Elvis jumped away, grumbling, as Thorne stood up and walked across to the front door. He opened his bag and took out the small black book that had remained unopened since Ian Clarke had handed it to him.

The dirge from the bathroom seemed, thankfully, to have abated. Thorne carried the diary back across to the sofa. He picked up the remote and muted the volume of the TV as he sat down again.

When the pins and needles started, Chamberlain moved from the edge of the bath to the toilet seat. She turned her head so that she couldn't see herself in the mirror. It was half an hour since she'd come upstairs, and she wondered how much longer she was going to have to sit there before she stopped feeling like a silly old woman.

She'd spent the weekend going over the cold case she was supposed to be working on for AMRU: a bookmaker, stabbed to death in a pub car park in 1993. A dead man and a family who deserved justice as much as anybody else, but Chamberlain was in no fit state to help them get it.

She was finding it hard to care about anything . . . about anything else . . .

The Jessica Clarke case had been one she'd been close to. As close as she had ever been to any case.

And she'd got it wrong.

Three nights earlier, on the last train home after the evening round at Tom Thorne's, she'd almost convinced herself that she was being stupid. What could she have done differently? Rooker had confessed, for heaven's sake. There was no earthly reason why they should ever have looked for anyone else . . .

Sitting on that all-but-deserted train, she'd *almost* convinced herself, but wrong was wrong, and it still hurt. She felt the pain of professional failure, and another, much worse pain, that comes from knowing you've let down someone very important.

Another train had begun rushing past, and she'd turned to watch. Her reflection had danced across the windows of the train as it flashed by. After it had gone, she'd stared at her face, floating in the darkness on the other side of the glass, and noticed that she was crying.

The most painful thing, of course, was feeling useless. Being surplus to requirements. It was knowing that she'd got it wrong, and that she would play no part in putting it right again.

She'd heard the swish of the carriage door as it slid back, and watched the man moving towards her, reflected in the window. Watched as he'd weaved slowly back towards his seat with a bag from the buffet. Watched as he'd stopped at her table . . .

'Are you all right, love?'

In the bathroom, Chamberlain raised her head as she heard footsteps on the stairs. They stopped, and she heard Jack call out her name.

There'd been a few days, a couple of weeks earlier, when she'd begun to feel like a copper again; when she went in with Thorne to see Gordon Rooker; when the two of them had confronted Billy Ryan outside his arcade. Then, once they'd begun to deal with Rooker, she'd been eased gently aside, and it had felt as bad as when she'd handed in her warrant card seven years before. It was only to be expected, of course. Friday night round at the flat in Kentish Town – Thorne showing her the CCTV footage – had been a favour and nothing else. She knew that there weren't likely to be any more . . .

She dropped slowly to her knees and reached into the cupboard under the sink for the cleanser and a cloth.

If anybody else was going to sort things out for Jessica Clarke, she'd be happy for it to be Tom Thorne. But she didn't want *anybody else* to do it . . .

The footsteps on the stairs started again, and grew closer. She held the dry cloth under the tap for a few seconds, told herself to start worrying about dead bookies and stop being so bloody ridiculous.

The knock came, softly, as she squeezed a thick line of pale yellow cleanser around the rim of the bath.

'Are you all right, love?'

14 March 1986

Taking over a year out of school is really starting to cause a few problems. Now that Ali and Manda and the rest have moved up, I'm stuck with people who are younger than me that I didn't really know before. I can talk to most of the girls in my own year about everything. About the ops and the grafts and all the rest of it. But I only see them in the playground at lunchtime, and some of them are already a bit distant because they're one year higher up the school and are acting like they're one year older or something.

The girls in my class are trying too hard. I think that's basically the problem. I know bloody well they've been spoken to about what to say and what not to say. I also happen to know that someone from the hospital came to the school to see the teachers the week before I came back, and some of them are better at appearing natural about it than others.

My new class teacher is pretty cool, though.

There are a <u>couple</u> of girls I think are OK in the new class, but a lot of the time I can't stand most of them. Maybe I'm being unfair because I know it's a bit awkward. I remember feeling a bit strange around a girl in junior school who had a harelip. I can remember trying <u>not</u> to ignore her, then gabbling when I spoke to her and going red. Actually, with some of the girls it's really hard to tell the difference between fear and shyness. There's a few, though, who are just going way over the top in trying to be my new best friend and a couple are just ignorant bitches.

Maybe things will settle down a bit in time.

Shit Moment of the Day

Hearing it go quiet when I took my shirt off before PE.

Magic Moment of the Day.

Mum thinking she was being subtle when an advert for the Nightmare on Elm Street *video came on, and she stood in front of the TV so I wouldn't see Freddy Krueger's face.*

FOURTEEN

The elegant row of substantial Victorian houses would not have been out of place in Holland Park or Notting Hill, when, in point of fact, it was part of a conservation area in the middle of Finchley. The sunlight could easily have belonged to a warm August day, but the temperature was in single figures, and the first day of spring was still a fortnight away. The man on the green enjoying the afternoon with his dog might have been a pillar of the community. As it was, he was anything but.

Walking towards him, watching him smile as the Jack Russell ran and slid and jumped at his knees, Thorne doubted that Billy Ryan enjoyed as uncomplicated and loving a relationship with any other living creature.

'I'm surprised,' Thorne said. 'I'd've thought a Rottweiler or a Doberman. Maybe a pit-bull . . .'

Ryan didn't look overly concerned to see him. 'I've got nothing to prove. I don't have an undersized cock to compensate for. And I like small dogs.'

Thorne watched Ryan shake his head and wave to someone behind him. He turned to see his friend the receptionist climbing *back* into a Jeep parked at the other side of the green. Thorne gave the man a jaunty salute but got nothing very friendly back.

'Afternoon off, Mr Ryan?'

'Perk of being the boss.' He smiled, adjusting the frames of his lightly tinted sunglasses. 'I reckon I've earned it.'

'Right . . .'

Ryan bent to take a slobber-covered ball from the dog, who growled and wrestled until it was torn from his mouth. Ryan faked throwing the ball in one direction, then threw it in the other. Once the dog had started chasing it, Ryan walked slowly after him.

Thorne moved alongside him, nodding towards the car. 'Is he all you've got?'

'How d'you mean?'

'I'm sure he's tooled up and all that, but even so. Surely you must think you're a target *now*, Billy.'

Ryan was wearing a long black cashmere coat over a red wool scarf. He pulled the scarf a little tighter to his neck. 'Now?' he said.

'After Moloney.'

Ryan gave him a sideways look, but turned away again before Thorne could even begin to read anything into it. 'That was a shame,' he said.

'A shame how he died? A shame that he was killed? Or a shame that he was a copper?'

'Pick one.'

'You didn't send a wreath,' Thorne said. Moloney had been buried quietly the weekend before. His wife had refused the full Police Service funeral that had been offered.

Ryan shrugged, expressionless. 'Shitty way to go, I'll grant you. Not exactly a hero's death. But he did rather put himself in the firing line, wouldn't you say?'

'Who did the firing, do you reckon?'

'I'm not doing your job for you . . .'

The dog had returned with the ball. Ryan hurled it away again and carried on walking.

'Puts you in a tricky position though,' Thorne said. 'There's obviously a need to strike back, or at least be seen to strike back . . .'

'Strike back against who?'

'. . .when, actually, retaliation would be pretty bloody ironic.'

'Let's pretend you're not talking bollocks for a second.'

'Yes, let's.'

'Why would it be ironic?' The soft brogue had hardened suddenly. The end of the word bitten off and spat, as Ryan stopped and turned.

Reflected in the lenses of Ryan's aviators, Thorne could see the expanse of green at his back, and the tiny figure of the dog racing towards them. *Because it was you who had him killed, you murdering prick.* 'Because he was a police officer, obviously,' Thorne said.

This time, Ryan snatched the ball from the dog and stuffed it into his pocket. The terrier yapped a couple of times and then wandered off, its nose to the ground. He wasn't the only one on the scent of something.

'You didn't answer my question,' Thorne said.

'Which one?'

'About you being a target for the Zarif brothers.'

'The *who* brothers . . .?'

'You seem very relaxed, which is strange, considering you were bleating about protection the other day.'

'I've never bleated in my fucking life, and I was talking about my family.'

'My mistake . . .'

Ryan took off his sunglasses. As the sun had certainly not gone anywhere, Thorne could only assume that it was some kind of gesture. Maybe Ryan wanted Thorne to see his eyes.

'You don't get to the top in business by walking away when that business is threatened. You stand your ground or somebody takes it.'

'Kevin Kelly walked away,' Thorne said.

The sunglasses went back on. 'Before your time, son. You know nothing about it . . .'

Thorne smiled. 'I know people who were there.'

'Aye, right, course you do. Where *is* Miss Marple today, anyway?'

'Kevin Kelly walked away and handed the whole shebang over to you. Pretty lucky, considering you hadn't done much to deserve it. The way I understand it, there were others in the firm who might have had a greater claim. Faces who'd done a bit of time, got a decent reputation, you know? Still, it's up to the boss, and when he decides he's had enough, he gives it all to you. You must have done some serious brown-nosing to get the nod, Billy . . .'

Ryan said nothing. The sun highlighted the sheen of lacquer on his hair.

'So, Kevin Kelly buggers off to the country, thankful that *his* little girl isn't the one who looks like the Phantom of the Opera, and the Kelly family becomes the Ryan family.'

'The old woman's memory must be going,' Ryan said. 'I remember different . . .'

'What happened at that school, terrible as it was, *disgusting* as it was . . . did you a bit of a favour, I'd say.'

Somewhere in the trees at the edge of the green, a dog was barking, but Ryan didn't take his eyes from Thorne. He nodded knowingly. 'I wondered when you were going to bring up Gordon Rooker again.'

Thorne looked equally knowing. 'I didn't,' Thorne said.

He didn't need to see Ryan's eyes to know that they had darkened. Ryan began walking towards the trees, quicker this time.

Thorne stayed a pace or two behind, raising his voice as he followed: 'I don't know whether you heard what happened to Mr Rooker. You know, seeing as you mention him. He was attacked in prison apparently. Stabbed in the stomach. While he was *painting*, of all things. He's all right now, in case you were worried. He's *safe* now . . .'

Ryan stopped. He was trying to smile, but his lips were pursed, his teeth well out of sight. 'Is this official?'

Thorne considered the question. He noticed that Ryan was shuffling his feet and remembered that he'd done the same thing outside the arcade, waiting for his car. 'Well, I'm being *paid* for it . . .'

'Because there's really no fucking point to it, is there? Whatever it is you're expecting me to say, even if I say it, it won't get you anywhere. Not unless you're recording it and, to be honest, mate, even then, there are people getting paid by *me* who make sure that kind of shit doesn't stand up. So, I think we're done chatting . . .'

'I'm not recording anything,' Thorne said. 'Really, I'm just interested in where you stand on a few issues, and I'm trying to be upfront about it.' He grinned, pushing his hands deep into the pockets of his leather jacket. 'Who can be arsed going round the houses? The term we use is "being lawfully audacious".'

'The term *I* use is "pushing your fucking luck".'

Ryan stuck two fingers in his mouth, and whistled as he marched off towards the car. Thorne wasn't sure whether he was whistling for his driver or for his dog.

Either way, both came running.

Outside, it was cold and dark, and the traffic on the North End Road was nose to tail. Inside the car, Thorne was warm, and in a remarkably good mood.

The rest of the day, back at Becke House, had gone pretty well, notably because Tughan and the rest of the Projects Team were spending it over at Barkingside. Thorne had begun scaling a mountain of paperwork. He'd got up to speed on some of the cases that had been nudged on to the back burner over the past few weeks.

He had also caught up on the investigation Holland and Stone had been making into the visitors on the Park Royal security tape.

'Sod all of any significance,' Holland had said. 'The wife and the daughter are what you'd expect: neither of them's Mother Teresa, but

I think they're harmless enough. Philip Simmonds, the prison visitor, is definitely a bit spooky, but most of those types are, if you ask me . . .'

Stone had nodded, added his own observations: 'Wayne Brookhouse, the youngest daughter's ex-boyfriend, is a bit dodgy. No less than you'd expect from a mate of Rooker's. Nothing worse than that, though. Tony Sollinger's dead. Bowel cancer, three weeks ago.' He'd looked up from his scribbled notes. 'How did it go with Ryan, Guv?'

Thorne had been pleased with his afternoon stroll in Finchley, and so too was Brigstocke, having finally succeeded in persuading Tughan that they should at least be letting Billy Ryan know that they were still around. It was predictable that Tughan had needed talking into a slightly more forceful approach. It was also ironic, as in theory that was just what the Projects Team was supposed to have. It was the team's bad luck that its DCI thought 'pro-active' was something you took for constipation.

As it happened, most of the teams that made up the Serious and Organised Crime Unit were pro-active to some degree. The Flying Squad – TV's Sweeney – were the most well known. Using carefully nurtured intelligence sources, they could occasionally prevent armed robberies from taking place, or even catch the villains with the guns in their hands – *going across the pavement* – which was the most highly prized result of all.

For Thorne, and others on murder squads, the situation was slightly different. Those who hunted killers could only ever be *reactive*. You could find out where a robbery was going to take place or which security van might be getting blagged, but you never knew where a body was going to turn up. Usually, of course, you never knew *when*, either, but, as things stood, Thorne could hazard a guess that one or more would be turning up sooner rather than later . . .

He was coming down through Belsize Park, past the overpriced delicatessens and organic greengrocers', when he suddenly decided that he was going to have an early dinner. He took a left just before Chalk Farm tube station, then cut across to Camden and pointed the BMW towards the Seven Sisters Road. He called Hendricks as he was approaching Manor House and told him that he would be eating out.

The food was delicious, and the size of the portions decidedly non-nouvelle . . .

Arkan Zarif hovered at the table, watching as Thorne took the first mouthful of his main course. Thorne had chosen a dish he'd never seen before – spiced lamb meatballs wrapped in a layer of potato. He chewed, nodding enthusiastically, and the old man beamed with delight. 'I picked out the meat,' he said. 'Of course, I cooked it also, but picking out the meat is the important part.' He watched for a few moments more, his mouth gaping, smiling as another forkful went in. 'OK, I leave you to enjoy your dinner . . .'

Thorne swallowed and pointed to the seat opposite. 'No, please. Join me. It's not often you get a chance to eat with the chef.'

Zarif nodded. 'I drink a glass of scotch with you.' He turned and spoke in Turkish to his daughter, who stood, scowling, behind the counter. She looked at Thorne, who smiled sweetly back. The old man frowned as he sat down and leaned across to whisper. 'Sema is permanently miserable,' he said. 'It is not your fault.'

Thorne watched her pouring a glass of Johnny Walker for her father, and topping it up with mineral water from a plastic bottle. 'Are you sure? I do tend to have that effect on women.'

Zarif had a wheezy laugh. He repeatedly slapped a huge hand against his chest until it had died away.

Sema brought the drink to the table, then moved back behind the counter without a word.

'*Serefé*.' Zarif held up his glass.

Thorne was drinking beer. He raised his bottle of Efes.

'It means "to our honour".'

171

'To our honour,' Thorne said, as the bottle touched the glass.

In the minute or so of silence that followed, Thorne devoured most of what was on his plate. He sliced off huge chunks of the meatball, spooned up the rice, washed it down with the cold beer.

Zarif took small sips of his Scotch and water. 'You like the lady's thigh,' he said.

Thorne looked up, chewing. He grunted his confusion.

'This dish is called *kadinbudbu*. This means "lady's thigh". So, you like the lady's thigh. I joke that if you don't enjoy the *kadinbudbu*, then maybe you don't like ladies. You see?' The wheezy laugh erupted again.

'What about vegetarians?' Thorne asked.

Zarif picked up the menu, gave him a look like *that* just proved the joke was true. 'All the dishes on the menu mean something. Turkish names always have meaning. What was your starter?'

'The fried aubergine . . .'

Zarif pointed to the dish on the menu. '*Imam bayildi*. This means "the priest fainted". You see? When this dish was given to the priest, he enjoyed it so much that he fainted from pleasure.'

'I'm sorry I didn't faint,' Thorne said, 'but it was very good . . .'

'*Hunkar begendi*.' Zarif stabbed at the menu again. 'This is a dish I make very well. Diced lamb in white sauce. This means "the Emperor loved it".'

'Did he love it as much as the priest?'

Zarif didn't get the joke. 'All names mean something, but some have bad translations. Funny translations, you see? We have English customers who ask why the names are always in Turkish. I tell them if they were in English, my menu would have dishes called *rubbish kebab* and *stuffed prostitute*.'

Thorne laughed.

'No, really this would put people off . . .'

'Only some people,' Thorne said. 'Others might come in specially.'

Zarif laughed loudly, slapping his chest again, the drink spilling over the edge of his glass.

Thorne suddenly thought about his father. He thought about how much he would have enjoyed this conversation. He pictured him laughing, scribbling down the names of the dishes . . .

'What about people's names?' Thorne said. 'Do they always mean something?'

Zarif nodded. 'Of course.'

Thorne had finished eating and pushed away his plate. 'What does Zarif mean?'

The old man thought for a few seconds. 'Zarif is . . . "delicate".'

Thorne blinked and saw a breath of blood across Anaglypta wallpaper. The body of Mickey Clayton bent over a kitchen chair. Gashes across his back . . .

'Delicate?' he asked.

Zarif nodded again. He waved to get his daughter's attention, and, when he had it, spoke quickly to her in Turkish. The scowl grew more pronounced as she moved across to a small refrigerated cabinet to one side of the counter.

'Now, my first name, Arkan? This is the best joke of all. It has two meanings, depending on where you are, how you say it. It means "noble blood" or "honest blood". This sounds nice, you see? But it also means "your backside". It means "arse".'

Thorne laughed, swilling the last of the beer around in the bottle. 'My name means different things to different people as well.'

'Right.' Zarif waved his fingers in the air, searching for the words. 'A thorn is small, spiky . . .'

'Irritating.' Thorne drained the bottle. 'And it can be difficult to get rid of . . .'

Sema arrived and put down a dish in front of Thorne. He looked at Zarif for explanation.

'That is *suklac*. On the house . . .'

It was a simple rice pudding – set thick, creamy and heavily flavoured with cinnamon.

'This is gorgeous,' Thorne said.

'Thank you . . .'

Thorne saw the old man's expression change the second he heard the door open. He half turned and from the corner of his eye saw two men enter. The look on Sema's face told him that the two Zarif brothers he had yet to meet – Memet and Tan – had popped in to introduce themselves.

Arkan Zarif stood and walked over to the counter, where the men took it in turn to lean across and kiss their sister. They began talking in Turkish to their father. Thorne watched them while pretending to look around. He stared at the ornate arrangements of tiles, mounted and hanging on the walls next to Health and Safety certificates in cheap clip-frames.

Both brothers, unlike Hassan and their father, had very little hair. Memet, who Thorne put somewhere in his early forties, had a receding hairline and had chosen to wear what little he had left very short. He also had a goatee, thicker than Thorne's, but also more clearly defined, and like Thorne's, failing to hide a double chin. Tan, younger by maybe fifteen years, was shorter, and whip-thin. He wasn't losing his hair but had shaved it anyway – aping his eldest brother, Thorne guessed. He too had facial hair, but it was little more than a pencil-line running along his top lip and around the edge of his chin, in the style George Michael had worn for a while until someone pointed out that it looked ridiculous. Tan clearly fancied himself as something of a hard man and stared across at Thorne while Memet did all the talking.

Knowing that Thorne wouldn't understand, Memet Zarif made no attempt to lower his voice as he spoke to his father. He smiled a lot and patted the old man's shoulder, but Thorne could hear a seriousness in the voice.

At the mention of his name Thorne glanced up. He remembered what Carol Chamberlain had said when she'd been talking about Billy Ryan. About these people knowing as much about you as you did about them. Knowing more . . . Thorne returned Tan's

174

thousand-yard stare for a second or two before going back to his pudding.

It was disconcerting, *exciting* even, to think that one of these men – Thorne was putting his money on Memet Zarif – had probably given the order to have Mickey Clayton and the others executed. If he, or his brothers, thought that the law was going to go easier on them because they hadn't wielded the gun or the knife themselves, they hadn't learned as much as Thorne presumed they had. And, though Thorne had his own ideas, the received wisdom was that the Zarif brothers were also responsible for the death of DS Marcus Moloney. Whatever he thought of Nick Tughan, Thorne knew that he would make Memet, Hassan and Tan pay for that.

When Thorne looked up from his *suklac* again, Memet and Tan were at the table.

'What is it you want?' Memet Zarif asked.

Thorne took another mouthful, then loaded his spoon again. When he answered the question, it was as if he'd just that second remembered he'd been asked it. 'I *wanted* some dinner, which I'm actually still having, so maybe you should think about being polite and leaving me in peace to finish it. If you want me to get as annoyed as I *should* be and cause a scene in your father's restaurant – you know, maybe turn over a table or two – I suggest you carry on with the attitude.' He turned to the younger brother. 'And if that look is supposed to be intimidating, you'd better get a new manual, son. You just look like a retard . . .' Thorne turned away before the two men had any chance to react. He leaned round them, caught their sister's eye, and scribbled in the air – the universally accepted gesture when asking for the bill.

Memet and Tan walked to a table in the corner, where they were quickly joined by another man, who came scuttling from the back of the room. Sema brought them coffee and biscuits dusted with sugar. They lit cigarettes and spoke a mixture of Turkish and English in hushed voices.

Arkan Zarif carried Thorne's bill across on a plate. 'You will stay for some coffee . . .?'

Thorne took a piece of Turkish delight from the plate and examined the bill. 'No, thank you. Time to go, I think.' He dug around in his wallet for some cash.

Zarif looked towards the table in the corner, then back to Thorne. 'My sons are suspicious of the police. They have bad tempers, I know that, but they stay out of trouble.'

Thorne chewed the sweet, and decided that the old man's thinking was only marginally less divorced from reality than that of his own father. He dropped a ten and a five on to the plate. 'Why the suspicion of the police?' he said.

Zarif looked uncomfortable. 'Back in Turkey, there were some problems. Nothing serious. Memet was a little wild sometimes . . .'

'Is that why you left and came here?'

Zarif waved his hands emphatically. 'No. We came for simple reasons. All Turkish people want is bread and work. We came to this country for bread and work.'

Thorne stood and picked up his jacket. He thanked the old man, praised the food, then walked towards the door, thinking that you could work for bread, or you could just take somebody else's . . .

Common sense told his feet to keep on walking past the table in the corner, but another part of his brain was still thinking about names.

Irritating. Difficult to get rid of . . .

The three men at the table fell silent and looked at him. The blue-grey smoke from their cigarettes curled up towards the ceiling, floating around the hanging lamps like the manifestation of a dozen genies.

Thorne pointed upwards at the swirls and strands of smoke, then leaned down to address Memet Zarif. 'If I was you, I should start making wishes . . .'

He was still smiling as he made his way back to the car, taking out his mobile and dialling the number as he walked.

'Dad? It's me. Listen, I've got a great one for you. Actually, we can do a whole list, if you like, but I think you should do this one as a trivia question first. Right, have you got a pen? OK, what sort of . . . No, make that: *where would you be* if you ordered a stuffed prostitute?'

FIFTEEN

Rooker had been moved earlier that week to HMP Salisbury, one of a handful of prisons in the country with a protected witness wing. He'd pronounced himself delighted with the move. Now he was rattling around with only half a dozen other cons for company and not a paintbrush in sight.

'How did Billy Ryan first approach you?' Thorne asked. 'How was the idea of killing Alison Kelly first brought up?'

The purpose-built interview suite had freshly decorated pale yellow walls, but was still a lot less glamorous than it sounded. Whoever had designed and equipped the place hadn't put in a long day: a table, chairs, recording equipment, an ashtray . . .

Rooker cleared his throat. 'I'd met Ryan a couple of times . . .'

'Like when you got the original contract on Kevin Kelly?'

'I'm not talking about that.'

'Ryan hired you for that as well, though, didn't he?'

'I thought we'd got past this . . .'

'It's amazing he came back to you after you'd messed that one up.'

Rooker sat back in his chair and folded his arms. He looked like a sulky kid.

'Listen,' Thorne said. 'This is going to get brought up in court. Ryan's brief is going to be all over you, doing as much as he can to discredit your statement. You're not exactly a model citizen, are you?'

Rooker leaned forward slowly, pulled his tobacco tin across the table and began to roll up. He was a different character from the one Thorne had first met at Park Royal a month before. It was clear that he had still not fully recovered from the stabbing, but also that his initial cockiness was far from being the whole story. Thorne knew very well that survival in prison was all about front. All about what others *thought* you were. Pretence could be every bit as useful as a phonecard or a stolen chisel.

'The point is that I was perfect,' Rooker said. 'The word was that I *had* been the one hired to do Kevin Kelly the year before . . .'

'Right. The word.'

'Like I said, that's what everyone *thought*. Which made me the ideal choice for Billy Ryan when he decided to do the daughter.'

'The perfect cover.'

'Exactly.'

Rooker's cigarette was already alight. Thorne watched the smoke rise, remembering the words he'd spoken to Memet Zarif a week before, envious now, as he had been then. As he was around anyone who still had the joy of smoking. Some of Thorne's more prosaic dreams were filled with smoke-rings and nicotine and the glorious tightening in the chest as it hits . . .

'So, how did Ryan make the approach? He couldn't risk being seen with you.'

'Not straight away, no. It was all arranged by a third party. A face called Harry Little. He's dead now . . .'

'In suspicious circumstances?'

'Not as far as I know. He was in his late fifties back then, I think.'

'Go on . . .'

179

'We met in a pub in Camden. It might have been the Dublin Castle, I can't remember. Anyway, Harry was all over me. Very friendly. We'd never been particularly matey, so I knew he was after something, and I knew it was something heavy because he had a reputation, you know? He starts talking about Billy Ryan, going round the houses with it. I mean, we're getting through a fair few pints, know what I mean? Eventually, he says that Billy wants a meet, and that he'd be in touch with when and where and what have you, and it was obvious even then that this was something a bit special.' He saw enough of a change in Thorne's face to qualify what he'd said. 'Special as in *different*, you know? From the normal run of things.'

Thorne nodded. *The normal run of things.* Putting a bullet in the back of somebody's head, or throwing them out of a window, or beating them to death . . .

'Where did the meet with Ryan take place?'

Rooker stubbed out his fag and pushed his back chair. 'Listen, can we take a quick break? I really need to have a piss . . .'

While Rooker was gone, Thorne stood and stretched his legs. He walked to the far wall, leaned against it and closed his eyes. The faces shifted around in his mind, jockeying for position: Billy Ryan, Memet Zarif, Marcus Moloney, Ian Clarke, Carol Chamberlain. The dead faces of Muslum and Hanya Izzigil. The face of their son, Yusuf.

The two faces of Jessica Clarke . . .

A prison officer opened the door and ushered Rooker back into the room. Thorne rejoined him at the table.

'Have you got any children, Mr Thorne?'

'No.'

Rooker sat and shrugged, as though whatever he was going to say was no longer relevant, or would not make any sense.

Thorne was curious, but keener still to crack on. To get out. He hit the red button on the twin-cassette recorder that was secured to the wall. 'Interview commencing again at . . . eleven forty-five a.m.' He looked at Rooker. The lid was already off the tobacco tin again. 'Tell me what happened when you met with Billy Ryan.'

'It was a track through Epping Forest, up near Loughton. I just got the call from Harry Little one night and drove up there . . .'

'There were just the two of you?'

Rooker nodded. 'We sat in Ryan's car and he told me what he wanted.'

'He told you that he wanted you to kill Kevin Kelly's daughter, Alison.'

Rooker looked directly into Thorne's eyes. He knew this was the important stuff. 'Yes, he did.'

'What did you think?'

Rooker seemed confused.

'Well, like you said, this was different from the normal run of things.'

'Everybody knew that Ryan was a bit mental . . .'

'But still, a *child*?'

'He wanted a *war*. He wanted to do something that would send the whole fucking lot spinning out of control, you know?'

Thorne blinked and remembered Ryan's face close to his own, the cheeks almost as red as his scarf. The eyes glassy. The faintest quiver around the small mouth as he spoke: '*I think we're done chatting . . .*'

'Was it Ryan's idea?' he asked. 'The burning?'

'Christ, yes.' Rooker ran a hand through his hair, sending a shower of tiny white flakes floating down to the table. 'He thought that since it was something I'd done before, I might be more comfortable with it.'

'*Comfortable?*'

'I told you. He was mental . . .'

'It was something you were known for, though? The fire? The lighter fluid? So, when Ryan suggested it as a method, didn't you hear any alarm bells?'

'What?' Rooker grinned. 'Fire-alarm bells, you mean?'

Thorne's face was blank. 'Look at me, Gordon. I'm pissing myself.'

'Sorry . . .'

'Weren't you even a little bit suspicious?'

Rooker took a long drag, then another, held the smoke in.

'Come on, it was obviously going to point to you, wasn't it? Are you seriously telling me that while you were busy thinking how mental Ryan was, you didn't for one moment think that he might be planning to set you up?'

The smoke drifted out on a noisy sigh. 'Later I did. I realised afterwards, after it had happened and I was being fingered for it anyway. Yeah, *then* it was fucking obvious, and I knew I'd been stupid, but it was a bit late. I was in the frame and Ryan had his excuse to come after me. By then, of course, I knew damn well that he really needed me out of the way to shut me up.'

'So, what did you think when he asked you?'

'I thought, No fucking way.'

'Because it was risky?'

'Because it was a fucking kid.'

Thorne leaned towards the recorder. 'Mr Rooker slams his hand on the table. For emphasis.' He flashed Rooker an exaggerated smile. 'I'm saying that just in case anybody thinks that was the noise of me hitting you with a chair or something . . .'

Rooker grunted.

'So, what happened when you turned Ryan down?'

'He wasn't happy . . .'

'What did he say?'

'He said that he'd find somebody else to do the job. I remember him saying exactly that when I got out of his car just before he drove away: "There's always somebody else . . ."'

And Thorne could picture Ryan saying it. He could picture Ryan's face as he said it, and he felt something tighten in his stomach, because Ryan would have known that it was true. Bitter experience had taught Thorne that it was one of the few things that you could rely on. There's always somebody else willing to do what another won't.

Something darker and more depraved. Something inexplicable. Unimaginable . . .

Thorne announced, for the tape, that he was formally suspending the interview.

Then he punched the red button.

'We'll carry on after lunch,' he said.

Thorne was just shy of Newbury when he turned off the M4 and pulled slowly into the car park at Chieveley Services. A car flashed its lights as he approached and Thorne parked the BMW next to it. Holland got out of a car-pool Rover, leaned against it and waited for Thorne to join him.

Thorne had received the call just after seven on the M3 as he was heading home from Salisbury. He'd turned off at the next services to pick up a sandwich and consult the road atlas. The traffic had been heavy on the A road that had taken him across to the M4, and even worse for the journey back west.

Holland offered Thorne a bulky torch. Thorne took one look at it and plumped instead for the Maglite he kept in his boot, taking his gloves out at the same time. Torches sweeping the ground ahead of them, they began to walk towards the farthest corner of the car park.

'How did we get hold of this so quickly?' Thorne asked.

'Swift and harmonious cooperation between ourselves and the lovely lads from Thames Valley.' Holland smiled at the incredulous look on Thorne's face. 'I know, hard to believe. They found the lorry this morning, ran the number plate and at the end of a very long paper-trail – half a dozen different companies – whose name should pop up? A flag on their computer system alerts the Thames Valley lot, tells them it's a name we're very interested in, and Bob's your uncle . . .'

'What, they just called us?'

'Amazing, isn't it, forces working so well together? Someone should get hold of Mulder and Scully . . .'

The lorry stood in almost total blackness. The light from the restaurant and shopping complex five hundred yards away died just short of it, leaving the two Thames Valley woodentops standing watch as little more than dark shapes. As Thorne and Holland got nearer, their torches picked out the reflective bands on the officers' uniforms, and the fence of fluttering blue crime tape that had been erected around the vehicle.

Pleasantries were exchanged with the two officers, who gratefully accepted the offer to go inside and get themselves some tea. Thorne and Holland walked slowly around the outside of the truck.

It was a white Mercedes cab, fitted with what looked like a twenty-five, or thirty-foot solid-sided body. Dirty, dark green. No company logo or markings of any sort.

Thorne climbed up to the passenger door, gingerly took hold of a handle.

'I think the Thames Valley boys have been over a lot of it already,' Holland said.

Thorne pulled open the door. 'Well, I hope they were careful. We'll need to get SOCO down here.'

'They're on their way . . .'

Thorne shone his torch around the cab's interior. There were papers scattered across the seats and in the footwells. Whoever had gone through it hadn't been too careful. It was unclear whether that was the fault of the officers who had discovered the abandoned vehicle, or those responsible for hijacking and then dumping it.

'What was it carrying?' Thorne asked, jumping down from the cab. 'What was it *supposed* to be carrying?'

'Well, the manifest they found in the cab says DVD players. Full load, top of the range, well worth nicking.'

'Well, whatever was in there, I wouldn't bet against Billy Ryan already having his hands on it. Looks like he's decided to hit the Zarifs where it's really going to hurt them. What about the driver?'

'No sign. Not so much as a Yorkie bar . . .'

'What d'you reckon?'

'Your guess is as good as mine,' Holland said. 'Maybe the hijackers took him . . .'

Thorne was on his knees, shining his torch underneath the truck. Oil, dirt and nothing else. 'Or maybe they just beat the shit out of him and he's gone running back to the Zarif brothers. Either way, I don't fancy his chances.'

A couple of teenage lads who'd obviously seen the torchbeams came wandering down from the direction of the restaurant carrying burgers and Cokes. Thorne shone his torch towards them. They shouted and put their hands up to shield their eyes.

'Go and tell them to piss off, will you, Dave?' Thorne watched Holland walk towards them, then turned back to the lorry, thinking that, for once, the old cliché about there being 'nothing to see' was absolutely spot on. The rear doors were obviously not locked, but had been pushed together. After trying and failing to open one of the huge doors with one hand, Thorne put his torch on the ground, grabbed hold with both hands and pulled.

The stench of piss hit him immediately. He bent to retrieve his torch and pointed it inside, jumping slightly as Holland stepped around from the side of the truck.

'Fuck . . .'

'Sorry,' Holland said, grinning. He added the light from his own torch to Thorne's, revealing, little by little, the interior of the empty box. 'Smells lovely, doesn't it? Tramp's been in there overnight, I reckon. Kids maybe . . .'

Thorne lifted a leg and reached up. 'Give us a hand, will you?'

Holland locked his fingers together, making a cradle for Thorne's foot. Thorne stepped into it and heaved himself up into the back of the lorry. The smell was even worse inside.

'Jesus . . .'

'Maybe somebody was very pissed,' Holland suggested. 'Thought it was a new kind of Portaloo. Makes a change from doing it in phone boxes . . .'

Thorne played the torch across the scarred metal floor. The light caught slick trails where the liquid had run, puddles where it had pooled.

Having seen quite enough, he turned, ready to jump down, when the Maglite caught something. There were markings high up on the side of the box, near the driver's cab. Thorne trained the beam on the spot and moved slowly towards it.

'Has anybody else been in here?' he shouted. He knew the answer already. Nobody could have missed this in daylight . . .

'I'm not sure,' Holland said. 'I think they just opened the door, saw that it was empty . . .'

The scratches were recent, Thorne was sure of it, the marks bright against the dull, dark metal.

Holland was leaning into the truck, fixing his torch on Thorne. 'What's the matter?'

It was a single word. The language was unfamiliar. Scored in broken lines deep into the side of the box with a knife. A nail maybe.

UMIT.

'It wasn't tramps or kids in here,' Thorne said. 'And the Zarifs aren't smuggling dodgy videos.' He turned towards the open doors and the figure of Holland standing in the darkness. 'They're smuggling people.'

'What? Illegal immigrants?'

'It could be trafficking for prostitution, but I doubt it. I'm guessing these people were perfectly willing. Paid their life savings on the strength of some gangster's promise . . .'

Holland said something else then, but Thorne couldn't make it out. He spun around slowly on the spot, the circle of light from his torch dancing lazily across the dirty walls. Miserable, remembering . . .

The woman on the tube, that first day. A baby and an empty cup.

Arkan Zarif's words.

Bread and work . . .

★

It was well after midnight by the time Thorne turned into Ryland Road and pulled up behind a dark blue VW Golf. He felt wiped out. He was walking past the Golf towards his flat when he noticed a man asleep in the driver's seat. Thorne slowed his pace and leaned down to take a closer look. There was some light from a lamp-post twenty feet away, but not a great deal. The man in the car opened his eyes, smiled at Thorne and closed them again.

Thorne continued on towards his door, reached into a pocket for his keys. Perhaps he'd rattled Billy Ryan more than he'd realised . . .

Hendricks had already made up the sofa-bed and was lying there reading a paperback with an arty-looking cover.

Thorne filled him in on the day's events.

As far as work on the case went, Hendricks had not been involved practically since the post-mortem on Marcus Moloney, but it was important that he remain part of the team. Besides, Thorne was certain that his particular skills would be required again before it was all over.

'There's a message on the machine for you,' Hendricks shouted through to the kitchen. 'Sounds interesting . . .'

Thorne wandered in with his tea, pressed the button, sat on the arm of the sofa-bed to listen. The message was from Alison Kelly. She asked if he was free the following evening and left a phone number.

Hendricks put down his book. 'Was that who I think it was?'

Thorne turned off the living-room light and walked towards his bedroom. 'Hard to be sure,' he said. He was smiling as he opened the bedroom door. 'I don't know who you think it was, do I . . .?'

A few hours later, Thorne padded back into the living room, as awake as he'd been when he'd left it. He moved slowly towards the window. As he edged past the end of the sofa-bed, he banged his foot against the metal rail.

Hendricks stirred and sat up, woken by the impact, or the swearing.

'It's four o'clock in the morning . . .'

'Yes, I know.'

Though there was no one left in the room to disturb, the darkness dictated that they spoke in whispers.

'What are you doing?' Hendricks moaned.

Thorne was feeling irritable, and the throbbing pain in his foot was not helping matters. 'Right now, I'm thinking that it's getting a bit bloody crowded in here.' He stepped across to the window. 'How long can it possibly take to get rid of a bit of damp anyway?'

Hendricks said nothing.

Thorne pulled back the blind and looked out into the street. The Golf had gone.

18 May 1986

Ali and I went into town today. We just hung around really. Ali bought a bag and a couple of new tops and I got some LPs. Afterwards we got a burger and sat on a bench outside the library. A couple of lads were messing around and they were both staring. I started joking around with Ali, asking her which one of us she thought they fancied. It's only the sort of thing I would have said to her before. (Ali was always the one lads fancied, by the way!) She looked uncomfortable and threw her burger away, and I know I should have left it, but I was just trying to make her laugh. I told her that it was obviously true what they say about how good-looking girls always hang around with an ugly mate, and then she started to cry.

Now I feel guilty that I've upset her, but also angry because her feeling sad or guilty or whatever it is she feels seems so fucking trivial when I look into the mirror on the back of the bedroom door, and half my face still looks like the meat in her burger.

I know I'll feel differently about today by the morning and Ali and I will be best mates again before the end of school on Monday, but it's difficult not to feel a bit low when I'm writing this stuff down and it's my own fault. I always write at night, staring out of the window and listening to the Smiths or something equally miserable. Maybe I should have bought some cheerier music when I was in town. The soundtrack to tomorrow's entry will be courtesy of Cliff Richard or the Wombles or something . . .

Shit Moment of the Day

The stuff with Ali.

Magic Moment of the Day

A comedian on the TV making a joke about burn victims sticking together.

SIXTEEN

A single word was written on the whiteboard in red felt-tip pen.

UMIT.

'It means "hope",' Tughan said. 'In Turkish . . .'

Feet were shifted uncomfortably, and awkward looks exchanged. Thorne thought that if the people who'd been taken from the back of that lorry were now being handled by Billy Ryan, hope was something they would almost certainly have run out of.

It was Saturday morning, the day after the discovery of the abandoned lorry. The SO7 team was back at Becke House to work through this latest development. All that was *actually* developing was a sense of frustration . . .

'Customs and Excise are all over this now,' Tughan said. 'Not sure what they'll get out of it, but it'll probably be a damn sight more than we do . . .'

Thorne stood with Russell Brigstocke and the rest of the core team – Kitson, Stone, Holland and their SO7 counterparts – in a corner of the Incident Room. They watched as Tughan wore out a small strip of carpet in front of one of the desks. Weekend or not, there were always those who made no concessions to casual wear, but, despite the sharp and predictably well-pressed suit, Thorne thought that Tughan was starting to look and sound a little tired. Maybe not as tired as Thorne himself, but he was getting there.

'In terms of the Zarif brothers, you mean?' Thorne asked.

Holland held up his hands in a gesture of exasperation. 'Surely there must be something tying them to this? Something that will at least give us an excuse to make their lives difficult . . .'

Tughan put down his coffee and began to flick through a hastily assembled report on the hijacking. 'It's like six degrees of fucking separation,' he said. 'Between this lorry and the Zarifs there are any number of haulage companies, leasing agencies, freight contractors. They own the vehicle, *theoretically*, but if we spend a lot of time trying to tie them to whatever the vehicle was carrying, *we'll* be the ones whose lives are difficult.'

'I bet they're laughing at us,' Holland said. 'Them *and* the bloody Ryans.'

Tughan shrugged. 'Without any bodies, without the people who were inside the lorry, we've got sweet FA.'

'I can't believe they've got everything covered.' Holland looked around for support, found a little in the way of nods and murmurs.

'I've had a thought,' Brigstocke said. All eyes turned to him. 'Have we checked to see if that lorry's tax disc is up to date?'

The joke got a decent, and much needed, response, even if some of the laughter was lost in yawns.

'Do we know what was inside the lorry?' Kitson said. 'Specifically, I mean. Are we ever going to know how many?'

Tughan shook his head. 'Anywhere between a dozen and, I don't know . . . fifty?'

'There were that many found dead in the back of that lorry at Dover, weren't there?' Holland said.

'There were more,' Thorne said. He remembered the smell when he'd stepped up into that box the night before. He wondered what it must have been like for whoever had opened a pair of lorry doors a few years earlier and stared as the sunlight fell across the tangled heaps of crushed and emaciated dead. Fifty-eight Chinese immigrants, crammed like sardines into a sealed lorry, and found suffocated when it was opened on a steaming summer's afternoon. Their clothes in nice, neat piles. Their bodies in considerably less ordered ones . . .

There had, of course, been a major outcry at the time. There were demands for tougher controls, for positive action to curb this barbaric trade. Thorne knew very well that more *might* have been done had the corpses in the back of that lorry been those of donkeys or puppies or kittens . . .

'How can that many get through?' Stone asked. 'Don't these lorries get searched?'

'Sometimes,' Tughan said. 'They can hide in secret compartments or behind stacks of false cargo . . .'

Stone was shaking his head. 'You'd think they'd check the lorries a bit more thoroughly after all that business at Dover, though.'

Thorne knew that it wouldn't have taken a particularly thorough search to have found those Chinese immigrants earlier. To have saved their lives. They'd tried to hide behind a few crates of tomatoes . . .

'The smugglers aren't stupid,' Tughan said. 'They'll try to avoid the ports that have got scanners, but even those that *do* have them are overrun. They can't possibly check any more than a handful or you'd have queues fifty miles long waiting to board the ferries.'

Thorne knew Tughan was right. Unable to sleep the night before, he'd booted up his rarely used computer and surfed the Net for a couple of hours. He'd gone to the NCIS site and taken a crash course in Turkish organised crime. He'd looked at the way the gangs and families operated both in the UK and in Turkey, and had followed the link from there to the NCIS pages on people smuggling.

It had made for grim reading. It hadn't helped him sleep . . .

Customs and Excise were still more concerned with finding illicit alcohol and tobacco than they were with the smuggling of and, worse still, the *trade* in people. Though a few scanners had been installed, it was simply too big an undertaking to check anything more than a small random sample of vehicles passing through most ports. Seven thousand lorries a day came through Dover; on a good day, 5 per cent of them might be searched. It was little surprise that often no effort at all was made to conceal the people being smuggled. Those doing the smuggling knew full well that they could afford to be brazen.

Tughan talked some more about the hopelessness of trying to curb the growing trade in desperate people. He mentioned the valiant efforts being made by the police, the immigration services, the NCIS and Customs. He described an operation, yet to yield substantial results, involving MI5 and MI6 agents infiltrating the businesses of those responsible . . .

Thorne listened, wondering if he should jump in and help. After all, it wasn't often that he had the facts and figures at his fingertips. He was not usually the one who'd done his homework. He decided not to bother, figuring that it might be a bit early in the morning for some people to handle the shock.

Yvonne Kitson had brought a flask of Earl Grey in with her. She poured herself a cup. 'So, until we find these people, find out what Ryan's done with them, we won't know who they are or how they got here.'

Brigstocke pointed to the whiteboard, to the single word, scrawled in red: *Hope*. The colour of crushed tomatoes . . .

'Well, we can be pretty sure that at least some of them are Turkish,' Brigstocke said. 'Kurds, probably.'

Thorne knew the most likely route: 'From Turkey and the Middle East through the Balkans.' He ignored the look of surprise from Brigstocke, the look of amused horror from Tughan, and carried on, 'Then across the Adriatic to Italy.'

Tughan took over. 'The smugglers have a range of options. They change the routes to keep the immigration services on their toes, but there are a few key places – Moscow, Budapest, Sarajevo are all major nexus points . . .'

Thorne smiled. *Nexus points!* Nick Tughan was not a man to let himself be outdone. Thorne half expected him to march across like a teacher and write it on the whiteboard.

'But Istanbul is the big one. It's smack on the most direct route to the West from most of the major source countries.'

'Right,' Brigstocke said. 'And where the Zarif brothers have got plenty of friends and contacts.'

Holland rubbed his eyes. 'What about getting in here?'

'I already told you,' Tughan said, 'the smugglers aren't stupid.'

Neither am I, Thorne thought. 'They've got a few choices at this end as well,' he said. 'They can risk a major port or try a back-door route like the one through Ireland. There's another way in that's becoming quite popular – via Holland and Denmark, then over to the Faroe Islands, the Shetlands and across into mainland Scotland.' Thorne wasn't sure whether the short silence that followed was *considered* or simply *astonished*.

It was Yvonne Kitson who eventually spoke up. 'All right,' she said, turning to him, mock-aggressive. 'What planet are you from, and what have you done with Tom Thorne?'

DC Richards – the tedious Welshman who had so enjoyed making his 'concentric circles' speech – cut off the laughter before it had really begun. 'What are we actually going to *do*, sir? About the Zarifs and Billy Ryan?'

Tughan gave a thin smile, grateful to one of his own for passing the baton back to him. Back where it belonged. 'It's tricky, because both sides have got good reason to lie low for a while. The Zarifs know we're looking at their smuggling operation, and Ryan's got any number of immigrants to dispose of.'

'I can't see Memet Zarif and his brothers lying low for very long,' Thorne said. 'They'll want to hit back at Ryan for this. Close to home, maybe . . .'

Tughan considered this for a second. 'Maybe, but I think we've got a bit of time to play with. I want a full-on policy of disruption. Let's make it hard for them to do *any* business; let's fuck them both around.' He pointed at Holland, reminding him of what he'd said earlier. 'Make their lives difficult . . .'

Thorne knew that 'disruption' essentially meant arresting, or, at the very least, hassling a variety of low-rank workers in the two organisations: drug dealers, debt collectors – those in DC Richards' outer circles. It was time-consuming, heavy on manpower and, worst of all, as far as Thorne was concerned, it had little effect on the people they should be really going after. It was a policy that could produce results in the right circumstances, but there were just too many bodies around this time. It made him feel like a glorified VAT-man, and he resented it. He wanted to hurt Billy Ryan and the Zarif boys in more than just their wallets . . .

'Not convinced, Tom?' Tughan asked. Obviously, Thorne's face was giving away as much as it usually did.

Thorne hated the eyes on him, the barely suppressed sighs from those without the bollocks or the brain power to speak up. 'It's like we're trying to catch a killer,' he said, 'and while we're waiting for him to do it again, we're busy cutting up his credit cards. Nicking a few quid out of his wage packet . . .'

Tughan's response was remarkably calm, gentle even. 'We're not dealing with everyday criminals, Tom. These men are not ordinary killers.'

Thorne traded small shrugs with Brigstocke, exchanged a 'what the hell' look with Dave Holland. He knew that Tughan was right, but it didn't make him feel any happier, or any less lost.

Thorne had never thought the day would come, but he was starting to yearn for a decent, honest-to-goodness psychopath . . .

There was a message from Phil Hendricks on Thorne's mobile: he'd be spending the night at Brendan's. Thorne texted him back: he was sorry for being a miserable sod the night before, and hoped that wasn't the reason Hendricks was staying away.

'What's Ryan going to do with them?' Kitson asked.

The pair of them were back in their own office, working their way through paperwork, while, up the corridor, Tughan and Brigstocke were still hammering out a plan for 'disruption'. Thorne put his phone down and glanced at his watch before he looked up. Another fifteen minutes and he'd head home.

'Probably exactly the same as the Zarifs would have done,' he said. 'He'll exploit them. The poor sods hand over every penny they've got, and when they arrive here they find that they owe these "businessmen" a lot more. In the time it takes them to get people smuggled into the UK they might be working with criminal organisations in half a dozen different countries. It might take months, even years, and the smugglers are incurring extra costs on the way. Palms need to be greased all along the route, and the cost of that gets passed on to the people in the backs of the lorries.'

Kitson shook her head. 'So, even if they get here in one piece, they're up to their eyeballs in debt . . .'

'Right. But, luckily, people like that nice Mr Zarif have lots of jobs they can do to work their debts off. At one pound fifty an hour it should only take them a couple of years . . .'

'And they can't do anything about it. They can't kick up a fuss.'

'Not unless they want to get reminded, forcibly, of just who they're dealing with. I mean, there're so many of these buggers over here, aren't there? Nicking our jobs or claiming our dole money. Who's going to notice if a couple of them disappear?' Thorne's voice dropped, lost its ironic swagger. 'Or there's worse. Don't forget, back where these people have come from, the smugglers have plenty of friends who know *exactly* where their families are.'

Kitson sighed, a slow hiss of resignation. 'It's a great new life . . .'

Thorne thought about all the clichés. It was hard to think of hope as something that sprang eternal, but easy to see it being crushed and dashed. Hope died violently. It was bludgeoned and it was burned.

Hope was something that bled.

He dropped some papers he hadn't bothered looking at into a drawer, and slammed it shut. The action distracted him from the face of the woman on the tube train. The sound drowned out the noise of nothing rattling in the bottom of her chewed polystyrene cup.

Thorne had read plenty the night before about trafficking. He knew about women being kidnapped, forced into heroin addiction and the vice trade. He guessed that the Zarifs were involved in that particularly lucrative area of human trading.

He knew that there were worse things than begging . . .

At the sound of raised voices outside the door, Thorne looked up. Holland knocked and stuck his head in. 'They've found the lorry driver,' he said. He pushed the door further open and stepped into the office. 'In some woods behind a lay-by on the A7.'

'How?' Thorne asked.

'Shot in the head . . .'

'Nice.'

'But not until they'd smashed half of it to pulp with a dirty great tree branch.'

'The A7,' Kitson said. 'That's the main road between Edinburgh and Carlisle. My ex had family up there . . .'

Holland had his notebook in his hand and began flipping through the pages.

Thorne had been right on the nail at the morning briefing. It looked like the lorry had been hijacked after coming into Scotland on the route he'd described. The cargo would have been loaded on to another vehicle, then the original lorry driven south and dumped at Chieveley.

Holland had found what he was looking for. 'Right,' he said. 'The lay-by was just north of Galashiels. It was the Lothian and Borders boys who found the bodies.'

'Found the *what*?' Thorne said.

'There were two other bodies. Three altogether.' Holland looked from Thorne to Kitson. 'No identification on them. Gunshot wounds to the head.'

Kitson spat out the breath in her lungs like it had suddenly become foul. She took a mouthful of fresher air. 'A couple of them put up a fight, maybe?' She looked to Thorne.

He nodded. 'Or tried to run.'

'I think that's the theory they're working on,' Holland said.

Thorne immediately pictured the two men thrashing desperately through woods in the dark. Tearing, breathless, through wet leaves and sprawling over rotting stumps. He saw them fall before the echo of the shots had died away. He knew that whatever last word passed through their heads the second before the bullet did, it had certainly not been *umit*. He had been taught a Turkish toast; maybe he should go back and learn a few Turkish prayers.

The door opened wider and Holland stepped aside as Brigstocke and Tughan marched in.

'Ten bodies now,' Tughan said. 'Double figures. This has to stop . . .'

Double figures? Tughan was making it sound as if the Ryan–Zarif turf war had now exceeded some unspoken quota of acceptable victims. Thorne had known stranger things to be true, but, for whatever reason, he had the impression that the plan to 'disrupt' had been superseded in light of the news from north of the border. Tughan certainly looked as if he now had something rather more direct in mind.

Brigstocke swept a hand through his thick, black hair, nudged his glasses with a knuckle. 'Ten bodies, and the civilian victims are starting to outnumber the soldiers.'

'Let's stop pissing around with monkeys then,' Thorne said. 'Go straight for the organ-grinders . . .'

Tughan held up a hand. 'That's exactly what we're going to do.'

'All right.' Thorne was thinking: I've got a date later, but there's still time. I needn't hang around too long. Finchley is a bit of a schlep, and trickier in terms of just dropping by, but Green Lanes isn't too far out of my way . . .

'We *will* put Billy Ryan away,' Tughan said. 'We'll get him with the Rooker case, and we'll get the Zarif brothers as well, eventually. Right now, our top priority has to be preventing any more deaths.'

'Eventually' was one word that Thorne hadn't wanted to hear.

'I'm going to the detective chief superintendent in the first instance and he may well have to take it higher. We'll make an official approach to Ryan, almost certainly through his solicitor, and we'll do the same thing to the Zarif family, probably via a community leader, or perhaps a priest.' Tughan was nodding to nobody in particular, as if he were trying to convince himself of something. 'Things have got to the point now where intervention might well do us as much good as investigation. Sitting down with these people is not something we do every day of the week, but if getting them around a table might help us put a stop to this fucking chaos, I'm happy to do it.'

Thorne looked thoughtful for a second or two before he spoke. He was thinking it was no great surprise that Tughan was not exactly proposing to kick anybody's door in.

'Do we have to provide the sandwiches?' he said.

'Where you going?' The man behind the simple wooden counter asked the question with only the most cursory glance up from his newspaper. The thick accent transformed the three words into one: '*Werrugoeen?*'

'I'm not going anywhere,' Thorne said, 'but you're going back there to tell your boss that somebody wants to have a quick word with him.' Thorne looked hard at the man who was now giving him his full attention. He pointed back over the man's shoulder towards the dimly lit space behind him. He knew that a second man, sitting on a tatty armchair in the corner behind and to the left of him was also studying him intently.

Thorne held up his warrant card. 'Quick as you can.'

The man slapped down his paper, snorted back phlegm and disappeared into the gloom.

The minicab office consisted of little more than a waiting room the size of a cupboard. An unpainted door to the right of the hatch led back into any number of rooms behind. Thorne guessed that the drivers themselves would be sitting nearby in their dodgy Vauxhalls and Toyotas, or perhaps waiting in the Zarifs' café next door. He turned and watched a few seconds of a film he didn't recognise on the TV bolted above the front door. The local news might be on the other side, might be showing the three goals Spurs had put past Everton earlier in the day. He let his eyes drop to the man on the armchair. The latter raised an eyebrow as if they were both just frustrated customers waiting for a lift home. He held Thorne's stare for longer than was strictly necessary before standing and walking through the side door towards the rear of the office.

A few seconds after it had closed, the door opened and Memet Zarif stepped into the waiting room. At the same time, Thorne was aware of the man he'd first spoken to resuming his position behind the counter. A few feet further back, hovering in the shadows, stood the man who'd been sitting in the armchair.

'You want a cab, Mr Thorne?' Memet said. He wore a simple white shirt, buttoned at the collar, over black trousers and tasselled loafers.

Thorne smiled. 'No, thanks. I think I'd like to get home in one piece. Last minicab I took, the driver didn't know that a red light meant stop . . .'

'My drivers know what they're doing.'

'You sure?'

'Of course.'

'They know how to fill out insurance forms, do they?'

Memet laughed, glancing across to the men behind the counter and nodding towards Thorne. The man from the armchair moved forward and stood at the shoulder of the receptionist. He spat some Turkish in Thorne's direction.

Thorne whipped his head round and smiled. 'Same to you,' he said. He turned back to Memet, still smiling at the tremendous fun they were all having. 'So, you don't think it would be worth my while getting a few officers round here, checking that all your cars and all your fantastic drivers are fully insured?' Thorne was fighting against the sound of gunfire from the TV set. He raised his voice: 'I'd be wasting my time, would I?'

The noise from the TV suddenly dropped enough for Thorne to hear Memet sigh. 'Do you think we are stupid?'

It seemed to Thorne that everyone was awfully keen to tell him that the likes of Memet Zarif and Billy Ryan were anything but stupid. He didn't doubt that they were *careful*, but he refused to buy into a myth that he and his team were up against the gangland chapter of Mensa. Thorne had caught his fair share of supposedly clever villains, and he knew equally that plenty were thick as shit and doing very nicely for themselves. He knew that, actually, the most successful villains got by on instinct, like many of those who were out to catch them.

Instinct was fallible, though, as Thorne knew only too well.

Do you think we are stupid?

Memet was certainly clever enough to load a simple question with meaning. He was no longer talking about a minicab firm . . .

Thorne moved past Memet, talking as he pushed open the wooden side door and stepped into a dimly lit corridor. 'I like what you've done with this place,' he said. Through the thin wall, he could hear the men behind the counter moving round to intercept him.

Memet was following as Thorne walked calmly along a strip of greasy linoleum. The place smelled faintly musty. Flakes of magnolia paint crackled under his shoes.

'Did you do it yourself, or did you get professionals in?'

'What do you want, Mr Thorne?'

They walked past the doorway that led to the reception hatch. The two hired hands stared at Thorne, then looked to Memet for instructions. At the end of the corridor was a small, gloomy living room. The three men sitting around the table put down their playing cards and looked up as Thorne approached. Hassan Zarif made to stand up, then relaxed as he saw his older brother looming at Thorne's shoulder.

Thorne took the scene in fast. The two other men at the table were Tan, the youngest brother, and the heavyset man he'd seen at the café with Hassan when he'd been in there with Holland. For a few seconds, the only noise was the muffled soundtrack from the TV in the waiting room and the bubbling of the air filter in a large tank of tropical fish sitting on an oak sideboard.

Thorne pointed to the table. The pile of crumpled five- and ten-pound notes in the middle was about to spill on to the carpet. 'I could make up a four for bridge if you fancy it,' he said.

Memet pushed past him and took the empty seat at the table. 'Just say what you've come to say.'

'It's funny, you talking back there about drivers. It reminds me: they found the driver of your lorry.'

Memet shrugged, looked confused. 'Our lorry . . .?'

Hassan leaned across and spoke to him in Turkish. Memet nodded.

'The police at Thames Valley called me about it yesterday morning,' Hassan said. He spoke to Memet and Tan as if he were filling them in on some minor business glitch. 'The lorry wasn't damaged, as far as they can tell, and the haulier will claim for their lost load, so I didn't think there was any need to contact our insurance company.' He looked up at Thorne. 'I haven't had the chance to talk to my brothers about it yet, but it's fairly trivial.'

'Pass on our gratitude to the officers who found it,' Memet said.

Thorne had to concede that they played it well. 'It wasn't very trivial for the driver,' Thorne said. 'They found him with half his head missing.'

The heavyset man failed to conceal a smile. He looked down and began to tidy up the notes when he saw that Thorne had caught it.

Hassan ran a hand back and forth across his prominent chin. The stubble rasped against his palm. 'Well, that clears one thing up at least,' he said. 'We can assume that the driver wasn't in league with the hijackers.'

Memet did a convincing enough job of looking shocked and saddened, though Thorne knew very well that the news would have come as something of a relief. A dead driver was a driver who wouldn't be telling the police anything. 'They killed him?' he said, turning to Hassan. 'For what? What was this lorry carrying?'

Playing it *very* well. Certainly far from stupid . . .

'I think the police said it was CD players,' Hassan said.

Thorne corrected him. '*DVD* players, actually. The good news is that they didn't get the entire load.'

The heavyset man carried on straightening banknotes, but now the three brothers looked directly at Thorne. Memet's face was a blank. Hassan was trying too hard to look no more than innocently curious. Tan was persevering with the hardman glare.

'That's right,' Thorne said. 'Apparently, a couple of the DVD players were shot, trying to run away.'

Only Memet Zarif was able to hold the look, to continue to meet Thorne's eye.

'Don't worry, I'll get straight in touch if we find any more,' Thorne said. 'Just thought you'd be interested in what we'd established so far.'

More bubbles from the fish tank. Voices from the TV along the corridor.

As Thorne turned to leave, he became aware of another figure seated in the corner to his right and a little behind him. He stared until the man leaned slowly forward and his face moved from shadow into light. Thorne recognised him as the son of Muslum and Hanya Izzigil.

Thorne took a step towards the boy. 'Yusuf . . .'

It may just have been the light, but the boy's eyes seemed changed. The previous month, with his parents dead in the next room, they had brimmed with tears, but that was not the only difference that Thorne could see. There was a challenge in their stillness, in their *dead*ness, and in the set of the boy's shoulders as he stared at the man who'd failed so miserably to provide him with any justice.

Clearly, there had been others who'd made him promises they had more chance of keeping.

'We are taking care of Yusuf now,' Hassan said.

Thorne stared at the boy for a few seconds more, looking for a sign that some part of him might not yet have become theirs. He saw only that the boy was lost. He turned, and moved slowly back the way he'd come in. 'I'll let you get back to your game . . .'

'Are you sure you don't want that cab home?' Memet asked.

Thorne said nothing, his back to them.

Tan Zarif spoke up for the first time. 'We'll do you a very good price,' he said. 'Green Lanes to Kentish Town for a fiver. How's that sound?'

Thorne felt something tighten in his gut at the revelation implicit in the simple details of the journey. He turned and looked deep into Tan's eyes, trying to swallow back the panic and sound casual. 'I thought we'd talked about this,' he said. 'Drop the "we know where you live" hardman shit or change the look.' He drew a finger from ear to ear along the line of his jaw, the same line marked out on Tan by his pencil-thin beard. 'The George Michael thing is scaring nobody . . .'

Thorne took a deep breath and held it as he walked quickly back along the corridor, through the empty reception area and out on to the street. He let the breath out and turned to see Arkan Zarif staring at him from the doorway of the café.

The old man raised his hand as Thorne came towards him, brought it up to his mouth. 'You come inside for coffee? For *suklak*, maybe . . .?'

Thorne slowed his pace, but kept on heading towards his car. 'I can't. I've got to be somewhere . . .'

It was true that he had less than an hour to get home, shower and change, but that wasn't the only reason why he'd refused the old man's invitation. Even if he'd had the time, Thorne knew that the coffee would have tasted even more bitter than usual.

When he thought about the burning girl, he often thought about the others, too. About her friends.

They'd been the first to see it, of course, to spot the flames. The one who had been standing closest, the one who really was Alison Kelly, screamed like it had been her who was on fire. He'd jumped slightly, perhaps even cried out as the scream had moved through him like a blade. He'd turned his head towards the noise then, and seen the flames reflected in the girl's eyes. They were dark brown and very wide, and the flames that were growing, that were climbing up the girl who was actually burning, seemed tiny, dancing in her friend's eyes in that second before he'd turned and run. He still remembered how small they had seemed, flickering against the dark brown. How far away.

As he'd rushed away down that steep hill, careering towards the car, that scream had followed him. He could feel the echo of it at his back, rolling down the hillside after him, all but knocking him off his feet as he went. Then the screams had grown, of course, louder and more hysterical, pushing him downhill even faster.

He'd stood still for just a second or two before jumping into the car, and he remembered that moment now vividly. Remembered the shortness of breath and the picture on the backs of his eyelids. He'd closed his eyes and the shape of the flames had still been there, imprinted. Gold and red edges bleeding into the blackness.

A snapshot of the flames. The ones he'd seen jumping in the eyes of the girl he'd been sent there to kill.

SEVENTEEN

'How did you get my number, anyway?' Thorne asked.

Alison Kelly put down her glass, tucked a strand of hair behind her ear. 'On your card?'

Thorne smiled and shook his head. Like everyone else on the job, he had a generic Metropolitan Police business card. It gave the address of Becke House, together with the phone and fax numbers at the office. It bore the legend 'Working for a safer London', printed in blue as a jaunty scribble. It left a space to write in mobile, pager or other numbers.

'I never write down my home phone number,' Thorne said. 'You didn't get it out of the phone book, either . . .'

She still wasn't giving anything away.

'You got my number the same way you found out everything else, right?'

They were sitting in a corner of the Spice of Life at Cambridge Circus. Alison nursed a large gin and tonic. Thorne was on the Guinness, and enjoying it. The lounge contained acres of red velvet, far too many brass rails and, inexplicably, was crammed with annoyingly healthy-looking Scandinavian tourists.

Thorne tore open a packet of crisps, grabbed a handful. 'I'm not going to get a straight answer, am I?'

'I was a gangster's daughter until I was fourteen,' she said. 'Then everything changed. *Everything*. Dad walked away from it all and took us and a great big bag of his tasteless "new" money with him. Spent the rest of his life playing golf and doing crosswords in his conservatory. A couple of years later, Billy and I were together, but once that marriage was over, I was completely out of it. I was out of the life, and that's how I wanted it. Gangland was just something Mum and I saw on the TV, and I was just a lowly legal secretary with a private-school accent and a pony. Now, I'm a slightly better-paid legal secretary with less of an accent and no pony. And I'm *still* out of it. But . . .'

'*But?*'

She grinned, picked up her drink. 'I've still got a few friends who are very much *in* it.' She drained her glass. 'We'll have a girls' night out a couple of times a year. You know the kind of thing – family-run restaurant, shed-loads of booze on the house, I complain about work and they complain about how long their husbands and boyfriends are getting sent down for.'

'Sounds like a fun evening . . .'

'One or two of them may or may not know certain police officers pretty well and can call in a favour if they're asked nicely. Getting a copper's phone number is hardly rocket science.'

'I *should* be shocked,' Thorne said, 'but I'm too busy thinking about another round.'

She picked up Thorne's empty glass and pushed back her chair. 'Another one of those . . .?'

For the next hour or so they talked about the difficulties of doing, or not doing, what was expected of you. It was soon obvious that this was something they both knew a great deal about.

Thorne told her that if he were the sort to do what was expected, or at the very least encouraged, he wouldn't be there drinking with her.

Alison told Thorne about her reluctance to do bugger all and sit on her arse spending her old man's money. She told him about upsetting her mother by refusing the offer to set her up in a business.

'Sounds like you were trying to distance yourself,' Thorne said. 'From the money. From everything that *made* the money. Like you blamed it for what happened to Jessica.'

Her pale complexion flushed a little. 'If my dad hadn't been who he was, *what* he was, then it wouldn't have happened. That's not a delusion . . .'

They both took a drink to fill the short pause that followed. By now, she'd moved on to white wine. Thorne had moved on to his next Guinness.

'Why did you marry Billy Ryan?' he asked.

She thought about it for a few seconds. Just rising above the buzz and burble of pub chat, the voices of the latest boy-band drifted through from the jukebox in the bar next door.

'It sounds like I'm joking,' she said, 'but it really did seem like a good idea at the time.'

'He must have been . . . what? Mid-thirties?'

'Older. And I was only eighteen.'

'So who the hell thought that was a "good idea"?'

She smiled. 'Not my mum, for a start. She thought the age difference was too big. I mean, Billy's son was only ten years younger than I was, for God's sake. But Dad was all for it. I think there were a few people who thought it was a good thing, you know, some of the old boys who'd been around a bit. Even though Dad had been out of it a few years by then, and Billy was running the show, some people thought it was a good way of . . . building bridges, or something. The old guard and the new guard.'

'You make it sound like it was arranged.'

She shook her head. 'I wish I had that as an excuse. I'd like to say I married him to make everybody else happy. And I knew that I *was*, to some extent. But the simple fact is that I loved him.' She paused, but looked as if she needed to say something else. She searched for the right words. 'He was impressive, back then.'

Thorne thought about the Billy Ryan he'd so recently encountered. There would be some who might still describe him as impressive, but lovable was not a word that sprang to mind. 'What went wrong?'

She took a good-sized slurp of wine. 'Nothing . . . for a while. I mean, I never really hit it off with Stephen, who was a right little sod even then, but he wasn't the problem. His old man was. There were two sides to Billy.'

Thorne nodded. He didn't know many people without at least a couple . . .

'There was part of him', she said, 'that just wanted to have fun. He liked to have friends over or go out to parties. He used to take me into all the clubs. He wanted to dress up and show off and hang around with actors and pop stars. People writing books. He loved all that . . .'

'I bet the actors and pop stars loved it as well.'

'When it was just the two of us, though, he could be a whole lot different. If it was just him and me and a bottle of something, he became somebody else, and I was on the receiving end. Maybe he was still having fun, I don't know . . .'

Thorne saw her eyes darken and knew what she meant. He remembered the feet, dainty inside highly polished shoes, but also Ryan's shoulders, powerful beneath the expensive blazer.

Two sides. The dancer and the boxer.

'It's a pretty good reason to leave someone,' he said.

'He was the one who left.'

'Right . . .'

'He said he couldn't cope with the problems I had. All the stuff with Jess I was still trying to deal with.'

Thorne had to fight to stop his mouth dropping open. *Problems? Stuff?* All of them, all of it, the result of what her husband had done.

Alison saw the look on Thorne's face, took it as no more than mild surprise. 'I did have some bloody awful mood swings, I know I did.

Billy wasn't exactly what you'd call supportive, though. He kept saying I was neurotic . . . that I needed help. He kept telling me that I hated myself, that I was impossible to live with, that I needed to get over what had happened when I was in that playground.'

When a man paid by Billy Ryan had come to her school to kill her. When flames had devoured her best friend in front of her eyes.

'No,' Thorne said. 'Not exactly supportive.'

She swirled around the last of her wine in the bottom of the glass. 'He was right about me needing help, of course, but I needed a damn sight more after a couple of years with Billy. I got through a bit of that money my mum had been offering then. Pissed a lot of it away paying strangers to listen. Any number of the buggers at fifty quid an hour.'

Thorne stared at her.

Her eyes widened when they met his. 'I'm all right now, though,' she said.

'That's good . . .'

As she downed her drink, she contorted her face into a series of deliberately comical twitches and tics. It wasn't particularly funny, but Thorne laughed anyway.

She put down the glass and reached for her handbag. 'Let's go and get something to eat . . .'

Rooker stared at a spider on the ceiling, wishing things were noisier. It was always noisy in prison, always. Even asleep, five hundred men could make a shitload of noise. During the day, it could be unbearable. The pounding of feet in corridors and on stairs, the clank of metal – buckets and keys, the slash and smash of voices echoing from cell to cell, from landing to landing. Even a tiny noise – a fork on a plate, a groan in the night – was magnified somehow and charged. It was like the anger floating around the place had done something to the air itself, made it easier for sound to move through it and carry. Distorted, deafening. It was something you got used to. It was something *Rooker* had got used to.

Here, though, it was like the bloody grave.

Even the relative peace of the VP wings he'd been on was like a cacophony compared to this. There, the shuffling nonces made noises all of their own. Same thing went for the old fuckers they got lumbered with. They always stuck the very old fellas on the VP wings. The stroke victims and the doolally ones, and the ones who had problems getting around. They were no trouble, most of them, but, Christ, once the lights went out, the hawking and the coughing would start, and he'd want to put pillows over all their pasty, lopsided faces.

He missed it now though. The silence was keeping him awake.

He allowed himself a smile. There would be plenty of noise in a few weeks when he was out – when it was all over and he was home, wherever that would be. There would be silence when *he* wanted it, and noises he hadn't heard in a very long time. Traffic, pubs, football crowds.

When it was all over . . .

The sessions with Thorne and the rest were wearing him out. Thorne especially had a way of digging at him, of pushing and pushing, until the effort of remembering and repeating it over and over again was like shovelling shit uphill. He knew it had to be done, that it would be worth it, but he'd forgotten quite how much he hated them. Even when you were supposed to be helping them, when you were supposed to be on the same side, the police were a pack of mongrels.

He felt a familiar flutter in his gut that was coming often now, whenever he thought about life on the outside. It was like a bubbling panic. He'd imagined being out for so long and now that it was within his reach he realised that it scared the living shit out of him. He'd known plenty of cons who'd done a lot less time than him and couldn't hack it on the outside. Most were fucked up on booze and drugs within a year. Others all but begged to be sent back to prison, and, eventually, they made sure they got what they wanted.

It wasn't going to be easy, he knew that, but at least with Ryan out of the way he would have a chance. He would have the time to adjust.

If he ever felt a moment's doubt, wondered about changing his mind and telling Thorne and the rest to stuff it, he just had to remember that night in Epping Forest, one of the last times he'd ever clapped eyes on Ryan. He just had to remember the look on Ryan's face.

Getting out scared him, but Billy Ryan scared him more.

Rooker turned on to his side to face the wall, wincing at the jolt of pain in his belly. It was still sore. On balance, he preferred the pain to the panic, but still, he decided that once he'd got out and away, once he'd let the dust settle, he'd do some ringing round. He'd call in a favour or two and get that shitbag Fisher sorted out.

Thorne looked across at the clock on his bedside table. 5.10 a.m. Only ten minutes later than the last time he'd looked.

He turned and watched Alison Kelly sleep.

She was dead to the world, and had barely stirred since she'd finally drifted off for the second time. Thorne knew he would have no such luck. He had scarcely blinked since being woken nearly three hours before by the sobbing.

He watched her sleep and thought about what he'd told her . . .

For a while, he'd been unable to get a word out of her. Every attempt at speech caught in her throat, was strangled by the heave of her chest that seemed to shake every inch of her. He'd held her until she'd calmed a little, then listened as it began to grow light outside, and the tears and snot dried on his arms and on his neck.

She'd asked some of the questions he'd already heard, and others he'd seen in her eyes when she'd spoken about her past. The whispers and the sobs had added a desperation he'd heard before only in the voices of the recently bereaved, or from the parents of missing children.

What could she have done differently?

Why did Jessica burn?

When was she ever going to stop feeling like she was burning herself?

So, Thorne had held on hard to her, and finally given her the only answer he had, hoping that it might serve as the answer for all of her questions.

The tears had stopped quickly after that, and she'd seemed to grow suddenly so tired that she couldn't even hold up her head. She'd dropped slowly down on to the pillow, her face turned away from him, and Thorne had no idea how long she'd lain staring at his bedroom wall. He'd known it would be wrong to ask, even in a whisper, if she was still awake . . .

Now, staring up at his cheap lampshade, he wasn't sure why he'd told her. Maybe it was what she'd said in the pub about Ryan. Maybe it was a simple desire in him to give something. Maybe it was a belief in the plain goodness of fact, in its power to smother the flames of doubt and guilt. Whatever the reason, it was done. Thorne knew he'd moved into strange territory and he wasn't at all sure how he felt about it.

Knowing that he would not get back to sleep, he eased himself to his feet and moved towards the door. Standing on Alison's side of the bed, he looked down at her face. He saw half of it, pale in a wedge of milky light bleeding into the room through a crack in the curtains. The other half was in darkness, where shadow lay across it like a scar.

6 June 1986

We all drove out to a country pub today. The weather was nice enough to sit outside, which was probably a good idea. It was crowded in the pub anyway and I didn't want to put anyone off their ploughman's lunch. I don't think I'm ever really going to be great with lots of people around.

Mum and Dad let me have half a lager, which was another very *good reason to be outside!*

There were lots of wasps buzzing around the food, which was pissing everyone off. I kept perfectly still, hoping that one might settle on me, settle on the scar. I wanted to know what it felt like, or even if I could feel it at all. But Dad was flapping his arms around and swearing and none of them came near me.

Dad had brought his new camera along and insisted on taking loads of pictures. We both smiled like always, like it was perfectly normal and I pretended that I was fine about it so Dad wouldn't be upset. Afterwards I made a joke about the woman at Boots getting a nasty shock when she developed the photos and Mum went a bit funny for a while.

Ali rang later to tell me she's got to dress up and help out at some swanky dinner party her parents are having. She says she's dreading it. She says there's probably going to be <u>several</u> hardened criminals sitting around trying to make polite conversation and eating Twiglets. That made me laugh and I wanted to tell someone, but Mum and <u>especially</u> Dad have still got a real problem with Ali and her family. I don't even tell them when me and Ali are meeting up outside school.

Shit Moment of the Day

In the pub garden, there was a family a few feet away from us, on one of those wooden tables with a bench attached on either side. They had a teenage boy with them, and a girl of four or five, and she stared at me for ages. I pulled faces at her. I rolled my eyes and stuck my tongue down behind my bottom lip. I kept trying to make her laugh, but she just looked frightened.

Magic Moment of the Day

I was in the kitchen after tea and we had the radio on. Mum was out in the garden having a fag, and Dad was drying up. The new Smiths single came on, and I was singing along. I was waving my arms around like Morrissey, wailing in a stupid high voice and messing around. When I got to the bit about knowing how Joan of Arc felt, Dad looked across at me with a tea towel in his hand. There was a pause and then we both just pissed ourselves laughing.

EIGHTEEN

If Thorne were to make a list of the places he least liked to be beside, the seaside would come fairly near the top. Admittedly, British seaside resorts were marginally less attractive than those slightly more glamorous ones in Australia say, or Florida, but even then, Thorne was far from keen. The sea might be warmer, bluer, *cleaner*, but it had its own drawbacks.

Margate or Miami? Rhyl or Rio? As far as Thorne was concerned it pretty much came down to a choice between shit and sharks . . .

Having said that, what he'd seen of Brighton so far that morning hadn't been too unpleasant. A ten-minute taxi ride from the station to Eileen's house. A five-minute walk from there to the pub.

Thorne's father, and his father's best friend Victor, had travelled down together from St Albans the day before. Victor had rung while Thorne was getting ready to go out and meet Alison Kelly. They'd arrived in one piece, Victor had told him. His father was excited, but fairly well behaved. He was looking forward to a weekend away.

Thorne had wanted to catch an earlier train, but getting himself together and out of the flat that morning had been complicated. Alison

215

had caught him looking at his watch as they'd shared breakfast in the kitchen, and it had only heightened the awkwardness that hung between them, heavy as the smell of burned toast.

What had been said in the early hours . . .

That was far harder to deal with, and certainly to talk about, than what they'd been doing to each other a few hours earlier. The sex had been snatched at and sweaty, the two of them equally needy, physically at least.

The morning did its job on them, muggy, thick-headed and cruel. It shone a fresh, harsh light on what was now unsayable.

Thorne belched, tasting last night's Guinness. Victor laughed. Eileen tried to look disapproving. His dad appeared not to have noticed.

'Sorry,' Thorne said. He knew that he was looking slightly rough, knew that Eileen could see it. 'I had a bit of a night . . .'

She sipped her tomato juice. 'That explains why you got here so late.'

By the time Thorne had reached his aunt's house and got a cup of tea down him, there'd been nothing left to do except head off for a quick drink before Sunday lunch.

'It won't be easy to get into a decent restaurant,' Eileen said. 'They'll all be full if we don't get a move on.'

Thorne said nothing. Eileen had been a life-saver since his dad's illness had kicked in, but she could be a bit prissy when she felt like it. He hoped she wasn't in that sort of mood.

'Beer or birds?' Jim Thorne said suddenly.

Thorne stared at his father. 'What?'

'Your "bit of a night". On the beer or on the birds?'

Thorne wasn't sure which was throwing him more, the question or the way it was couched.

'Maybe both,' Victor said. He grinned at Thorne's father and the two of them began to laugh.

Victor was probably the only friend that Thorne's father had left.

He was certainly the only one Thorne ever saw. He was taller and thicker-set than his father, especially now, as Jim Thorne was losing weight. He had much less hair, and false teeth that fitted badly, and the two old men together often reminded Thorne of some bizarre, over-the-hill double act.

'Maybe,' Thorne said.

His father leaned towards him. 'Always a good idea, I reckon. Get a few pints down you and even the ugly ones start to look . . . woss-name . . . the opposite of ugly?'

Victor supplied the word his friend was searching for. 'Pretty? Attractive?'

Jim Thorne nodded. 'Even the ugly ones start to look attractive.'

Thorne smiled. A bizarre double act: the straight man occasionally needing to provide a bit of help with the punchlines. He glanced across the table at Eileen, who shook her head and rolled her eyes. There wasn't too much wrong with her mood.

Victor raised his glass, as if proposing a toast. 'Beer goggles,' he said.

'The same goes for women, you know,' Eileen said. 'We can wear wine goggles.' She pointed towards Thorne's father. 'I reckon Maureen probably had a pair on the night she got together with you.'

Thorne watched his father. They hadn't talked much about his mother since her death. Almost never since the Alzheimer's. He wondered how the old man would react.

Jim Thorne nodded, enjoying it. 'I think you're probably right, love,' he said. 'Bloody strong ones an' all.' He raised his glass until it covered the bottom half of his face. 'I was stone-cold sober . . .'

Once the drink had been supped and the glass lowered, Thorne tried and failed to catch his father's eye. The old man's gaze was darting around all over the place.

The pub was old fashioned in the worst sense and half empty, probably as a result. They sat in a tiny bar – the sort of room that might once have been called a snug – around a rickety metal table near the door. The absence of anything like atmosphere was mostly due to the strip lighting. It buzzed above their heads, washing everything out. It made the place feel like a waiting room that smelled of beer.

Thorne knew why they'd chosen this particular pub: his father liked places that were brightly lit. He was forever wandering around his house turning all the lights on, even in the middle of the day. It might have been forgetfulness, but Thorne thought that the old man was simply trying to keep the darkness away, knowing it was creeping up on him and struggling to stay in the light, where he could see. Where he could still be seen . . .

'Who's for another one?' Victor asked.

Eileen shook her head, slid her empty glass away from her. 'If we want to get proper Sunday lunch somewhere . . .'

They began to gather their things together – bags, coats, hats. As Eileen, Victor and his father moved slowly, one by one towards the door, Thorne checked under the table to make sure no one had left anything behind.

He was wishing he was somewhere else. He was thinking about the case; about Rooker and Ryan and two men running for their lives through a dark wood. He was picturing Alison Kelly and Jessica Clarke; faces on his pillow and in a drawer beside his bed.

Beneath her chair, Thorne found Eileen's umbrella. He grabbed it and followed her to the door. Now he thought about it, perhaps a day out was a good idea. Feeling like a youngster being dragged around by three, slightly strange, grown-ups, might be just what he needed.

They walked towards the seafront. Thorne dragged his heels and stared at things he wasn't really interested in to avoid getting too far ahead of his father and the others.

Spring was a few days old but hadn't found its feet yet. It was grey – the type of day Thorne associated with the seaside. He couldn't help thinking that the picture would be complete if Eileen had a reason to put up her umbrella. This was, he knew, a little unfair on the city of Brighton. Expensive and deeply fashionable, with a thriving music scene and a reputation as the gay capital of Britain, it was hardly the typical coastal resort. Still, prejudice was prejudice, and, as far as Thorne was concerned, if you could buy rock with the name of a place running through it, he was happy to stay away.

As if to confirm his preconceptions, there were people 'sunbathing' on the beach. Several families were encamped on the pebbles, windbreaks flapping around them, the goosepimples visible from a hundred yards. Stubbornness, optimism, stupidity – you could call it what you liked. It seemed to Thorne as perfect an embodiment of Englishness as he'd seen in a while.

'Look at those daft sods,' Eileen said. 'In this weather!'

Thorne smiled. There were other things, of course, that were even more English . . .

'It's getting bloody cold, if you ask me.' Eileen pulled her coat tight to her chest. 'Ten or twelve degrees at most, I should think. Colder, with the wind-chill factor.'

The wind-chill factor. A concept oddly beloved of forecasters in recent years. Thorne wondered where it had come from, and if they used it in places where the wind-chill might actually *be* a factor . . .

'Well, here in Spitzbergen it's minus forty degrees, but with the wind-chill factor, *it's officially cold enough to freeze the bollocks off a zoo-full of brass monkeys . . .'*

They moved on, Thorne listening to his father witter on about how many years, how many workmen and how many thousand gallons of gold paint it had taken to complete the Royal Pavilion, until they reached the restaurant. Eileen put on her poshest voice to ask the waiter for a table. When they sat down, Thorne, who had already decided that he was going to pay for lunch, checked the prices. They all went for the three-course Sunday afternoon special. It wouldn't break the bank.

'This is nice,' Victor said.

Eileen nodded. 'I normally cook a big lunch for everyone on a Sunday, but Trevor and his wife are away and Bob's off playing golf, so I decided not to bother. Besides, it's a treat to go out, isn't it?'

219

Thorne grunted, thinking that, at less than a tenner a head, 'treat' might be putting it a bit strongly. 'Shame we won't see Trevor and Bob,' he said. Trevor was Eileen's son, and Thorne guessed that he probably hadn't gone anywhere. Lunch with barmy Uncle Jim wasn't exactly a tantalising prospect. It almost certainly explained husband Bob's game of golf, hastily arranged once he'd found out that the dotty brother-in-law and dotty brother-in-law's mate were coming down for the weekend . . .

'I know,' Eileen said. 'They both said how much they were looking forward to seeing you.'

Thorne suddenly felt enormously sorry for Eileen. For having to lie. For the shit she had to put up with from his father. For doing all that she did and getting nothing in return. Thorne couldn't remember if he'd ever really thanked her for anything. 'Maybe next time,' he said.

Eileen nodded towards Thorne's father. He was staring at the table, tapping the blunt end of a knife against his teeth. 'I think your dad's having a good time,' she said.

Victor reached across for the water jug. 'He's having a brilliant time, definitely.'

'Did we thank you for bringing him down?' she asked.

Victor beamed. 'It's fine, really. It's fun for us both to go on a bit of a jaunt.'

'Thank you anyway, though. I couldn't get up to fetch him down and he wouldn't have been able to get here without you . . . you know, keeping him company.'

'He's no trouble, honestly.'

Thorne knew that both of these people loved his father, that they sacrificed a great deal for him, but it still set his teeth on edge to hear them talk about him as if he were not there.

'He's trouble when he wants to be,' Eileen said.

Victor laughed and poured Jim Thorne a glass of water.

Thorne tuned out the conversation and looked away, searching to see if there was any sign of their first course. He felt a hand on his arm and saw that it belonged to his father.

'You look like you've got a lot on your mind, son,' the old man said.

Thorne nodded. In his mind a young girl's arms were thrashing, as she whirled across a playground, as she danced around a kitchen, as she tumbled through the air from the roof of a multi-storey car park . . .

Jim Thorne leaned in close and whispered, 'Sometimes, I think you've got it worse than I have.' He jabbed a finger into the side of his head. The hair at his temple was white, whereas his son's was grey. 'You want to try this, Tom. Can't recommend it highly enough. However bad you feel, however much it hurts to think about something, half an hour later and you can't remember fuck all. Just like that, *whoosh*, it's gone. Excellent. Goldfish brain . . .'

Thorne stared at his dad for a few seconds. He couldn't think of a single thing to say. He was rescued by a waitress who materialised at their table with four bowls of watery-looking soup.

'Four and three, forty-three . . .'

When Eileen had suggested bingo, Thorne had felt almost suicidal, and the enthusiasm of Victor and his father had done nothing to change his mood. They walked past what little was left of the West Pier, now all but derelict having caught fire with suspicious regularity. They carried on to Brighton Pier, formerly the Palace, but now renamed as it was the only functioning pier the city had left. Thorne sulked all the way there.

Bingo. It was right up there with karaoke and poking red-hot needles into your eyes . . .

'Two little ducks, twenty-two . . .'

Now that he was *playing*, though, the excitement of the game was getting to him. Even though the prizes on offer – an oversized teddy-bear and a giant, inflatable hammer – hardly justified his increased heart rate.

'On its own, number seven . . .'

'*Bingo!*'

The call came from an old woman sitting a few feet away. Thorne swore under his breath and sat back hard in his chair at the same time as everybody else. He slid back the blue plastic squares that had been covering all but two of his numbers.

He was sitting next but one to his father.

The old man leaned across Eileen and grinned. 'If you've got a hundred old women, how d'you make ninety-nine of 'em shout "fuck"?'

Thorne shook his head. 'Don't know.'

'Get the other one to shout "Bingo".'

Thorne had heard the joke before, but laughed anyway like he always did.

'How many numbers did you need?' Eileen asked.

'Just the two,' Thorne said.

'Imagine what it's like in a big hall. Tens of thousands of pounds they play for sometimes. More on a national game . . .'

Thorne decided immediately that he'd best not venture into one of those places. If the excitement was relative to the money up for grabs, he'd probably drop dead on the spot.

Where they were, in an arcade at the end of the pier, couldn't have been much different to one of the grand bingo halls that were still dotted around London. Most were former cinemas, but several still retained the grandeur of the Victorian music halls from which they'd been converted. Thorne and the others sat on uncomfortable moulded chairs around a small podium with the plastic grids in front of them, and slots into which to shove their pound coins. It was quick and easy. There was no cash to be won. It was bingo-lite.

'Your next full house in just one minute . . .' The caller's voice echoed through the cheap sound system.

Thorne looked up at him. He was stick-thin and balding. The huge microphone that was pressed against his mouth masked the bottom half of his face. The oversized sunglasses hid the rest of it. Shoddy as the set-up was, the concession to form in the shape of a frilly shirt and wilting bow-tie was something to be admired.

Thorne put his coin into the slot for the next game.

'Come along now, ladies and gents, only a few places left . . .'

Thorne looked around. There were no more than half a dozen people in the whole place. The bloke had more front than Brighton.

'Eyes down for your first number . . .'

Thorne leaned forward, fingers hovering, ready to flip back the plastic squares. A few feet to his right, he could hear that his father was still laughing at his 'bingo' joke. He saw Eileen lean over and whisper, then pick up a coin and push it into the slot for him.

'Five and six, fifty-six . . .'

Thorne's father began to laugh louder. The old woman who'd won the previous game shushed them and shook her head. There were increasingly loud mutterings and murmurs from Thorne's right. He turned at the same moment as Eileen reached for his hand and implored him for some help.

'Two and four,' his father shouted suddenly, 'your mother's a whore!'

Victor giggled, and Thorne saw the colour drain from Eileen's face. He reached across and took hold of his father's arm. 'Dad . . .'

'Three and six, cocks and pricks!'

Thorne stood up and stepped around the back of Eileen towards his father. He heard sniggering, then a voice of encouragement from somewhere behind him. 'Go on, mate, why don't you get up there and have a go?'

Thorne lowered his head until it was close to his father's. The look of excitement, of *glee*, that he saw on the old man's face made him catch his breath.

'Two fat ladies,' his father announced, 'I wouldn't fuck either of them!'

There was a whistle of feedback as the caller put down his microphone. Thorne was shocked to see that the man had no teeth and was at least twenty years older than he'd taken him for. From the corner of his eye, Thorne could see a man in a dark suit – the manager, he guessed – marching towards them with a walkie-talkie in his hand. Thorne knew he should compose himself, should prepare the usual excuses and explanations, but he was far too busy laughing.

The coffee he'd bought at Brighton station had gone cold. Thorne stared out of the carriage window into the blackness as the train moved far too slowly back towards London. He let his head drop back and closed his eyes, wondering why it was that he so rarely felt this tired in bed, when he should sleep.

He pictured his father and Victor, lying in twin beds in Eileen's spare room and talking about the day they'd had. Laughing about what had happened on the pier. In truth, he had no idea whether his father knew what he was doing at moments like that. Were they events he could objectively look back on and enjoy? Thorne hoped that they were, and imagined his father struggling to hold on to the memory of his bingo-calling exploits before it slipped away from him.

Whoosh, it's gone. Excellent. Goldfish brain . . .

Earlier in the day, Thorne had imagined himself as a child with a gaggle of eccentric adults. He knew of course that this was a momentary illusion, that in reality the reverse was true – that trying to look after his father was as close as he'd come, as close as he might *ever* come, to being a parent.

He didn't bother stifling an enormous yawn. When he'd finished, he caught the eye of a woman sitting opposite and smiled. She looked equally knackered and smiled back.

He'd heard plenty about parenting. From seasoned campaigners like Russell Brigstocke and Yvonne Kitson. From Dave Holland, who still had milky sick-stains on his lapels. Everything they'd told him seemed suddenly relevant to his situation . . .

Nobody could prepare you for it.

You never stopped learning.

There was no right way and no wrong way.

Thorne knew from talking to these people, from listening to their conversations, that there were times when you needed to come down hard. And times when you did, only to feel shitty later, when you realised that you'd got it wrong. Now, Thorne understood what they meant. Sometimes, though they might not like what their children were doing, or the effect that their behaviour was having on other people, it was important to accept that the child was simply having fun. He pictured the look on his father's face as he was shouting out obscenities . . .

Thorne wondered if it was too late to call Alison Kelly. He decided it probably was. Then he reached for his phone and dialled anyway.

'Hi, it's Tom. Hello . . .?'

'Hi . . .'

'Sorry if it's late. I was wondering how you were.'

'I'm tired.'

'Me too. It was quite a night.'

She laughed. 'Yes, it was, wasn't it?'

Thorne pictured her naked. Pictured her crying. Pictured her turned away from him, trying to take in what he'd said. 'I was wondering how you were about what I told you.'

Static crackled on the line. Thorne thought he'd lost the signal, looked at the screen on his phone.

'I'm fine about it,' she said finally. 'I'm . . .grateful.'

'I shouldn't have said anything.'

'You told me the truth . . .'

'You were upset . . .'

'I needed the truth. I *need* the truth.'

Thorne noticed the woman opposite turning her head away. He lowered his voice. 'Some truths are harder to handle than others.'

There was silence.

'Alison . . .?'

'I'm a big girl,' she said. Another laugh, humourless. 'At least *I* got to *be* a big girl . . .'

'Do you want to do it again? Go out?'

He heard a breath let out slowly. 'Why do I think you're just being nice?'

'No, really . . .'

'Let's give it a few days, shall we?' she said. 'See how we feel . . .'

Because of the darkness on the other side of the window, it took Thorne a few seconds to realise that they'd entered a tunnel. He checked the phone. This time he had lost the signal. He stared into space for a few minutes, then reached across the aisle for a newspaper that had been discarded on a table. He turned it over and began to read.

He was asleep before he'd finished the back page.

NINETEEN

The waitress slid a plate of perfectly arranged biscuits into the middle of the table. She picked up the empty tray and moved back, stopping at the door to cast a somewhat perplexed glance back towards the group of men and women gathered in the conference room.

It was certainly an odd collection . . .

Detective Chief Superintendent Trevor Jesmond cleared his throat noisily and waited for silence. 'Shall we get started, ladies and gentlemen . . .?' Tea and coffee were poured as Jesmond made the introductions.

There were seven people around the long, rectangular table. Jesmond was at the head, with a Turkish-speaking uniformed WPC adjacent to his right. Further down the same side of the table sat Memet Zarif, who was next to an elderly man, described as a well-respected Turkish community leader. Opposite them sat Stephen Ryan and a smartly dressed woman named Helen Brimson, introduced by Jesmond as the solicitor representing Ryan Properties. The last person to be introduced sat sweating beneath his leather jacket, a pen in his hand and a sheaf of paper in front of him.

'DI Thorne will be taking notes. Keeping minutes of the meeting . . .'

Helen Brimson sat forward and cut in: 'I presume these proceedings will be subject to a valid Public Interest Immunity Certificate?'

Jesmond nodded, and kept on nodding as she continued.

'I want it confirmed that any notes taken will form the basis of an internal police document *only*, that they will not be disclosed in open court should any action arise at a later date . . .'

Thorne scribbled without thinking, hoping that there wouldn't be too much more of this legal bullshit to wade through.

'This meeting is purely part of an ongoing process of community consultation,' Jesmond said. He held out his arms. 'I'm grateful that everyone has agreed to take part, and to come here this morning . . .'

'Here' was a bland and anonymous hotel just outside Maidenhead. A businessman's hotel, like any one of a hundred others around the M25. Easy enough to reach and far enough away from the spotlight.

This was what Tughan had been talking about a little over a week before – getting them around the table, trying to put an end to it.

Zarif placed a hand on the shoulder of the man next to him, the 'well-respected community leader'. The pair of them wore smart suits and tidy smiles. 'My brothers and I have been asked, through our good friend here, to assist the police in any way we can,' he said. 'I would like to think that we were already doing everything in our power to aid these investigations, but if there is anything else we can do, of course we shall be happy to do it.'

Jesmond nodded. Thorne scribbled. There was clearly going to be a *lot* of bullshit flying around.

'The same goes for myself,' Stephen Ryan said. A thick gold chain hung at his throat. A pricey suede jacket over the open-necked shirt. 'It goes for my father and for everyone connected with Ryan Properties. An important business meeting has meant that my father can't be here today, but he wanted me to stress his disgust at these killings . . .'

Thorne could barely believe his ears. He thought about Alison Kelly. It had been just over a week since their phone conversation on the train. There had been no contact between them since . . .

'. . . and his desire to prevent any further bloodshed.' Ryan looked along the table at Thorne. 'Are you going to write that down?'

Thorne thought, I'd like to take this pen and write something across your face, you smug little shitehawk.

He wrote: Ryan. Disgust. Desire.

Jesmond snapped a biscuit in half, careful to shake the crumbs on to the plate. 'I don't need to tell any of you that this is what we want to hear. But we need *action* if anything's going to change. If this bloodshed you refer to is really going to stop.'

'Of course,' Zarif said.

Ryan held up his hands: *Goes without saying.*

Jesmond put on his glasses, reached for a piece of paper and started to read the names printed on it. 'Anthony Wright. John Gildea. Sean Anderson. Michael Clayton. Muslum Izzigil. Hanya Izzigil. Detective Sergeant Marcus Moloney.' Jesmond paused there, looked around the table. 'Most recently, Francis Cullen, a long-distance lorry-driver and two as yet unidentified bodies found along with his.'

Thorne looked at Ryan, then at Zarif. Both wore serious expressions, suitably sombre in response to the roll-call of victims. Those they had lost. Those they had murdered.

'These are the deaths we know about,' Jesmond said. 'These are the murders we are currently investigating, all of which, to some degree, have involved your families or your businesses . . .'

Ryan's solicitor tried to cut in.

Jesmond held up a hand. 'Have, at the very least, *affected* your families or your businesses. Miss Brimson?'

'I have advised my client that, for the purposes of this meeting, he should say nothing in relation to any specific case on which you might ask him to comment.'

'Who's being specific?' Thorne asked.

He received an icy smile. '"Might", I said. *Might.*'

'I'll make sure I underline it,' Thorne said.

Zarif poured himself a second cup of coffee. 'It's a shame that this is your attitude, Mr Ryan. It is people's refusal to speak about these things, to get involved, that is so dangerous. It's what makes these murders possible.'

The old man next to him tugged at his beard, nodding enthusiastically.

'There are some in my community who are afraid to speak up,' Zarif said. He looked towards Jesmond. 'We had thought that those in Mr Ryan's . . . circle might be a little less fearful.'

Zarif was pressing all the right buttons. Ryan's anger was controlled but obvious.

For a long ten seconds no one spoke. Thorne listened to the sound of the cars on the nearby motorway, the rattle of a fan above one of the ceiling vents. The weather had taken a turn for the better in recent days and the room felt arid and airless.

'These killings, whoever and whatever the victims might have been, are simply unacceptable,' Jesmond said eventually. 'They hurt people across a wide range of communities. They hurt people and they hurt businesses . . .'

Thorne wrote, thinking, They hurt your chances of promotion . . .

Ryan smiled thinly. 'Sometimes they're the same thing.'

'I'm sorry?' Jesmond said.

'People and business.' Ryan leaned forward, looked hard at Zarif across the table. 'Sometimes, your business might actually *be* people. You know what I mean?'

Now it was Zarif's turn to exercise some control. He knew that Ryan was talking about the people smuggling, about the hijack. He turned to the old man next to him and muttered something in Turkish.

When Zarif had finished, the Turkish-speaking officer translated for Jesmond. 'There was some swearing,' she began.

Thorne looked at Zarif's face. He wasn't surprised . . .

'Mr Zarif said that some people should think a little about what they were saying before they opened their mouths . . . opened their *stupid* mouths.'

Thorne looked from Ryan to Zarif, in the vain hope that the two of them might clamber on to the table and get stuck into each other. Go on, he thought, Let's end it here and now . . .

Jesmond thanked the WPC. Thorne looked across and caught her eye. He'd forgotten her name. He knew that she was there to ensure that any incriminating statement could be noted, however inadmissible it would later prove to be. He knew there was fat chance of *anything* much that mattered being said by *anybody*. This was politics and pussyfooting. The whole seemingly pointless exercise was about what was *not* being said.

'We need to be united in our efforts,' Jesmond said. He looked around the table until he was satisfied that tempers were being held in check.

'There seems little point in continuing', Brimson said, 'if my client has to sit here and be insulted.'

Thorne glanced at her and Ryan. Their arms were touching, and he idly began to wonder if they might be sleeping together. He knew Brimson was only doing her job, but surely there had to be some other reason why the bile wasn't rising into her mouth. 'Would Mr Ryan prefer to sit *here* and be insulted?' he said.

Ryan didn't bother looking up. 'Fuck you, Thorne.'

Thorne turned innocently to Jesmond. 'Should I write that down . . .?'

'I want to get two messages across to you this morning,' Jesmond said. 'The first, and I want there to be no mistake about this, is that, as far as the murders I have already mentioned are concerned, we are *in no way* scaling down any of those investigations.'

'No way,' Thorne repeated.

Jesmond glanced at him, nodded. 'Some of you will already know this, but DI Thorne is one of the officers actively involved in seeking those responsible.'

Thorne was tempted to give a little wave.

'The second message is by way of a direct appeal.' Jesmond removed his glasses, slid them into his top pocket. 'We want this level of consultation to continue, for everyone's benefit. On behalf of the Commissioner, I'm appealing to you directly. We want you to use your influence. As businessmen. As important members of your communities. We want you to do whatever you can to prevent further loss of life.'

Thorne's pen moved across the paper. He was struggling to keep up with Jesmond's speech. He sat there, hot and headachey, fighting the urge to doodle.

Fifteen minutes later, the waitress knocked and entered. She asked if the biscuits needed replenishing, but the meeting was already starting to break up. Ryan and Zarif left a minute or two apart, each chatting animatedly with his adviser.

Jesmond gathered up his papers. 'How would you say that went, Tom?' He didn't wait for the answer, perhaps guessing that it would be a long time coming. 'I know. These kind of meetings are buggers to get right.' He snapped his briefcase shut. 'Let's just hope we get something out of it.'

With the possible exception of writer's cramp, Thorne doubted it . . .

Methodical in this, as she was in everything – up one aisle then down another, missing none of them out – Carol Chamberlain steered her way past a small logjam near the checkouts, and turned towards detergents, kitchen towels and toilet roll.

Jack appeared, grinning at the side of the trolley, and dropped large handfuls of shopping into it. 'Do we need dog food?' he asked.

Chamberlain nodded, then watched her husband head up the aisle and disappear round the corner. She moved on slowly, picking things off the shelves. Reach, drop, push. Methodical, but miles away . . .

'When we get Ryan, he's going to tell us who took his money twenty years ago and burned Jessica. He's going to give me a name.'

Thorne had made her a promise. He'd told her he was going to find the man who'd been responsible for what had happened twenty years before. He'd told her that he was going to put right her mistake.

He'd told her what he thought she wanted to hear.

That had been more than a fortnight ago, round at his flat, and she hadn't seen Thorne since. She hadn't spoken to him on the phone for almost as long. She knew he was busy, of course, knew that he had far better things to do than keep *her* up to date.

Reach, drop, push . . .

Her cold case from 1993, the murdered bookie, was going nowhere. There was nothing in it to get the blood fizzing in her veins. Nothing to distract her.

Naturally, it was how Jack preferred it. He relished the calm at the end of the day, the fact that she had nothing, of any shape or form, to bring home. He was happier now that she rarely needed to be away from home *at all*. She loved him fiercely, knew that he felt as he did only because he loved her just as much. She'd have been lost without him, helpless without the anchor of his concern. But, feeling as she felt now, as she'd felt since this had all begun, that anchor was starting to pull her down.

She wanted this to be over.

Reach, drop, push . . .

Tom Thorne was the man in whom she'd placed her hopes. She'd had no choice but to do so. Much as Chamberlain liked and respected him, she hated feeling beholden. Hated the fact that it was out of her hands.

Hated it.

She wanted to load up her trolley, pile it high with heavy bottles and tins, and charge, shouting, down the aisle. She wanted to watch the families and the shelf-stackers scatter as she ran at them. She wanted to hear the rattle of the trolley and the squawking of two-way radios as she burst past the tills and flattened the guards, and rushed at the plate-glass windows . . .

Jack came hurrying towards her, clutching cans of dog food to his chest. As soon as they'd tumbled noisily into the trolley, she reached out and slid her arm around his. They moved together towards the next aisle.

23 August 1986

The new Smiths album is awesome. It's got 'Bigmouth Strikes Again' on it and Dad still puts his head round the door if he hears it, and laughs when it gets to the 'Joan of Arc' line.

Ali's got a boyfriend! She met him at some club. I don't know when she went clubbing, or who she went with, but apparently this bloke just walked up to her and asked if she wanted a drink. I met him the other day and he seems nice enough, but when he said hello to me, like everything was normal, he kept looking at Ali, so she could see how 'sensitive' he was being, like he was checking to see what she thought of him.

I don't know if they've really <u>done anything</u> yet.

There's another bloke who she says she's got a big crush on as well. Ali has a crush on somebody different every week. This one's much older than she is, which is why she's so keen, if you ask me. Also, he used to work with her dad, which means that he's probably got a nickname like Ron 'The Butcher' or something. Ali always used to joke about trying it on with one of those blokes, one of her dad's friends. You know, flirting with them and saying, 'Is that a gun in your pocket, or are you just pleased to see me? Oh, it's a gun . . .'

There's another song on the album called 'I Know It's Over'.

I was listening to it on my headphones and there's a bit where Morrissey is singing about feeling soil falling over his head. Like that's how it feels when this relationship he's been in has finished, when he's been dumped or whatever. I was trying to imagine it. Like I'd been with someone and he'd finished with me. I was lying there with it on loud and my eyes closed, putting myself in that position. For a while, it made me feel deep and romantic, like some poet or something.

Then, suddenly, I started feeling angry and stupid and I couldn't stand to listen to it again. I always skip that track now. The words and the melody were making me cry, making me _want_ to cry, but the feelings weren't real. The emotion behind it was fake. I'd thought that pity from other people was painful enough, but when I start pitying myself, that's just about as bad as it gets.

I'm not likely to have a fucking relationship, that's the simple truth, and if by some miracle I did, you wouldn't need to be Mastermind to figure out why it might not work. Unless I got it together with some other Melt-Job, of course. You know, our eyes meet across a crowded plastic surgeon's waiting room . . .

No chance of that. Just because I look like I do, doesn't mean I have to fancy other people who look the same, does it?

Being dumped wouldn't make me sad. It would make me want to kill whoever I'd been having the relationship with for being such a wanker. Such a cowardly shithead.

I don't want to have a relationship anyway.

Reading all that back, it sounds _so_ pathetic. Like I'm some brat and I'm pretending that I want to be on my own because I'm really feeling so sorry for myself. I can't help how it sounds. I know what I think.

Shit Moment of the Day
Decided not to bother with this any more because it's stupid.
Magic Moment of the Day
Ditto.

TWENTY

'Tell me again about the meeting with Ryan. Tell me what he said that night in Epping Forest . . .'

Rooker was wreathed in cigarette smoke. His sigh blew a tunnel of boredom through the fug. 'Is there nothing else you could be doing?' he asked. 'It's not as though I'm suddenly going to remember something I haven't already told you, is it?'

Thorne stared at the tapes in the twin-cassette deck. Watched the red spools spinning. 'I don't know . . .'

'Not after twenty years. Do you not think I've had enough time to remember?'

'Or enough time to forget.'

'Oh for fuck's sake . . .'

It had been nearly a month now since the attack on the girl in Swiss Cottage. Nearly a month since the Powers That Be had agreed to take Gordon Rooker up on his offer to give evidence against Billy Ryan. Tughan had told Thorne the day before – the day of the round-table session in Maidenhead – that, all being well, Ryan was likely to be charged within a week or so.

The case was being carefully built on a number of fronts; many of the people connected with Rooker and Ryan back in 1984 had been sought out and questioned. Some were still in the game. Some had long since sloped off to the suburbs. Others had gone even further, to countries with better weather and more attractive tax systems. A few had talked, but not enough for Tughan and his team to feel confident.

Omerta, the Mafia called it: the code of silence. The foreign language and associations made it sound honourable, dignified even, but there was no honour or dignity in the lives of these people, hiding out in villas, mock-Spanish and otherwise, shitting themselves. Thorne would have liked to spend some time with a few of these old fuckers, these fossilised hardmen in Braintree and Benidorm. He wanted to slap their stupid, perma-tanned faces and press a picture of Jessica Clarke up close . . .

'Like I told you before,' Rooker said, 'I got the call from Harry Little and drove up to meet Ryan in Epping Forest. A track near Loughton . . .'

One way and another, Rooker's testimony was going to be key, and, as with all evidence from convicted criminals, it would not be hard to discredit. If it was given any credit in the first place.

Whatever happened, they had to be sure it was nailed down tight . . .

'You got into his car . . .' Thorne said.

'I got into his car.'

'What kind of car was it?'

Rooker looked up, stared at Thorne like he was mad. 'How the fuck should I know? It was dark. It was twenty years ago.'

Thorne sat back, like he'd proved a point. 'Details are important, Gordon. Ryan's defence team are going to slaughter you if you give them a chance. If you can't remember the car, maybe you can't really remember *exactly* what Ryan said. Maybe you were confused. Maybe you thought he was asking you to do something when he wasn't. You with me?'

'It might have been a Merc. One of those old ones with the big radiators.'

'Do you understand what I'm saying? This is why we have to do this.'

Rooker nodded, reluctantly. 'I wasn't confused,' he said.

The door opened and Thorne muttered his thanks as a guard stepped in with drinks. Tea for him. A can of cheap cola for Rooker. The guard closed the door behind him. The drinks were taken.

'This is warm,' Rooker said.

'When you got into his car, did Ryan come straight out and say what he wanted or did you talk about other stuff first?'

'He wasn't really the type to chat about the weather, you know? We might have talked about this and that for a couple of minutes, I suppose. People we both knew . . .'

'Harry Little?'

'Yeah, Harry. Other faces, what have you. I don't remember him beating around the bush for very long, though.'

'So, he asked if you'd be willing to kill Kevin Kelly's daughter, Alison?'

Rooker puffed out his cheeks, prepared to trot out the answers one more time. Thorne asked the question again . . .

'Yes.'

'In exchange for money that he would give you.'

'Yes.'

'How much? How much was he proposing to pay you to kill Alison Kelly?'

Rooker looked up quickly, stared at Thorne. A charge ran between them, flashed across the metal tabletop. Thorne realised, shocked, that this had not come up before.

Rooker seemed equally taken aback. 'I think it was about twelve grand . . .'

'You *think*? *About*?'

'It *was* twelve grand. Twelve thousand pounds.' He said something else, something about what that sort of money might be worth now.

Thorne had stopped listening. Now he knew what Alison Kelly's life had been worth. He was wondering whether he would have told her – the exact amount – had he known it on the night he'd started whispering truths to her in the dark. Thinking that he probably shouldn't have said anything at all . . .

'Did Ryan say why he wanted you to do this?'

'He was trying to get at Kevin Kelly, wasn't he?' Rooker said. 'He wanted him to take on the other firms. He wanted to take over . . .'

'I know all that. I'm not talking about that. Did he say why he was trying to do it by killing a child? You said yourself that it was extreme. That it was out of the ordinary.'

'Right. Which is why I walked away. But, beyond what I've already told you, I don't know anything else. Same with all the jobs I did back then. *Why* was never my business.'

Thorne took a slurp of tea. He opened his mouth to ask something else, but Rooker cut him off.

'How many more times do we have to do this?'

'This is probably the last time,' Thorne said. 'The last time *we* need to go over it, at any rate. I'm not saying there won't be further interviews with other officers . . .'

'Tell me about afterwards.'

'The trial?'

'*After* the trial. Tell me about what happens to me.'

It was Thorne's turn to sigh. This was an area which Rooker seemed keen to keep going over . . .

'I've told you,' Thorne said. 'I don't have any say in what happens, where you end up, any of that. There's a special department that takes care of that stuff.'

'I know, but you must have some idea. They'll presumably move me a good way away, right? Don't you reckon? A whole new identity, all that.'

'There are different . . . *levels* of witness protection. I think it's safe to say you'll probably be top level. To start with, at least . . .'

Rooker seemed pleased with what Thorne had told him. Then he thought of something else. 'Can I pick the name?' he asked.

'What?'

'My new name, my new identity. Can I choose it?'

'Got something special in mind, have you?'

'Not really.' He laughed, reached into his tobacco tin. 'Don't want to go through all this then end up with some twat's name, do I?'

Thorne felt something start to tighten in his chest. The cockiness that he'd first seen in Park Royal was back. Rooker was talking to him as if he were a mate, as if he were someone he liked and trusted. It made Thorne want to reach across the table and squeeze his flabby neck.

Thorne looked at his watch, bent his head to the recorder. 'Interview terminated at two-thirty-five p.m.' He jabbed at the button.

'Are we done, then?' Rooker asked.

Thorne nodded towards the recorder. 'We're done with *that*.' He leaned forward. 'What did it feel like, Gordon?'

'Come again . . .'

'When you killed someone for money. When you carried out a contract. I want you to tell me how it felt.'

Rooker continued to roll the cigarette, but slower, the yellowed fingers suddenly less dextrous than before. 'What's this got to do with anything?' he asked.

'We already know that *why* wasn't your business, so I was just wondering what *was*. Did you get job satisfaction? Did you take pride in your work?'

Rooker made no response.

'Did you *enjoy* it?'

Rooker looked up then, shook his head firmly. 'You enjoy getting the job done clean, that's all. Getting the money. If you start to enjoy the *doing*, if you start to get some sort of kick out of it, you're fucked.'

Thorne had to disagree. The X-Man clearly relished what he did, and he hadn't made too many mistakes yet.

'So what, then?' Thorne said. 'You just turn off? Go on to some sort of automatic pilot . . .?'

'You focus. Your mind goes blank . . . No, not blank exactly. It's like it's fuzzy, and there, right in the middle, is a point of light. It's really sharp and clear. Cold. You relax and stay calm and move towards that. That's the target, and you don't let anything take you away from it . . .'

'Like guilt or fear or remorse?'

'You asked me, so I'm telling you,' Rooker said. 'It's the job . . .'

'You talk about it in the present tense.'

Rooker put the completed cigarette into the tin. He snapped the lid back on. 'I'm still living with it.'

'A lot of people are still living with it,' Thorne said.

Phil Hendricks was doing some teaching at the Royal Free, and Thorne had arranged to meet him after work. He'd caught the train to Hampstead and they'd eaten at a Chinese place a stone's throw from the hospital. Afterwards, they'd crossed the road to the nearest pub and sunk a couple of pints each inside fifteen minutes. Neither had said a great deal until the edges had been taken off . . .

'Don't let Rooker wind you up,' Hendricks said. 'He's trying to make it sound like some fucking Zen mind-control thing. He just killed people. There's no more to it than that.'

'I wasn't in the mood for him, that's all.' Thorne smiled, raised his glass. 'Just one of those days . . .'

One of those days that seemed to roll around every month or so. When, for no good reason, Thorne stopped and caught himself. When he saw what he did, looked at the people he was dealing with every hour of his life. When, after ticking along for weeks, doing the job without thinking, he was suddenly struck by the stench and blackness of it all. It was like waking up briefly only to find that real life was far worse than the nightmare.

Thorne decided that in some ways, when things became extreme, his own life was similar to his father's. There were times when he heard himself saying things – to killers, and to their victims – that were every bit as bizarre, in their way, as anything that his father ever said.

'Six and nine,' Thorne said, grinning at Hendricks. 'Your face or mine?'

It had become a running joke between them since Thorne had told him about what had happened in Brighton: they had been exchanging filthy bingo calls by phone and text message all week.

Hendricks got up to fetch another round. He grabbed his crotch, sniffed his hand as he turned towards the bar. 'All the threes, I smell cheese . . .'

Thorne looked around. The place was busy, considering that it was only a Tuesday night. It's proximity to the hospital meant that the place was probably full of medics. Thorne knew very well that many of them would have their own edges to take off . . .

He was trying, and failing, to think up another bingo call when a fresh pint was plonked on the table in front of him.

'You know that the body loses weight after death?' Hendricks said.

'This sounds good . . .'

Hendricks sat down, drew his chair closer to the table. 'Seriously. You weigh a bit less dead than you did when you were alive and kicking.'

Thorne picked up his glass. 'It's a bit drastic, don't you think? As diets go . . .'

'Shut up and you might learn something. You can lose anything from a fraction of a gram upwards. Sixteen grams or thereabouts is the average.' Hendricks shook his head, took a sip of lager. 'The students I was talking to today looked about as interested as you do.'

'Go on then, what causes it?'

'No one's a hundred per cent sure. The air in the lungs, probably. But, this is the good bit . . .'

'Oh, there's a good bit, is there?'

'People used to think it was the weight of the soul.'

The phrase rang in Thorne's head. He nodded. Waited to hear more.

'In the eighteenth century they constructed elaborate scales, designed to weigh terminally ill patients in the moments just before and just after death.' Hendricks let the words sink in, relishing his tale. 'It was a big deal back then – trying to measure the soul's weight as it left the body. Trying to isolate it. They were still doing similar things in America in the early 1900s, and there was a famous experiment in Germany just twenty-five years ago . . .'

Thorne was amazed. A century or more ago and it was easy to put such a theory down to lunatics in fancy dress, to mumbo-jumbo masquerading as science. But *twenty-five* years ago?

'But it's just the air in the lungs, right?'

'That's the best guess,' Hendricks said. 'Unless you go for the soul theory . . .'

Thorne smiled across the head of his beer. 'Did you start drinking before you finished work, or what?'

They drank in silence for a minute or more. Thorne was beginning to feel light-headed. He'd only had a couple of drinks and knew it was tiredness more than anything.

There were pictures forming, dissolving and forming again in Thorne's head. Bodies and scales. Men in wigs and duster coats loading vast weights on to wooden beams. Monitoring the death throes of the wheezing, whey-faced dying, and scratching figures into notebooks. Eyes wide, raised up from inky calculations and then higher, far beyond their primitive laboratories . . .

Thorne looked across at Hendricks. It was clear from the grin, and the faraway expression, that his friend had gone back to thinking about numbers, and rhymes and dirty jokes.

Hampstead Heath was only a couple of stops on the overground from Kentish Town West. They were walking towards the station when Thorne's mobile rang.

243

'Tom . . .?'

Thorne looked at Hendricks, raised his eyebrows. 'Bloody hell, Carol, it's a bit late for you, isn't it?'

'I know, sorry. I couldn't sleep.'

'You haven't had any more calls, have you?'

'No, nothing like that . . .'

A huge lorry roared past and Thorne lost whatever Chamberlain said next. There was a pause while each of them waited for the other to say something.

'I just called to see how you were getting on.'

'I'm OK, Carol . . .'

'That's good . . .'

'*Everything's* OK. The case is more or less where it was the last time I spoke to you, but it's coming together.' He'd known straight away of course, that this was what she really wanted to know. 'I'm sorry,' he said. 'I meant to call.'

'Don't be daft. I know you must be busy. Listen, I'll leave you to it . . .'

'How's Jack?'

'He's fine. It's fine, Tom . . .'

Hendricks pointed to his watch: the last train was due in a few minutes.

Thorne nodded, picked up speed. 'Why don't we meet up next week?' he said. 'Come down and we'll go for lunch. I'll whack it on expenses.'

'Sounds great. I'll speak to you next week, then . . .'

'Take care, Carol. Phil says hello . . .'

She'd already gone.

At the station, they sat on a bench, waiting for the westbound train. On the other side of the tracks, three teenage boys drifted aimlessly up and down the platform.

'Sixteen grams on average, you said?'

Hendricks looked blank for a moment or two, then nodded.

'Yeah . . .'

'That's for what? A man of medium height and weight?'

'Right. A woman of medium build would be around twelve grams, I suppose.'

So, a child would be less, Thorne thought. Three quarters as much, maybe eight or nine grams. That didn't make sense, though, did it? Thorne's head was starting to spin. Surely the soul of a child would weigh *more*. It's only as we grow older that we become corrupted, soulless . . .

Eight or nine grams.

Their train rumbled into the station. Thorne spoke over the noise of it, to himself as much as Hendricks.

'A handful of rice,' he said. 'Christ, no . . . *less*. A few grains . . .'

TWENTY-ONE

3 November 1986

If another person leers at me and winks or says something moronic like 'soon be legal', I might have to do something drastic. It's like they're really saying 'as soon as you're sixteen, you can have sex, you know, which is absolutely normal'. I feel like grabbing them by the wrists and saying, 'Thanks a million, I hadn't realised that. All I need now is to find someone who's desperate enough and a big fucking bag to go over my head.'

Why do people presume I'm <u>interested</u>?

Why do people <u>always</u> presume?

I've been frantic for days, wondering how to tell M & D that I'd rather die than go to this party they've been so busy planning for tomorrow. First birthday since the recovery, since the final op. It's like it's such a big deal and I know they just want me to have a good time and do normal things and I can't make them understand.

I don't want a party. I don't want the attention. The falseness of all that.

When I get angry they just fucking smile at me. They indulge me <u>all</u>

the time and it makes me want to scream and smash something. While Ali and the others would be getting grounded or whatever, I get treated with kid gloves.

Like all of me's scarred. Like none of me can be touched.

I want to be shouted at and punished. I want to tell them to stick their party up their arses just to see them lose their tempers for once and tell me that the whole thing's off. Whenever I do start being a bitch, they just stare at each other and they have this look that kills me, as if they're thinking that this behaviour's acceptable and should be forgiven. You know, black clothes and black moods, like it's all perfectly normal for your average, horribly disfigured teenage girl.

When I try to tell them how I feel about this birthday, I know they think it's just some trauma I'm having, some understandable reaction after everything I've been through, and that I don't really mean it.

I do really mean it.

This party, just the thought of it, makes me sweat and makes me ache. Nobody has a clue. Even Ali doesn't seem to get what I'm talking about. She keeps telling me that it'll be a laugh, that I'm just being a stroppy cow, and asking me if there's going to be any tasty men there.

I know M & D have probably spent a fortune on hiring the hall and the disco and everything, and I love them to death for doing it. If I thought for a second that I could get through it, I wouldn't be making a fuss. Watching my mates dance and drink and get off with people sounds great, but I know bloody well what would happen.

I know that, eventually, someone would want to say something.

I've imagined it for weeks now, ever since they told me. Ever since they announced that they wanted to throw a party and looked a bit upset when I told them to throw it as far away from me as possible. Sometimes I imagine it's Dad and other times it's one of my friends, usually Ali. The music stops and there's this howl from the speakers as they grab the DJ's microphone. They start to make this speech. They say something about bravery and make some crap jokes and people

247

pretend to find them funny. Then there's that awkward few seconds of silence that you get after a speech. Then they all start to clap and everyone stares.

Everyone. Stares.

And the pale half of my face, the smooth half, reddens until the blush becomes the colour of the scar. Both halves matching as I burn all over again.

Singing 'Happy Birthday', and Mum and Dad are hugging each other and a few of my mates are crying, and they're all watching me standing in a circle of light in the centre of the room, with looks on their faces like I'm six years old.

Like I'm <u>*special*</u> *. . .*

Thorne closed the diary, lay back and pressed it to his chest. He opened it again, took out the photograph he'd been using as a bookmark. Pictured her slipping away into the darkness on a bleak November night.

The music, a Wham track, fading behind her as she walks away from the hall, from the party, moving towards the lights of the town centre.

Unmissed still. Her friends dancing, shouting to one another above the music while she climbs.

The smell of exhaust fumes and the sound of her shoes echoing off the grey concrete stairwells.

A voice of concern, the first few worried looks from her friends as, half a mile from them, she steps out into the cold. Into fresh air. The desperate rush of the black towards her. The night kissing both sides of her face as she tumbles through it . . .

Thorne jumped slightly when the phone rang, the sudden movement sending Elvis careering from the end of the bed. Thorne looked at the clock: 4.35.

Brigstocke wasted no time on pleasantries. 'We're getting reports of an incident at an address in Finchley . . .'

Thorne was already out of bed. 'Ryan's place?' he said.

'Right. Uniform are on the scene, but there's some confusion. At least one person injured, by all accounts, but beyond that we don't know much.'

'Zarif sent the X-Man after Ryan, you think?'

'You know as much as I do, mate . . .'

Thorne was moving quickly around the bedroom, snatching up socks and underpants, grabbing at a shirt. 'Are you on your way up there?'

'Tughan's got it,' Brigstocke said, 'but you live a lot nearer than he does, so I reckon you'll probably beat him to it.'

'Cheers, Russell. I'll call you when I get there . . .'

Thorne moved into the living room to find that Hendricks was already sitting up in bed. Thorne told him what was happening.

'Want me to come along?' Hendricks asked.

Thorne had gone into the kitchen. He came out shaking his head, gulping down a glass of water.

'You sure? I can be dressed in one minute . . .'

Thorne picked up his jacket, felt in the pockets for his keys. 'No point. We don't know exactly what's happened yet,' he said. 'But I wouldn't bother going back to sleep, if I was you . . .'

The streets were all but deserted as Thorne drove up towards the Archway roundabout and turned north. He knew he might be over the limit to drive, but he felt clear-headed and focused. He was seeing the tail-lights early, anticipating the few cars that were coming at him from side-streets. Thinking a long way ahead.

He chose the route through Highgate, avoiding the road that ran parallel, that would have taken him under Suicide Bridge. The iron footbridge that had long since replaced John Nash's viaduct – the original 'Archway' – was the preferred jumping-off point for many of the city's depressed. Thorne did his best to avoid it when he could, unable to drive beneath it without unconsciously bracing himself for the impact of a body on the roof of the car.

Tonight, he was in a hurry, but with the pages of a dog-eared diary still dancing in front of his eyes, he would have done almost anything to avoid the bridge.

His mobile rang again as the car flashed across a red light and on to the North Circular. Thorne checked the display, saw 'Holland Mob' flashing . . .

'I know,' he said. 'I'm on my way to Ryan's place now.'

Holland laughed. 'I'll see you there . . .'

If the Zarifs had hit Ryan, there was no way of knowing how things would pan out. Thorne guessed that Stephen would take up the reins, and he didn't seem the sort to forgive and forget. Then again, from what Thorne had seen, there might be nothing to Billy's son and heir *except* a temper. He might go to pieces, leaving Ryan Properties to implode and the Zarifs with new possibilities for expansion. The whole messy business might have started out as a reaction to Ryan's firm moving into their territory, but Thorne couldn't believe that Memet and his brothers would have gone to all the trouble they had without wanting something substantial out of it. Whichever way things went, there were likely to be big changes ahead. *Messy* changes . . .

Thorne reached the Finchley conservation area within fifteen minutes. He swung the BMW hard around the green and recalled his encounter there with Billy Ryan a fortnight before. He didn't know what he was going to find when he reached Ryan's house, but something told him that somebody else was going to be walking the dog for a while.

It was a three-storey detached house at one corner of the green. There were two squad cars parked outside, but no sign of an ambulance. Thorne showed his warrant card to the PC at the door and stepped inside. He was looking at the trail of blood that snaked along the hall carpet when a second uniformed officer appeared in front of him.

'I'm DI Thorne. Where's the ambulance?'

'It came and went away empty, sir. The victim was already dead when they arrived. Dead when they were called, if you ask me . . .'

Thorne wondered if Hendricks had got himself dressed yet. 'Where?'

The officer pointed to a doorway down the hall.

Thorne moved towards it, wishing he'd taken some gloves from his boot. 'Any ID?'

'Yes, sir. According to Mrs Ryan, the dead man is her husband, William John Ryan.'

Thorne stepped carefully around the bloodstains that grew bigger as he neared the doorway. The door was ajar. He nudged it all the way open with his shoe.

Ryan was on the kitchen floor, curled close into a corner, one hairy forearm streaked with red and propped up oddly against a cupboard. His white shirt was sopping – dark patches soaking through the silk at the shoulder and beneath the arm. The good-sized gash in his neck still wept a little blood, the lines of grout running red between the terra-cotta floor-tiles.

You didn't need a medical degree . . .

Thorne was aware that the uniform had joined him at the door. He glanced at him, then looked back to Billy Ryan. 'So, what's the story?' he asked.

'The story's a bloody odd one. She just walked in and stuck a knife in him, by all accounts. Over and over again.'

Thorne swung around, stunned. 'His *wife* killed him?'

'No, sir. Not his wife.' The uniform turned, nodded towards the doorway from which he'd first appeared. 'The other woman . . .'

Thorne pushed past him, moved down the corridor without a word. He could feel the breath rushing from his lungs, could hear a noise that grew louder in his head, like wasps trapped beneath a cup. He knew what he was going to see . . .

The two officers sitting on the sofa stood up, their faces grim-set, when Thorne entered the living room. The woman, handcuffed to one

251

of them at the wrist, had little choice but to rise with him. A WPC on the other side of her stared at Thorne, waiting, her hand clasped tight around Alison Kelly's elbow.

Thorne opened his mouth to speak, then closed it. There was nothing he could think of to say. Alison looked at him for a second or two.

He was sure she gave him a small nod before she lowered her head.

APRIL

IMMORTAL SKIN

TWENTY-TWO

A couple of years before, while driving to work early one morning, Thorne had been shaken by the sight of a horse-drawn hearse coming at him out of the mist. He'd pulled over and stared as the thing had rattled by. The breath of the horses had hung in front of their soft mouths like smoke before drifting back through the black feathers of their plumes.

The genuine spookiness of that moment came back to Thorne now as he watched the undertakers slide the coffin from an almost identical glass-sided carriage. If there was one person he would not wish to be haunted by, it was Billy Ryan.

St Pancras Cemetery was the largest in London. While not as well known as Highgate or Kensal Green, and with fewer grand monuments or famous residents, it was nevertheless an impressive and atmospheric place. Thorne watched as the pall-bearers hefted the coffin on to their shoulders and began to move slowly away from the main avenue. The vast acreage, shared with Islington Cemetery, stood on the site of the notorious Finchley Common, once the killing ground of highwaymen Dick Turpin and Jack Sheppard. It was an appropriate place, too, Thorne decided, for Billy Ryan to go into the ground and rot.

The hearse could go no further. The beautifully tended beds near the cemetery entrance had given way quickly to overgrown woodland that in places was virtually impenetrable. The elegant displays of daffodils, tulips and pansies had been replaced by nettles, brambles and a jungle of ivy that crept across the doorways of burial chambers and grasped the stone wings of smiling angels.

'Pardon me, sir . . .'

Thorne stepped aside to let one of the funeral directors pass. He and three others beside him were hurrying to catch up with their colleagues. They each carried vast floral tributes: crosses, wreaths, arrangements that spelled out 'DAD' and 'BILLY'. Dozens more were already being lined up at the roadside. A great day for Interflora . . .

Thorne had glanced at the noticeboard near the entrance as the procession had swung in through the main gates. There were half a dozen other funerals taking place that morning. Three were listed as being for babies, with the words 'No Mourners' handwritten beneath their typed entries on the timetable.

The Ryan bash was definitely the main event.

Times had certainly changed for the Ryan family and those like them. There was still a profit in vice and gambling, but the big money was in drugs. It was a dirty business in every sense and had only got dirtier since Johnny Foreigner had moved in and dared to stake a claim. The rule-book had been well and truly torn up, but, though the good old gorblimey days when you could leave your door open in the East End and villains 'only killed their own' were long gone, some things remained the same.

They still loved their mums and they still loved an honest-to-goodness, old-fashioned funeral: curly sandwiches and warm beer and well-worn tales of plod, porridge and pulling teeth for fun and profit.

The brown moss was damp and springy underfoot as the cortège made its way towards the centre of the cemetery. The crowd had thinned out. Only close family, friends and certain police officers would be present at graveside. Thorne looked at these people with whom he had spent the best part of the day: sniffing through the moving tributes in the church; processing slowly through Finchley; muttering about how pleased Billy would have been with the turnout.

Thorne had watched from inside the dark, unmarked Rover at the back of the line. He'd stared as pedestrians had bowed their heads or tipped their hats, unaware to whom they were showing respect. Thorne had found it funny. Respect was, after all, very important to a certain type of businessman . . .

Those carrying Billy Ryan's body moved awkwardly along the narrow grove, struggling to retain the necessary degrees of dignity and balance as they stepped across gnarled roots and around leaning headstones. One of their number walked two steps ahead of the coffin to push aside overhanging branches. The mourners followed gingerly, in single file.

Thorne was not the only police officer present. Tughan was a little way ahead of him, and a fair number of SO7 boys were knocking around somewhere. Thorne recognised plenty of other faces, too. These were a little harder, the eyes that bit colder. He wondered how many mourners were carrying weapons; how many years the pall-bearers had done between them. He wondered whether the killer of Muslum and Hanya Izzigil might be the man next to him.

It occurred to Thorne that, with the exception of the vicar and the blokes in the black hats, there were probably no men there without either a warrant card or a criminal record. Come to think of it, even the vicar looked dodgy . . .

They rounded a corner and the track widened out towards a freshly prepared grave. A green cloth lay all around the hole, garish against the clay. It was a decent-sized plot, expensive, with room for a fitting memorial. More flowers were already laid out, waiting. There were a few recently filled graves here, among many that were far older, the gleaming black headstones and brightly coloured marble chippings incongruous next to the weathered stones. The epitaphs were gold-edged and vulgar alongside the faded names that belonged to another age: Maud, Florence, Septimus . . .

The vicar spoke to begin the service:

'Oh God . . .'

It pretty much summed up the way Thorne felt.

On the far side of the grave Stephen Ryan was clutching his mother's arm. His eyes were bloodshot; whether from cocaine or grief, it was hard for Thorne to tell. The eyes flashed Thorne a look, intense and loaded, but impossible to read.

Thank you for coming . . .

What am I supposed to do now . . .?

What the fuck do you think you're doing here . . .?

Get ready . . .

Thorne looked from the son to the mother. Ryan's wife stared, unblinking, at the coffin. Thorne had not had the pleasure. He remembered something Tughan had told him, and if the rumours were to be believed, any number of gardeners and personal trainers certainly *had*. The botox and plastic tits had clearly been doing the trick, and now she'd have much more money to spend on keeping herself desirable. When she raised her eyes towards him and then higher to the trees beyond, Thorne could see that they were dark and dry beneath the heavy make-up.

The vicar droned on, the occasional word lost to the caw of a crow or the rumble of a passing plane.

Thorne wondered if Billy Ryan had kept those old boxing skills sharp by practising them on the second wife as well as the first. It was, he decided, highly probable. Either way, the fucker had finally been made to pay for everything he'd done to Alison Kelly.

But had he *really* paid for Jessica Clarke?

Thorne stared at the widow and the heir as the coffin was lowered into the grave. He couldn't be sure, but Ryan's wife looked like she just wanted to be certain he was never coming out. Stephen began to sob, and Thorne realised that *he'd* been holding on to his mother for support, not vice versa.

When various armed robbers began stepping forward to sprinkle dirt on to the coffin lid, Thorne decided it was about time to move in the opposite direction. He turned and walked slowly back along the rough, narrow track towards the main avenue. As he did, he read the headstones, in the same way that it was impossible not to look through a lighted window as you wandered along a street. Many of those resident beneath his feet seemed to have 'fallen asleep', which struck him now as always as childish and silly. But it was perhaps understandable that there were nearly as many euphemisms here as there were bodies. 'Passed into rest' and 'gone to a better place' were, even Thorne had to admit, marginally more acceptable than 'hit by a truck' or 'fallen down a lift shaft'. Certainly better than 'knifed several times in his hallway, then again in his kitchen'.

Thorne emerged on to the wide road that ran down to the cemetery gates. He stopped by the hearse to rub the muzzle of one of the horses. A shiver ran down the animal's flank before it whinnied, and released a series of turds which splattered on to the tarmac.

One bad memory well and truly exorcised . . .

Moving along the line of cars, Thorne walked past a number of serious-looking characters in long black coats, many of whom he knew to have written best-selling true-crime memoirs. They were doubtless greatly honoured to be policing Billy's service. Security, along with a healthy smattering of soap stars and minor sporting figures, was a prerequisite of the traditional gangland funeral.

Thorne stopped next to a large, metal litter-bin. It was overflowing with plastic bags, plant pots and dead flowers. Leaning against it was someone he hadn't expected to see. 'Is there really any point you being here?' Thorne asked.

Ian Clarke was clutching a large wreath of white lilies. He was wearing jeans and a dark blue jacket over a brown polo shirt. He clearly found Thorne's question highly amusing. 'No point whatsoever,' he said. 'I went to Kevin Kelly's funeral, too. It was the least I could do . . .'

Thorne found himself wondering if Clarke could possibly know about Ryan's part in what had happened to his daughter. He dismissed the thought, wondered instead if he should tell him. That idea was sent packing even quicker. If he hadn't opened his mouth once already, they wouldn't be standing in a cemetery at all.

He looked over towards the gatehouse. A gardener was moving slowly around the edge of a flower bed. One hand manoeuvred a strimmer, the other pressed a mobile phone to his ear.

When Ian Clarke began to speak, it was so quietly, and with such an absence of emotion, that it took Thorne a few seconds before he realised that he wasn't talking to himself. Once he'd begun to listen, Thorne could tell that he might just as well have been.

'It's the few days just after the burn that are the worst. Not just . . . emotionally, but that's when all the real damage gets done, the *peak* damage. The progression of the injury can be ten times worse than the burn itself. Did you know that? That's what really causes the scarring . . .

'She couldn't open her eyes or her mouth after it happened. She couldn't bite. The screaming came out through her teeth, like a sound I'd never heard before. Like a noise that was bleeding out through what was left of her skin. There was a lot of screaming in those first few days.

'She had to wear a mask, a clear mask to keep a steady pressure on the damaged skin. It's basically to reduce the final height of the scars. To keep them supple. Over a year she wore that hideous bloody thing. Over a year, she wore it and hated it for twenty-three hours a day. Pointless in the end, though, because it hadn't been fitted properly and the damage had already been done. She had to keep still, you see, utterly still, absolutely fucking motionless while they put Vaseline across her face, and then this jelly stuff. She couldn't move a muscle while it set . . .

'I could have let them anaesthetise her. *Should* have done. I didn't want her to have another operation, though. You understand? She'd already had six skin grafts and twenty-five blood transfusions by then. Some of the junior doctors used to joke, you know? They used to say she spent more time in the bloody hospital than *they* did.

'That mask I was talking about, the pressure mask, they do it all with lasers now, you know. They scan the face with these lasers and it's always a perfect fit. No doctors or parents to mess it up. The treatment of burns is so much better now than it was then. Everything's moved on. Now they use hyperbaric oxygen therapy to reduce the scarring in the early days. Amazing things, new techniques, new discoveries all the time: microdermabrasion, laser skin resurfacing, chemical peeling, you name it. There are sites I've got bookmarked on the computer at home, you know? Medical newsgroups, chatrooms you can join. You can find just about anything on the Internet if you're interested enough, or nerdy enough, depending on how you want to look at it, and you've got the time. I'm quite the expert on all the new developments.

'These are good days to get burned . . .

'The grafts are amazing now, really amazing. Single-sheet grafts, that's what's really made the difference. Back in our day, they only did split-skin grafts. You understand what I'm saying? They took shavings from different areas and it was virtually impossible to stop it contracting. To stop the scar tissue tightening. Now, they've got artificial skin which they can use for temporary grafting. It's amazing stuff, you know? Made from shark skin and silicon. Back then . . . God, listen to me, talking as if it was a hundred bloody years ago . . . *Back then*, they used cadaver grafts. Just the name makes you go a bit funny, doesn't it? Skin harvested from the dead.

'Skin from corpses. On my girl's neck. Lying across her face . . .

'They can even grow skin in labs now. They can *grow* it. Skin that's as near as damn it the same as the stuff we were born with. It's as thick as human skin, that's the real step forward. They call it "immortal skin". "Immortal" because the cells never stop growing. *Ever*. Did you know that there's only one naturally occurring human cell in which immortality is considered normal? Do you want to guess? It's the cancer cell . . .'

'Now, they've got immortal skin . . .'

Finally, he paused.

Thorne took half a step towards him. 'Ian . . .'

'Bad guys have scars. Monsters and murderers in films and on TV. The Phantom of the fucking Opera and the Joker and Freddie Krueger.'

'Maybe we've moved on from that kind of rubbish, too,' Thorne said.

If Clarke heard what Thorne had said, he chose to ignore it. 'It's like wearing a mask you can never take off,' he said. 'Jess wrote that in her diary.'

'I read it . . .'

Clarke looked up, his eyes bright, his voice suddenly cracked and raw. 'What she said about the party? You remember what she wrote that last day, about the speech someone was going to make on her birthday? It was exactly what I was planning to do. *Exactly*. Even down to the crap jokes . . .'

Thorne found it hard to meet the man's gaze, as he had that day in the house off Wandsworth Common. He dropped his eyes slowly to the ground. Down past the fists that had tightened around the edge of the wreath, the knuckles white as the petals that had fallen at Ian Clarke's feet.

TWENTY-THREE

'I think you're an idiot, Tom.'

'Cheers. Thanks for that . . .'

'I think you're a *fucking* idiot.'

'Jesus, Carol . . .'

The shock of hearing Chamberlain swear – not an everyday occurrence – somehow softened the blow of the comment itself.

Chamberlain's pithy character assassination simultaneously managed to kill the conversation stone dead; to thicken the space between them. After half a minute spent tearing up beer mats and avoiding eye contact, Thorne held up his empty glass. Without fully shifting her gaze from the back of a stranger's head, Chamberlain nodded. She slid her empty wineglass across the table.

Thorne walked across to the bar, ordered a pint of Guinness and a glass of red.

They were in the Angel on St Giles High Street. The pub, pleasantly tatty and old fashioned, stood on or around the site of a tavern which, several hundred years before, had been on the route from Newgate Prison to the gallows at Tyburn. The condemned man's final journey, which took him along what was now Oxford Street, involved stopping at the tavern for a last drink. The drink was given free, the joke being that the customer would pay for it 'on his way back'.

Thorne handed over his ten-pound note, knowing that he wouldn't receive a great deal of change. The concept of free drinks certainly belonged in a bygone age, like smallpox or press-gangs. These days, you could crawl into a pub on your hands and knees with two minutes to live and you'd be lucky to find so much as a complimentary bowl of peanuts on the bar.

Those who knew the history of the pub also knew that the custom for which it had once been famous had spawned the phrase so beloved of publicans and pissheads alike. Thorne walked back to the table, put down the drinks. 'One for the road,' he said.

Chamberlain understood the reference. Her smile managed indulgence and disapproval at the same time. 'Right, and we all know who's likely to be the one swinging, don't we?'

Thorne's face, save for the moustache of froth, was a picture of innocence. 'Do we? I can't see why.'

He could see perfectly well why, but felt like arguing about it. He was less certain about why he'd told Carol Chamberlain what he'd said to Alison Kelly in the first place. He'd actually decided to tell Chamberlain, to *confide* in her, well before this evening. Well before Alison had killed Billy Ryan even. So he could hardly blame the beer . . .

'The sex part I understand,' she said.

'Oh, good . . .'

'After all, you *are* a bloke.'

'Right. I'm a mindless brute in helpless thrall to my knob.'

Chamberlain reddened slightly. 'You said it.'

The blush made Thorne smile. 'I didn't tell her because I slept with her,' he said.

'So why, then?' She answered the question herself. 'Because you're an idiot.'

'Let's not start that again . . .'

She shook her head, exasperated, and took a slug of red wine.

Thorne wondered if the things she'd seen, that she surely must have heard, had made Chamberlain blush back when she was on the force. Perhaps it was simply a reaction that suppressed itself in certain situations, like a bookmaker's pity or a whore's gag reflex. She was certainly a damn sight less worldly than she often pretended.

'You're pissed off because it wasn't *you*,' Thorne said. 'Because you had nothing to do with it.'

'I'm pissed off because of a lot of things.'

It didn't sound like an invitation to pry, or a willingness to share. Thorne held his tongue and waited to see where she wanted to go.

'You're right, though,' she said. 'I knew I could never play a part in bringing Ryan down. However much you indulged me . . .'

'Carol, I never . . .'

She silenced the protestation with the smallest movement of her hand. 'Still, knowing I wasn't going to be involved didn't stop me imagining certain . . . scenarios.'

'Ryan dead, you mean?'

'Not just dead. I thought about killing him myself. I thought about it a lot.'

Thorne raised an eyebrow. 'How was it?'

'It was great.'

'The way you killed him or the way it made you feel?'

'Both.'

'And the reality isn't quite as good as you'd imagined it . . .'

She pulled a tissue from her sleeve, dabbed at a ring of wine left on the table. 'It's not the right result, Ryan being dead.'

Thorne had turned the same thing over and over in his head, looked at it from every angle, examined it in every conceivable light. 'Do you not think he's paid for what he did?'

Chamberlain said nothing.

'Look, the law could have taken its course, and Tughan, or somebody

265

like him, might have got lucky and maybe, five years from now, Billy Ryan would have been cock of the walk in Belmarsh or Parkhurst. I'm not necessarily saying that what happened was right or that he got what was coming to him. How the hell could I, knowing . . . what I had to do with it? I just can't find it in myself to feel the slightest bit gutted that he's dead.'

The flash that had been in Chamberlain's eyes when she'd talked about killing Billy Ryan had gone. It had been replaced by something warmer, more muted. 'I'm not exactly heartbroken myself,' she said.

Thorne lifted his glass. 'Let's not overlook the substantial saving of taxpayers' money. Of *our* money. Or the fact that overpaid solicitors might have to wait that bit longer for flash cars and luxury holidays . . .'

Chamberlain did not come close to returning his smile. 'It's not the right result, because with Ryan dead we'll never get him, will we? How will we ever know who Ryan gave that money to? How will we ever know who burned Jessica?'

The beer was suddenly vile in Thorne's mouth. He swallowed it quickly, tasting it thick and brackish as it moved down his throat. He felt it settle in his stomach, black and heavy, like doubt. Like guilt.

'Why did you tell her, Tom?' Chamberlain asked. 'If it wasn't just a post-coital thing?'

Thorne shook his head. 'I honestly have no idea.' And he honestly didn't. 'Not beyond a simple, strong feeling that she needed to know.'

'"She needed to know", or you needed to tell her? They might have seemed like the same thing at the time.'

'It felt good to tell her. I won't pretend it didn't.'

'What about now?'

Now felt like a world away from *then*, though it was less than three weeks since he and Alison Kelly had slept together. Ten days since she'd stuck a blade into Billy Ryan. *Now* seemed infinitely confused and uncertain. *Then*, it had all seemed straightforward. Then, there had only been light and shadow, and a simple choice between a hot, hard knowing and an ignorance that looked and sounded anything but blissful.

Thorne blinked before answering Chamberlain's question, remembered the inscription on a headstone he'd walked past at Billy Ryan's funeral a few hours before.

In life, in death, in dark, in light. We are all in God's care . . .

It was supposed to be simple. Life was light and death was darkness. But for some souls, the situation was always going to be more complex. There could be little doubt that Ryan's had been a life lived in darkness. Through it and for it. Right now, Thorne was not so certain where *he* stood . . .

'Now? I wish to God I'd kept my mouth shut,' he said. 'Not for Ryan's sake . . .'

'For hers.'

'She'll spend a long time in prison.'

'There's a lot for the court to take into account . . .'

Thorne shook his head. 'A *long* time. And she's not hard, you know? She must *think* she is. She made a decision to do what she did. She *chose* prison.'

'Same as our friend Gordon Rooker,' Chamberlain said. 'Maybe we're not making these places scary enough.'

'Right.' It was an automatic response, meaning nothing. Alison Kelly would find it tough enough.

Chamberlain put down her glass, leaned forward. '"She *chose* prison." You said it yourself. You didn't put the weapon in her hand, Tom . . .'

'In a way, I did.' He took a sip of Guinness. It wasn't really tasting any better. 'Didn't somebody say that knowledge is a dangerous thing?' Feeling his brain start to fuzz up just a little. Breathing a bit more heavily.

Thinking: knowledge is a knife . . .

'Probably,' Chamberlain said. 'Some smart-arse.'

The dour look on her face, the way her soft Yorkshire accent suited the word so perfectly, made Thorne laugh. A hole was punched through the murk that had been settling about their heads and sucking away the joy that was normally there between them.

'How's your cold case going, anyway? The case of the punctured publican . . .'

'It wasn't a publican, it was in a pub car park and "cold" doesn't come close. There's icicles hanging off the bloody thing. Mind you, I've not exactly been giving it my undivided attention.'

'Maybe now you'll be able to focus a bit more.'

'Maybe . . .'

Thorne touched his glass to her hand. 'Billy Ryan. Jessica Clarke. You need to let it go now.'

Slowly, her eyes widened. '"Let it go". Right. And the names Bishop, Palmer and Foley mean nothing to you . . .'

Thorne's hand moved to his scrubby beard and his thoughts to the cases Chamberlain was talking about. Cases that had left their mark on him. Carved deep, but never less than fresh, never less than tender. How had one fifteen-year-old put it? 'Like a mask you could never take off.'

'I think', he said after a few moments, 'that I preferred it when you were insulting me . . .'

Tottenham Court Road tube station was pretty handy for both of them. Thorne would take the Northern Line up to Kentish Town. Chamberlain could change at Oxford Circus, just two stops away from Victoria Station and the last train back to Worthing.

They walked past the church of St Giles in the Field. It had been founded at the start of the twelfth century as a leper hospital, and its parish records contained the names of Milton, Marvell and Garrick. The burial grounds that lay behind the spiked metal fence contained many of those who'd met their end at Tyburn tree and whose final taste of alcohol had cost considerably less than Thorne and Chamberlain had just spent.

They crossed the road at Denmark Street and turned towards the

Charing Cross Road. To the north of them, the skyline was dominated by Centre Point. The office block – once thought smart, and even stranger, tall – had stood totally empty for some time after it was first erected, and a charity for the homeless, as an ironic gesture, had taken its name. The building rose above an area that a hundred and fifty years before had been the city's most notorious and overcrowded slum. The Rookery had been a maze of filthy alleyways, rat-runs and courts where the poor had lived in squalor, and where crime had been as endemic as the disease. A sprawling network of so-called 'thieves kitchens' and 'flash houses' had made it a virtual no-go area for the police officers of the time.

Thorne outlined the history of the place as they walked. It had flourished, if that was an appropriate word, for over a century, before being demolished to make way for what was now New Oxford Street some time in the mid-nineteenth century. Thorne couldn't remember the exact date.

'You and I seem to talk about history a lot,' Chamberlain said.

Thorne laughed. 'Some of it not quite so dim and distant.'

'Why do you think that is?'

Thorne considered the question for a moment. 'Maybe because we think we can learn from it.'

'Can we?'

'We *can*. I'm not sure we *have*. I'm not convinced anything's changed very much.'

Chamberlain said something, but her words were lost beneath the wail of a siren as a police van rushed past them towards Leicester Square. Thorne shook his head. Chamberlain waited for the noise to die down before she repeated herself. 'Perhaps that's reassuring.'

Gazing through the windows of Internet cafés and computer stores, Thorne couldn't help but picture the gutters running with sewage, families packed into cellars. Men and women driven to prostitution and theft to maintain a standard of living that could only be described as inhuman.

'Have you read *Oliver Twist*?' Thorne asked. It was the iniquity of life in the Rookery, and places like it, that Dickens had described, perhaps a touch romantically, in his creation of Bill Sikes, Fagin and his gang of under-age rogues . . .

Chamberlain shook her head. 'I've only seen the musical. Shameful, isn't it?'

Thorne had taken a few steps before he decided to make his confession. 'I was in a production of *Oliver!* at school. I was the Artful Dodger . . .'

Chamberlain took his arm. 'Now *that* I would have paid good money to see.'

'You'd have felt very ripped off . . .'

Thorne had actually enjoyed himself. He'd done his turn, shown off and clowned around, blissfully unaware that the real people on which the characters were based did somewhat worse than pick a pocket or two.

'Can you remember any of the songs?' Chamberlain asked. She began to hum 'Consider Yourself', but Thorne didn't join in.

'I remember I had a battered top hat that you could squash, and then it would pop up again. I remember my nan waving at me on the first night when I walked on. I remember spending the whole time trying to cop off with a girl from the sixth form who was playing Nancy.'

They turned into the entrance to the tube station. Walked down the stairs towards the turnstiles.

'Right,' Chamberlain said. 'So you were in helpless thrall to your knob even then . . .'

Back at the flat, Thorne sat at the kitchen table waiting for the kettle to boil. He called his father but the line was permanently engaged . . .

He was still getting used to having the place to himself again. Hendricks had moved back into his flat the week before, and, if he was being honest, Thorne missed having him around. It *was* good to have some peace and quiet, though, and he certainly didn't miss the discarded trainers dotted about the place or the disparaging comments about his record collection.

After five minutes he rang the operator, asked them to check his father's line. His dad's phone had been left off the hook.

It was nice to have some privacy back too. Although Hendricks had shown no such inhibitions, Thorne had felt somewhat uncomfortable about being less than fully clothed in front of his friend. He knew he was being stupid, or worse, but the journey from bathroom to bedroom had occasionally been a little awkward.

Thorne carried his tea through to the living room. He put some music on and, while he was up, took a well-thumbed encyclopedia of London from the shelves.

The Rookery of St Giles had been demolished in 1847.

He drank tea and listened to Laura Cantrell, and to the hum of distant traffic between the tracks. He sat and read . . .

While various King Georges had come and gone, while science and revolution were changing the world beyond recognition, the deprivation and crime in the worst areas of the capital had reached incredible levels. The poor and the sick had robbed and murdered one another, and sold their children to buy gin, while the law had more or less left them to get on with it.

Two centuries on, the drugs were different. The gun had replaced the cudgel and the cut-throat razor. The Rookeries were called housing estates.

Thorne remembered what Chamberlain had said when the siren had stopped screaming.

'*Reassuring*' was definitely *not* the word . . .

TWENTY-FOUR

'So, come on,' Rooker said. 'What level of protection do I get?'

He looked from Thorne to Holland and back again, searching their faces for some hint. The two detectives looked at each other, milking the moment.

To say that the SO7 case – specifically the part involving the testimony of Gordon Rooker – had been thrown into confusion would be an understatement. The concept of witness protection did, after all, become a little pointless when the individual from whom you were providing protection had been carved up by an ex-wife. As Thorne had explained to Rooker before, there were different levels of protection, each appropriate to the perceived threat. Rooker had clearly grasped the concept, and, with the prison jungle drums going mental, had been on the phone before Ryan's death had so much as made it into the papers. He'd ranted and raved and demanded to know where he stood. It had been explained to him through appropriate channels that, in the immediate aftermath of Billy Ryan's murder, *his* peace of mind was pretty low on everybody's list of priorities.

Now, face to face with Thorne for the first time since Ryan's death, Rooker was still looking for an answer. '*Well?* What level do I get?'

Thorne sniffed, nodded thoughtfully. 'I think maybe a more basic method of disguise, as opposed to a completely new identity, and perhaps some means of raising the alarm should you feel threatened.'

'Come again?'

Holland smirked. 'A wig and a whistle.'

'Oh, fuck off and behave yourselves . . .'

On a practical level, no one had so much as decided where Rooker should even go. He was still on the protected witness wing in Salisbury, which did seem pretty stupid. He could be transferred back to the VP wing at Park Royal or even, it had been suggested, back into the general prison population elsewhere, now that he was obviously in no danger from Billy Ryan. This idea had thrown Rooker into such a furious panic that the solicitor who'd passed on the information had briefly feared for his physical safety. In the end, unable to make a quick decision, they'd decided to leave him where he was. It was where he wanted to be, but Rooker still seemed far from content . . .

'I don't understand,' Holland said. 'I thought you'd be delighted that Billy Ryan was six feet under.'

Rooker sucked his teeth. 'Ten feet would be better. Yeah, if I had one, I'd've raised a glass to Alison Kelly for sticking a knife in the cunt, course I would. Shame it wasn't a paintbrush . . .'

'So, why are we here?' Thorne asked. 'Frankly, we've got better things to do.'

'How d'you know I'm not still a target?'

Thorne pretended to rack his brains. 'Oh, I don't know. Maybe because Billy Ryan's pushing up daisies in St Pancras Cemetery . . .'

'What about Stephen?'

'What about him?' Holland said.

'Nobody knows what he's likely to do.'

Thorne glanced at Holland. He had to admit that Rooker had a

273

point. Since his father's murder, a great deal of time had been spent fruitlessly speculating as to exactly how Stephen Ryan was going to react.

'He might decide to play the big man,' Rooker said. 'Come after me because of his father.'

Holland picked at a fingernail. 'Can't see it, Gordon. I know Steve's not the sharpest tool in the box, but even he knows you didn't top his old man.'

Rooker's eyes narrowed. 'You know perfectly fucking well what I mean.'

Holland's mood changed in an instant. 'Watch your mouth.'

'Sorry. Look, I just think that now might be a good time to tie up a few loose ends, you know? And I think they'll use someone a bit more reliable than Alun Fisher next time.'

'I really don't think so,' Thorne said. 'We aren't the only ones with better things to do. Stephen Ryan's got quite enough to worry about at the moment . . .'

The man on the motorbike pulled over to the pavement and waited. He sat letting the traffic move past him, revving the bike for no good reason. Letting his breathing grow shallower.

It was a hot day and he'd have been sweating under his gear anyway, but in those places where the leather met flesh, the two skins slid across each other on a sheen of perspiration.

He raised the dark visor just a little and took a few gulps of air that was anything but fresh. He swallowed petrol fumes and hot tar. He could taste the flavoured grease from the seemingly endless parade of fast-food outlets on this stretch of the Seven Sisters Road.

The bike, which had been his only since that morning, had cut easily through the traffic, and he was well ahead of schedule. He thought about parking up and grabbing a Coke but knew that he'd be taking a stupid risk. He had a bottle of water in the box on the back, along with a few other bits and pieces. There'd be somewhere better to stop up ahead. Maybe he could take a stroll around Finsbury Park, kill some time before delivering the message.

This was a big job, his biggest yet. He'd told his wife to pack for a spring break. All the swimming things and plenty of high-factor sun cream for the kids. He'd told her that it was a surprise, knowing that she'd be thrilled to bits with the amazing place he'd booked for them all in the Maldives. Four weeks, fully catered, would make a big hole in what he was getting for the job, but there'd still be a decent amount left for other things. They'd been talking about shelling out to send their eldest private. The secondary schools in his part of Islington were a disgrace, and going private was a damn sight cheaper than upping sticks and moving. They'd have enough to cover three or four years at least, and still have some left over to tart up the house a bit. A conservatory maybe, or a loft conversion. He knew a few builders, people who'd give him a good price and still do a top-notch job.

Doing a good job without charging silly money. It was simple really. He thought that he could build a decent reputation for himself by doing the same thing. He knew there were others, a few foreigners especially, who asked for more, but he believed that pitching yourself somewhere in the middle was the best policy long term.

He flicked on his indicator, edged the bike's front wheel towards the road.

Not the cheapest, but one of the best: that was what he wanted people to think. All anyone really wanted was to believe they were getting value for money, wasn't it? Everyone loved a bargain.

A lorry's horn blared as it rumbled by him. He pulled out into the stream of traffic, accelerated, and overtook it within seconds.

Rooker was standing. Maybe he thought it gave him some authority. 'We had an agreement,' he said.

Thorne leaned back in his chair. He knew exactly how much authority *he* had. 'I'm a police officer, and, unless I'm much mistaken, you're a convicted felon. This is a prison, not a gentleman's club, and the only part of you I'd ever consider *shaking* is your neck. Are we clear?'

Rooker ground his teeth.

'Any agreement you might have thought you had is worth precisely less than fuck all,' Holland said.

Thorne shrugged. 'Sorry.'

Rooker sloped across the room, dragged back his chair and sank on to it. He pushed a palm back and forth across white stubble, the loose skin beneath his chin shaking gently. 'There's stuff I know,' he said. 'Stuff about plenty of people. I told some of it to DCI Tughan's boys, but there's other bits and pieces. There's a few things I kept back.'

'Why was that, then?' Thorne asked.

'Because I wasn't sure you lot were being completely straight with me . . .'

Holland laughed. 'Straight with *you*?'

'I was right as well, wasn't I?' Rooker smiled thinly. His tongue flicked the spit away from his gold tooth.

Thorne could well believe that Rooker hadn't told them everything. He could equally well believe that Tughan had kept a few pieces of information back from the team himself. Thorne didn't really give a toss on either score.

'Whatever you may, or may not, have told SO7, the deal was based on you helping to put Billy Ryan away . . .'

Holland took over. 'Now that he's been put away for good, you're not a great deal of use.'

'I want to talk to Tughan.'

'You can talk to whoever you like,' Thorne said. 'I'm sick of listening to you . . .' He reached behind for the leather jacket that was draped across the back of the chair.

Rooker slid a hand forward, slapped a palm down on the scarred metal tabletop. It was a gesture of frustration as much as anger. 'I need to get out. I was *supposed* to get out.'

'You'll be out soon enough,' Holland said.

Rooker spoke as if his mouth were filled with something sour, with something burned. 'No. *Not* soon enough.'

'Unfortunate turn of phrase, Holland.' Thorne pulled on his jacket.

'Without your say-so I'll never get through the DLP next week. Those evil bastards'll make sure I die inside.'

'You'll get out eventually,' Holland said. 'Think how much more enjoyable it'll be. Things are always better when you've looked forward to them for a while.'

Thorne tried to catch Rooker's eye. The irises, green against off-white, darted around like cornered rats. 'Especially now you don't have to worry about Billy Ryan paying someone to put a bullet in your spine.'

'Well *you* certainly won't be worrying about it,' Rooker said.

Holland stood, tucked in his chair. 'I reckon you've probably still got time to do something useful,' he said. 'Why not squeeze in a quick degree? Come out with a few letters after your name . . .?'

Rooker muttered curses.

Thorne watched as he snatched the lid from his tobacco tin, dug into it. 'Why are you so *very* keen to get out, Rooker? Got a little something stashed away?'

Rooker spat back the answer without so much as raising his head. 'I told you before.'

'Right. Some desperately moving crap about fresh air and wanting to watch your grandson play football.'

'Fuck you, Thorne.'

'You never know, Gordon. If the pair of you avoid injury, you might be out in time to watch him score the winning goal in the FA Cup Final. Although, with him playing for West Ham . . .'

The motorcyclist idled the bike, steady against the kerb, waiting out the final minute.

Trying to focus. Deciding to go half a minute early, to take into account the probable wait for a gap in the late afternoon traffic. Trying to clear his head. Trivial thoughts intruding, sullying the pure white horizon of his mind in the final few moments. They'd need to set aside enough for school uniforms. They weren't cheap when you needed to buy four or five of everything. Did the all-inclusive package in the Maldives include booze? He'd need to check. That could make a big difference . . .

He let one car pass, two cars, a pushbike, before accelerating away hard from the kerb and swinging the machine across both lanes in a wide U-turn. He pulled up outside a dry cleaner's, two doors along from the address he would be visiting. Then, within fifteen seconds, the moves he'd gone over in his mind a hundred times or more in the last few hours.

He flicked the bike on to its stand, left the engine running.

He walked quickly to the box on the back. It had been left unlocked.

He reached inside, withdrew his hand as soon as it had closed around the rubberised grip of the gun, and turned away from the street.

The arm swung loose at his side as he walked, quickly but not *too* quickly from kerb to shopfront. Without breaking stride, he turned right into the open doorway of the minicab office.

He was two large paces towards the counter before the man behind it looked up and by then the gun was being levelled at him. A man in an armchair in the corner lowered his newspaper and executed a near-perfect double-take before crying out. Hassan Zarif cried out too as a bullet passed through him. The spray of blood that fell across the calendar behind him was somewhat overdramatic in comparison with the gentle hiss from the weapon that had caused it.

The motorcyclist fired again and Zarif fell back, dropping behind the wooden counter. The gun bucked in his hand, but only slightly. No more than it might recoil had it brushed the surface of something hot to test the temperature.

As he strode forward, his target having disappeared from sight, the door to the right of the counter burst open, and the motorcyclist turned just as the gun in Tan Zarif's hand began to do its work. The bullet smashed through the plastic of the darkened visor. By the time the first passer-by had spilled his shopping, and others – who knew very well that a car was not backfiring close by – were starting to run, the man in the leathers had dropped, with very little noise, on to the grubby linoleum.

For a few seconds inside the tiny office, there was only the ringing report of the unsilenced gunshot. The high-pitched hum of it rose above the deep rumble of a bus, passing by outside on its way towards Turnpike Lane.

Tan Zarif shouted to the man in the armchair, who jumped up and ran past him through the doorway that led to the rear of the office. Zarif stepped smartly across to the body. And it *was* a body, that much was obvious: the ragged hole in the visor and the blood that poured along the cushioned neck of the helmet and down, made it clear that the man on the floor would not be getting up again.

It didn't seem to matter . . .

The man who had been sitting in the armchair, the man who was now behind the counter bending over the bloodied figure of Hassan Zarif, clapped his hairy hands across his ears as Hassan's younger brother emptied his gun into a dead man's chest.

The first part of the drive back had been pleasant enough. They'd moved through the Wiltshire and Hampshire countryside quickly, but with enough time to enjoy the scenery, to laugh at the signs to Barton Stacey and Nether Wallop. Once they'd joined the M3, however, things had quickly become frustrating. It was one of those journeys where drivers had decided to sit there, beetling along at seventy or below in *all three lanes*. As usual, Thorne sat in the outside lane, grumbling a good deal and damning those ahead of him for the selfish morons they were. He never for a moment entertained the possibility that he might be one of them.

A couple of weeks into spring, and summer weather seemed to

have come early. The BMW's fans were chucking out all the cold air they could, but even in shirtsleeves it was stifling inside the car.

Holland took a long swig from a bottle of water. 'Still pleased you bought this?'

Thorne was singing quietly to himself. He reached across, turned down the volume of the first Highwaymen album. 'Say again?'

'The car.' Holland fanned himself theatrically. 'Still think it was a good move?'

Thorne shrugged, as if the fact that they were all but melted to the leather seats was unimportant. 'When they made these, cars didn't have air conditioning. It's the price you pay for a classic.'

'I'm surprised they had the wheel when this thing was made . . .'

'Good one, Dave.'

'And what you pay to keep this on the road for a year would buy you a car with A/C.'

Thorne drew close to the back of a Transit van and flashed his lights. He slammed his palm against the wheel and eased his foot off the accelerator when the signal was ignored.

'Rooker's not easy to like, is he?' Holland said.

'Probably the right reaction, considering you're one of the Met's finest and he kills people for a living. Not that I haven't met plenty of murderers I could sink a pint or two with . . . and more than a few coppers I'd happily have beaten to death.'

'Right, but Rooker's an arsehole, whichever way you look at it.'

'You do know that bit about "the Met's finest" was ironic, don't you . . .?'

Holland opened his window an inch, turned his face towards it. 'Absolutely.'

'Rooker was a touch more likeable when I had something he wanted,' Thorne said. 'And he'd probably say the same thing about me.'

He pulled across into the middle lane but was still unable to get ahead of the Transit van. It had a sticker on the back that read: 'How am I driving?' Thorne thought about calling the phone number that was given and swearing at whoever was at the other end for a while . . .

'Tell me about some of them,' Holland said. 'The murderers you got on with.'

Thorne glanced into his rear-view mirror. He saw the line of cars snaking away behind him. He saw the tension, real or imagined, around his eyes.

He thought about a man named Martin Palmer; a man who, in the final analysis, had killed because he was terrified *not to*. Palmer had strangled and stabbed, and his final, clumsy attempt at something like redemption had been made at a tragic price. He had changed Tom Thorne's thinking, not to mention his face, for ever. Thorne had not 'got on' with Martin Palmer. He had despised and abused him. But there had been pity, too, and sadness at glimpsing the man a murderer could so easily have been. Thorne had been disturbed, was still disturbed, by feelings that had asserted themselves; and by others that had been altogether absent when he'd sat and swapped oxygen with Martin Palmer.

Then there was last year: the Foley case . . .

The murderers you got on with . . .

'I don't really know where to start,' Thorne said. 'Dennis Nielsen was all right if you got to know him, and Fred West was quite a good laugh, till he topped himself. Talking of which, I remember one night, I was playing darts with Harold Shipman. Harry, I used to call him . . .'

Holland let out a loud, long-suffering sigh. 'If you're going to try to be funny, can you turn up the music again?'

They drove on, the car barely getting into top gear for more than a few minutes at a time. The monotony yielded only briefly to drama when Thorne spent too long watching a kestrel hovering above the hard shoulder, and came within inches of rear-ending an Audi.

'How's Sophie and the baby?' he asked.

'They're good.'

'What is she now?'

'Nearly seven months. It feels like we're getting our lives back a bit, you know?'

Thorne shook his head. He had no idea at all.

'There's not so much panic,' Holland explained. 'I mean, it's still bloody scary, and we're knackered all the time, but we know more or less what we're doing.' He paused, glanced across at Thorne. 'Well, Sophie always did, but now *I* know, more or less what I'm doing. You should come round and see her . . .'

'So, you're fine with it all, then? The dad bit. I know you had some worries.' Thorne remembered a conversation they'd had the previous summer. Bizarrely, it had been on the very day he'd bought the BMW. Holland had been drunk, had confessed to feeling terrified. He'd told Thorne he was worried that he might resent the baby when it came, that Sophie might make him choose between the baby and the job.

'I was being stupid,' Holland said. He turned to Thorne, grinning. 'Chloe's brilliant. She's into everything, but she's fucking brilliant . . .'

'I'm glad it's working out,' Thorne said.

'Tell you the truth, the last couple of weeks have been great. A chance to recharge the batteries, you know? The only problem is that Sophie's starting to get used to having me around again . . .'

The officers on the investigation had all been spending more time with loved ones in the fortnight or so since the Ryan murder. The job had recently involved a lot of paperwork, much of it from other cases, and a good deal of time sitting on arses waiting for somebody – Stephen Ryan in particular – to get off theirs. To make a move. The investigation had wound itself down, or spiralled into chaos, depending on your point of view.

'D'you reckon Stephen Ryan is going to do anything?' Holland asked.

Thorne grunted, but only with pleasure as the Transit van finally indicated and moved inside. Thorne swerved back into the fast lane and powered past it, gaining a pointless thirty feet but enjoying it nonetheless.

He had no idea that, twenty miles ahead of him, uniformed officers were taping off the area around a minicab office on Green Lanes. Others were gathering witnesses and starting to take statements. Phil Hendricks was already on his way to the crime scene, while an ambulance was moving in the opposite direction, its services clearly not required.

Stephen Ryan had made a move.

TWENTY-FIVE

Wednesday morning in the Major Incident Room. Two days after the fatal shooting at the Zarifs' minicab office. A team back on its feet, but yet to get the feeling back in its arse . . .

'We've had word from Immigration,' Brigstocke said. 'They think a few more from the lorry might have turned up. I say "think" because the individuals concerned aren't telling anybody very much.'

'Where?' Thorne asked.

Brigstocke glanced at the sheet of paper he was holding. 'A car wash in Hackney. One of those places where there's half a dozen of them on your car at once, you know? With sponges and chamois leathers, inside with vacuums . . .'

Stone nodded. 'There's one near me. Inside and out for a tenner. Plus a tip . . .'

'The owner's being questioned,' Brigstocke said. 'So far, surprise, surprise, he's pleading ignorance. There'll be a connection to the Ryans somewhere down the line, but I don't think it'll be much different from the others . . .'

A man and a woman, suspected of being from the hijacked lorry, had been detained the previous week in Tottenham, having been discovered working in a restaurant kitchen. Two men had been seized a few days before that from a shopfitting wholesalers in Manor House. In both cases an astonishing bout of amnesia seemed to have struck all concerned. Arrests had been made, but none would lead to anything other than deportation orders for the illegals and fines for their employers. There would be enough red tape to stretch back to where the people in the lorry had originated and nothing to incriminate those who mattered in the Ryan *or* the Zarif organisations.

Tughan took over from Brigstocke. 'Let's move on to the shooting in Green Lanes. What about the witnesses, Sam? Any luck?'

Karim shook his head. 'Hard to believe, I know, but we still can't find *anybody* who saw *anything* that contradicts Memet Zarif's story. We've even got a couple who conveniently noticed a man in a balaclava carrying a gun and running away after the gunshots had finished.'

'Yeah, right,' Thorne said.

Holland let out a grunt of laughter. 'That's one couple who won't go short at Christmas, then . . .'

According to Memet Zarif and the others in the minicab office at the time, the man in the leathers who had shot and wounded Hassan Zarif had *himself* been shot dead by a mysterious second gunman who'd followed him inside and fled once he'd killed him. The police knew it was cock and bull. They guessed that the 'second' gunman was Memet or Tan Zarif, but with no murder weapon or corroborating witness, there was little anyone could do to prove it.

'We are sure about one thing, though,' Tughan said. There was a certain amount of laughter, which he acknowledged with uncharacteristic good humour. 'I know, I've already alerted the media. We have a name for the victim: the *dead* one, that is. He was Donal Jackson, thirty-three. A known associate of Stephen Ryan.'

This last fact came as no surprise to anyone.

'Is he the bloke who did the Izzigils, do we think?' Stone asked. 'Same gun . . .?'

Tughan opened his mouth but Thorne was quicker. 'No chance,' he said. 'It's the same *type* of gun, that's all. Whoever was hired to kill the Izzigils was good. Clinical, you know? This idiot got himself killed and didn't even manage to take anybody with him . . .' He trailed off, his mind focusing suddenly on the failed attempt to kill an innocent four-teen-year-old girl. Now, twenty years later, the son of the man behind that had fucked up a hit of his own.

'DI Thorne's probably right,' Tughan said. 'Word is that Jackson was pretty new to contract stuff. Picked up the job because he was Stephen Ryan's mate, because Ryan wanted to go a different way from his old man. Also, according to the people we've spoken to, Jackson was pretty cheap.'

Stone snorted. 'Pay peanuts, you get monkeys.'

'You'd've thought shelling out for a decent hitman was pretty basic,' Kitson said.

Others picked up on her sarcasm, mumbled their agreement.

'Haven't these people heard of a false economy?'

'You just can't get the staff.'

'He'll pay for it in the end,' Thorne said. 'What he did, what he *failed* to do, is going to cost him.'

'Think it's all going to kick off?' Holland asked.

'I think Ryan should have dug into his pocket and hired a trio of hitmen.' Thorne was only half joking. 'One for each brother. He should have done it properly and killed all three of them.'

'This might be a good time to announce that in terms of the joint operation, we're going to be scaling things down a bit,' Tughan said.

Thorne stared at him. Surely he was joking. 'You what?'

'We've had results, some good ones, but the fact is that the Job can't see us getting too much more out of this. We're wrapping it up.'

Thorne looked across at Brigstocke, eyes wide. The look he got back told him that there was nothing worth arguing about. This was for information, not discussion.

'Billy Ryan, one of our main targets, is no longer a worry, even if, sadly, we can't claim credit for that. In point of fact, from now on, there's not going to be much in the way of results that we won't have to share with Immigration or the Customs and Excise mob. There are one or two loose ends that we've yet to tie up and there'll be a few more arrests, but the pro-active end of it just isn't justified in terms of resources . . .'

'How can we pull out of this now?' Thorne asked. 'After what just happened?'

Tughan was already putting papers into a briefcase. 'It was Stephen Ryan's last hurrah. He messed it up. It's a war he's going to lose, and then hopefully things will settle down again . . .'

'*Hopefully?*'

'Things *will* settle down again.'

'Meanwhile, we just look the other way. We do some paperwork and nick a few nobodies and let them kill each other . . .?'

Tughan turned to Brigstocke. 'I want to thank Russell and his team for their cooperation and for their hospitality. We've done some good things together. We've achieved a lot, really, we have, and I think I'll be borne out on that in the weeks and months to come. Anyway, I'm sure you'll be looking forward to getting back to work on your own cases. To getting your offices back, at least.'

There was a smattering of unenthusiastic laughter.

'We'll have a pint or two later, of course, and say our goodbyes. Obviously, we won't be vanishing right away. Like I said, there are a few loose ends . . .' And he was moving away towards the door.

Brigstocke cleared his throat, walked a few paces after Tughan, then turned. He looked to Thorne, Kitson and the rest of his officers. 'I'll be getting together with DS Karim later. Re-assigning the case-work.' His parting words were spoken like a third-rate manager trying to gee up a team who were six–nil down at half time. 'There's still plenty of *disorganised* criminals out there who need catching . . .'

For a few seconds after Brigstocke had left the room, nobody moved or spoke. One of those uneasy silences that follows a speech. Gradually, the volume increased, though not much, and the bodies changed position, so that in a few subtle turns, half paces and casual shifts of the shoulder, the single team became two very separate ones. The officers from each unit began to huddle and look to their own, their conversations far from secret, but no longer to be shared.

The members of Team 3 at the Serious Crime Group (West) stayed silent a little longer than their SO7 counterparts. It was Yvonne Kitson who sought to break the silence and change the mood at the same time. 'How's the philosophy going, Andy? Nietzsche is it this week, or Jean-Paul Sartre?'

Stone tried to look blank, but the blush betrayed him. 'Eh?'

'It's all right, Andy,' she said. 'All blokes have tricks. All women too, come to that.'

Stone shrugged, the smile spreading. 'It works . . .'

'Obviously you have to use whatever you've got.' Holland lounged against a desk. 'Only some of us prefer to rely on old-fashioned charm and good looks.'

'Money goes down quite well,' Karim said, grinning. 'Failing that, begging usually works for me.'

'Begging's excellent,' Kitson said.

Holland looked to Thorne. He was six feet or so distant from them, the incomprehension still smeared across his face like a stain.

'What about you, sir?' Holland asked. 'Any tricks you want to share with the group?'

Stone was laughing at his joke before he even started speaking. 'I'm sure Dr Hendricks could get his hands on some Rohypnol if you're desperate . . .'

But Thorne was already moving towards the door.

'Can't you be predictable just once in your life,' Tughan said. 'I thought you'd be glad to see the back of me.'

Tughan stood in the doorway to his office. Brigstocke was nowhere to be seen.

'Look, we can't stand each other,' Thorne said. 'Fair enough. Neither of us loses a great deal of sleep about that, I'm sure, and once or twice, yes, I've said things just to piss you off. Right? But *this*' – he gestured back towards the Incident Room, towards what Tughan had said in there – 'is *seriously* stupid. I know you're not personally responsible for the decision . . .'

'No, I'm not. But I stand by it.'

'"Ours is not to reason why". That it?'

'Not if we want to get anywhere.'

'Career-wise, you mean? Or are we back to results again?'

'Take your pick . . .'

Thorne leaned against the door jamb. He and Tughan stood on either side of the doorway, staring across the corridor at the wall opposite. At a pinboard festooned with Police Federation newsletters and dog-eared photocopies of meaningless graphs. At an AIDS-awareness leaflet, a handwritten list of last season's fixtures for Metropolitan Police rugby teams, a torn-out headline from the *Standard* that said, 'Capital gun crime out of control', at postcards advertising various items for sale: a Paul Smith suit; a scooter; a second-hand PlayStation . . .

'It's the timing I don't understand,' Thorne said. 'Now, I mean, after . . .'

'I think this decision was made *before* the shooting in the minicab office.'

'And that didn't cause anybody to rethink it?'

'Apparently not.'

Richards, the concentric-circles man, came along the corridor with a file that was, by all accounts, terribly important. Tughan took it with barely a word. Thorne waited until the Welshman had gone.

'When we found that lorry driver dead and those two in the woods with bullets in the backs of their heads, you were fired up. "This has got to stop," you said. You were angry about the Izzigils, about Marcus Moloney. You were up for it. There's no point pretending you weren't . . .'

Tughan said nothing, clutched the file he was holding that little bit tighter to his chest.

'How do these people decide what *we're* going to do?' Thorne asked. 'Who we target and who we ignore? Which lucky punters have a chance when it comes to us catching the men responsible for killing their husband or their father, and which poor sods might just as well ask a traffic warden to sort it out? How do these people formulate *policy*? Do they roll a fucking dice every morning? Pick a card . . .?'

Tughan spoke to the pinboard, scratched at a small mark on the lapel of his brown suit. 'They divvy up the men and they dole out the money as they see fit. It goes where they think it's most needed, and where they think it might get a return. It's not rocket science, Thorne . . .'

'So, which deserving cause came out of the hat this time?'

'We're shifting direction slightly, looking towards vice. The Job wants to crack down on the foreign gangs moving into the game: Russians, Albanians, Lithuanians. It's getting nasty, and when one of these gangs wants to hit another operation they tend to go for the soft targets. They kill the girls . . .'

Thorne shrugged. 'So, Memet Zarif and Stephen Ryan just go about their business?'

'Nobody's giving them "Get out of Jail Free" cards.'

'Talking of which . . .'

'Gordon Rooker will be released by the beginning of next week.'

Thorne had figured as much. 'Right. He's one of those loose ends you were talking about.'

'Rooker can give us names, a few decent ones, and we're going to take them.'

'Define "decent".'

'Look, there'll be better results, but there'll be plenty of worse ones.

Right now, this is what we've decided to settle for.' Even Thorne's sarcastic grunt failed to set Tughan off. He'd remained remarkably calm throughout the entire exchange. 'You're a footie fan, right? How would you feel if your team played beautiful stuff all bloody season and won fuck all?'

If Thorne had felt like lightening the atmosphere, he might have asked Tughan if he'd ever seen Spurs play. But he didn't. 'You won't be offended if I don't hang around for the emotional goodbye later on?' he said.

'I'd be amazed if you did . . .'

Thorne pushed himself away from the door, took half a step.

'I'm the same as you,' Tughan said. 'Really. I want to get them all, but sometimes . . . no, *most* of the bloody time, you've got to be content with just some of them. Not always the right ones, either – nowhere near, in fact – but what can you do?'

Thorne completed the step, carried on taking them.

Thinking: *No, not the same as me.*

He'd found nothing suitable in Kentish Town and fared little better in Highgate Village, where there seemed to be a great many antique shops and precious little else. He'd carried on up to Hampstead and spent half an hour failing to find a parking space. Now, he was trying his luck in Archway, where it was easy enough to park, but where he wasn't exactly spoiled for choice in other ways.

Having decided – with no idea what else to get for a seven-month-old baby – to buy clothes, Thorne couldn't really explain why he was wandering aimlessly around a chemist's. As it went, it was no ordinary chemist's and had quickly become Thorne's favourite shop after he'd discovered it a few months earlier. Yes, you could buy shampoo and get a prescription filled, but it also sold, for no reason Thorne could fathom, catering-sized packs of peanuts past their sell-by date, motor oil, crisps, and other stuff not seen before or since in a place you normally went for pills and pile cream. It was also ridiculously cheap, as if the chemist were just trying to turn a quick profit on items that had been delivered there by mistake. Thorne might have wondered if somewhere there wasn't a grocers with several unwanted boxes of condoms and corn-plasters, if it weren't for the fact that there were a number of such multi-purpose outlets springing up in the area.

Maybe small places could no longer afford to specialise. Maybe shopkeepers just wanted to keep life interesting. Whatever the reason, Thorne knew a number of places where the astute shopper could kill several birds with one stone, even if it might not otherwise have occurred to him to do so. One of his favourites was a shop that sold fruit and vegetables . . . and wool. Another boldly announced itself as 'currency exchange and delicatessen'. Thorne could never quite picture anyone asking for 'fifty quid's worth of escudos and a slice of carrot cake' and was sure the place was a front for some dodgy scheme or other. He remembered a small shop near the Nag's Head which had seemed to sell nothing much of anything during its odd opening hours. The owners, a couple of cheery Irish guys, appeared uninterested in any conventional definition of 'stock', and no one was hugely surprised when the place closed down the day after the IRA ceasefire.

It was easy for Thorne to imagine places and people as other than they seemed. It was in his nature and borne of experience. It was also, for better or worse, his job.

In the chemist's, Thorne finally realised that, though disposable nappies would be useful, they were really no kind of a present. He looked at his watch: the shops would be shutting soon. After a few words with the woman behind the counter, who he was seriously starting to fancy, Thorne stepped out on to the street.

He stood for a minute, and then another, letting people move past him as the day began to wind down. It wasn't that he had any grand moral notions about *serving* these people. He didn't imagine for one second that he, or the thousands like him, could really *protect* them.

But he had to side with those of them who drew a line . . .

He knew from bitter experience that some of them might one day be his to hunt down. Some would think nothing of hurting a child. Some would wound, rape or kill to get whatever it was they needed.

That was a fact, plain and terrible.

Most, though, would know where to stop. They would draw a line at round about the same place he did. Most would stop at cheating the tax man or driving home after a few drinks too many. Most would go no further than a raised voice or a bit of push and shove to blow away the cobwebs. Most had a threshold of acceptable behaviour, of pain and fury, of disgust at cruelty that was close to his own.

These were the people Thorne would stand with.

The lives of these people, to a greater or lesser extent were being affected every minute of every day by the Ryans and the Zarifs of the world. By those who crossed the line for profit. Some would never even know it, handing over a cab fare or the money for a burger without any idea whose pockets they were lining. Whose execution they might unwittingly be funding. Some would be hurt, directly or through a loved one, their existence bumped out of alignment in the time it took to lose a child to drugs. Twisted by those few moments spent signing the credit agreement. Smashed out of existence in the second it took to be in the wrong place at the wrong time.

They worked in banks and offices and on buses. They had children, and got cancer, and believed in God or television. They were wonderful, and shit, and they did not deserve to have their lives sullied while Thorne and others like him were being told to step away.

Thorne thought about the woman he fancied in the chemist's and the bloke who lived in the flat upstairs, and the man passing him at that very second yanking a dog behind himself. He remembered the Jesus woman and the reluctant security guard who'd thrown her out of the supermarket.

I suppose there are worse crimes.

The lives of these people were being marked in too many places by dirty fingers . . .

He turned as the chemist stepped out of his shop and pressed a button. They both watched as a reinforced metal grille rolled noisily down over the door and window. Thorne looked at his watch again and remembered that the Woolworth's across the road sold a few kids' clothes. He couldn't remember whether it closed at five-thirty or six.

TWENTY-SIX

Chamberlain stood in the doorway watching Jack at the cooker. She loved her husband for his attention to detail and routine. He wore the same blue-striped apron whether he was making a casserole or knocking up cheese on toast. His movements were precise, the wooden spoon scraping out a rhythm against the bottom of the pan.

He caught her looking at him and smiled. 'About twenty minutes. All right, love?'

She nodded and walked slowly back into the living room.

The paper on the walls came from English Heritage – a reproduction of a Georgian design they'd had to save up to afford. The carpet was deep and spotless, the colour of red wine. She let herself drop back on to the perfectly plumped cushions and tried to remember that this was the sort of room she'd always dreamed of; the sort of room she'd imagined when she'd been sitting in dirty, smoke-filled boxes trying to drag the truth out of murderers.

She stared at the watercolour above the fireplace, the over-elaborate frame suitably distressed. She'd pictured it – or something very like it –

years before, while she'd stared at the photos of a victim; of the body parts from a variety of angles.

She pulled her stockinged feet under her and told herself that these walls she'd once coveted so much weren't closing in quite as quickly as they had been.

What had Thorne said?

'*Billy Ryan. Jessica Clarke. You've got to let it go.*'

She was trying, but her hands were sticky . . .

As it went, she knew that Ryan would quickly become little more than the name on a headstone.

She could keep on trying, but Jessica would always be with her.

And the man who'd stood looking up at her bedroom window – the flames dancing across the darkness of his face – would become, if he were not *actually* the man who had burned Jessica, a man who they were never going to catch. In her mind, he was already the one who had touched the flame to a blue cotton skirt, all those years before.

In the absence of cold, hard fact, imagination expanded to fill the spaces. It created truths all of its own.

Jack called through from the kitchen, 'Shall we open a bottle of wine, love?'

Fuck it, Chamberlain thought.

'Sod it,' she said. 'Let's go mad . . .'

Thorne stared at the screen, his eyes itchy after an hour spent trawling the Net for useless rubbish. He wrote down the name of an actor he'd never heard of and reached for his coffee . . .

His father had called while Thorne was still in Woolworth's, struggling to make a decision.

'I'm in trouble,' Jim Thorne had said.

'What?'

Thorne must have sounded worried. The impatience on the face of the girl behind the till had been replaced, for a few seconds, by curiosity.

'Some items for lists I'm putting together, maybe for a . . . *thing*. Bollocks. Thing people read, get in fucking libraries. A *book*. Other stuff, trivia questions driving me mental . . .'

'Dad, can I talk to you about this in a few—?'

'I was awake until three this morning trying to get some of these names. I've got a pen by the bed, you know, to jot things down. You saw it when you were here. Remember?'

Thorne had noticed that the girl on the till was staring at her watch. It was already five minutes after closing time and there were no other customers in the shop. He was still holding two different outfits in his arms, unable to decide between them.

He had smiled at the girl. 'Sorry . . .'

'Do you remember seeing the pen or not?' His father had started to shout.

The girl had nodded curtly towards the baby clothes Thorne was carrying. Her eyes had flicked across to an angry-looking individual standing by the doors, waiting to lock up.

'I'd better take both of them,' Thorne had said. He'd handed over the clothes, returned to his father. 'Yes, I remember the pen. It's a nice one . . .'

His father had spat down the phone. 'Last night the bloody thing was useless. Needs a . . . new pen. Needs a new bit putting in. Fuck, you know, the thin bit with fresh ink you put in . . . when the fucker runs out . . .'

'Refill . . .'

'I need to go to a stationer's. There's a Ryman in the town.'

The girl had held out a hand. Thorne had put a twenty-pound note into it. 'I'll call you when I get home, Dad, all right? I can go online later and get all the answers.'

'Where are you now?'

'Woolworth's . . .'

'Like the killer . . .' his father had said.

'*What?*'

'It was the Woolworth's Killer who did Sutcliffe in Broadmoor. Remember? He'd killed the manager of a Woolworth's somewhere, which is how he got the name, and then, when him and the Ripper were inside together, he stabbed the evil fucker in the eye. With a pen, funnily enough. A fucking pen!'

'Dad . . .'

'We got your bike from Woolworth's in 1973. Can't remember who did the Christmas advert that year. Always big stars doing the Woolies Christmas ads, you know – TV stars, comedians, what have you. Always the same slogan. "That's the wonder of Woolworth's!" Fucking annoying tune went with it, an' all. I'll bet Peter bastard Sutcliffe wasn't singing *that* when the pen was going in and out of his eye.'

Then his father had started to sing. '"That's the wonder of Woolworth's . . ."'

The girl behind the counter had all but thrown Thorne's change at him. The security guard by the door had held the door wide and glared.

'". . . that's the wonder of good old Woolies . . ."'

Thorne had just listened . . .

He'd bought the computer cheaply the year before, stuck it on a table underneath the window in the living room. One of the old-model iMacs, it was 'snow' white when he'd bought it, but was now distinctly grubby. Thorne listened to the low hum from the monitor and thought about the inside of his father's head.

Did the words get lost somewhere between the brain and the mouth? If they made it out of the brain, did they just take a wrong turn? If his father could *hear* the word he wanted inside his head, if he could *see* it perfectly well, then the frustration must have been unbearable. He imagined his father as a tiny, impotent figure, raging inside his own skull. He imagined him standing next to a pair of enormous speakers that blared out the word he was unable to speak. Dwarfed by its illuminated letters, fifty feet high.

Swearing and shouting and a certain amount of public embarrassment – under the circumstances, they were the very least you could expect. Jesus, Thorne was amazed his father hadn't smashed his own brains out against a wall. Bent down to finger the grey goo as it leaked from his head, and tried to pick those elusive words out of the soup . . .

A new page was downloading. Thorne waited for a list to appear on the screen, then scribbled down the names of the ten tallest buildings in the world. He'd call his father in the morning, give him all the useless information he'd asked for.

'*The Job can't see us getting too much more out of this* . . .'

Thorne leaned back in his chair, cradled his coffee cup and thought about the team celebrating that night in the Oak. Tughan would have made a speech, rather more fulsome than the one he'd given in the office. They'd have drunk toasts to their results. Arms thrown around shoulders as they lifted glasses of lager and malt whisky, and drunk to lies. To what they'd been told to settle for.

He pictured other glasses being raised elsewhere, by those who *really* had something to celebrate. Those who would be extremely happy if they knew – and there was every reason to think that they would know – that for the time being the police were off their backs.

Thorne had only a mug of lukewarm coffee, but he raised it anyway.

To *some* of the police . . .

He reached forward to turn the computer off but then paused. He typed 'immortal skin' into the search engine and waited. Eventually, a site appeared that gave all the details Ian Clarke had told him about. The page was dense with information, closely typed, difficult to read.

Thorne's eyes closed and he dreamed for a few minutes, no more than that, of holes in flesh that healed. Of scars fading like the words written in sand, and of lines etched into skin that vanished; the X replaced by smooth, fresh flesh that smelled of babies . . .

When he jolted awake, the screen had frozen. He swore at the computer for a few seconds, then pulled out the plug.

And went to bed.

TWENTY-SEVEN

The car containing Memet and Hassan Zarif pulled away from the traffic lights at Stoke Newington station and accelerated across the Stamford Hill Road.

Sitting three cars behind them, Thorne was still unsure where the brothers were heading. They were driving in the general direction of the restaurant and minicab office, but it wasn't the route Thorne would have chosen. They were a little too far south.

Thorne made it through the lights with a few seconds to spare. He turned up the soundtrack to *O Brother, Where Art Thou?* and sat back. Wherever the Zarifs were going, he was along for the ride.

He'd tried the minicab office first, but none of the brothers had been around. The same surly individual he'd encountered on his first visit there had shaken his head and invited Thorne to search the premises. The man had shrugged and drawn phlegm into his mouth when Thorne had turned to walk back out of the door.

Outside, Thorne had stood for a moment, considering where to go next. A smart black Omega had pulled up and one of Zarif's drivers had asked if he needed a lift. Thorne had shaken his head without giving the driver a second glance. His decision made, he'd marched towards his car. Looking through the windows of the restaurant as he'd passed, Thorne had seen Arkan Zarif and his wife moving about in the half light, setting up the tables for lunch.

The cars crossed the Seven Sisters Road at the bottom end of Finsbury Park, heading north again.

Memet Zarif's BMW was somewhat newer than Thorne's, and now, sitting no more than fifty feet behind it, he wondered if its occupants were aware that they were being followed. His car was fairly distinctive – both in shape and colour – and if they knew where he lived, the chances were they also knew what he drove.

Thorne decided that it didn't really make a fat lot of difference. They'd be stopping somewhere eventually and he only needed a quick word . . .

After leaving the minicab office, he'd driven a mile or two east, to Memet Zarif's home address. It was an ordinary-looking, semi-detached house in Clapton, with a view across the River Lea to the Walthamstow Marshes beyond. There were plenty of pricier places around, but Thorne guessed that, somewhere, Zarif had other property they were as yet unaware of.

Thorne had spent forty minutes loitering with a newspaper, then watched as the front door eventually opened, and Hassan Zarif had emerged. His arm was in a sling, the only visible sign of the bullet that had shattered his collarbone. As Hassan had waited on the drive near the car, his elder brother had appeared, a wife and child next to him on the doorstep. Memet had kissed his family goodbye, and Thorne had walked back towards the side-street where he'd parked up.

When the dark blue BMW had moved past him a few minutes later, Thorne had eased his car slowly out and fallen into the stream of vehicles behind it.

They moved through heavy traffic into Stroud Green and then dropped down towards the somewhat better-preserved environment of Crouch End. This was an area popular with creative types who were not quite in the Highgate and Hampstead league. Despite the lack of a tube station, property prices had gone through the roof in recent years, and the place was crammed with trendy restaurants and bars. The majority of its better-than-averagely heeled shoppers tended to ignore the handful of less salubrious establishments: the adult magazine shop; the working men's caff; the massage parlour . . .

The main road divided either side of the clock tower, and Thorne watched as Zarif took the right-hand fork, then pulled sharply across and parked on a double-yellow line. Thorne cruised past as the brothers stepped out of the car, and swung into a side-street as they crossed the pavement towards a door.

The sign in the window flashed red after dark. At half-past eleven in the morning, the letters spelled out 'sauna' in grime. The girl on reception probably looked a little better herself once the daylight had disappeared; a little less pasty and pissed off. The smile she'd slapped on when Thorne came through the door became a scowl as soon as he produced his warrant card.

'Oh, for fuck's sake,' she said.

'Nothing like that going on here, is there?' Thorne walked towards the door in the far corner, tipping his head from one side to the other. 'Neck's a little bit painful,' he said. 'Got anybody through here who can do something about stiffness . . .?'

'Sorry if I don't piss myself.'

Thorne reached for the handle. The girl was either too lazy, or too scared or too engrossed in her magazine to try and stop him.

The room on the other side of the door was clearly designed to be a lounge, but it had not been expensively decorated. Thorne guessed that this wouldn't bother most customers, as the eye would quickly be drawn from the multicoloured carpet to whatever hardcore activities were taking place on the big-screen TV. Right now, a blonde in popsocks was engaged in an enthusiastic bout of fellatio. The permed stallion on the receiving end, eyes tight shut in cutaway, looked suitably grateful . . .

Hassan Zarif was sitting, side on to the door, in a velour armchair. A red towelling robe gaped open across his chest and he was using his one good arm to flick through the pages of a *Daily Mirror*. He let out a sound somewhere between a grunt and a moan when he looked up and saw that he had company.

'That's a shame . . .' Thorne said, nodding towards the sling. 'You could have a wank *and* read the paper if you hadn't gone and got yourself shot . . .'

Hassan shifted uncomfortably in his chair, caught between a desire to stand and the need to hide his erection.

'Don't get up,' Thorne said.

It didn't take too long for Hassan to recover his composure. He crossed his legs, pulled the robe across his chest. 'If you've come here for a freebie, I'll see what I can do,' he said. 'I'm pretty sure a number of police officers get VIP treatment in here . . .'

Thorne walked slowly across the room. He picked up a remote from a glass-topped table, flicked off the TV. 'Sorry, but the slurping makes it really hard to concentrate.'

'I presume you do *want* something . . .'

'This one of yours, is it?'

'I'm sorry?'

Thorne held out his arms. 'This place part of the Zarif Brothers empire?'

Hassan smiled. 'No. This business is owned by an acquaintance, but we may, in fact, be looking to invest in similar premises . . .'

'Right. So this is . . . what? Research?'

'This is exactly what it looks like. I'm not certain you can *arrest* me for it, but go ahead and try if you like. I'm happy to let you make a fool of yourself.'

Thorne nodded. 'How happy would you be if I stepped over there and snapped your other arm? How *happy* would you be with somebody else wiping your arse for a while . . .?'

Hassan stuck out his prominent chin and pointed towards the

ceiling. Thorne looked up at the tiny camera mounted high above a flap of peeling Anaglypta.

'You'd be amazed at how easily a videotape can go missing in an evidence room,' Thorne said. He moved towards the archway on the far side of the room, leaned against a plastic pillar and stuck his head through. To his left, a number of rooms – 'suites', as they were advertised on a poster in reception – ran off a carpeted corridor.

Thorne turned back into the lounge, looked across at Hassan. He thought he'd got the three brothers fairly well worked out: Tan, the youngest, was the hard man – the one with a short fuse; Hassan was the one that made business plans and worked out where to hide the money. Neither was the one Thorne needed to speak to.

He gestured back towards the archway. 'Big brother through there, is he?'

'I presume you followed us here, so you know he is.'

'You're sitting here waiting for sloppy seconds, that about right?'

Hassan said nothing, but his jawbone moved beneath the skin where the teeth were clenching.

'You *presume?*' Thorne said. 'So you didn't see me? That's good news. It's been a while since I've tailed someone and I thought I might have lost the knack.'

Before he stepped through the archway, Thorne picked up the remote and turned the movie back on. The blonde woman resumed her performance.

'This one's a classic,' Thorne said. 'Don't worry, I won't tell you what happens at the end, in case you haven't seen it . . .'

Rooker turned the phonecard over and over in his hand as he waited for his turn to make a call. He had a fair amount of credit left that he'd never get the chance to use up now. Phonecards were always in demand in prison, were as good as hard currency to those with people to talk to. He'd swap this one for a few fags before he left.

He'd made more calls than usual in the last couple of months, but before that there hadn't really been many people he'd wanted to speak to. Fewer still who had wanted to speak to him.

The man in front of him swore and slammed down the phone. Rooker avoided making eye contact as he stepped forward to take his turn. He slotted in the card and dialled the number.

When the call was eventually answered, the response was curt, businesslike.

'It's me,' Rooker said.

'I'm busy. Be quick.'

'You know I'm coming out in a couple of days . . .?'

The man on the other end of the line said nothing, waited for Rooker to elaborate.

'I'm just checking, you know, confirming that we still have an agreement . . .'

There was a grunt of laughter. 'Things have changed a little.'

'Right, and whose doing well out of that? You're quids in now, right?'

'Let's hope so.'

'Course you are. Competition's out of the way, aren't they?' Rooker cleared his throat, did his best to sound casual, matey. 'Listen, I'll be relocated. I don't know where yet, but I'll let you know as soon as I do.'

There was a long pause. Rooker could hear voices in the background. The man he was talking to spoke to somebody else, then came back to the phone. 'That's fine. I hope it all works out, all right?'

'Hang on, I want to know that you're guaranteeing me protection.'

'From who?'

'From whoever . . .' Rooker was trying to control his temper. This was the same conversation he'd had with Thorne, for Christ's sake. Unbelievable . . .

'Don't worry. We had an agreement, as you say.'

'Good. Great.' Rooker saw his own grin; a lopsided reflection in the battered metal plate above the phone. 'So you were joking just now, right?'

'Just joking . . .'

'I mean, anything could happen, couldn't it? The deal was that you'd look after me. That you'd take steps . . .'

'You have that guarantee.'

Steel crept into Rooker's voice. 'If anything happens to me . . .'

It was there too in the voice of the man on the other end of the line. In the words he repeated before ending the call: 'You have that guarantee.'

What had been described in reception as the 'VIP Suite' was little more than a large bathroom with a sofa in one corner. The walls were panelled in glossy, orange pine that ran with moisture. Red bathrobes hung on hooks, and a pink, plastic jacuzzi took up most of the available space. The wall-mounted TV, probably set up to show the same film that was playing in the lounge, was switched off. Memet Zarif had no need of such visual stimulation. The real thing was being eagerly supplied by the woman sharing his bathwater, though, in the absence of an aqualung, she was providing manual rather than oral relief.

The woman, whose enhanced breasts bobbed in the water like buoys, stopped what she was doing the second she saw Thorne.

Memet reached for her wrist, dragged her arm back beneath the water. He spoke to her, but his eyes never strayed from Thorne's. 'Carry on.'

For a few tepid seconds nobody did much, then, finally, with a splash, the woman yanked her hand away and climbed out. Dripping, she walked behind Memet and pulled on a bathrobe, her lack of shyness as obvious as the scars and stretch-marks. She slipped her feet into sandals and turned back to Zarif. 'Do I need to fetch someone?'

Memet shook his head, unconcerned.

The woman sized Thorne up like she was working out how big a stick she'd need to scrape him off the bottom of her sandal.

'Am I a copper or a hired thug?' Thorne asked. 'Or both? I know you're finding it hard to decide.' He nodded towards Memet. 'Your friend in there's helping me with my inquiries, so why don't you go somewhere and wash your hands . . .'

The woman slipped the scrunchie from her hair, shaking it loose as she crossed the room. She stopped for just a second to hiss at Thorne, before stepping out into the corridor.

'Tosser . . .'

'You're a fine one to talk,' he said.

When Thorne turned back to Memet, he had disappeared under the water. Thorne waited, watched as he lifted up his balding head and shook the water from it like a dog.

'Sorry to interrupt . . .'

'She was right,' Memet said. 'You *are* a tosser.' The accent made the word sound a good deal more serious than when the woman had said it.

'I just thought you might like to know that we found a couple more of your missing DVD players,' Thorne said.

Memet smiled, but the effort was obvious. 'Well done.'

'They're turning up all over the place. This lot were working in kitchens and cleaning cars. Maybe one day we'll find out exactly where they came from. What d'you reckon?'

'Good luck . . .'

'Where's Tan, by the way?'

Memet wiped water from his eyes, grunted a lack of understanding.

'Well, Hassan's out there waiting his turn like a good boy, and I know how close the three of you are, so I was just wondering where the baby of the family had got to?'

'My brother's on holiday . . .'

'Oh, right.' So, Tan was almost certainly the one who had put six bullets into Donal Jackson. Thorne wasn't hugely surprised. 'A sudden urge to get away, was it? You can get some very good last-minute deals if you shop around.'

'He was upset after what happened. After the shooting.'

'I'm sure it was very traumatic for all of you . . .'

Memet's face darkened suddenly. 'Hassan was nearly killed. In the middle of the day, a man walks in with a gun.'

'I know. Not very sporting, was it? Thank heavens for that mysterious second gunman. You sure it *was* a gunman, by the way? It couldn't have been Batman or Wonder Woman, could it?'

Memet said nothing. He moved his arm back and forth through the water. The banter was done with.

The plastic tiles squeaked beneath Thorne's shoes as he took a step towards the jacuzzi. 'So, here's the thing: I think Stephen Ryan's a shitbag, and I'm not a great deal fonder of you. In fact, if Ryan was sharing your bathwater right now, I'd be head of the queue to chuck a three-bar fire in . . .'

'Am I supposed to be upset?'

'You're supposed to *listen*. There's not going to be any retaliation for what happened in the minicab office, do you understand? It's over. You boys can all put your guns down now.'

'You don't know what you're talking about . . .'

'I don't care what the "policy" is on this. I don't give a toss about efforts being concentrated elsewhere, about resources being redistributed or even about the fact that you fuckers are doing us all a favour by killing each other. I'm just telling you this: if any more bodies turn up, if Stephen Ryan's cousin's auntie's best mate's brother-in-law so much as twists his ankle, I'll start making a major nuisance of myself. Whatever the *official* position on this might be, *I'm* not going anywhere . . .'

There was amusement in Memet's voice, but also genuine confusion and curiosity. 'Why are you taking all of this so . . . personally?'

Suddenly, Thorne felt helpless, like the tiny, impotent figure that he'd imagined his father to be. The words he wanted to say were vast and deafening. They were made to be roared or screamed. To be sucked up and spat like powerful poison. Instead, Thorne heard them departing from his mouth as little more than murmurs, half hearted and sullen. 'Because you don't stop where other people do,' he said. He looked at the floor as he spoke, sweat stinging his eyes. He stared at the strip of grubby mastic where the tiles met the base of the jacuzzi. 'Because you don't have a *line* . . .'

There was a long moment of silence, of stillness, before Memet heaved himself on to the edge of the bath. Water gathered in thick droplets on his round shoulders. It ran through the dark hair clinging to the fat on his chest and belly.

'I will talk to those with some influence in the community . . .'

'Don't start with that "pillar of the community" bollocks.' Thorne wasn't murmuring now. 'I heard enough of it at that hotel.'

'My family has done all that was asked of us . . .'

'Does Mrs Zarif know about these lunchtime hand-jobs, by the way?'

'You're starting to sound very desperate.'

'Whatever it takes . . .'

Memet sat and dripped.

'Talk to me about what you *do*,' Thorne said. 'Here and now, come on. Tell me about the killing, and the buzz or whatever it is, that you get from controlling people's lives. It can't just be about the money . . .' He paused as Memet climbed to his feet and stared at him, a defiance in his stance, some strange challenge in his nakedness. 'There's nobody worth hiding from in here, is there?' Thorne said. The water was cooling, but the room seemed to be growing hotter by the second. 'It's just the two of us. I'm not writing anything down, my memory's not what it was and I haven't got a tape recorder in my pocket, so it stays in this room. Every bit as discreet as everything else that goes on in here. Talk to me about it *honestly*. Just once . . .'

Slowly, Memet reached for the towel that was draped across the arm of the sofa and began to dry himself. 'That day in my father's café,' he said. 'You told me to make a wish, remember?'

Thorne remembered the lamps hanging from the ceiling, the cigarette smoke dancing around them like a genie. He recalled his parting shot as he'd walked out of the door. 'So, did you make one?'

'I made one, but it didn't come true . . .'

Thorne beat Memet to the punchline. He smiled, but felt the sweat turn to ice at his neck as he spoke.

'Because I'm still here.'

TWENTY-EIGHT

'I knew I should have got a toy or something.'

'Don't worry, I'm sure we can exchange them.'

'You'll be lucky. I've chucked the bloody receipt away . . .'

They spoke quietly, conscious of the baby asleep in a Moses basket beneath the window.

'We can just hang on to them, you never know . . .'

Thorne had known as soon as he'd clapped eyes on Holland's baby that all the clothes he'd bought were far too small. Holland was holding up the tiny outfits, trying and failing to find something positive to say about them.

'What, are you going to have another baby?' Thorne asked.

'Well . . .' Holland laughed and sipped from a can of lager.

Thorne, furious with himself, eventually did the same.

'Sophie's had to nip out and see a mate,' Holland said. 'She'll be sorry she missed you. Said to say "hello" . . .'

Thorne nodded, feeling himself redden slightly. He knew very well that Holland was lying, that his girlfriend would have done her level best to make herself scarce on learning that Thorne was coming

311

round. For all he knew, she might have been hiding in the bedroom, waiting for him to leave.

They were sitting on the sofa in Holland's living room. The clutter made the first-floor flat seem even smaller than it was. Thorne looked around, thinking that if the rest of the place was as cramped, then Sophie wouldn't have had the room to hide . . .

Holland read his thoughts. 'Sophie thinks we should find a bigger flat.'

'What do you think?'

'She's right, we should. Whether we can afford to is a different matter . . .'

'Rack up that overtime, mate.'

'Well I *was*. God knows whether there'll be any on the cards now.'

Though Thorne had brought the beer, he didn't feel much like drinking. He leaned over, put his can down by the side of the sofa. 'Don't worry about it, Dave. The SO7 thing might have gone, but there'll be some nutter out there somewhere putting a bit of work our way soon.'

Holland nodded. 'Good. I hope he's a real psycho. We could do with three bedrooms . . .'

The joke was funny only because of the dark truth that fuelled it. Thorne knew all too well that in a world of uncertainties, in a city of shocking contrasts and shifting ideas, some things were horribly reliable. House prices climbed or tumbled; Spurs had bad seasons or average ones; the mayor was a visionary or an idiot.

And the murder rate went up and up and up . . .

'What d'you reckon about the operation just getting called off like that?' Holland asked. 'I know you and the DCI weren't exactly best mates, but still . . .'

Thorne didn't fancy rehashing the conversation he'd had with Tughan the day before. Instead, he told Holland how he'd spent the morning.

'I reckon they'd booked the entire massage parlour for themselves.'

'Like when they close Harrods so some film star can go shopping,' Holland said. 'Only with prostitutes . . .'

Thorne described the confrontations in the lounge and the VIP Suite, playing up the comedy in his exchanges with Hassan and Memet Zarif. He exaggerated the moments that had felt like small victories and glossed over those that were a little more ambiguous.

He left out the fear altogether . . .

'Will it do any good, d'you think?' Holland said.

'Probably not.' Thorne looked across at the baby. He watched for a few seconds, counted the breaths as her tiny back rose and fell. 'But we can't let these fuckers just . . . swan about, you know? Most of the time, they'll run rings round us, I know that, but every so often we've got to give them a decent tap on the ankles, just to let them know we're still there . . .'

Thorne lifted his eyes to the window, saw that it was rapidly darkening outside. 'I thought it would do *me* some good,' he said.

The baby began to stir, crying softly and kicking her pudgy legs in slow motion. Holland moved quickly to her and squatted down next to the basket. Thorne watched as he pulled the dummy from his daughter's mouth, gently pushed it back in, and repeated the action until she was peaceful again.

'I'm impressed,' Thorne said.

Holland returned to the sofa. He picked up his beer. 'Can I ask you something?'

'As long as it doesn't involve nappies.'

'There's a rumour going around . . .'

Thorne hadn't bothered taking his jacket off. It was warm in the flat, but he'd been unsure how long he would be staying. Suddenly, it felt as stifling as it had been standing next to that jacuzzi a few hours earlier.

'Right . . .' Thorne said.

'Did you have a thing with Alison Kelly?'

A variety of images, hastily constructed denials and straightforward lies flashed through Thorne's head in the few seconds before he spoke.

Where had the rumour come from? It didn't really matter. There was only a headache to be gained from worrying about it, or trying to work it out . . .

Thorne didn't want to deceive Dave Holland. He didn't want to look him in the face and make shit up. In the end, though, he chose to tell the truth because he couldn't be arsed to lie, as much as anything else. 'I slept with her, yes.'

Holland's expression rapidly changed from shock to amusement. Then it became something different, something ugly, and that was when Thorne decided to tell him everything else. He wouldn't stand for Holland sitting there looking *impressed*.

When Thorne had finished the story, when the words had moved from the simple repetition of things said over a pub table to those that best described Billy Ryan's body, bleeding on a kitchen floor, they sat and watched Chloe Holland sleep for a minute or two.

Holland drained his can, then squeezed it very slowly out of shape. 'Are we just talking here? This is off duty, right?'

'If you mean "Can we forget about rank?" then yes.'

'Right, that's what I mean . . .'

The sick feeling that came with thinking he shouldn't have said anything was, for Thorne, becoming horribly familiar. 'Don't forget that it's only temporary, though, or that I can get pissed off very quickly, all right?' He was smiling as he spoke, but hoped that the seriousness beneath was clear enough. He knew that Holland thought he was every bit as much of a *fucking idiot* as Carol Chamberlain had, but he didn't want to hear it again . . .

Holland weighed it up and did what Thorne had repeatedly failed to do. He kept his mouth shut.

Thorne spent most of the drive back from the Elephant and Castle thinking about Alison Kelly. Bizarrely, it had not occurred to him until now, but he began to worry about whether she would say anything to anyone. He began to ask himself what might happen if she did . . .

314

If she were to mention to her solicitor the conversation with a certain detective inspector, they would certainly recommend that she go public with the information. After all, it could only strengthen a diminished-responsibility plea. Wasn't it reasonable to conclude that the balance of a person's mind might be disturbed after they'd just been told that their ex-husband had tried to have them burned to death when they were fourteen years old? That he'd been responsible for setting fire to her best friend? Wouldn't that make *most* people go ever so slightly round the twist?

Mutterings from the public gallery and nodding heads among the jury . . .

Why on earth should the accused have believed such an outlandish tale?

Well, Your Honour, she was told it by one of the police officers who was investigating her ex-husband. Told it, as a matter of fact, in that very police officer's bed . . .

Gasps all around the courtroom . . .

In reality, Thorne had no idea what would happen to him were the truth to get out. He certainly felt in his gut that there would be some form of action taken against him, that he should probably resign before that could happen. Another part of him was unsure exactly what rule he'd broken. Maybe there were guidelines in that manual he'd never bothered to read. He could hardly go to Russell Brigstocke and ask.

The more he thought about it, the simpler it became. Would she tell anyone? Would Alison Kelly, either alone or on the advice of others, sacrifice him in return for a lower sentence, or even a nice cushy number in a hospital?

He thought, as he drove across Waterloo Bridge, that she might well.

Going around Russell Square, he decided that she probably wouldn't.

By the time Thorne pulled up outside his flat, the only thing he knew for certain was that he would not blame her if she did.

All thoughts of Alison Kelly flew from his mind as he approached his front door, then stopped dead with his keys in his hand. He stared at the scarred paintwork and pictured the face of Memet Zarif, the water running slowly through the heavy, dark brows. He stared at the gashes in the woodwork, at the ridges and clinging splinters picked out by the glow from the nearby streetlamp. He felt again the chill at his neck, and knew that Memet had made a decision. When wishes were not enough, action needed to be taken.

Thorne stared at his front door; at the ragged 'X' carved deep into it.

TWENTY-NINE

Thorne was dragging the car around and flooring it back towards the main road within a minute, spitting his fury out loud at the windscreen as he drove. His heart was dancing like a maniac in his chest, his breathing as rapid as the baby's he'd been watching only an hour before.

It was important to try to stay calm, to get where he was going in one piece. He had to hold on to his anger, to save it up and channel it against Memet Zarif when he finally got hold of the fucker . . .

He shouted in frustration and stamped on the brake, his cry drowning out the squeal as the wheels locked and the BMW stopped at the lights with a lurch. He watched his knuckles whiten around the wheel as he waited for red to turn to green.

Watching a taxi drive past. Feeling his chest straining against the seat-belt over and over. Listening to the leather move against the nylon, the spastic thumping of his heartbeat . . .

The realisation was sharp and sudden, like a slap, and Thorne felt the stinging certainty spread and settle across him. Slowly, he leaned forward and flicked on his hazard lights, oblivious to the cars snarling round him and through the traffic lights.

A taxi . . . a minicab . . .

He recalled the face he'd barely registered that morning behind the wheel of a black Omega – the driver outside Zarif's place on Green Lanes who'd asked if he needed a cab. He remembered where he'd seen that face before.

Thorne waited until the lights had changed again, turned the car around and cruised slowly back towards his flat.

Why was this man driving a cab for Memet Zarif? Would he still be working this late in the day? It was certainly worth a try . . .

Thorne's mind was racing every bit as fast as it had been before, adrenalin fizzing through his system, but now a calmness was making its presence felt, too, flowing through him where it was needed.

The calmness of decision, of purpose.

He was dialling the number before the BMW had come to a standstill outside the flat. He listened to the call going through as he stepped out on to the pavement.

The phlegm-hawker who answered was no more polite on the phone than he had been in person.

'Car service . . .'

'I need a cab from Kentish Town as soon as you can,' Thorne said.

'What's the address?'

'Listen, I need a nice one, a good-looking motor, you know? I've got to impress someone. You got a Merc or anything like that?'

'No mate, nothing like that.'

Thorne leaned back against his car. 'You must have *something* nice. A Scorpio, an Omega, that kind of thing. I don't mind paying a bit over the odds . . .'

'We've got a couple of Omegas.' The man sounded like he resented every syllable of the conversation.

'Yeah, that's great. One of those. Which driver is it?'

'What's the difference?'

Was there a hint of suspicion in the question? Thorne decided it was

318

probably just a natural sourness. 'I had one of your lot a couple of weeks ago and he wouldn't shut up . . .'

Thorne was told the driver's name and felt the buzz kick in. 'That's perfect,' he said.

'What's your address, mate?'

Thorne stared at the 'X' on his front door. There was no way he was going to give them an address they would clearly be all too familiar with. The very last thing he wanted was for the driver to know who he was picking up. He named a shop on the Kentish Town Road, told the dispatcher he'd be waiting outside.

'Fifteen minutes, mate . . .'

Thorne was already on his way.

The fifteen minutes was closer to twenty-five, but the time passed quickly. Thorne had plenty to think about. He couldn't be certain that when the driver had spoken to him that morning outside the minicab office, he hadn't done so knowing *exactly* who he was. Thorne could only hope that the man he was now waiting for had simply been touting for business, and that he'd just been viewed as a potential customer.

When the Omega pulled up, Thorne looked hard at the driver. He saw nothing that looked like dissemblance . . .

Thorne climbed into the back of the car, knowing full well that he'd been wrong about these things before.

'Where to?' the driver asked.

It was the one thing Thorne hadn't considered. 'Hampstead Garden Suburb,' he said. It was a couple of miles away from them, beyond Highgate. Thorne was hoping it was far enough away, that he'd have got what he needed well before they arrived . . .

The driver grunted as he steered the Omega into the traffic heading north along the Kentish Town Road.

They drove for five minutes or more in complete silence. Perhaps the dispatcher had mentioned that the customer was not fond of chit-chat. Perhaps the driver had nothing to say. Either way, it suited Thorne perfectly. It gave him a little time to gather his thoughts.

He'd recognised Wayne Brookhouse – had finally remembered his face – from the CCTV tape of Gordon Rooker's visitors. He remembered Stone and Holland laying out the black-and-white stills on his desk. Brookhouse, if that was his real name, wasn't wearing the glasses any more and his hair was longer now than it had been when he'd last visited Rooker. He was supposed to be the daughter's boyfriend, wasn't he? Or ex-boyfriend, maybe . . .

What had Stone said about Brookhouse after he'd been to interview him? '*A bit dodgy*'? Thorne had good reason to believe that the young man driving him around was rather more dodgy than anyone had thought.

The soft leather seat sighed as Thorne relaxed into it. 'Busy day, Wayne?'

Brookhouse looked over his shoulder for as long as was possible without crashing. 'Sorry, mate, do I know you?'

'Friend of a friend,' Thorne said.

'Oh . . .'

Thorne watched the eyes move back and forth from road to mirror. He could almost hear the cogs whirring as Brookhouse tried to work out who the hell he'd just picked up. Thorne decided to give him some help . . .

'How's your love life, Wayne? Still giving Gordon Rooker's daughter one? What's her name again?'

Thorne watched Brookhouse's back stiffen, felt him struggle to figure out what might be the 'right' answer, given the circumstances. Thorne was starting to doubt that Brookhouse had ever even *met* Gordon Rooker's daughter.

'Who the fuck are you?' Brookhouse said. He'd clearly decided that aggression was his safest option.

'You won't be seeing a tip with an attitude like that . . .'

'Right, that's it.' Brookhouse indicated and began to pull over to the kerb.

'Keep driving,' Thorne said. His tone of voice made it obvious that he did not respond well to aggression.

Brookhouse swerved back towards the centre of the road and they drove on past the tennis courts at the bottom of Parliament Hill.

'Who put you up for the part?' Thorne asked. 'I can't work out whether you were already one of Memet's boys and he suggested you to Rooker, or whether you did have some kind of connection with Rooker and he was the one who found you the job driving the cab.' He waited for an answer. Didn't get one.

'It's not vital information,' Thorne said. 'I'm just curious. Either way, you were clearly just passing messages backwards and forwards. Popping in to see Rooker, playing the part of the harmless tearaway who used to shag his daughter, giving him messages from Memet . . .'

There were still a great many questions that needed answering, but Thorne had worked one thing out: whatever deal Rooker had been trying to strike with him, he had been busy setting up another with Memet Zarif. If he was going to hand over Billy Ryan, Rooker had clearly decided to play it very safe indeed.

'Rooker told us you were a car mechanic. Is that bollocks, Wayne? Would you know a big end from a Big Mac? You certainly convinced my DC when he interviewed you . . .'

'You're Thorne.'

'Spot on. And *you're* fucked . . .'

Through the gap between the seats, Thorne watched Brookhouse's hand slide across, reaching for something on the passenger seat. Thorne leaned forward, grabbed a good handful of Brookhouse's hair and pulled his head back.

'*Ow, Jesus!*'

Thorne looked and saw that Brookhouse had been reaching for a mobile.

'Look, I was just pretending to be a visitor,' he said. His voice had risen an octave or two. 'Like you said, I was just delivering a bit of information, nothing important, I swear. I know fuck all about fuck all, that's the truth.'

Thorne stared at the tiny mobile phone, small and shiny, nestled in the folds of a dark blue anorak that had been neatly laid across the seat. Wayne Brookhouse had posed as a car mechanic, and as the ex-boyfriend of Gordon Rooker's daughter. Thorne suddenly wondered if he might not have played *another* role.

'*Now* you can pull over,' Thorne said. 'Anywhere . . .'

'What for?'

Thorne barely registered the cry as he dragged Wayne Brookhouse's head a little further back. 'I need to make a call . . .'

Chamberlain reached for the phone, both eyes still on the TV programme she was trying to lose herself in.

Thorne's voice concentrated her thoughts.

'Oh, hello, Tom . . .'

Thorne spoke quickly and quietly, and her expression changed when she heard the edge in his tone. From his armchair, Jack looked across at her, concern in every line of his face. He pointed the remote control, turned down the volume on the TV.

Thorne told her to listen.

Chamberlain smiled at her husband and shook her head. It was nothing . . .

Thorne pressed the handset hard against Brookhouse's ear until he began to moan in pain.

'Now, say it again,' Thorne said. 'Like you mean it.'

Brookhouse winced and took a deep breath. 'I burned her . . .'

Thorne yanked the phone away, his fingers still clutching Brookhouse's hair. Something in the near silence on the line, a horror in the gentle hiss, told him that Carol Chamberlain had recognised the voice.

'Carol . . .?'

'There's a train from here in less than fifteen minutes,' she said. 'I can be there in an hour and a half . . .'

Thorne felt a second or two of doubt, but no more. He had been fairly sure what Chamberlain's reaction would be as soon as he'd decided to make the call. 'Give me a ring when you're coming in,' he said. He flicked his wrist sharply to one side, smacking Brookhouse's head against the window. 'There'll be a cab there to meet you.'

THIRTY

Wayne Brookhouse's face – open and attractive beneath the mop of thick, dark hair – broke into a smile. He looked relaxed and happy. Only the redness, livid around his right ear, and the expressions on the faces of the two people sitting opposite him indicated that anything might be out of the ordinary.

'How much longer we going to carry on with this?' Brookhouse said.

It was not far short of midnight, and in the two hours since Thorne had first confronted him, in the time spent waiting for Carol Chamberlain to arrive and travelling back to Thorne's flat, Brookhouse had recovered his confidence.

'Hadn't really thought about it,' Thorne said.

'That much is fucking obvious . . .'

Chamberlain looked at Thorne. They were sitting next to each other on kitchen chairs. Brookhouse was a few feet in front of them in the middle of the sofa. 'I don't think there's any time limit, is there?' she said.

Thorne shook his head, stared for a few seconds at Brookhouse before speaking. 'Tell us how it worked between you, Rooker and Zarif.'

Brookhouse's smile didn't falter. 'They clearly aren't paying you enough,' he said, looking around. 'This place is shit.'

'Why were you pretending to be responsible for the attack on Jessica Clarke?'

Thorne knew this was not going to be easy. In the time that Brookhouse had honed his cocky act, Thorne had put a few pieces of the puzzle in place. He was now working up to the really important questions by asking a few to which he already knew the answers.

'It smells as well,' Brookhouse said. 'It stinks of curry . . .'

Whoever had put the idea together – and right now Thorne's money was on Gordon Rooker – had been intent on putting the ball into the police's court. Drawing the police to him. And, like mugs, they'd come. Brookhouse had made the calls and, sent the letters and sure enough, eventually some idiot had gone along to have a word with Gordon Rooker and started the ball rolling. They'd pressed Rooker until, finally, he'd confessed his innocence, and told them about Billy Ryan. Then he had them . . .

Some idiot . . .

'So, Rooker was sorting out a deal with us, and at the same time making sure he had a slightly different kind of protection from Memet Zarif, right? Is that right, Wayne?'

'You came to my house.' Chamberlain crossed her legs, smoothed down her skirt.

Thorne glanced at her, imagining for a bizarre moment that the two of them were interviewing Brookhouse for a job.

'You stood in my front garden and looked up at me, didn't you?'

Brookhouse stretched out his legs, knocked the toes of his trainers together. 'This is *so* fucked up,' he said. He nodded towards Chamberlain. 'Look at her. She's not a copper. She's like my fucking auntie or something . . .'

'*I'm* a copper,' Thorne said.

'So? You wouldn't be with her if this was anything official. It's obvious you aren't going to arrest me. This is something . . . private. Right?'

Thorne shrugged. 'So what are you going to do, Wayne? You want to call the police?'

Brookhouse leaned forward, his forearms braced across his knees. 'I might call a solicitor, yeah.'

'The phone's by the front door . . .'

The man on the sofa held Thorne's stare for a few seconds, then, slowly, the smile reappeared. 'You can't do shit to me.' He started to laugh softly in short, high-pitched bursts, and Thorne could see that the amusement was real. The little fucker really found the situation funny. He genuinely believed that they could not touch him, that he was protected.

'You're absolutely right, Wayne. This is private, which means that I won't lose my job if I come over there and kick your balls up into your throat.'

Thorne's threat, or perhaps it was his expression as he made it, was enough to stop the laughter, but no more than that.

'Fine,' Brookhouse said. 'It's probably the only way this can end up, right?'

'That's up to you . . .'

Brookhouse sat up straight. 'It's OK with me if it means we can get this shit over with. I'll take a pasting if I have to, but I'll hurt you at the same time, man, I swear.' Another nod towards Chamberlain. 'She going to have a crack as well, is she? 'Cos I tell you, I've got no fucking problems with giving her a slap as well.'

The confidence vanished for a second as Chamberlain stood suddenly and stepped towards him, shouting: 'No fucking problems with trying to set fire to a young girl at a bus stop, either, have you?'

'No idea what you're on about . . .'

Thorne knew now that the attack in Swiss Cottage had been made to up the stakes, had been the only option left when it looked like

Rooker's offer had been rejected. It had certainly done the trick, leaving the police no option but to agree to Rooker's deal.

'That was you, too, wasn't it, Wayne? At that bus stop?' Chamberlain stood, red-faced, above him. 'That's attempted murder, and you're looking at the same sentence Rooker got . . .'

Brookhouse stared at her, calmly bringing up his hand to wipe her spittle from his cheek.

'Jack of all trades, aren't you?' Thorne said. 'Are you the only one Memet's got who can do all these things? Or has the family blown all its money on hookers and expensive hitmen?'

Brookhouse said nothing . . .

Thorne leaned forward. This was an important one. 'Who put the cross on my door, Wayne?'

The answer came at the back end of a yawn. 'Piss off . . .'

Thorne's fingers curled into fists at the exact moment that Chamberlain turned to him, suddenly composed again.

'Have you got any handcuffs knocking about?' she asked.

Gordon Rooker was shopping.

He'd spent a lot of money already. He'd splashed out on smart new clothes and several pairs of fashionable shoes. He'd got drinks in for a bar-full of strangers who were now his closest friends. He'd bought the latest mobile phone, a nice radio and a massive flat-screen TV that he'd seen in a magazine and planned to put in the corner of his new living room. He didn't know where that living room was going to be yet, or how much money he'd have to buy all these things when he *really* got the chance, but he relished the planning. He savoured the dream of *owning* again, the joy of the notes passing through his hands.

Lying on his bunk in the dark, he tried to imagine the future. This was something he'd done countless times before, of course, when there was even a sniff of hope that he might be let out, but this time it was different. He could taste, smell and touch the freedom that was no more than a few days away.

He ate an expensive meal – three courses and a fancy bottle of wine – in a restaurant that was almost certainly no longer in business. He left a large tip and walked out of there feeling like his shit would taste of sugar . . .

Money had been mentioned back when Ryan was still alive. It had been part of the deal then, even though they'd been a bit coy about exactly how much. He was likely to cop for a bit less now than he would have done originally, but they still had to give him *something*, surely. They couldn't just dump him in a strange town or city, point him towards the nearest dole office and tell him to get on with it, could they?

He'd tried getting some straight answers out of that bastard Thorne, but it had been like trying to piss up a rope. There was still so much that was unsettled, and it was disconcerting after twenty years of routine, but he could live with it. A release date, in black and white, was all the certainty he needed.

He bought books, dozens of them: spy thrillers and biographies. He'd learned to lose himself in them and looked forward to choosing his own.

He bought a season ticket at Upton Park. Wherever he ended up, he'd sneak back now and again to watch his grandson play.

And he bought himself a woman. Inside, you developed strong wrists, but cash handed over to lie back and watch a tart doing the work could only be money well spent.

In his cell, Rooker drifted towards sleep thinking about big, soft beds, and about flesh beneath his fingers that was not his own.

THIRTY-ONE

Thorne hadn't known Wayne Brookhouse for long, of course, but this was definitely a look he'd not seen before. The eyes bulged. The face seemed stiff and yellow as old newspaper.

Thorne knew Chamberlain's features far better, but they were distorted by an expression that to him was equally as strange.

'This is *so* . . . fucking . . . out of order,' Brookhouse said. He panted out the words, his head twisting from side to side, the bed shaking as he fought against his restraints.

One wrist was cuffed to the metal bedstead, the other lashed to it with a black tie which Thorne normally only dug out for funerals. Thorne was sitting across his prisoner's legs, holding tight to the rail at the foot of the bed to avoid being pitched off as Brookhouse struggled and bucked.

Chamberlain finished unbuttoning Brookhouse's shirt and reached towards the bedside table. The appliance she picked up was plugged into a red extension reel, which in turn ran to a socket in the corner of the room. She flicked the cable aside as she took a step towards the head of the bed. 'It's funny,' she said, 'because, normally, I bloody hate ironing . . .'

Brookhouse spat out a string of curses. He was doing his very best to appear unafraid, to make the fear look like rage, and he wasn't making a bad job of it. Maybe it would have been harder to disguise if Thorne had been holding the iron. Perhaps, much as he was struggling, Brookhouse found the sight of a woman in her mid-fifties playing amateur-hour torturer faintly ridiculous.

To Thorne, the only ridiculous thing was that Brookhouse wasn't a damn sight *more* scared. Thorne could see something in Carol Chamberlain's eyes that he'd never seen before. Or maybe something that was usually there was *missing* . . .

'Tell us about the X-Man,' Thorne said.

Brookhouse screwed his eyes shut. 'I can't . . .'

Chamberlain lowered her arm. The face of the iron was no more than six inches above Brookhouse's chest. 'This is heavy,' she said.

Thorne stared at Chamberlain. They were busking this. *He* couldn't tell whether she meant it, so Brookhouse certainly couldn't. 'Come on, Wayne . . .'

Brookhouse winced. It was obvious, though the iron was not touching him, that he was starting to feel its heat. 'He's gone, he's gone.' He began to shout, to gabble his words. 'He got out of the country. All right?'

'Where?' Thorne asked.

'I don't fucking know, I swear. Serbia, maybe. I think he was a Serb . . .'

'Give me a name.'

'I don't know his name, I never met him . . .' He tensed as the iron dropped another inch. 'Look, I saw him in the café once, that's all. He was just sitting on his own in the corner, smiling. Dark hair, you know, same as they all fucking look. Smile like a film star, loads of fucking teeth, I remember that . . .'

Thorne remembered the man in the car outside his flat. He remembered that smile. He wondered how close he'd come to feeling a blade against his back; the brightness of its edge, teasing before the blackness of the bullet . . .

'When did he leave, Wayne?'

'A while ago. A few weeks after he did the last one. After the copper.'

Moloney . . .

So, Thorne had been wrong about Billy Ryan having Marcus Moloney killed. It *had* been Memet Zarif who had ordered the killing, without realising he was targeting an undercover officer. The murder of Moloney had, in Thorne's mind, been one more thing Ryan had paid for with his own death. One more thing that had justified Thorne telling Alison Kelly what he'd told her. Now, Thorne had to take Moloney's death off that list, but it didn't make much difference. There were still plenty of things Billy Ryan had needed to pay for . . .

'If he's gone,' Thorne said, 'who put the "X" on my door?'

'It could have been anyone.' The sweat left a stain on Thorne's sheets when Brookhouse turned his head. 'It was just to put the shits up you a bit, that's all.'

'Who ordered the killings?' Chamberlain asked. 'Was it Memet?'

Brookhouse shook his head.

'Is that a "no"?' Chamberlain moved the iron to her left hand, shook out the right for a few seconds, then moved it back. 'Or a "no comment" . . .?'

Thorne steadied himself as Brookhouse's knees jerked up into his backside. He rode out the struggle, thinking about the dead and about those who had taken money to arrange their deaths. Those for whom knives and guns were the tools of their trade: the butcher who had murdered Mickey Clayton, Marcus Moloney and the others; the man who had shot Muslum and Hanya Izzigil; whoever who had gunned down Francis Cullen and the two still unidentified immigrants who had been dragged from the back of his lorry and had tried to run for their lives.

The men who'd got away with it.

Like a man whose tools had been a naked flame, and a can of lighter fuel . . .

Thorne looked at Brookhouse, wondering just how close he might have got to Gordon Rooker. Rooker probably trusted him a damn sight more than he'd ever trust a police officer. Thorne asked himself how much Rooker might have had to reveal, how much he'd had to give up before his arrangements with Memet Zarif were finalised. It couldn't hurt to ask.

'Who burned Jessica Clarke, Wayne?'

Thorne saw something flicker, just for a second, in Brookhouse's eyes. A spark of *something,* that he immediately did his best to hide, like a small boy caught stealing and jamming the booty far down into his pocket. Thorne glanced at Chamberlain and knew immediately that she'd seen it, too.

'You *know*, don't you?' she said.

Thorne watched as Chamberlain let the iron fall a little further. He could see the tendons stretching on the inside of her forearm as she took the weight of it, the concentration on her face as she moved it, as slowly as she could.

'You won't . . .' Brookhouse said.

Thorne watched, compelled, as Chamberlain reached down and turned the dial on the iron to its highest setting. A drop of water fell from it on to Brookhouse's chest. He flinched as if it were boiling.

'You're imagining the pain as something quick,' Chamberlain said. 'A moment of agony as I press the iron down and then release it. Just a second or two of hissing and then it's over, right? OK, I want you to think about how it would be if I let the iron go. If I just left it sitting there on your chest. Sizzling on your chest, Wayne. How long do you think it would take to start sinking in . . .?'

When Brookhouse took his eyes from the iron and looked at Chamberlain's face he started to talk. 'Jesus, how fucking thick are you people? There was no other man. There was only me, pretending to be him.'

'Pretending to be the man who really burned Jessica . . .?'

'*Him*. Rooker. Rooker *was* the man.'

332

And Thorne could see it: bright as a flame and certain as a scar. In the walk and in the fucking wink of him, and in the cunt's fingers moving through his greasy, yellow hair. In the tongue that slid across a gold tooth and in that sly smile before Gordon Rooker bent to snap the lid from his tobacco tin . . .

Thorne had known from the moment he'd recognised Brookhouse that Rooker had been lying. But not about *this*. It was obvious that Brookhouse couldn't have burned Jessica, but Thorne had never presumed that the man making the calls – the man on Chamberlain's front lawn – had been the real attacker. He'd always thought that there was someone else, and that Rooker had probably known who he was . . .

'Tom . . .?'

Everything had been built upon the belief, *his* belief that Rooker had been innocent. Wasn't it him that had put the pressure on Rooker in the first place, *forced* him to admit that he wasn't the one?

Chamberlain had raised the iron and stood looking at him, waiting for something. Guidance, perhaps.

The vast, dreadful stone of his own stupidity crashed onto the floor of Thorne's gut. Its weight exactly equalled the elation of knowing, of finally getting the name. He felt hollow and bloated; cancelled out . . .

Almost every single thing that Rooker had told them was true. He'd only changed one, tiny fact. When Billy Ryan had asked him to kill Alison Kelly, he'd said yes.

'He was perfect . . .'

Chamberlain still hadn't got it. 'What?'

Rooker had almost certainly been involved in the earlier attempt to get rid of Kevin Kelly. Billy Ryan, as Kelly's number two, had a very good reason to want Rooker dead. It made him the ideal choice to carry out a contract on Kelly's daughter . . .

'Maybe Ryan offered to lift a contract he had out on Rooker,' Thorne said. 'In return for Rooker doing him one small favour.'

Chamberlain looked unconvinced, but it didn't really matter either way. What was beyond dispute was Rooker's fear of Billy Ryan, a fear based on the knowledge that Ryan did not forgive those who fucked up. It had driven Rooker to confess, to condemn himself to prison and to a life spent with only the fear itself for company. It grew with every attack, with every beating in the showers, until it dictated everything Rooker did. Fear was what drove him. It was what eventually gave shape to a scheme that might protect him when he finally came to start life again outside prison.

Which he would be doing just a few days from now . . .

Thorne decided that Brookhouse could kick as much as he wanted. He swung his legs around and slid off the bed. 'What's Rooker's arrangement with Memet Zarif?'

Again something flashed in Brookhouse's eyes. This time, there was no mistaking genuine terror.

'A lot more scared of Memet than he is of us,' Chamberlain said.

Thorne watched Brookhouse's eyes dart to meet his own. He saw the tears begin. He saw the hope that their meaning might not be understood. Thorne began to suspect that he may have been wrong about which of the Zarif brothers was pulling the strings.

'*Not* Memet?' Thorne asked.

There was a moan which seemed to come from Brookhouse's belly as he started to thrash around on the bed.

'Hassan . . .?'

Thorne repeated the name, raising his voice over the noise Brookhouse was making to blank him out. There was still no response. Thorne nodded to Chamberlain, who moved the iron back into position. 'Who is it, Wayne?'

As the iron descended again towards his chest, Brookhouse gradually began to grow still. The sobbing died away, his body stiffened and his eyes closed tight shut. It was clear that he was waiting for the pain, that he was prepared for it.

Something . . . some*one* frightened him a lot more.

Chamberlain held the iron an inch above his chest. Thorne watched

334

the skin begin to redden, saw the translucent edges of blisters gaining definition.

'Looks like you're happy to let us get on with this, Wayne,' Thorne said. 'Maybe we should just go down to the station. You might be less happy about going to prison for attempted murder . . .'

Brookhouse gasped out his words on snatched breaths. 'The girl at the bus stop was just for show. So the deal would happen. I was never going to do it . . .'

'It's not much of a defence . . .'

'Doesn't matter, does it?' Brookhouse opened his eyes. He looked, glassy-eyed, at the edge of the iron, then up at Thorne. 'We're not going to the station, are we?'

Thorne stared back at him. Terrified as he was, Brookhouse knew very well that this was never going to get as far as paperwork.

'You're right, we're not.' Thorne turned to Chamberlain. 'Burn him . . .'

The flippancy with which Thorne had issued the instruction was in stark contrast to the way he felt. It was as if the blood were poised to explode from beneath every inch of his skin. The tendons in his neck felt ready to snap, and things had stirred, and begun to jump and slither in his stomach.

Burn him . . .

The pair of them had struggled to overpower Brookhouse, to drag him through to the bedroom and tie him down. Since that moment, Thorne had stood outside himself, impotent as he'd followed Carol Chamberlain further into the shadows. She'd told him to fetch the iron and he'd done it. He'd watched her weighing up ends and means in an instant of rage, and her decision had taken him with it. He'd been borne along with her, exhilarated and appalled, deferring to something far beyond a rank that had been long since taken from her.

He watched the steam drifting from beneath the iron like the breath of funeral horses. He listened to the scrape of the handcuffs against the metal rail as Brookhouse strained against his bonds.

'Get a towel under him,' Chamberlain said. 'When there's contact he'll probably piss himself . . .'

Thorne was not sure if this was a simple practicality or a last attempt to scare Brookhouse into talking. He looked into Chamberlain's eyes and knew one thing: if he *didn't* talk, she *was* going to press a hot iron on to his chest.

Brookhouse said nothing.

The iron moved towards the scarlet skin in slow motion . . .

Chamberlain had obviously reached the point where she thought she had nothing left to lose. Thorne watched her about to torture a man, and tried to decide if what *he* had was worth holding on to.

There was scarcely any air between metal and flesh . . .

Thorne knew that the sound and the smell of it could be no more than a moment away. He tried to speak, but once more he'd become as his father was. The words 'no' and 'stop' refused to come. He heard the hairs on Brookhouse's chest begin to crackle. He put out a hand.

'Carol . . .'

Brookhouse screamed hard and sucked in his chest, then screamed louder still as the mattress pushed him back up again, into the steaming base of the iron.

Chamberlain moved as if her's was the skin kissed by hot metal, and when she and Thorne had finished shouting, they could only stand still, pale and stiff as corpses, looking away while Brookhouse sobbed and spat bubbles of nonsense.

'Ba . . . ba . . .'

Thorne listened to Brookhouse's gibberish. He watched him kick a leg, slowly, as Holland's baby had done.

'Ba . . . ba . . . ba . . .'

Thorne looked across the bed at Chamberlain. He was unable to tell if the horror on her face was at what she had done with the iron or at something she could see stuck to the flat of it.

It was perhaps an hour after Wayne Brookhouse had gone. The two of them were sitting in darkness, unable to drink fast enough – when the word suddenly danced into Thorne's head.

'What are we going to do about Rooker?' Chamberlain asked. 'With what that fucker did to Jessica? We can't let him come out . . .'

Thorne wasn't paying much attention. He was trying to place a word, recalling precisely where he'd seen it on a page. *No*, on a screen . . .

Brookhouse had not been talking nonsense at all.

Thorne had seen the word a month or so before on the NCIS website. On a night when he'd been unable to sleep, when he'd sat at his computer and absorbed the miserable realities of human trafficking. That same night he'd trawled through pages of information about organised crime in the UK and in Turkey. He'd speed-read dense blocks of text about the set-up of Turkish gangs, the customs and the hierarchies of the most powerful families in Ankara and Istanbul . . .

A word that looked to English eyes as though it should mean *baby* or *child* and meant exactly the opposite.

'Tom? What about Rooker . . .?'

Baba . . .

Thorne felt it where the hairline brushed the nape of his neck. He knew that Gordon Rooker was not the only person he'd misjudged.

THIRTY-TWO

Thorne waited nearly a week before going back to Green Lanes.

He'd spent the days at work, going through the motions – pushing paper around his desk as one case wound down and others moved up a gear. All the time he was weighing up everything he'd learned about what had been done and who should pay for it, and waiting in vain for something that might change the most depressing fact of all. There was nothing he could do . . .

It was just after eleven-thirty on a warmish Thursday night. The café had not been closed very long when Thorne pressed his face against the glass in the door. He could just make out Arkan Zarif alone at a booth towards the back. He could see Zarif's daughter Sema moving back and forth behind the counter.

Thorne banged on the glass.

Zarif looked up, peered to see who it was. From outside, Thorne couldn't read the expression on the old man's face when he recognised who was at the door. Zarif nodded towards his daughter and the girl came from behind the counter, unlocked the door and held it open for Thorne without a word.

The main lights in the place had been turned off, but a number of the lanterns overhead were glowing: orange and red bleeding through coloured glass and slats in metal. There was music playing at a low level, a woman singing in Turkish. Thorne couldn't tell if she was in love or in despair.

Zarif held up his glass, shouted something to his daughter as Thorne approached his table. Thorne turned to the girl and shook his head. She moved back behind the rows of cups and glasses.

'No wine?' Zarif said. 'Coffee then . . .?'

Thorne slid into the booth without answering.

For a few moments they studied each other, then Zarif emptied his wineglass. His hand seemed huge around the stem. He reached for the bottle and poured himself another.

'*Merhaba, Baba*,' Thorne said. Hello . . .

Zarif smiled and raised his glass. '*Merhaba* . . .'

'We sat in here once and talked about what names meant, remember?'

Zarif said nothing.

'We joked about how they can mean more than one thing. Like the word *baba* . . .'

'The meaning of this word is simple,' Zarif said.

'I know what it *means*, and I also know how it's used. I know the respect that it inspires back in Turkey. And the fear.'

'*Baba* is "father", that's all.'

'Father as in "head of the family", right? Father to your children, and to your friends, and to those who earn you money. Father to those who kill for you and father to those who you wouldn't think twice about *having* killed if it suited you.'

'I look after my wife and children . . .'

'Of course you do. You're just running a small family business while others are out with the guns and knives you put into their hands. How does it work, *Baba*? You run things until you croak or you're past it and then the boys take over?'

Zarif swilled wine around his mouth, then swallowed. 'When business

339

no longer interests me, I will retire. Now, things are still interesting. It's a good arrangement . . .'

'It's a *great* arrangement. Memet and his brothers front it up, handle all the attention from the likes of me, while you're just the harmless old boy in the kitchen, chucking meat on the grill.'

Zarif folded his hands across his gut. He was wearing the same grubby, striped apron Thorne had seen the first time he'd come into the café. 'These days, I truly enjoy the cooking more than . . . other parts of my business. It's easy to be at the heart of things here. I'm in the kitchen, people know where I am.'

It struck Thorne suddenly that Zarif's accent was less pronounced than when they'd spoken before. There was little, if any, groping for the right word. The act had been dropped.

Sema Zarif stepped from behind the counter and walked past them. She glanced at Thorne as she moved towards the stairs, and for the first time Thorne caught the trace of a smile. As if he were no longer someone to be worried about . . .

'You must have thought I was such a fucking idiot,' Thorne said. 'Sitting at your table, eating with you . . .'

'Not at all. If you want to feel better, you must know that you are a man far from the one I took you to be.'

The white parts of Zarif's thick moustache were stained red with wine. Thorne stared at it, thinking that it looked like Zarif had been feasting on something raw; wishing that he'd said yes to a drink; wanting to know what the hell Zarif was talking about.

'A man who would torture to get what he wants,' Zarif said. 'The performance with the hot iron was . . . remarkable.'

Thorne felt something clench beneath his breastbone. 'When did you speak to Wayne Brookhouse?' he asked.

Zarif raised his glass to his mouth, answered quietly across the top of it. 'It was several days ago, I think . . .'

When Brookhouse had left Thorne's flat, in the early hours of the previous Friday morning, the goodbyes had been less than fulsome.

Chamberlain had said nothing as Thorne had untied him. The two of them had stood and watched without a word as he'd rushed, swearing and stumbling, towards the door. Only at the last moment had Thorne taken Brookhouse to one side, held him against the back of the door and tried to press some good advice upon him.

'Don't go back,' he'd said. It had been hard to make himself understood, to be sure his words were being heard and taken seriously, but Thorne knew that he had to make the effort. 'Are you listening, Wayne? Go home, pack a bag and make yourself very fucking scarce . . .'

Thorne watched as Zarif took another sip of wine. Wayne Brookhouse had not been nearly as clever as he'd thought he was. He'd made the decision to go back to Zarif and tell him what had happened, and Thorne knew that he almost certainly hadn't received the sympathy or the respect he thought he deserved. Thorne could imagine Brookhouse showing Zarif the burn on his chest, cursing those responsible and assuring his boss that he'd done what was expected, that he'd said nothing.

Thorne could imagine the artfully faked concern on the *Baba's* face, the stone-cold resolve as he'd made the only decision possible.

'Where is he now?' Thorne asked.

'I haven't seen Wayne for a day or two. He's gone away, maybe.'

'If a body turns up, you know I'll be back.'

'It won't turn up.' Zarif made no effort to hide the smile or to disguise the double-meaning. He knew that he was safe, and seeing that knowledge smeared across his fat face was like a blade sliding back and forth across Thorne's chest. He said nothing and tried again to convince himself that he'd done the right thing. If not the right thing, then the *only* thing he could have done.

He felt sure that even if he'd done the sensible thing a week earlier – if he'd asked Wayne Brookhouse to drive his taxi to the nearest police station – it would have made no difference. Brookhouse would have said nothing. Zarif's lawyers would have had him back picking up customers within a few hours. The police would have been left with nothing but a few awkward questions to throw at Gordon Rooker, and even less to link the Zarif family to anything worth talking about.

Even if Thorne were to come clean now – if he were to go to Brigstocke or Tughan or Jesmond and tell him what he knew and how he knew it – there would be little to gain. He could admit to torturing a witness and with his next breath explain that the witness had now disappeared; that the witness was, in all likelihood, dead and buried. The only person on the end of any awkward questions after *that* would be Thorne himself.

And he'd been asking himself plenty of those already.

'Mr Rooker was released yesterday, so I understand.'

'You know he was . . .'

'This was a surprise.' Zarif raised his thick grey eyebrows. 'Knowing that he told you a number of lies, you still chose to let him out of prison.'

Thorne tried hard to draw some spit up into his dry mouth. 'I chose not to take the steps that might keep him there . . .'

I chose not to reveal what I'd discovered. I chose not to tell anyone that I'd kidnapped a suspect, that I'd held him against his will and done nothing as this information was forced from him with extreme violence. I chose not to reveal the extent of Gordon Rooker's brutality, or of my own.

I chose to keep the truth quiet and to protect myself . . .

'I wonder what Rooker is doing?' Zarif asked.

'If he's got any sense, he'll be watching his back. You're not fond of leaving loose ends lying around, are you?'

Zarif looked genuinely hurt. 'You've got it wrong. Rooker has nothing to fear from me. We had an agreement, we had shared interests.'

'Right. He helps you deal with Billy Ryan and in return you look after him once he's out. What are we talking? Money, I presume. Protection? Something above and beyond what we can provide . . .'

'An *agreement*, which I fully intend to honour.'

Thorne ran his hand along the surface of the table, scraped salt into the palm of his hand. 'Honour, right. That's important, isn't it? I remember you touching glasses with me and drinking to it. How much honour was there for Marcus Moloney? Sliced up and shot in the head in his car.' He dropped the salt on to the floor. 'Was that an honourable way to die, do you think?'

'Did he behave honourably?' Zarif asked. 'Doing what he was doing?' He flicked a fingernail against his glass. 'Have *you*?'

Another question Thorne had asked himself, and answered, a thousand times in the previous few days. 'When I came down to your level, no.'

Zarif looked up at the sound of his daughter calling to him from the top of the stairs. He answered her, watched her go, then turned back to Thorne. He emptied the last few drops of wine into his glass. 'Time for you to leave . . .'

Thorne reached across the table, grabbed the wineglass and pushed it hard into the old man's face. He felt the glass break and ground it through the soft hair of Zarif's moustache, blood springing bright to the surface and running down as Thorne twisted and pressed.

'We need to lock up.'

Thorne blinked away the fantasy and stood up. He walked to the counter, leaned back against it. 'You got the message I gave to Memet about retaliation for the shooting?' He pressed on before Zarif could answer. 'Of course you did. Hence the message of your own on my front door.'

Zarif spread his arms wide. Sweat stains darkened the white nylon of his shirt. 'I'm sorry for that, really. That was Hassan's doing.'

This was a genuine surprise. 'Hassan?'

'He is normally the most cautious of my sons, but you upset him.'

'Well now he's upset me.'

'I will be sure to tell him.'

'Do that.'

Zarif grunted, began to slide his bulk along the seat. 'Have you replaced your door?'

Thorne shook his head.

'Please' – Zarif gestured casually towards the counter – 'take some money from the till.'

He got to his feet and fixed Thorne with the same expression of vague amusement that had recently been on his daughter's face. 'Go ahead, help yourself . . .'

Thorne wondered if perhaps there was more on offer than just a few tenners to cover the cost of a new door. Zarif had already admitted that Thorne was not the man he'd thought he was. Was he pushing a little, perhaps, trying to find out just what sort of a man Thorne *really* was . . .?

Zarif's smile was returned with bells on. 'I think I'll let you owe me,' Thorne said.

Zarif shrugged and stepped towards the door. He held out a hand in front of him, beckoning Thorne to leave. Thorne pushed away from the counter and walked slowly back the way he'd come in. He felt the faintest flutterings of pride, but at the same time knew that he was kidding himself. He guessed that the feeling would probably not last as far as the pavement.

'Blood and money,' Thorne said.

'What?'

'You told me that you came to this country for bread and work. Blood and money. I think that's closer to the mark . . .'

Zarif stepped around Thorne and opened the door. The breeze began to stir the lanterns above their heads. Diamonds and stars of colour danced gently around the walls. 'That first time, when we talked about names, about what they meant, we talked about yours also,' Zarif said. 'Thorne. Small and spiky, and difficult to get rid of.'

Thorne remembered. 'It depends on how seriously you take that kind of thing.'

344

'I take my business *very* seriously . . .'

'Good, because I'd rather not see your face again, unless it's in a courtroom. I don't want to come back here, however good the food is.'

Zarif nodded. 'We understand each other.'

'Fuck me, no,' Thorne said. He caught Arkan Zarif's eye, and held it. 'Never.'

Thorne turned towards the street, opening his mouth to suck down the fresh air. A few seconds later, he heard the door close behind him with a gentle click.

He'd been right about the pride not lasting very long. It was a warm night, but Thorne was shivering as he walked back towards his car.

He imagined it . . . he *felt* it, as a frenzy of metal wire, tangled and tightly wound somewhere deep inside him. Each time he'd managed to work a piece of it loose, he would pull at it in desperation, succeeding only in winding the coils even tighter, making the snarl that much harder to unravel . . .

Thorne had put some music on, then turned the volume down. He'd opened a bottle of wine and left it untouched. Nothing made it easier. Nothing helped him make sense of the mess, or understand his own part in creating it. There'd been so many bodies and so much grief, and so little to show for it.

He asked himself what else he could have expected. Hadn't he always known that the likes of *Baba* Arkan Zarif were fireproof? They had complex mechanisms in place that protected them, soldiers who would sacrifice themselves and any number of men and women on the right side of the law who would keep them untarnished. Still, the knowledge that nobody was answerable, that no one would pay for a fraction of the carnage, was horribly corrosive.

A few of Ryan's people were dead and a couple of Zarif's. Business had been hit on both sides. Life moved easily on, but not for Yusuf Izzigil, who'd lost both parents. Nor for the family of Francis Cullen, nor for Marcus Moloney's widow, whose name Thorne had never even bothered to learn . . .

And there were the other deaths, those for which, for good or evil, Thorne himself would always be responsible.

Billy Ryan and Wayne Brookhouse.

Thorne felt the knots inside tighten a little further. He thought about where lines were drawn. He wondered whether his had just moved further away, or if he'd long since overstepped it and was moving on. Moving to a much darker place where people couldn't quite make out his face and the lines had disappeared.

He looked at the telephone . . .

He closed his eyes and saw the face of Gordon Rooker. It was starting to regain its colour, the smugness reddening in the fresh air. Thorne saw the gold tooth catch the light as Rooker bought fruit from a market stall. As he sat with other men around a pub table. As he smiled at something he was reading in a magazine.

And there was always the burning girl.

Her arms windmilling as she tumbled through blackness towards the street.

Her face in the photograph her father had given him; the features ravaged, the smooth skin overwritten by rough, discoloured ridges.

Her voice in the diary. Funny and furious. Deserving to be listened to . . .

He got up from the sofa and walked across to the table near the front door . . .

He dialled a Wandsworth number and exchanged a few cursory pleasantries with the man on the other end. He made arrangements to return a diary and some photographs. Then, he told him to get a pen.

Gave him an address.

Thorne turned the music up then, and poured himself a drink. He sat back down on the sofa, pulled his feet up and considered the weight of his soul. He wondered if it might be possible to exercise it, to beef up the soul, to strengthen it by working out spiritually. If

346

so, then bad deeds would surely *cost* you weight. Those who were truly wicked would wind up with souls that weighed next to nothing.

He reached for the wine bottle.

Wondering, in light of the phone call he'd just made, if his soul had gained a little weight. Or lost it.

MAY

IGNORANCE

THIRTY-THREE

It was the day before the Cup Final – a little over a month since the man who used to be known as Gordon Rooker had been found murdered by an intruder in his own home – when Thorne received the call . . .

Three weeks into May and it was gently drizzling. Everything else was equally as predictable.

While the Zarif and Ryan investigations had become little more than a couple of dozen boxes stacked on metal shelves at the General Registry, other cases had arrived to fill the void. Other victims that cried out for attention, that demanded action. There was never a shortage of rage, or lust, or greed. Or of bodies, when the chemistry that was there to control such things turned everyday feelings into something murderous.

Disfigured them.

Tom Thorne had read the *Murder Investigation Manual* in an hour and forgotten the whole thing almost as quickly. He knew he was adept at forgetting what didn't really matter; what there simply wasn't room for. Every day there were a thousand new pieces of information that needed good, clean space – that needed the chance, however slim, to move together, around and within one another, to spark and create the idea or the ghost of an idea that might just help to catch a killer.

But many other things were far from forgotten. They just got shifted around, crammed into smaller spaces in Thorne's head and in his heart. And in that other place that there wasn't really a name for, where the coils just got wound that little bit tighter . . .

On the couple of occasions he'd seen Carol Chamberlain, or spoken to her, they'd talked happily enough about their respective cases: his ongoing and hers long unsolved. Only their immediate past was jointly understood to be off limits.

Individually, and alone, it was far harder to escape.

Alison Kelly had phoned one afternoon and they'd talked for a few minutes. Thorne had asked her how she was. The talk had been so small, so pathetically prosaic, that he'd almost asked her *where* she was. As the time passed, he thought of her face and body less than he thought of the knife in her hand, but each time she came into his mind he thought of the inscription carved into the foundation stone of Holloway Prison, where she waited for the trial that was only a matter of weeks away:

'May God . . . make this place a terror to evil-doers.'

Thorne knew there was no God-given reason for Alison Kelly to be terrified . . .

Going home time. Sheltering beneath a concrete overhang in the car park of Becke House, Thorne breathed in the smoke from Holland's cigarette and watched the rain make a mess of the car he'd cleaned only that morning.

'Why don't you come round tomorrow?' Thorne asked. 'Watch the game with me and Phil . . .'

Despite Thorne's best efforts, Holland's enthusiasm for football was still no more than lukewarm. 'I can't get excited about it,' he said.

'Excited? It's the Cup Final . . .' Thorne was conjuring a tirade of sarcastic abuse when his phone rang.

Something in Eileen's voice froze the smirk on Thorne's face. Chased the blood from it.

'Tom . . .?'

'What's happened?'

Thorne started walking towards his car, his pace quickening with every second of silence that passed before Eileen spoke again.

'There was a fire . . .'

'Jesus, again?' Thorne used a shoulder to press the phone to his ear, dug frantically in his pockets for the car keys. 'Is he all right?'

From behind him, Thorne could hear Holland shouting something. Thorne raised a hand without turning. 'Eileen? Is he all right?'

'I'm sorry, Tom.' She started to cry. 'They found him in the bed-room.' She sounded like a small girl.

Thorne leaned hard against the car. He gasped out his pain, then smothered it quickly, before it became a scream. He was instantly all too aware of how much time he would have. He told himself that, now, Eileen needed to be comforted.

He yanked open the car door and climbed in. 'Eileen, don't.' He stabbed the key into the ignition.

A fire . . .

He thought about the cooker he'd never got around to removing from his father's house. It would only have taken a phone call. Five minutes of his time. Victor would have been happy to take care of it. Eileen could have found someone to take the thing away, had *offered* to, but Thorne had promised that he'd get it organised.

He hadn't even put a lock on the kitchen door . . .

It was down to him.

'Where is he, Eileen? Where have they taken him?' Thorne listened carefully, but his aunt's words were fractured by sobs. 'It's OK, Eileen. I'm coming . . .'

Then another thought that hit him like a wrecking-ball. It smashed him back in his seat and held him there, his hand shaking against the steering wheel.

He pictured Arkan Zarif across a table, remembered what had been said when they'd talked about the deal to protect Gordon Rooker.

'An agreement which I fully intend to honour . . .'

The agreement had certainly involved a degree of protection. Could it also have included retribution should anything happen to Rooker.

Thorne was sure the tightness across his chest was all that was preventing the contents of his stomach rising into his mouth.

An accident, or one that had been arranged? Would they be able to tell which it was? Would Thorne ever *know . . .?*

Either way. Down to him . . .

He glanced to his right and saw a figure coming towards the car, moving fast through the drizzle. Holland raised his hands, mouthing, *'Everything OK?'*

Thorne felt like he'd forgotten how to breathe.

He nodded slowly and started the car.

ACKNOWLEDGEMENTS

In researching this novel I learned a huge amount from two books in particular: *Gangland Britain* by Tony Thompson (Hodder & Stoughton 1995) and *Gangland Today* by James Morton (Time Warner Books 2002). My gratitude is due to both these authors.

For their time and patience I am once again grateful to DI Neil Hibberd, and to DCI Jim Dickey as well as to Richard Baldwin, the cemeteries manager for the London Borough of Camden. For their joke, I owe Phil Nichol and Carey Marx one large drink between them.

Enormous thanks are due to Vedat Suruk Deniz and his brother Sedat Suruk Deniz of the Archgate Café in London N19, for the warm welcome, the good advice and of course for the wonderful *sucuk*. For his extensive knowledge of the Turkish language and for help with matters of translation I have to thank Hikmet Pala.

In bringing a side of London to the US that the tourists rarely see, HarperCollins and William Morrow continue to astonish me with their faith and brilliance. I especially want to thank Claire Wachtel, Michael Morrison, Lisa Gallagher, Sharyn Rosenblum, George Bick, Kevin Callahan and Angela Tedesco.

And of course, a debt is owed as always to: Sarah Lutyens, Susannah Godman, Lucinda Prain, Mike Gunn, Alice Pettet, Paul Thorne, Peter Cocks and Wendy Lee.

As ever the biggest thankyou goes to my wife Claire, for support and saintly patience.

And coffee.